P9-CJJ-222

Received On

NO LONGER PROPERTY OF
SEATTLE PUBLIC LIBRARY

DEC -- 2018

THE
SANS PAREIL
MYSTERY

Received On

OHC — 2018

ALSO BY KAREN CHARLTON

DETECTIVE LAVENDER MYSTERY
The Heiress of Linn Hagh

INDIVIDUAL WORKS
Catching the Eagle
Seeking Our Eagle (non-fiction)
The Mystery of the Skelton Diamonds (short stories)
'The Piccadilly Pickpocket' *(short story)*

KAREN CHARLTON

THE SANS PAREIL MYSTERY

THE DETECTIVE LAVENDER MYSTERIES

 THOMAS & MERCER

The characters and events portrayed in this book are fictitious. Any similarity to real persons, living or dead, is coincidental and not intended by the author.

Text copyright © 2015 by Karen Charlton

All rights reserved.

No part of this book may be reproduced, or stored in a retrieval system, or transmitted in any form or by any means, electronic, mechanical, photocopying, recording, or otherwise, without express written permission of the publisher.

Published by Thomas & Mercer, Seattle

www.apub.com

ISBN-13: 9781503947825
ISBN-10: 1503947823

Cover design by Lisa Horton

Printed in the United States of America

Debby Elsey

Thank you for always being there for me with your unconditional love, ferocious support and awesome accountancy skills.

Love you, Sis.

xxx

Chapter One

'Me Ma says send a constable! Quick! They're murderin' a woman at Raleigh Close on 'Art Street!'

A hush fell over the crowded and noisy hallway entrance of Bow Street Magistrates' Court and police office. Everyone turned in the direction of the ragged urchin with the big voice and distinctive red spiky hair, who stood framed dramatically in the open doorway. The clerks at the desk paused, quills held in midair. Even a few of the drunks slumped against the grimy walls were stirred by the boy's shrill tone and the cold draught from the open door.

'Hurry up!' urged the boy. 'Or she'll be dead.'

Detective Stephen Lavender assessed the scared expression on the child's pale and freckled face and decided he was genuine. 'I'll go,' he said to Magistrate Read, and put on his hat.

As Lavender moved towards the boy, James Read grabbed his arm. 'There's a horse patrol just arrived outside – take them with you.'

Lavender nodded and quickly followed the boy down the steps onto Bow Street. The bitter cold slapped him in the face. Ned Woods and three other constables had just dismounted from their horses onto the busy pavement and were brushing the dust of the Holborn Road from their blue coats and scarlet waistcoats. Two grooms gathered up the reins of the sweating animals ready to lead them round the back to the stables.

'Come with me!' Lavender said. 'There's an incident on Hart Street – possibly murder.'

'Shall we ride?' asked Woods.

'No. It's too crowded. It'll be quicker to go on foot.' Lavender set off at a pace with the constables behind him. He had already lost sight of the carrot-topped urchin who had darted through the stream of heavy carts and wagons that rumbled ceaselessly up and down Bow Street, to and from Covent Garden market. The boy had narrowly missed a trampling by a heavy brewer's dray.

Fortunately, Lavender knew Raleigh Close. Offset from the salubrious Hart Street, it was a three-sided, Elizabethan dwelling, which was overshadowed by the taller Georgian buildings surrounding it. An abandoned remnant of a bygone age, it was in danger of falling down.

As the Bow Street officers turned down Hart Street, their pace slowed. The narrow street heaved with crowds of shoppers, flower sellers, gangs of urchins and swaying drunks, who staggered from one tavern to another. It was a sea of bobbing heads, hats and bonnets. Whores leant out from the overhanging casement windows of the brothels, enticing customers to come up to their beds.

Lavender sidestepped the refuse and steaming piles of horse dung. He bumped into an old woman and apologised before he regained his stride. The officers moved purposefully towards Raleigh Close. A large, stationary crowd now blocked their way ahead. Everyone was staring at the dwelling.

If a murder is taking place, thought Lavender. *At least there are plenty of witnesses.*

Fishing out his tipstaff from his coat pocket, he held the short, gilt-topped baton aloft and pushed his way to the front of the crowd. The mob recognised his badge of office and the uniform of the constables, and parted to let them through.

The freckled youth who had summoned them stood beside a plump, indignant woman at the front of the crowd. The thick pile of faded red hair beneath her mob cap left Lavender in no doubt that this was 'Ma'. The woman was berating an official gent in spectacles and a smart topcoat. The object of her derision looked worried and clutched a sheaf of papers in his gloved hands. The furious matron ceased her cursing and gesticulation and glanced up as Lavender arrived by her side.

'Detective Stephen Lavender from Bow Street,' he announced. 'Who summoned us, and why?' He sensed the burly figure of Constable Woods at his right shoulder.

'About time, too!' snapped the ruddy-faced matron. 'This fellah is about to kill a gal.' The crowd behind them murmured in anger.

'What does he plan to do?' asked Woods, loudly. 'Beat her to death with a piece of paper?'

Laughter rippled around the crowd. Lavender resisted the urge to smile. His experienced constable had a great knack for diffusing tension. Woods had the common touch, a trait Lavender lacked. The detective glanced around and took in the situation at once. A group of labourers armed with shovels and picks and the long hooks they used to pull down rotten-timbered buildings stood beside large, empty carts.

'I'm Algernon Price from the Duke of Bedford's estate office,' the official protested. 'This building is due to be demolished and this woman – these people – are hindering us in our work.' His neck flushed red with embarrassment as one or two in the crowd jeered his words.

The feisty woman beside him jerked a flour-whitened finger in the direction of Raleigh Close. 'There's a young gal inside there,' she told him. 'They're goin' to bring the buildin' down on top of 'er 'ead and kill 'er!'

Now a murmur of dissent rose around them.

Lavender switched his gaze to the rotten two-storey structure before him. Overgrown with weeds and ivy, the ancient building sagged. Large sections leant perilously forward. It looked like one strong gust of wind would topple the lot.

'The place is derelict and empty,' Price continued. 'It hasn't been used for years – except by vagabonds and rogues – and the Duke of Bedford's estate has instructed me to demolish it.'

Lavender nodded. He heard the creak and strain of the crumbling structure from where he stood. Most of the thatched roof was gone or hung down in black, mouldy clumps from the smoke-blackened beams. A large flock of starlings and some crows had made their home amongst the rafters, no doubt attracted by the insects in the ivy that smothered most of the building. The birds fluttered in and out of the gaping holes in the roof and the glassless windows. Lavender could smell the stench of decay from the street.

'This young woman – why haven't you asked her to leave?' he asked.

'Or removed her by force?' Woods added.

'Because we can't find her,' said the exasperated official. 'Every time we enter the building she runs away from us and hides. The rooms and corridors in there are like a rabbit warren. We've shouted and shouted, but still she hides.'

'She's probably terrified of yer,' said the indignant matron.

'Who are you, madam?' Lavender asked.

'Jacquetta 'Iggin,' she informed him. 'I own the bakery on the other side of the street.' She jerked a thumb behind them. 'This is my son, Nathanial.' She patted the tousled head of the young boy who had summoned them. A cloud of flour rose then settled onto his hair.

'Who is this mysterious young woman, Mistress Higgin?' Lavender asked.

'Well, I don't rightly know – but I know she's in there.'

'What about you, Mr Price?'

'I have no idea. We haven't caught sight of her yet. She eludes us every time.'

'Well, how do you know she's in there, if you haven't seen her?' Constable Woods sounded bewildered. His comment echoed Lavender's own thoughts.

'Because of the infant!' Mistress Higgin's voice rose with exasperation.

'The infant?'

'Yes, we can 'ear its piteous cries as she runs from room to room, carryin' the child.'

'Why do you think she is running, madam?' Lavender asked.

Mistress Higgin scowled and gave him a look of contempt. ''Tis obvious. The poor gal is terrified. She might be a furriner and not speak the King's English.'

As if on cue, the desperate and pitiful wailing of a newborn babe drifted towards them on the chill breeze. The hairs on the back of Lavender's neck next stood up. There was something unearthly about that cry. Something not quite right.

The crowd behind them groaned and cried out spontaneously.

'Aw bless!'

'Poor child!'

'The sound came from the right,' Lavender said. 'Woods take a man and see if you can locate it. You two officers' – he gestured to the other men from the patrol – 'you enter the building on the left. Get on both floors, move round, and check every room. Then meet in the middle. If the woman runs, you should trap her.'

'We've tried that already,' said Price. 'Yet somehow she stays out of sight and eludes us.'

The constables followed Lavender's orders. An expectant hush fell on the crowd as the four officers separated into two groups and clattered across the uneven and mossy cobbles of the courtyard. They stooped, pushed back the water-swollen doors and entered the building. For a few moments there was a silence apart from the chirping and cawing of the birds and the distant rumble of traffic on Bow Street. Lavender thought he caught a glimpse of movement through the gaping windows. He heard nothing, but the birds did. They rose in a great flock and wheeled across the sky before they noisily settled again on another part of the building.

Suddenly, an upstairs window, directly opposite to them, was jerked open. Constable Woods' close-cropped grey head appeared. 'There's no one here, sir,' he called out. 'We've checked the entire place. It's a flash-ken for rogues and it reeks like hell – but there is no sign of life.'

At that precise moment, the wailing infant began its piteous cry once more – from the exact spot that Woods and the other officer had first entered the building.

'She's there! She's there!' The crowd now became animated. Frantic hands reached out and pointed. 'She's there!' They gestured the officers back to the entrance. Woods cursed, withdrew his head and disappeared back inside.

A few moments later, the men reappeared from the same door they had entered.

'There's no one there, sir,' Woods repeated as he returned to Lavender's side. 'No woman with a nipper.'

'Good,' said Price. 'Now maybe we can get on with our job and demolish the place.' He turned towards the group of labourers behind him but as he opened his mouth to instruct them, the sound of a mewling infant once again emanated from the dwelling.

'Stop! Stop!' screamed Mistress Higgin.

'This is ridiculous!' Price snapped.

'It came from the left-hand side this time,' said Lavender, thoughtfully.

'Gawd's teeth, sir!' Woods said. 'I swear to you, there is no woman or child in that buildin'!'

'I think you're right,' said Lavender. 'I don't think it's human.'

'What, a ghost? A spirit?' interrupted Mistress Higgin. 'Some poor lost soul, you think?'

The rest of the crowd now took up the cry.

'A ghost!'

'The detective thinks it's a ghost!'

''Tis a poor woman and child who died in there!'

'Was she murdered?' someone asked.

Exasperation flashed across Lavender's face and he turned to address the agitated crowd behind them. 'No,' he shouted. 'There's no such thing as ghosts – and certainly not in broad daylight. This is *Gracula religiosa*.'

'It's a foreign ghost!' someone yelled.

'Catholic most like,' said another.

'Speak English, sir,' Woods suggested, gently.

But it was too late. The seed of superstition had been planted in the mind of the mob.

''Tis the spirit of the dead!' one woman shrieked.

''Tis witchcraft!' screamed another.

Suddenly, Lavender pulled out his pistol and fired a shot into the air above their heads. Many of the hysterical mob squealed and stepped back in alarm. The starlings rose in a beautiful, swirling murmuration. They circled above their heads and settled once again on a dilapidated corner of Raleigh Close.

In the shocked silence that followed, Lavender pointed his smoking pistol towards the flock of birds and raised his voice again.

'The next time we hear the wailing, the sound will come from over there.'

Woods' shaggy eyebrows met in consternation: 'How do you know that?'

Lavender's reply was interrupted as the plaintive cry drifted towards them from the far side of the building; from the area Lavender had predicted.

'Good grief!' exclaimed Price. 'How did you know that?'

The crowd fell silent now. Many leant forward to hear Lavender's response.

'Look among those starlings,' he said, loudly. 'There's one with a green gloss to its plumage and a purple tinge on its head and neck.'

'Where?'

'What is it?'

'Where?'

'It's *Gracula religiosa*, a distant relative of the starling from the Asian subcontinent.'

'English, sir,' Woods reminded him.

'It is also known as the mynah bird; it can mimic human sounds.'

'I can't see it!'

'What's he call it, again?'

'Is it valuable?'

'Shall we trap it?'

'What is it doing here – in Covent Garden?' Price asked.

'I suspect that it will have been imported by the East India Company, bought by a family in London and then escaped from its cage.'

'Why a family?'

'They mimic the sounds they hear,' Lavender explained. 'Its owners must have had an infant.'

'Ahh,' said Woods. 'I've heard of them birds.'

The writhing crowd strained their necks and pointed. Everyone was trying to catch a glimpse of the mynah bird.

'Fire your pistol again, Detective!' someone yelled. 'Make it move!'

'Mind you,' Woods added, 'the owners probably released it on purpose. If I had a creature like that, I'd soon get rid of it. Damned thing would have me teeth on edge night and day with that wailin'.'

'And there speaks the family man,' said Lavender with wry smile.

'It's because I have nippers that I know what I'm talkin' about,' said Woods, grimly. 'There's nothin' more distressin' in the world than a cryin' child.'

'Can we begin the demolition?' asked Price.

'Yes,' said Lavender. 'The starlings and the mynah bird will move on to another roost when you pull it down.'

As if triggered by an unseen signal, the starlings rose once more into the sky and wheeled around gracefully. The expectant crowd was not disappointed. There was an unusual flash of white beneath the mynah bird's wing, which made it distinct from the rest. They pointed it out to each other and 'oohed' and 'ahhed'. Now they knew what to look for, the bird was clearly visible.

Constable Woods turned round and addressed the milling throng. 'Right, you've heard what the detective said: there's no young woman or child in that buildin' – it's just a bird. It's time to get back to your business, the show is over.'

Satisfied, the crowd began to disperse.

'We should have sold tickets,' Woods added under his breath. 'We've had a bigger crowd than Drury Lane Theatre. We'd have made a tidy sum.'

Mistress Higgin and her son remained at Lavender's side. Lavender could see by her frown and compressed lips that the woman wasn't wholly convinced by his explanation.

Algernon Price breathed a sigh of relief and beckoned his labourers forward. 'Thank you for solving this mystery, Detective,' he said.

Lavender watched the workmen raise their long, hooked poles to the sagging timber on the upper storey of Raleigh Close. They hooked a beam and anchored the sharp end into the rotten wood. With several poles now in place, the men pulled hard. Sweat glistened on their straining faces. At first, the rotten timbers resisted, held in place by the tenacious ivy. Then, suddenly, the front of the building crumbled and gave way. A large section of the roof and the upper-storey facade crashed down onto the mossy, cobbles below. The men dashed away to avoid the falling debris. A huge cloud of dust from the crushed rendering billowed like smoke into the air.

Coughing, Lavender and the others stepped back a pace or two.

Suddenly, Mistress Higgin screamed. She pointed back into Raleigh Close. 'You've killed 'er!' she shrieked. 'I told you that you would! You've killed 'er, you stupid sapheads!'

Alarmed, Lavender followed the line of her trembling finger through the dust towards the mangled and swaying remains of the upper storey. The blackened ceiling and wood panels of the interior room where Constable Woods had once stood were now visible.

There, dangling backwards over the jagged edge of the upper floor, was the body of a young woman. She was on her back. Her lifeless eyes stared up towards the cold February sky. Raven hair, turned grey with dust, cascaded from her head down towards the courtyard below. One arm trailed helplessly and swayed in the breeze. Her lower extremities appeared to be trapped beneath the void of the floorboards of the room.

Lavender gasped and ran towards the entrance to Raleigh Close. 'Heaven and hell!' Woods pounded behind him.

'They've bloody killed 'er,' screeched Mistress Higgin behind them. 'I told those Runners there was a woman in there! Them Bow Street constables have killed that gal!'

Chapter Two

Raleigh Close heaved and complained loudly with the crack of wood and the groan of straining timber as Lavender and his men raced up the narrow, swaying staircase. Lavender stopped at the doorway of the half-demolished chamber and grasped hold of the doorjamb to steady himself. The stench of death overpowered him. He recognised it immediately. One glance at the corpse, only a few feet away, confirmed what his nostrils had already told him.

'Stop!' he instructed his men, some of whom were only halfway up the stairs.

'There's too many of us. It won't take our weight.' He pointed to the youngest and slightest of his constables. 'Barnaby – you stay with me. Someone fetch me a pick – and Woods, you sort out that hysterical Higgin woman and the rest of the crowd.'

'What shall I say?'

'Tell them that this girl's been dead for days. The body is decaying. Go and tell the mob before we have a riot on our hands. She's obviously been murdered and buried beneath the floorboards. It is nothing to do with the demolition of the building.'

His constables nodded and backed down the stairs, leaving him and young Barnaby alone. There was less movement now. For the moment, Raleigh Close had settled.

'What do you want me to do, sir?' asked the bright-eyed young man.

Lavender scanned the debris on the floor of the chamber. 'There might be evidence of her murderers in here. We need to search this room thoroughly and collect up every item. If we crawl and spread out our weight, it might work.'

'I'll do it, sir!' Before Lavender could stop him, Barnaby had dropped to the floor and squirmed across the blackened floorboards.

Lavender held his breath as he watched him, grateful for the boy's sharp eyes, his enthusiasm and the fact that he didn't have to ruin his own coat and breeches on the snags of the filthy floor.

It didn't take Barnaby long to gather up a few stale crusts and scraps of paper, a mouldy blanket, a chipped pewter mug and some pieces of rope.

'The rope may 'ave been used to bind her,' he said as he dragged his haul back to Lavender.

'Are there any fresh bloodstains on the floorboards?' Lavender asked.

Barnaby set off back across the floor. 'No. But there's fresh footprints in the dust from a man's boot and there's an overturned wooden chair right on the edge of the precipice,' he called back over his shoulder. 'Could it be a sign of a struggle, perhaps?'

'It's difficult to say,' Lavender said. 'When the wall fell everything turned upside down and shifted in this room. You've done well, Barnaby. Make your way back to the door now.'

Lavender glanced around and spotted a discarded pannier further down the hallway. It was the type used by flower sellers in Covent Garden. Like everything else in Raleigh Close, it was rotten and mouldy, but the flimsy article would serve to collect in the evidence retrieved by Barnaby.

One of the constables arrived with the pick Lavender had requested. 'Ned Woods has calmed down the mob,' the constable said. 'And 'e's sent off to Bow Street for a cart to take the body to the morgue.'

Lavender nodded, grateful for Woods' initiative. Now more confident in the stability of the building, he allowed this second constable to stay. 'We'll have to drag her backwards by the feet and pull her out this way,' he told them. 'If we do that we don't have to go near the edge; it could collapse at any moment.'

Moving cautiously just inside the door of the chamber, the three men prised up the floorboards. It didn't take them long to expose the feet of the corpse. There was something particularly helpless about those tiny, lifeless soles. The torn stockings were filthy and revealed little patches of skin beneath. Lavender felt a wave of sympathy wash through him for the victim.

'Where are her shoes?' he asked. 'Nobody in their right mind would walk into this place without shoes.'

Sharp-eyed Barnaby reached down into the void and pulled out a dusty pair of high-heeled, embroidered brocade evening shoes with silver buckles. There was a label inside them which he suspected denoted the name of the cobbler: 'Kinghorn and Naylor'.

'Dancing shoes,' said Lavender. He was thinking aloud. 'I suspect that this woman came – or was carried here – in the evening. The villains used darkness to cover their crime. It also looks like whoever stuffed her body beneath the floorboards threw in her shoes as an afterthought, determined to conceal evidence.'

The two constables glanced at Lavender quietly, waiting for further deduction. But this wasn't the time or place.

Lavender instructed the constables to grab the woman's ankles and pull her towards them. She didn't weigh much but their job was made more difficult because her muslin gown and short wool jacket kept snagging on the jagged timbers and rusty nails. Her clothes didn't look particularly warm and Lavender wondered how long she had been here in this freezing building. The stench increased as the rest of the corpse was gradually revealed. Lavender fought back his urge to gag.

Despite the filth and the dust which covered the corpse, Lavender saw that the woman had been very pretty and was probably aged about twenty-five. Her bloated face had once been oval-shaped. Beneath the pallor of death, her complexion was flawless. Large, brown eyes fringed with luscious black eyelashes stared up at him blankly. He saw the marks around her wrists where she had been bound – presumably by the rope they had retrieved – but there was no obvious sign of injury. Her throat wasn't cut, there were no bloodstains anywhere on her crumpled clothing and there were no stab wounds or tell-tale bruises from strangulation around her throat.

He knew that there was no time to further examine the body; Raleigh Close could disintegrate into a pile of rubble at any moment. He needed to get the corpse to the morgue at Bow Street.

'Barnaby, have another look in the space beneath the floor-boards. See if the killers have thrown in her reticule, gloves or anything else which might to identify her.'

Barnaby crawled on his stomach once more across the creaking floor. 'There's nothing else down 'ere,' he called. 'Oh, wait a minute – there's some money.'

The young man stretched down into the hole and then held up a gold coin, which glinted in the weak sunlight. Lavender was surprised to see that it was a newly minted Spanish *escudo*. He narrowed his eyes and stared at the small piece of metal.

What on earth are you doing here? he wondered as he pocketed the coin.

Chapter Three

Back at Bow Street, the corpse was placed into the morgue at the back of the building. Lavender went to wash off some of the grime and stench of Raleigh Close. As he brushed the dust from his black coat and splashed water onto his face, he frowned. He had intended to call on Magdalena tonight but he would have to return his rooms in Southwark to change before he made the visit. He allowed himself a wry smile as he imagined the shock in her beautiful eyes if she could see him now. Her fine, aristocratic nose would recoil at the smell and the filth. But as he smoothed his dark hair back from his temple, he frowned again. He realised with a pang of regret that he may have to postpone his plans: he had an unidentified corpse and a murder to solve. It could be a very long night. Sighing, he left the narrow washroom and made his way up to James Read's first-floor office.

When Lavender entered the spartan room, he found the chief magistrate of Bow Street at work at his cluttered desk. As usual, James Read's wig lay discarded amongst the inkstands, broken quills and piles of parchment.

'Am I disturbing you, sir?' Lavender asked.

'No, not at all, Stephen.' Read laid down his quill, scratched his greying head and gestured towards the piles of paperwork before him. 'I'm ready for a respite from this. The Home Department issues more and more demands every day. I can't keep up with it.'

Lavender sat down on the chair opposite.

'So what happened at Raleigh Close?' Read asked. 'I heard that you found the body of a young woman.'

Briefly, Lavender explained the situation. Magistrate Read smiled when he heard about the mynah bird. 'Trust you to work that one out, Stephen. You really are the best detective we have when it comes to solving bizarre mysteries. The story will be round Covent Garden by now and won't do your reputation – or ours – any harm. For a man born in London, you have remarkable knowledge of the flora and fauna of the natural world.'

'I had a good education,' said Lavender, 'and I find that reading helps accumulate knowledge.'

'So, this unidentified woman has no visible marks on her body?' Read asked. 'I shall request that the autopsy is carried out by a surgeon experienced in pathology from Guy's Hospital. We need to know how she died – along with where, why and at whose hand.'

'It would help if we could also find out who she is,' said Lavender, drily.

'Well, we have not received any reports here at Bow Street of a missing woman,' Read replied. 'I shall send a messenger to the magistrate's offices at Middlesex and Westminster to find out if they're missing a woman.'

'That's strange,' said Lavender. 'The putrefaction of the corpse will have been slowed by the cold weather, but she has obviously been dead for several days. Someone must have noticed she was gone.'

Read shrugged. 'Dozens of young women arrive in London every day, Stephen. They look for work, try to make their fortune on the stage or try to snare a rich husband. She might be a new arrival. Of course, most of them end up on the streets . . .' He stood up, stretched and walked across to stand at the drapeless window

17

behind the desk. His glance took in the markets, theatres and gin shops of the bustling and notorious Covent Garden. 'The great square of Venus,' he said, slowly.

'Excuse me?'

'Covent Garden,' Read explained. 'When Inigo Jones built his Great Piazza nearly two hundred years ago, he planned it to be a magnificent square based on the neoclassic style of the continent: the first of its kind in England, inhabited by the rich and the titled.'

Lavender was familiar with this history. 'I don't think he expected it to become the biggest market for fresh produce in the country.'

'No.' Read sighed sadly. 'And I think he would have been shocked to know that his precious Covent Garden is now also the greatest market for carnal flesh anywhere in the world.'

Lavender said nothing. The seedy underbelly of Covent Garden was a thorn in the side for Read. The proliferation of prostitution around the area over the last fifty years had been so great that the Bow Street Officers couldn't control it. Prostitution was against the law but unless the local whores were implicated in public disturbances, raucous behaviour, theft or other crimes, they were generally left alone to ply their trade.

'Do you think your victim might be a Covent Garden Nun?' Read asked, suddenly. 'Raleigh Close has long been a den of iniquity and the haunt of beggars and thieves. It wouldn't surprise me if a few of our nuns also take their clients there.'

Lavender smiled at Read's use of the colloquial term for a whore. 'She wasn't dressed like a trollop,' said Lavender. 'Her clothes were brightly coloured but not gaudy or provocative – and she showed no sign of the pox.'

Read nodded. 'I'm glad that the Duke of Bedford has decided to raze Raleigh Close to the ground and develop the area. How do you plan to proceed with your inquiries?'

'I shall question the neighbours in the street immediately sur- rounding Raleigh Close. I'm not sure that this will yield much information. As you said, there was often insalubrious activity tak- ing place in that building but someone may have noticed her – or something suspicious. By the way, Barnaby found this at the scene of the crime.' Lavender pulled out the gold coin from his pocket. 'It's an *escudo*, minted in Spain only last year. Is it significant, do you think?'

Read turned the coin over in his hand and shook his head. 'Scurrilous traders often palm off foreign coins when they give change to their customers. The coins are passed from hand to hand and then end up in a beggar's bowl. A beggar spends the night at Raleigh Close and counts his takings. He discovers the foreign coin and tosses it away in disgust. It falls down between the cracks in the floorboards and is found by our sharp-eyed Constable Barnaby. Sorry, Stephen, I don't think it will be much help in your investiga- tion.'

Lavender nodded and put the coin back in his pocket.

'Is there anything else you need?' Read asked.

'Just the assistance of Constable Woods.'

'Now, why am I not surprised with that request?' Read smiled. 'Very well, take Ned Woods with you. I will deal with the com- plaints from the horse patrol about you filching – yet again – one of their best men.'

It was late afternoon before Sir Richard Allison, the surgeon from Guy's Hospital, arrived with his assistant. He immediately threw the clerks at the main desk into turmoil with his demands. He was a short, loud man with a brisk walk, a jowly chin and a bulbous nose. He had a thick mop of grey curly hair, brushed forward and volumised on top of his head in the latest Brutus style favoured by Beau Brummel. Allison was accustomed to being treated like royalty whenever he deigned to assist the officers at Bow Street, and took great delight in showing off his superior medical knowledge at every opportunity. He also had a vigorous enthusiasm for carving up dead bodies, which Lavender found slightly repulsive.

A pale and flustered clerk alerted Lavender and Woods to the fact that Sir Richard had arrived and already been taken across the back yard to the morgue. Lavender and Woods had just returned from a fruitless expedition to question the residents and traders of Hart Street. As predicted, no one remembered the deceased young woman, nor had anyone seen anything particularly suspicious at Raleigh Close over the last few days. The only person they had not been able to question was Mistress Jacquetta Higgin. Her bakery had been closed when they arrived, which was unusual for the time of day, and no one answered the door when they knocked.

The Bow Street morgue was in an airless room in a shed next to some of the cells. For the past two days it had held the decomposing body of an unidentified man hauled out of the Thames, and so it stank to high heaven. Now that the body count had doubled, the stench had magnified. The incarcerated prisoners complained vociferously through the grilles as Lavender and Woods crossed the cobbled yard.

However, none of this seemed to bother Sir Richard, who had already ordered more light, donned an apron and stripped the young woman naked by the time they arrived. Their unidentified victim was laid out on a slab in all her curvaceous glory.

'Ah! Lavender! Glad you could find the time to join me.'

Lavender shook hands with the eminent surgeon and ignored the slur about his punctuality. 'I'm glad *you* were able to find the time to help *us*, Sir Richard. I have to confess that cause of death in this case has left us bewildered.'

'I'm sure everything will become clear once I begin my autopsy. It's always my pleasure to assist you officers of the law with things you don't understand. I trust you and Constable Woods will remain for the procedure? It's not often I have the opportunity to dissect such a young and healthy woman. It should be a most educational experience; the internal organs will be in excellent condition.' He picked up an evil-looking hooked knife to emphasise his point.

Lavender felt Woods stiffen beside him. 'Alas, I'm afraid we have further inquiries to carry out regarding the case,' he said. Woods' sigh of relief was audible. 'I just wondered, before you start the autopsy, if there is anything else you can tell us about the cadaver.'

The surgeon's eyes gleamed. 'Nothing that I'm sure you haven't already worked out, Detective. There's no sign of obvious injury. No sign that she was ravished against her will and – apart from the marks on her wrists where she was bound – there are no other signs of abuse or physical violence on the body.'

'It must have been poison,' said Woods. 'There's no other way. That's how the bastards murdered her.'

'What makes you think she has been murdered, Constable?' asked Sir Richard.

Woods gasped and his broad, ruddy face darkened. 'Her body were shoved beneath the floorboards of an abandoned buildin' which was about to be flattened. That looks like a murder to me.'

'It's suspicious, yes, but not in itself proof of a murder. No, no, no, Constable. You mustn't jump to conclusions. There may be a dozen reasons for this woman's untimely demise. But only an *autopsia cadaverum* will provide the true answer.'

'We will leave you to your work, Sir Richard,' Lavender said, 'and call on you later to see if you have any news for us.'

'Oh, a procedure like this won't be finished until tomorrow – noon at the earliest. I must be thorough.'

'Tomorrow afternoon then,' said Lavender, and he turned to go.

'Before you go, Detective,' said Sir Richard, slowly. 'There are a couple of other things you might like to know.'

Lavender stopped and glanced back at the smirking surgeon. There was a glint in the man's eyes he didn't like. He braced himself for either bad or irritating news. 'Oh?'

'It might help you in your investigation to know that this woman has no wedding band on her finger and has never borne a child.'

'Thank you,' Lavender said.

'And her shoes don't fit.'

'Her shoes don't fit?' echoed Woods.

'They're a couple of sizes too large for her. And, judging by the shocking state of the soles of her feet, she hasn't been wearing them. If she walked in that chamber in the hours prior to her death, she did it in her stockings.'

'What about the rest of her clothing?' Lavender breathed a sigh of relief. The surgeon's pronouncements were not as bad as he had feared. 'What have you been able to determine from that so far?'

'Apart from the fact that the young woman liked bright colours and that she had urinated on her gown: nothing. They're not particularly good quality but then again, they're not the cheapest rags worn in London either. Your victim is no aristocrat, but she's no pauper either.'

'She wet herself?' Woods voice rose in surprise.

Lavender was thoughtful. 'This is in keeping with the idea that she may have been held captive in that room for some time,' he said. 'Perhaps her gaolers left her alone too long before they gave her access to the privy.'

'Or the poor gal pissed herself with fear.' Woods shook his head sympathetically. 'How long do you think she has been dead, sir?'

'Rigor mortis has been and gone and bloating has just started to swell the corpse. I would say two or three days at the most. I suspect that death occurred sometime on Friday night or Saturday morning.'

'Thank you, Sir Richard,' said Lavender. 'This information will surely help us to identify the woman and uncover the events which led to her death.'

A smile flitted around the edge of Sir Richard's mouth. 'Oh, you have no need to worry about her identity, Detective.'

'Why is that?'

'I already know who she is.' The surgeon pulled himself up to his full height and grinned from ear to ear.

Lavender was momentarily speechless. Woods had no such affliction. Bristling with indignation, he drew himself up to his full height. 'Gawd's teeth, man!' he exclaimed. 'Why didn't you say so before?'

Sir Richard smirked. 'You never asked, my good fellow.'

Woods' mouth fell open like a fish on a slab at Billingsgate Market.

'Well, who the hell is she?' Lavender snapped.

'Her name is April Divine,' Sir Richard said. 'She's an actress at the Sans Pareil Theatre. Despite the fact that she's not looking too chipper at the moment, an avid theatregoer couldn't fail to recognise Miss April Divine.'

'*Divine?*' Lavender queried.

Sir Richard waved a dismissive hand in the air. 'Oh, you know these actress types; they all work with a stage name. I take it that neither of you have ever seen her perform?'

Lavender shook his head.

'Lady Allison and I have had that pleasure several times,' the surgeon continued. 'Tut-tut, Detective. You've missed a treat – you really should go out into society more often.'

'I swear – one of these days I will punch that cocksure sawbones,' Woods exclaimed angrily as they walked out into the yard. 'He's a sly fellow and a fox.'

Lavender leant back against the brick wall and inhaled the familiar smells of horses and coal smoke, desperate to remove the stench of the morgue from his nostrils. The aroma of a thousand meat suppers simmering over London's cooking fires comforted him. It was already growing dark. One of the ostlers brought out lanterns and hung them on hooks on the side of the stable.

'Allison has a point though, Ned,' Lavender said. 'This suspicious death may not be attributed to murder alone – it looks like a kidnapping which has gone badly wrong.'

Woods wasn't in the mood to accept that Sir Richard had any redeeming qualities. 'And what was that nonsense about the shoes? Can you make head or tail of that?'

'Not at the moment,' Lavender said.

'The man is more of a hindrance than a help,' Woods declared hotly. 'So what's to do, now?'

'Now? Now I shall visit the Sans Pareil Theatre and question the manager about April Divine. At the very least, he should be able to furnish us with an address for the woman and provide the name and whereabouts of her family. I'll follow up any information I glean in the morning.'

'The manager's a she,' said Woods. 'There's a gal called Jane Scott who runs the Sans Pareil. Her pa invented washin' blue and magic lanterns, and made a fortune. He built the theatre for her. She writes most of the plays too.'

'Good grief,' Lavender said. 'I'd forgotten about that.'

'What do you want me to do?' Woods asked.

'You go home to your family tonight, Ned, and pay an early morning call on Mistress Higgin at the bakery. Oh, damn—'

'What's the matter?

'I had promised to call on Magdalena tonight.'

'You can still do that,' Woods said. 'Those theatres don't come alive until late anyway. In fact, she might want to go with you. You could both stay and enjoy the show.'

'That's hardly appropriate, Ned,' Lavender said. 'I'm a detective, investigating the case of a young woman murdered in distressing and suspicious circumstances. I can't sit down in the theatre where she worked and enjoy the show. Besides which, I'm not sure that a bawdy Covent Garden theatre is the place to take Doña Magdalena.'

Woods shrugged. 'Why not? Who's to know if you watch the show? And even your favourite surgeon said you should be more sociable. It is my opinion that you should be more adventurous in your courtin'.'

'You're full of advice about the ladies again, I see.' Lavender's tone was ironic. 'And as a matter of fact, Sir Richard is not my "favourite surgeon".'

'Well, you do need a prompt now and then.' Woods was a man on a mission and no amount or irony or sarcasm would deter him. 'Faint heart never won fair maid, sir. Besides which, Betsy said she's a lively gal who stays in her lodgin's most of the time and is weary of the boredom.'

'Betsy?' Lavender's head turned sharply. 'When did Betsy meet her?'

'Your Spanish widow called around at our home last Monday and introduced herself. They had quite a chat, I understand – though Betsy did complain later that she had arrived, unannounced, in the middle of wash day.'

'Good God.' Lavender tried to imagine the gracious and aristocratic Magdalena seated at a kitchen table, sharing a cup of strong tea with his constable's wife, surrounded by soapsuds and mountainous piles of dirty laundry. 'What on earth did they talk about?' He couldn't understand what the two women could have in common.

Woods paused for a moment and screwed up his broad face, trying to remember. Eventually, he said: 'Us. I think.'

'Us?'

'Yes.'

The two men stared blankly at each other. Lavender decided that this didn't bear thinking about. He'd known the diminutive and feisty Betsy Woods for as long as he'd known her loyal hulk of a husband. Betsy knew more about him than he cared to admit and he had a twinge of unease about what she might have told Magdalena.

'Anyway, Betsy said you should bring her round for supper some time but remember to give her some warnin'. Apparently, Doña Magdalena can be forgiven for turnin' up unannounced – but you won't be.'

Chapter Four

'He's here, the Señor Detective!'

Magdalena Morales sighed. She had spent many hours over the winter teaching the English language to her maid, Teresa, but despite this Teresa's grammar still left a lot to be desired. It always worsened when she was excited, and there was no doubt that Teresa found the visits from Detective Stephen Lavender very exciting. The girl had hovered by the large casement window that overlooked the street for the past half an hour.

'I make the coffee for the Señor Detective! Strong, *oscuro*, like him.' Teresa hung their battered copper kettle over the fire in the grate. She fussed with the coals and reached up to the shelf for their mismatched china cups and saucers.

Magdalena moved across to the window. Stephen stood in the bustling street by the hansom cab. He glanced around and frowned.

What was the matter? she wondered. When he smiled he was a very attractive man with genuine warmth in his brown eyes. Unfortunately, he didn't smile often. Her eyes roamed over his smart burgundy coat. She noticed how well it fitted his tall, slender frame. His slenderness belied the strength in his muscular shoulders and arms. She remembered the thrill she had experienced a few weeks ago when he had held her close to comfort her. It had been nearly a year since she had last seen her late husband. *A long time to be without a man*, she thought, and forgave herself for the guilty attraction she felt for Stephen Lavender.

Inevitably, Magdalena's eyes were drawn back to Lavender's figure. As usual, the cravat above his striped silk waistcoat was spotless and gleamed like cream in the soft lamplight. His boots shone with polish. He was smart and had exquisite taste. If only he would smile more often. But he was naturally serious, rather enigmatic and the responsibilities of his position as a principal officer with the Bow Street Magistrates' Court often weighed heavily on his shoulders.

Magdalena sighed. She had never paid much attention to men who worked for a living before: it wasn't the social class she had been born into, or generally cared much about. But Stephen was different. She enjoyed his intelligent companionship and his dry humour, and appreciated his generosity. But most of all she loved it when his mouth curled up into a smile and he teased or flirted with her. He was also a wealthy man – or so Betsy Woods had intimated last week. Magdalena had been startled to hear that the principal officers were paid a guinea a day in expenses when they went out into the provinces to help the local magistrates and landowners solve difficult crimes. As his assistant on these trips, Constable Woods was also generously rewarded. But the thought of the work Stephen did made her shudder slightly. What unpleasant crimes had he been forced to deal with this week? She braced herself, smiled and resolved to make him laugh tonight.

As Stephen disappeared into the ground floor of her building, she noticed that he had not let his hansom cab go. The driver remained outside in the street. Was something wrong?

Teresa was still crashing around with the crockery so Magdalena glided across their spartan room and opened the door to greet Stephen. The *dueñas* amongst her friends and family would have been horrified at this loss of status, but Magdalena didn't care any more. Her world had been turned upside down since she had fled her home in Spain and found refuge in these cramped lodgings in Spitalfields. She made her own rules now.

The young son of her landlady answered Stephen's knock at the main door downstairs. She heard movement, then the step of his boots on the flagstoned floor. Their voices drifted up on the chilly air towards her. Stephen's was deep, calm and polite. Then she heard the thunder of feet as the boy raced down the gloomy hallway to his own family's rooms. 'Ma!' he shouted. 'That papist bitch 'as got a gentleman visitor!'

Stephen's face was dark with anger when he rounded the bend in the narrow stairwell and came into view. She smiled sympathetically and moved towards him. He ignored her proffered hand, grabbed her elbow and pushed her firmly her back into her room, slamming the door shut behind them. Teresa glanced up startled, with a rattle of saucers.

'I hate you living here, Magdalena!' he said as he yanked off his gloves. 'It is deplorable that you should be subjected to that kind of insult.'

She smiled again, amused at his protectiveness and the ferocity of his anger. 'It is all I can afford, Stephen,' she said slowly. 'I'm a Spanish Catholic in Protestant London; there will always be some prejudice. I have got used to it – and you should too.' She shrugged. 'Besides which, these lodgings have a great blessing.'

He eyed her quizzically. 'Which is . . . ?'

She led him over to the tall, bare window and pointed out into the heaving street below. Despite the falling darkness, it was still a hive of activity. Market traders stamped their feet and clutched themselves against the biting cold behind their stalls, stubbornly determined to sell the last of their produce. Their icy breath billowed from their open mouths as they called out their wares. An

Italian organ grinder turned the crank of his ancient box as a tiny monkey bedecked in a little jacket trimmed with silver bells danced around to the delight of a group of street urchins. Beside the organ grinder an old woman turned hot chestnuts over in her brazier.

'After years of being buried in the countryside at our estate in Asturias, I finally have a window to the world. I spend hours here every day, Stephen. I have never seen such life, such activity and vitality.'

As intended, her enthusiasm distracted Lavender from his anger. The edge of his lips flickered with a smile. 'I had assumed that you spent most of your life in Madrid,' he said.

'No, no. For the first few years of my marriage, yes – but once Sebastián was born it suited Antonio for me to remain quietly in the country with my child and his parents.' She raised both her hands in a sharp, frustrated gesture. 'After Sebastián was sent to school and my father died, I found it was dull and tiresome. But now? Now I see life again. It is – how do you say it? – mesmerising.'

Magdalena saw one of Lavender's eyebrows twitch with disbelief, so she gestured to him to sit in one of the two old chairs by the window. Once they were both seated she pointed through the grimy panes to a fat, greying man with huge sideburns who sold vegetables at a stall on the opposite side of the street.

'He reminds me of Constable Woods,' she said. 'He has a friendly word for everyone – especially the children of this street. He's also a shrewd businessman. There is a woman, a customer, who owes him money . . .'

Lavender leant towards the window, his eyes searching for the woman Magdalena referred to. Magdalena caught the faint scent of his masculinity mixed with soap, as he moved closer to her.

'Oh, she's not there right now,' Magdalena said. Lavender fell back, a little disappointed. 'She shops in the morning and has many, many children whom she struggles to feed. I have seen the tension between her and the stallholder and assumed she owed him money. They have been eyeing each other awkwardly for weeks. She crosses over to the other side of the road, rather than risk being accosted by him for the debt. Then – last week – my suspicions were confirmed. I saw him cross the road to speak to her. At first she was alarmed but then the relief flooded across her face. I think he has written off her debt.'

'Why would he do that?'

Her lips curled up slowly into a smile. 'Because I now see him overcharging her. I know his prices and I see what she pays. She can't keep up with his addition. He overcharges her every time. Not a lot, just a penny here and a half-penny there.'

'It is possible he overcharges all of his customers.'

She shook her head. 'No, I have checked. I watch him every day.'

'An honest trader,' Lavender said, wryly. 'He must be the only one in London.'

'I think he's clever. He's slowly recouping his debt from the woman – and he still has the custom of one of the biggest families on the street.'

Finally, Lavender smiled. He sat back in the chair and observed Magdalena closely. 'He's a smart tradesman, in that case. And you can see and hear all that from here, from this window?'

'I listen and I watch the coins changing hands.'

'You're very vigilant.'

'Oh, there is more, far, far more.' Magdalena pointed to a young woman with wispy hair and a pale, thin face beneath a straw bonnet. The girl stood on the corner of the alley opposite. She seemed nervous and clutched her shawl tightly around her shoulders against the bitter night air.

He frowned. 'What is she?' he asked.

'I know what you're thinking.' Magdalena smiled. 'But she's no woman of the night. She's in love. Every evening she waits there for her sweetheart to finish work at the tannery and when he arrives her face lights up with joy. They link arms and walk home together for their supper.'

'How do you know she hasn't already eaten?'

'Because she's forever glancing at the hot chestnuts in the brazier and occasionally rubs her belly.'

Lavender was grinning now, his dark eyes soft and warm. 'What else do you see from your window to the world, Magdalena? Any crimes you would like me to solve?'

'Not really, Stephen,' she purred. 'There is nothing to concern a senior officer like yourself. Yes, there have been a few incidents of theft and I once saw a pickpocket steal a man's watch. But these are crimes for the constables – not for important detectives like you. Although, there is one mystery I can't fathom . . .'

'Oh?'

She knew that the word 'mystery' would never fail to get his attention. Magdalena pointed across the street to a shifty individual lurking against the wall of the tavern. Above his scarves, the man's face was ravaged with scars from the smallpox and haunted with an angry intensity. 'That man there – I think he's evil. He sells a greyish, white foodstuff, which I can't determine. His customers are some of the most haggard and starving of the beggars. They clamour for his product when he visits the street. They surround him, mob him and then devour this produce like vultures as they walk away. I don't know what it is.'

Lavender sighed. His frown returned but his voice was gentle. 'Stay away from him, Magdalena. It's opium.'

'Opium?' She was startled. 'Why do they want it so much? Are they in pain?'

'Pain of a sort. Opium reduces the pangs of hunger – and it is cheaper than bread for the poor beggars to buy. It is also addictive, which explains their desperation.'

Magdalena paused. Her mind reeled. Inadvertently, she had reminded him of the meanness of her neighbourhood, a fact from which she had tried to distract him. She also felt overwhelmed with her own ignorance. There was still so much about England and her new life that she needed to learn. Her descent into the position of poverty-stricken émigré, forced to live cheek by jowl with the criminal underbelly of London, had been swift and brutal.

Fortunately, at that moment Teresa arrived beside them with cups of steaming coffee.

'Thank you, Teresa,' Lavender said in Spanish. 'It is just how I like it – as usual.' He gave the maid a friendly smile, which made her blush with delight. She left them reluctantly and Magdalena had to lower her own head to hide her amusement.

Despite the heat of the beverage, Lavender drank it quickly. This urgency of movement was a new development and it reminded her of the cab waiting for him on the street.

'Alas, Magdalena. Unfortunately, I will be unable to stay much longer tonight.'

Disappointment washed over her, as he drained the last sips of coffee from his cup.

'I have to follow a line of inquiry at the Sans Pareil Theatre on the Strand. We discovered the body of one of the actresses today – she died in mysterious circumstances.'

Magdalena's hand flew to her mouth with shock. 'That is terrible news, Stephen. The poor girl – her poor family!'

'That is one of the reasons why I must go there tonight,' he said. 'We have only just identified the girl and as yet her family is unaware of her death. I called at the theatre on the way here but it was virtually deserted and the porter at the stage door suggested that I return later to interview the proprietor and the other actors.'

An idea began to form in Magdalena's mind. She mulled it over for a moment and chose her next words carefully. 'Might it not be better to speak to them *after* tonight's performance, Stephen? Your news may distress them and they will still have to work.'

A frown flickered across his forehead and she knew he was considering her suggestion. 'That may be how I should proceed,' he said. 'The porter also told me that the Duke of Clarence was due to attend the play tonight.'

This new and exciting information strengthened her resolve to push for the scheme that had formed in her head. She tapped his hand lightly. 'Then it is decided. You can't damage the performance of the actors and actresses with your bad news if royalty will be in the house. That would be unforgivable and may lead to your imprisonment in the Tower of London.'

He laughed and she decided to push her advantage. 'Tell me about this theatre. What kind of plays do they have?'

He shrugged. 'I believe they're licensed for all manner of musical entertainments, pantomime and burletta. They also perform melodramas, farces, comic operettas and historical dramas.'

'It sounds delightful, yes?' she said. 'I suggest that Teresa and I get our cloaks and accompany you to tonight's performance; we will wait in your cab afterwards while you question the manager and the actors.'

His mouth dropped open in surprise and she sensed that he was about to protest. She rose to her feet, and switched to Spanish to instruct Teresa to fetch her best cloak, bonnet and hand-muff.

'There won't be a problem, will there, Stephen? After all, any play patronised by the Duke of Clarence will be appropriate for Teresa to view, will it not? She's unmarried – we must not forget that. But if my understanding of the language of the French pigs is correct, *sans pareil* means "without comparison". Will this be a peerless performance, do you think?' She gave him her most beseeching smile, her head tilted to one side.

As he rose to his own feet she saw the amusement in his eyes. 'I'm sure it will be appropriate for Teresa – although, I suspect she won't understand half of it, anyway.' He glanced back at the murky panes of the tall window behind them. 'I think that you will find the theatre an exciting new window through which you can view the world; in fact, it will probably be a window to the world *without comparison.*'

Chapter Five

Lavender was well aware that Magdalena had beguiled him into taking her to the theatre. But he didn't care. It had been easy to dismiss Woods' suggestion earlier in the day but when confronted with the same idea from the attractive and confident ebony-haired beauty herself, the small voice of reason inside his head could barely squeak. The women clambered into his cab with a waft of delicious perfume, and when they were seated Magdalena's thighs pressed against his through their layers of clothing, causing his mind to fill with ungentlemanly thoughts.

When their cab slowed to a crawl in the heavy evening traffic of the Strand, Lavender attempted to distract himself from the close proximity of Magdalena's curvaceous body by pointing out the sights. The Strand was one of the better lit of London's thoroughfares and its mile of shops, houses, low taverns, theatres and coffee houses transected a part of the capital that had been occupied since Roman times. A popular high-class shopping area by day, some of the seedier nature of Covent Garden spilled over onto the Strand at night. The cab passed the royal mews with its long line of stables and approached the Sans Pareil from the east.

'Oh! Look at that funny little church marooned in an island in the middle of the street!' Magdalena laughed with delight.

'That is St Clement Danes,' Lavender explained. 'The road has been forced to go around it on both sides as the city expanded. There is the Dog and Duck tavern.' He pointed to an inn whose well-lit interior cast pools of golden light onto the crowded pavement below. 'The infamous Gunpowder Plot conspirators who tried to blow up King James the first and his Parliament met there.'

'It looks a lively place,' she said.

'Yes,' he said slowly. His tone left no doubt that there were other adjectives he probably would have applied to the Dog and Duck tavern. She glanced at him curiously. 'The Dog and Duck is notable for its song-and-supper evenings.' He hesitated for a moment before he continued, unsure how she would react to his next revelation. 'It also provides several tableaux of scantily clad women in lewd poses and other ribald shows.'

Magdalena laughed out loud. 'Then Teresa and I must make sure we don't inadvertently wander into those premises.'

Lavender smiled to himself in the darkness of the cab. Their carriage came to a sudden halt, this time in front of the neoclassical arches and colonnaded upper storeys of the magnificent Somerset House. Magdalena groaned in frustration. They were nose to tail with half a dozen hansom cabs.

'I think we may as well walk from here,' he said and rapped on the roof of the vehicle to attract the attention of their driver. Despite the boisterous and drunken behaviour of many in the crowd, their short walk to the Sans Pareil went without incident. Lavender kept his eyes open for pickpockets and steered the women away from the dirty gutter water sprayed up by the wheels of the traffic.

He felt a surge of pride in the beautiful and majestic woman who swept along beside him, her gloved hand resting lightly in the crook of his arm. She had begun to wear her hair in the

English style, he noted. The sombre mantilla and tortoiseshell *peineta* she had favoured when they first met were gone. Long, black curls now trailed over her shoulders beneath her bonnet and short ringlets framed her oval face in the Grecian fashion. Beneath her velvet cloak she wore the black dress he had bought her at Christmas. Magdalena was becoming anglicised. Her olive skin and striking dark eyes singled her out as a beauty rather than an Iberian; only her Spanish accent still marked her out as a foreigner.

He smiled to himself with amusement when he saw the four stone columns that supported the portico above the entrance to the Sans Pareil. They mirrored the four stone columns at the front of St Paul's Church in Covent Garden, also known as 'the actors' church'. When John Scott, the wealthy merchant, had converted these buildings into the Sans Pareil Theatre for his stage-struck daughter, he had clearly put some thought into the impression he wanted the architecture to create. Above their heads, the portico had been planted with trailing bushes and sweet-smelling jasmine that wound its way down the stonework towards their heads. A nice feminine touch, Lavender decided, and in keeping with the only theatre in London operated by a woman.

They were early and the foyer was empty. Lavender was able to purchase a box for himself, Magdalena and Teresa for four shillings each and he was thankful for that. Despite her obvious sympathy towards the poor and the semi-literate, Lavender suspected that Magdalena's tolerance might wear thin if she was forced to spend several hours bumping shoulders in the stalls with the smelly, London underclass, whom at this time of night would be befuddled with gin and ale.

Magdalena requested that they waited a while in the foyer before climbing the red-carpeted stairwell to their box. She wanted to watch the theatregoers arrive – especially Prince William, the

Duke of Clarence. While they waited, Lavender explained some of the brief history of the theatre.

'A woman?' she asked. Her dark eyes widened. 'A woman runs this theatre and writes the plays?'

'Yes, Miss Scott's father is a successful businessman who created this empire for his daughter. For years she ran a troupe of amateur actors at the back of one of her father's warehouses but three years ago he invested ten thousand pounds in these buildings and had them converted into a theatre for her to expand her ambition. His timing was impeccable. Two years ago there was a bad fire at Covent Garden Theatre and last year Drury Lane burnt to the ground. Although both companies have found smaller, alternative premises, many of the actors and actresses have found a new home here, which has added to the prestige and popularity of the Sans Pareil.'

'Fire?' Magdalena's eyes flicked warily towards the blazing chandeliers above their heads and the fat candles in their sconces, scattered amongst the framed playbills along the walls.

'Yes,' he continued. 'It appears to be a regular hazard for theatre proprietors in London at the moment.'

'Not arson, I trust?'

He shook his head. 'There's been nothing to indicate that an arsonist with a vendetta against theatres is roaming the streets of the capital.'

'And if there was, then Mr John Scott would have probably been at the top of your list of suspects,' Magdalena said. 'He seems to have been the main beneficiary of the misfortune of others.'

Lavender smiled. 'Meanwhile, Miss Scott has been described as "great artiste" by the theatre critics. Her plays have a tendency towards the melodramatic and the Gothic but there are several excellent singers in her cast so we shall not want for entertainment. If we're lucky we may see her perform tonight.'

'Is she beautiful?' Magdalena demanded.

'Er, no.'

The audience had now begun to arrive, so Lavender, Magdalena and Teresa were forced back against the wall. The foyer became a noisy gathering of men in smart topcoats and hats. Women in brightly coloured muslin dresses and bonnets hung on to their arms. Occasionally, there was a flash of scarlet as officers arrived and swept their regimental hats beneath their arms. Many people paused in the foyer to greet friends or, like Magdalena, to see the arrival of the prince. The air buzzed with excitement, hailed greetings and gossip; candlelight reflected from the brass buttons and glistening jewellery of the clientele.

As the temperature rose, Magdalena unbuttoned her cloak. Lavender was distracted from his admiration of the creamy skin of her throat and bosom by a crowd of drunken ruffians who pushed their way through the crowd towards the auditorium. They swung glass bottles by their side. 'Keep a firm grasp on your purse,' he advised. 'The theatre attracts every kind of person and pickpockets and opportunist thieves often circulate amongst the crowds.'

But the leader of the gang was interested in something else Magdalena possessed. He whistled when he laid eyes on her and bowed low in an elaborate gesture. His companions followed his courtly example.

'You're a beautiful gal,' the man said, before moving on.

Pink spots appeared on Magdalena's cheeks and she bowed her head regally to her new admirers.

Lavender scowled.

Suddenly, a fan rapped smartly on his arm. 'Good evening, Detective. I sincerely hope that you're here tonight for pleasure rather than business.'

He turned and found the sharp, grey eyes of the tall and willowy Lady Caroline Clare scrutinising him. A strikingly attractive redhead in her early forties, she had been injured in an accident in her youth and relied on a silver-topped walking cane for support. 'Good evening, your ladyship.' He bowed. 'I'm here to see the play.'

'Thank goodness for that!' Her pearl-studded turban topped with yellow ostrich feathers bobbed up and down as she nodded her head in satisfaction. 'We don't want the taint of criminal activity to spoil tonight's performance. You'd better introduce to me to that pretty girl, Lavender.'

'Lady Caroline, may I present Doña Magdalena Morales, widow of Don Antonio Garcia de Aviles, who fell at the Battle of Talavera. Magdalena, this is Lady Caroline Clare.'

Magdalena dropped a deep and regal curtsey, the grace of which momentarily caught him off guard. The candlelight caught the sheen of the glossy black curls on the top of her bowed head.

'It is a pleasure to meet you, Lady Caroline,' Magdalena said as she rose back to her full height.

'My condolences, my dear.' Lady Caroline's eyes were firmly fixed on Magdalena's face. 'I have buried two husbands and I know that your loss is recent. The Battle of Talavera was last summer, wasn't it?'

'Yes. Thank you for your kindness, your ladyship.'

'Oh, this damned, interminable war.' Her ladyship shook her head sadly. 'You're not the first woman to be widowed by it – and unfortunately you won't be the last. Your accent suggests to me that you're from northern Spain, am I correct?'

Lavender smiled. Caroline Clare was as sharp and intelligent as ever.

'Yes, I'm from Oviedo, although I have lived a while in Madrid.'

'A beautiful region, with a spectacular landscape and excellent light for artists,' Lady Caroline declared. 'I travelled the countryside of the Asturias with my first husband twenty years ago and he had to tear me away from your mountains. In fact, a painting of the Cantabrian Mountains still hangs in my drawing room. Would you like to see it sometime? It's very amateurish of course, but I understand homesickness. It might give you some pleasure.'

Magdalena's neck and face flushed. 'You're most kind.'

'Call on me one afternoon, preferably a Wednesday. I tend to have commissions on most other days.'

'Thank you.'

'Lady Caroline is often commissioned to paint portraits,' Lavender explained. 'I have seen your work, Lady Caroline, and you're a talented artist. You do not do yourself justice.'

She waved an elegant hand dismissively in the air. Her rings flashed in the light and he saw tiny flecks of oil paint on her fingers.

'You're charming as always, Lavender. Painting landscapes is my favourite occupation of course, but one has to go where the money is – and the money is definitely in portraits. Every wealthy man wants his dog, his horse or his children captured on canvas for prosperity. Besides which, I have a little trouble climbing the mountains these days.' She tapped her left leg with her walking cane. 'Lavender, I trust I can rely on you to give Doña Magdalena my address?'

He bowed his head again. 'Of course.'

'Then I shall leave you now, my dear. I'm a little slow and it may take some time for me to get into my damned seat. Henry? Come here! Give me your arm.'

A lanky young man stepped forward. He had hovered, unintroduced, behind Lady Caroline for the last few minutes. 'Henry, this is the famous Detective Lavender from Bow Street Magistrates' Court. I have told you about him before. This is his charming companion Doña Magdalena Morales. Lavender, meet Henry Duddles, nephew of Baron Lannister and my escort for tonight.'

Both men bowed and a huge shock of blond curls fell forward over Duddles's face. He hurriedly pushed them back into place and glanced sheepishly at Magdalena. Lavender smiled to himself. The lad was barely shaving. Caroline Clare always preferred them young.

Once Lady Caroline and her companion had departed, Magdalena couldn't contain her excitement. 'What a charming woman! So kind! And she has visited my country! Do tell me more about her.'

They were jostled by the crowd and Teresa yelped when someone stood on her foot. He motioned to the women to step further back.

He leant closer to Magdalena closer and lowered his voice.

'Lady Caroline was the younger daughter of the Earl of Kirkleven.'

'An earl!'

'Yes – an impoverished earl. The Kirklevens are an old Lancashire Catholic family who lost much of their fortune and influence after supporting the Jacobite cause.'

'Catholics!'

He smiled. That was an unexpected benefit for her, he realised – a commonality. 'She was motherless from a young age—'

'Like me. I barely remember my mother.'

'I believe she was a wild young thing.'

Magdalena's eyebrow rose and she smiled.

'Anyway, when she was eighteen she eloped with Victor Meyer Rothschild, a younger member of the great European banking family.'

'The Rothschilds? They're the Jewish bankers, yes?' Her smile fell. 'Such a marriage, across the religions, would not have suited their families, no?'

Lavender hesitated while he considered what more to tell Magdalena and what to leave out. She was so excited about her new friend that he didn't want to take the edge off her happiness. He wasn't completely convinced that Lady Caroline was a suitable companion for Magdalena, but he couldn't deny they had plenty in common. Nor would he deny the mutual attraction that seemed to have sprung up between the two women. He shrugged and made his decision. Magdalena was an intelligent woman who would make up her own mind. 'Both families disowned the couple and cut them off without a penny,' he said. 'They eloped to the continent, where I believe she made a living from her art. I suspect they supported themselves through Lady Caroline's painting.'

'She must have loved her husband a lot' – Magdalena's dark eyes shone with emotion – 'if she was prepared to give up everything for him – *and* work to provide the food on their table.'

'She's a remarkable woman,' Lavender said. 'However, their happiness was short-lived. They were involved in a coaching accident in northern France and Victor was killed. She was badly injured and, as you can see, has never fully regained her health, or her mobility, since then.'

'What happened next?'

'Her father brought her back to Kirkleven and arranged a new marriage for her to an elderly neighbour. She once told me that she was too ill and distraught to protest. I don't think Baron Clare was particularly wealthy or left her much income. She now supports her lifestyle in London through her portrait commissions. It is quite the fashionable thing to do, I understand, to have a portrait painted by the notorious Lady Caroline Clare.'

'Did they have children?'

'There are a couple of stepchildren, I believe, from the baron's first marriage.'

'They may have been some comfort to her.' He could see in Magdalena's eyes that she was thinking of Sebastián, her ten-year-old son, who was away at boarding school. The romanticism of Caroline Clare's history clearly fascinated her.

'I suppose the scandal of her elopement with Rothschild affected her chances of a making a more suitable second marriage.' Magdalena's tone was thoughtful, her words matter-of-fact.

'Yes, it was a great scandal, at the time,' he said.

Finally, she asked the question he was most concerned about. 'How do you know her so well, Stephen?'

'She required my services in a professional capacity a few years ago,' he said slowly.

'Oh?'

'She was being blackmailed by a young lover.'

Magdalena spluttered, threw back her head and burst into peals of laughter. Her whole body heaved in the most charming way. Several people turned in their direction, their eyes resting on the beautiful, laughing woman beside him. 'I never expected that,' she said.

'There are some who claim that Lady Caroline Clare is not a respectable woman.'

'I don't want to know,' she said. 'I shall be the judge of Lady Caroline's character – upon better acquaintance.'

Suddenly, her smile vanished. Her attention had been caught by a group of people across the foyer. Lavender glanced up. He realised at once from their dark complexions and alien clothing that they were foreign. Black lace covered the heads of the two frowning women, held in place by high combs. A tall, sour-faced man of about twenty-five with the shoulders of his black coat enhanced with the embroidered decorative pads in the style of a Spanish matador, glared back at Magdalena. There was no mop of foppish curls for him; his sleek black hair was pulled back into a ponytail. He had a long nose and prominent cheekbones beneath a swarthy face.

Magdalena smiled and bowed her head at the group but they turned their backs towards her and began to converse amongst themselves. He heard Magdalena gasp at the snub and felt her quiver with anger.

'Do you know those people?'

'Yes, that is Felipe Menendez and his sisters, Juana and Olaya. They were my neighbours back in Oviedo,' she said. 'I had no idea that they had also fled from Spain; I assume that they're now émigrés like me.'

'Your neighbours?' He was startled. 'Why on earth didn't they acknowledge you?'

She sighed. 'It is a long story, Stephen – and not a happy one. I will tell you some day. Let us take our seats in the theatre. I no longer wish to wait for the arrival of the duke.'

Chapter Six

Their burletta, *Mary, the Maid of the Inn; or, The Bough of Yew* was based on the tragic story of Robert Southey's poem 'Mary'. The story followed a young tavern wench, Mary, who accepted a wager to walk into a haunted abbey on a stormy night and retrieve a yew bough from the chancel. While Mary cowered beneath the ivy-clad ruins she witnessed her idle lover, Richard, and his companion burying the body of a man they had murdered. When Richard is later hanged for the crime, Mary sinks into madness and spends the rest of her life roaming the parish as a wild-eyed beggar.

Before the play began, they were entertained by Toby, the performing dog. The Jack Russell terrier wore a glittering, frilled collar, which matched that of his human handler. Toby walked on his hind-legs, played tricks on his human co-star and jumped through hoops in time to a lively Irish jig played by the theatre's orchestra. Teresa was enchanted with the little dog's antics. Flushed and excited, the young maid clapped her hands and rose to her feet with the rest of the boisterous audience to cheer and applaud when Toby bowed and made his exit. But Magdalena seemed unmoved and stared blankly at the stage.

'There was some trouble at this theatre last week,' Lavender told her. 'An audience threatened to riot when they didn't get the performance that had been billed. I suspect that the management have included the dog act to sweeten their clients.'

'It was charming,' she said, quietly. Her despondency contrasted sharply with the ebullient mood of most of the audience who chattered excitedly, waved across the theatre to their friends and consumed copious amounts of alcohol – and in some instances, food – in the stalls below. Apart from the traditional proliferation of oranges in the theatre, some patrons appeared to have brought picnics with them.

'What do you think of the theatre?' he asked.

'It's pretty,' she said, refusing to be drawn into further conversation.

Lavender glanced around and found that he agreed with her. The decorations and embellishments of this new theatre were in good taste: glittering gilt candelabras hung from the ceiling and broke up the pastel-coloured wooden inlays of the cream-coloured gallery, which reached around the walls of the auditorium. There was a light and airy feel to the whole place. It compared favourably to the bigger and now destroyed Drury Lane Theatre, where the management had the audience packed like sardines. At the Sans Pareil, their box was commodious and the red cushioned seats were comfortable.

Although melodramatic in the extreme, the play was enlivened by several solo renditions of songs written especially for the show. William Broadhurst, as the villainous lover, Richard, gave a particularly good performance. John Isaacs and Gabriel Gomez also stood out for their excellent singing. But Lavender was disappointed with the quality of Gomez's acting; the man clearly relied on his singing voice to make his way in the theatre.

Jane Scott herself took the role of Mary. She had both a confident and powerful stage presence and an excellent singing voice. As the actress wept and wailed her way through a sad ballad, Lavender heard several people in the audience sniffle. Even Teresa, whose English was limited, had tears glistening on her soft cheeks.

'Do you think she sings well?' he asked Magdalena. Her face was rigid; she was still angry about the incident in the foyer.

'She has the sweetest voice,' Magdalena commented, sharply. 'But I can tell by the way she moves that she was afflicted with rickets as a child.'

Magdalena was sullen and barely spoke while they waited for the curtain to rise on the final act. Lavender waited patiently for her mood to pass and silently cursed the Spaniards who had spoiled her evening. He wasn't in a rush to find out the cause of their open hostility towards the woman at his side. He already knew from something John Read had said and his subsequent inquiries that Magdalena had been forced to shoot her way out of Spain in order to escape with her son. He suspected that the two incidents were related. Magdalena would tell him about it when she was ready.

They had a good view of the Royal Box and its occupants from where they sat, although Magdalena only gave them a cursory glance. The Duke of Clarence and his party were sumptuously dressed in rich and colourful gowns and uniforms. The women glittered with jewels. The duke wore a silver badge with the insignia of an admiral on the lapel of his dove-grey velvet topcoat. Beside him sat a short man in the dark blue and gold-braided coat of a naval lieutenant. Lavender recognised him as the duke's aide, Sir Lawrence Forsyth, who now worked for the naval department in Whitehall. From the sour expression on his face, Forsyth wasn't enjoying the show. His close-set eyes narrowed with distaste at the performance on the stage. He seemed dwarfed in his chair sat beside the tall, stocky duke. Something about the aide's face and his long nose reminded Lavender of a weasel.

Prince William had a broad face and a double chin that wobbled above his high-necked cravat when he laughed. He was delighted with the show. He clapped his large hands loudly and boomed 'Encore!' at the end of each act. 'Damned cove!' he'd exclaimed when Richard's villainy was exposed. Lavender smiled to himself as he noticed that when the duke became animated, Forsyth dropped his sour expression and mimicked every action and every exclamation of the prince.

Magdalena followed his gaze and scrutinised the occupants of the Royal Box. 'That stout woman with the prince,' she asked, 'who is she?'

'Which one?' There were several women in the party.

'The one with the sequined headband and ostrich feathers in her frizzy hair.'

Lavender glanced across at the short, plump woman seated next to the duke. He lowered his voice. 'That is the famous actress, Dorothy Jordan. She's the duke's long-time mistress and the darling of Drury Lane. They have been together nearly twenty years.'

'I have heard of her,' said Magdalena. 'She was a great comedy actress, was she not? And quite famous for strutting across the stage in men's clothing.'

'Dorothy Jordan still acts occasionally and always draws huge crowds,' he said. 'Her popularity is undiminished.'

Magdalena's head turned sharply. 'She still acts? But she's the mistress of a prince! Why does she need to work?'

'The prince is heavily in debt,' Lavender explained. 'They have ten children back home in Bushy Park. It is rumoured that the money Mrs Jordan earns from theatrical tours and benefits is the only thing which keeps their home and the Duke of Clarence afloat.'

'I think your British women are very practical,' she said. 'Tonight I have been in the company of at least three talented women who support themselves – or their families – through their work.'

He nodded towards the stage. 'I don't think Jane Scott needs the money. Her father is wealthy.'

'No, she works in this theatre to satisfy her passion. I suspect that both Lady Caroline Clare and Dorothy Jordan also have a passion; they would not be so successful if they didn't.' She frowned and looked thoughtful. 'Maybe it is time I became more practical about my own situation.'

He sensed that she was pondering something but there was no time to enquire further about the meaning of her words because the curtain swept aside and the actors and actresses returned to the stage for the final sad act. Lavender didn't particularly enjoy melodrama. He grimaced throughout most of the act, especially when Mary killed herself from grief. Many of the audience dabbed at their eyes with their handkerchiefs but he was relieved when the final curtain fell.

Led by the upstanding and appreciative Duke of Clarence, the audience rose to their feet. The applause was deafening. The Hanoverian princes were a sentimental bunch, Lavender decided.

As she applauded, Magdalena pointed to the three huge candelabras, which still burned fiercely at the front of the stage. Each one must have held twenty fat candles. 'There were several occasions when I thought that Miss Scott's costume may catch in the flames.' She had to lean in to Lavender to make herself heard over the cheering and the applause. 'But I don't suppose that it would have been the first time an actress caught fire.'

'No, it wouldn't.' He enjoyed this enforced closeness to her warm body and the smell of her hair. 'It is quite common for an actor to catch fire during a performance. However, it does tend to liven up a dull play.'

She slapped him playfully on the arm with her fan and he thought he saw the glimmer of a smile at the corner of her lips. Relieved that her mood had lightened, he took his leave and arranged to meet her and Teresa in the foyer after he had finished his business backstage.

He went down to the stalls and, pushing his way through the tide of bodies trying to exit the theatre, made his way towards the exit at the side of the stage. A porter, resplendent in the green and gold livery of the theatre, barred his way but once Lavender explained his business the man led him through the dark maze of narrow passages backstage.

'Duke of Clarence and 'is party are coming backstage to congratulate the cast,' he told Lavender. 'Everyone's waiting for 'im in there in the green room.' He pointed to a door fifty yards down the corridor.

Lavender nodded. Even without guidance from the porter, he would have easily located the green room. Apart from the buzz of excited voices emanating from the crowded chamber at the end of the corridor, there was a constant stream of animated cast members going in and out. Every time the door opened, he caught a glimpse of the soft green interior walls, which according to tradition, helped to rest the cast's eyes after the glare of candlelight on the stage.

He grimaced inwardly. After such a successful performance and a visit from the Duke of Clarence, Lavender knew he would be as welcome amongst these people as the spectre at the feast. The news he carried about April Divine would dash their high spirits and ruin their night.

His guide obviously had the same idea. The porter stopped abruptly halfway down the corridor, and opened the door to a chilly office littered with props, discarded costumes and bookkeeping files. He gestured for Lavender to walk inside. A weak lamp glimmered on the battered desk. It smelt of paint and sawdust.

'If you can wait in 'ere for a while, Detective,' he said awkwardly. 'I'll get a message to Miss Scott that yer 'ere.'

Lavender glanced around at the cluttered space and nodded.

When Jane Scott limped stiffly into the cramped room her father accompanied her. Lavender stood up from the solitary chair in the room and offered it to Jane. She sank into it gratefully.

'My father is the general manager of the theatre,' she explained. 'If your business pertains to the Sans Pareil, then he needs to hear it.'

Jane Scott was tiny. Her magnificent stage presence had belied her diminutive stature. Beneath the heavy grease paint of her stage make-up, he saw the disfiguring marks of smallpox. She looked exhausted.

'Good grief! This is terrible!' she exclaimed, after Lavender had told them the reason for his visit. 'Poor April! What a dreadful way to die!' She put her face in her hands and began to sob. Her father placed a comforting arm round her quivering shoulders. After a few moments Jane lifted her head and wiped away her tears with a lawn handkerchief. Great smears of greasepaint and rouge came away on the material, further exposing her disfigured skin.

'We're not certain how she died,' Lavender said. 'We won't know until we have the results of the autopsy. But we can't rule out foul play.'

'Murdered? Oh, this is dreadful!' John Scott had a catch in his voice. His grey eyes were wide with shock. 'Who would want to kill the poor girl?'

'We're doing our best to find out,' Lavender said.

Scott was a tall, plain and balding man with a strong London accent. Lavender saw the intelligence in the eyes beneath his worried frown. Scott pulled himself together and cleared his throat. 'What do you need from us, Detective?' he asked.

'Firstly, I need the address of the girl's lodgings and any information you have about her family. Then I need you to share with me everything you know about Miss April Divine.'

'That probably won't be much,' John Scott said. 'She hasn't been with us very long. She joined us soon after the fire at Drury Lane. She's – was – a competent actress for minor parts but she was never destined for the leading roles.'

'When did you last see her?'

Scott paused for moment and glanced at his daughter. Jane Scott had now rallied herself. 'Last Thursday,' she said. 'April played one of Columbine's four female attendants in *The Necromancer*. We're not due to perform that play again until tomorrow evening.'

'We will have to organise an understudy to play the role for the rest of the season,' John Scott said quietly.

At that moment the door flew open and a flushed young woman strode into the room. 'Miss Scott!' she exclaimed. 'Helena has taken my rouge pot again. She won't give it back.'

'Not now, my dear,' Jane Scott's voice was strained and weary.

The actress glanced at Lavender and quickly dismissed him as unimportant. Ignoring the obvious distress of her employer she opened her mouth to protest and insist on immediate help with this alleged theft. John Scott spoke first: 'Come back later.' There was no arguing with his tone. The actress pressed her lips tightly together in a pout and retreated into the corridor.

'What manner of young woman was April Divine?' Lavender asked.

'Lively, vivacious,' the general manager replied. 'Like most actresses.'

'Did she have any enemies or great rivals?' Lavender asked.

A faint smile curled at the edges of Jane Scott's painted lips. 'As you have seen, there is always rivalry between actors in the theatre, Detective,' she said. 'On some nights, members of the cast stand in the wings and watch the performances of the others so they can later criticise them backstage and undermine their confidence.'

Lavender nodded and thought about the young woman who had just interrupted them.

'Whenever a new play is announced they vie with each other for the best parts,' John Scott added.

'Was there anyone in particular with whom Miss Divine had a disagreement?'

The Scotts both shook their heads. 'She had a cheerful disposition,' said Jane. 'And her roles were not big enough to attract jealousy. I'm not aware of a feud.'

'We have our petty jealousies within the theatre, Detective,' John Scott said. 'The actors squabble and have occasionally fought over a lost hairpin or a mutual admirer. But I can't see any of the cast taking their jealousy as far as murder.'

'Did she have a sweetheart, or a lover?' Lavender asked.

But before he could elicit an answer from the Scotts, the door flew open again. This time it was a heavy-set stagehand in an old hessian apron, stained with oil and filth. 'Miss Scott? Mr Scott? Begging yer pardon fer the interruption but I think yer should know that there's a problem with the 'oist for the scenery flats in the right wing.'

'I'll come in a moment,' John Scott said, and the stagehand disappeared.

'Did she have a sweetheart, or a lover?' Lavender asked again.

Jane Scott shook her head once more. 'I'm afraid I don't know, Detective. Our actresses receive a lot of flowers and gifts from admirers and are regularly invited out to supper by ardent men. Some of them are the mistresses of lords. I can't tell you about April. The other actors from Drury Lane may be able to tell you more about her private life. They knew her better.'

'I will call back to speak to them tomorrow when they have recovered from the shock of her death,' he said.

Jane Scott rose to her feet. Her face grimaced with pain. He suspected that it wasn't just physical. 'Yes, yes,' she said. 'Now I must inform the cast of April's death; they will be devastated.'

'We appreciate your discretion, Detective Lavender,' said John Scott. He held out his hand. 'Thank you. I'm glad you waited until after tonight's performance before you brought us this sad news. It is always a special night for us when the Duke of Clarence and Mrs Jordan are in the audience.'

Lavender bowed his head and shook Scott's hand. 'If I can just have the address of Miss Divine's lodgings and any information pertaining to her family, I would be grateful.'

'I will get the porter to fetch you her address immediately,' Jane said. 'As for her family, I assume that you have realised that Divine wasn't her real name?'

'I had suspected as much,' Lavender said.

'Most of our actresses have a stage name,' Jane Scott said. 'Her real name is – was – April Clare. She was the daughter of Baron Clare of Rochdale, and is the stepdaughter of Lady Caroline Clare who resides at Lincoln's Inn.' Her hand shot over her mouth and her eyes widened with horror at a sudden realisation. 'Poor Lady Clare! I do believe that she was in the house tonight!'

Chapter Seven

Lavender's mind was still reeling when the porter brought him the address of April Clare's lodgings. How the hell had the body of the daughter of an English aristocrat ended up shoved beneath the filthy floorboards of a condemned building?

He hated giving relatives the dreadful news about the death of their loved ones. It was the least favourite part of his job. Normally, he tried to approach this task with a certain degree of professional detachment. The fact that he liked and respected Lady Caroline Clare would make the grim job more difficult when he called on her tomorrow.

Lavender decided to use the rear stage door and walk around the outside of the theatre to meet Magdalena in the foyer. The smell of candlewax, unwashed costumes and body odour had become cloying and he wanted some fresh air to clear his head. As he climbed up the steps into the brightly lit foyer, he saw Magdalena and Teresa waiting for him at the bottom of a sweeping staircase that led up to the gallery and the boxes.

At that moment, the royal party, swathed in greatcoats, hats and fur-trimmed cloaks, descended the staircase. Several of the cast and audience were milling around. Many loitered, wide-eyed, on the landing, gawking at the prince and his guests. He raised an eye-brow when he saw the elderly Earl of Thornaby amongst them, rais-ing the hand of Helena Bologna, the theatre's Italian actress, to his lips. The woman simpered and giggled. Thornaby was a friend of Magistrate Read – and a married man.

Suddenly, a coarsely dressed ruffian with his hat pulled down over his face leapt down the stairs beside Mrs Jordan. He wrenched her reticule from her hand. The duke's mistress screamed but every-one was too startled to move. Many, including the duke, didn't see exactly what had occurred. The silk-snatcher leapt down the remain-ing stairs, two at a time, and belted towards the exit to the street.

Lavender moved swiftly to intercept him but Magdalena got there first. She hitched up her skirts, stuck out her boot and tripped the fellow up as he bounded passed. He landed on the foyer floor with a resounding crash. Magdalena pulled back her leg and cursed loudly in Spanish.

'*El cerdo! Aii, mi rodilla! Esta torcida!*' She screamed as she hopped from one foot to another.

The thieving cove scrambled to his feet. Lavender raced for-ward. Magdalena looked furious and for one dreadful minute he thought she would to try to grapple with the man herself.

'No, Magdalena!' he yelled.

The thief threw a couple of punches towards Lavender. The first missed its mark but the second caught him a glancing blow in his left eye. A sharp stab of pain sent an angry surge through Lav-ender's body. He grabbed the rogue and, marshalling his strength, threw him face down to the floor. He pinned him to the ground and viciously yanked the silk-snatcher's arm up behind his back.

'Yer brekkin' me arm, gov!' howled his prisoner.

Lavender didn't have to hold on for long. Within seconds, sev-eral burly theatre porters were by his side. They hauled him and his captive to their feet, grasped the still struggling villain and cuffed him several times around his head until he slumped motionless between them. As the porters dragged the thief away, an angry and indignant crowd gathered around Lavender and Magdalena. Sir Lawrence Forsyth swept Mrs Jordan's reticule up off the floor where it had dropped in the scuffle.

Lavender glanced quickly at Magdalena. She leant heavily on Teresa's arm. 'Take that silk-snatcher round to Bow Street and get him locked up in the cells,' he said to the porters. He brushed the dirt from his coat and tried to force open his left eye, which had begun to swell. 'Tell the clerks that Detective Stephen Lavender arrested him. I'll file the charges in the morning.'

To his intense embarrassment, the crowd suddenly burst out in applause.

'Lavender! Good God, man – I thought I recognised you!' The duke's voice cut through the babbling crowd. The cheering and applause died away. Everyone fell silent and stepped back as the Duke of Clarence descended the remaining stairs and strode towards Lavender, his party trailing in his wake. The duke's purposeful stride suggested that he was still an active man who hadn't succumbed to the unhealthy, hedonistic lifestyle of his two elder brothers.

Blinking his damaged eye, Lavender bowed his head. 'Your Royal Highness,' he said.

'Hells bells, man! Don't stand on ceremony here – you've just saved m'lady Dora's purse! We're damned lucky you were here.' He thumped Lavender on the shoulder in delight. The pain of the jolt shot through Lavender's jaw and into his eye socket. 'Our brother George often hires one of you detective fellahs to protect him from snivelling pickpockets – but I never thought I would see the day when I would need help from one of you.'

'It is my pleasure to be of service, Your Grace.'

'Is that where I've seen you before?' the duke asked. 'Protecting my brother?'

'Maybe, Your Grace, but I'm off-duty tonight.'

'Don't give me that, man,' said Prince William with a broad grin. 'You fellahs from Bow Street are never off-duty! You're England's finest – and we're damned proud of you.' He gave Lavender another punch on the shoulder, threw back his head and laughed at his own wit. Everyone laughed with him.

The duke's eyes now alighted on Magdalena and he emitted a low whistle. Lavender hid a smile. Clarence may be a prince but he still behaved like a midshipman on leave after a lengthy sea voyage. 'And who is this gracious lady with the nimble footwork who felled the rogue?' the duke asked.

Any injury Magdalena may have sustained in the incident was now ignored or forgotten. She turned and dropped down into the deepest and most graceful curtsey Lavender had ever seen. An appreciative hush fell over the crowd; everyone in that foyer was now aware that they were now in the presence of a lady of quality.

'Your Grace, may I present Doña Magdalena Morales, widow of Don Antonio Garcia de Aviles who fell at the Battle of Talavera,' he said. 'Her husband and his men fought alongside Sir Arthur Wellesley.'

'Wellesley, eh?' said the duke. 'Well, madam, we have cause to be grateful for our Spanish allies tonight. That was as nifty a piece of footwork as I have ever seen.'

'Yes, William, dear,' said a soft female voice, with an attractive Irish lilt. 'Doña Magdalena has saved the day.' Dorothy Jordan had now reached the duke's side. She slid her hand into the crook of his arm. Sir Lawrence Forsyth handed back her reticule with a stiff bow.

'I trust you have not hurt your ankle, my dear?' said the duke.

'No, Your Highness, my ankle is fine.' Magdalena gave him a brilliant smile. 'However, I fear that the rogue has scuffed and damaged my boots.' At that point she lifted her skirts again, raised her right ankle and twisted it provocatively in the air for his inspection.

The boot was indeed scuffed but if Lavender remembered correctly both this one and its partner had needed replacing for some time. He wondered what she was up to now.

Dorothy Jordan's green eyes narrowed at the sight of Magdalena's little trick. The duke, however, clearly appreciated the view.

'Damnation!' he cursed. 'We can't have that! We shall reward you with a new pair of boots, m'dear! Come, Dora. Be grateful – hand over the reward for saving your purse.'

'A new pair of boots for rescuing a purse which contains but a few pennies?' There was a sharp edge in Mrs Jordan's question.

The duke gave his mistress a scathing look. 'Such bravery and assistance towards the House of Hanover deserves a reward,' he snapped. 'Doña Magdalena will be the toast of the town by tomorrow morning when news of this unfortunate incident leaks out to those scoundrels in the press. We can't appear to be ungrateful.'

Dorothy Jordan hastily changed tack. 'Alas, my dear, I do not carry money of that value around with me. Perhaps Detective Lavender can call at Bushy House tomorrow and claim your reward.'

'I would be delighted, ma'am,' he said and bowed again. He wasn't sure if Magdalena was aware of the friction her little trick had caused but he was left in no doubt that money was a source of conflict in the Clarence household.

'Come now, William, it has been a long night. We need to return home.'

Reluctantly the duke tore his eyes away from the hem of Magdalena's dress. He offered his arm to Mrs Jordan and everyone bowed low again as the royal party swept towards the theatre door.

When they reached the exit, Dorothy Jordan turned back to Magdalena. 'When you go shopping to replace your boots,' she said, 'I would recommend the establishment of Mistress Evans on Long Acre.'

'Many thanks, ma'am, for your recommendation,' said Magdalena. 'I shall be sure to pay Mistress Evans a visit.'

'You do that,' said the actress. There was a glint in her eyes that reminded Lavender of a cat.

'Are you hurt?' he asked Magdalena when the royal party had gone. 'I heard you cursing about your knee.' He offered his own arm to support her, which she took gratefully.

'No, no. I twisted it when he ran into me but I will be fine.' Her cheeks glowed and her eyes shone with excitement. 'To meet a prince!' she exclaimed. 'Stephen! You never told me you knew the royal family!'

He smiled. 'I don't *know* them,' he said, 'but I have worked for the Prince of Wales on several occasions and Queen Charlotte. The principal officers are the only police officers allowed into Buckingham House. The heir to the throne has a particular attachment to a colleague of mine, John Townsend. On a few occasions when Prince George wanted additional security, Townsend was unavailable and I had to take his place. The Duke of Clarence has a remarkable memory if he remembers that.'

Suddenly, they were interrupted with a torrent of excited Spanish. With a flurry of black bombazine, the two women who had slighted Magdalena earlier now reappeared and surrounded her.

'*Magdalena! Magdalena! Cuanto me alegro de verte.*'

Beaming, they embraced her and kissed her cheek. He stepped back, barely able to follow the excited babbling of the women. Magdalena looked pleased but he sensed her surprise at this dramatic volte-face in their attitude towards her. *It's amazing*, he thought, *how a brief conversation with a prince can suddenly make one the most popular woman in London.*

He looked over the heads of the excited women and saw Felipe Menendez observing the group coldly. For a brief second, the

Spaniard glanced in his direction and shot him a withering look of hatred from down his aquiline nose.

Lavender's hackles rose but he said nothing. It wasn't often that he formed an instant dislike towards someone, but every fibre of his body told him that this arrogant man wasn't to be trusted.

Magdalena was animated and chatted non-stop all the way home. She plied Lavender with questions about the royal household and Lady Caroline Clare. As their cab neared her lodgings, Magdalena quietened for a moment and became serious. 'Tonight has been a wonderful experience for me, Stephen,' she said. 'Thank you for escorting me to the theatre. It may also turn out to be a night which will change my life.'

'Oh?'

'Yes. I have decided to do something about my poverty. After all, I can't rely on the whims of passing dukes to keep replenishing my wardrobe, can I?' She smiled. 'I have decided to take a lesson from those women we saw tonight. I think I will seek employment.'

'I'm not sure that you have the patience to be a governess,' he said, smiling.

'Oh, there are other ways to earn a living,' she said mysteriously. 'I have no idea how long I will have to remain in England before I can return to my estate in Spain and I have relied on the charity and generosity of my friends for support for too long. I also need to think about Sebastián's school fees for next year.'

'You could always marry again,' he said suddenly.

She turned her head sharply and stared at him. 'It is too soon, Stephen. I have to learn to become a widow before I can become a wife again.'

Silently, he berated himself for his insensitivity. 'I apologise,' he said. 'I spoke out of turn.'

'Not at all.' She smiled. 'You're a dear friend. I will be forever in your debt for all the kindness you have shown to Teresa and I.'

The cab had now stopped at her lodgings and the driver dismounted to hold open the door. But Magdalena had not finished. 'Earlier this evening you told me that the theatre would be a window to the world, without comparison. But you were wrong about that.'

'Oh?'

'It is not the theatre which is my window to the world. It is you, Stephen. Thank you for tonight.' With that, she leant forward, kissed him gently on his cheek and climbed out of the cab.

Chapter Eight

Tuesday 20th February, 1810

The faint pink fingers of dawn streaked slowly across the wintery sky above the smoking chimneys and spires of London. Constable Woods heard the distant peal of church bells and the hooters from the boats on the Thames as he walked down Hart Street. It was going to be another cold but dry day. The interminable rumble of traffic towards Covent Garden had begun and the Duke of Bedford's workmen were already hard at work at the ongoing demolition of Raleigh Close. He paused for a moment and watched as another gable of the ancient building crashed to the ground. The labourers stepped back and waited for the billowing dust to settle. Then they grabbed their pickaxes and shovels and began to break up the rubble and transfer it onto a wagon. Horses snorted and stamped impatiently in their jangling harnesses as dust irritated their nostrils.

Woods coughed, crossed the cobbled street and pushed open the low wooden door of Mistress Higgin's bakery. The smell of warm, freshly baked bread and pastries made his stomach rumble. Despite the disruption of the demolition across the street, it was business as usual.

Jacquetta Higgin stood at the shop counter, lifting dough and dropping it before once again thrusting her hands into the soggy mass. She glanced up and frowned when she saw his uniform. Beside her, the freckled face of her young son peered up at him through sleep-encrusted eyes. 'Ma! It's one of them Runners,' he said in alarm.

'Good mornin', Mistress Higgin,' Woods said pleasantly.

The sleeves of her gown were rolled back to reveal her strong, plump arms, which were dusted with flour. She gave Woods a hard stare. 'What d'you want?'

'I'm Constable Woods from Bow Street Magistrates' Court,' he said. 'We are investigatin' the death of that unfortunate young woman who died at Raleigh Close and I need to ask you some questions.'

'I can't 'elp you.' Mistress Higgin returned to her dough and continued to thump, lift and slap it back down on the counter with considerable force.

Woods paused, a little surprised by her open hostility, and then decided to change tack.

'Well, first of all, on behalf of Bow Street, I would like to thank you for your public spirit yesterday in summonin' us to Raleigh Close. Yes, that mewlin' child turned out to be a bird – a fact you couldn't possibly have known. If there had been a woman and a nipper in the buildin', they would have been seriously injured. That were very Christian of you.'

She said nothing but he thought he saw the rigid facial muscles of her jaw relax.

'As you know we then uncovered the dead body of a young woman and we're tryin' to find out what happened to her.'

'I can't 'elp you.' The dough slapped down on the counter.

'It is possible that you can. Maybe you – and your handsome young fellah here – have seen or heard something important. You may not even realise that you have valuable information which pertains to our inquiries . . .'

''Ave you seen or 'eard anythin' out of the ordinary, Nathanial?'

'No, Ma.'

'There you go, Constable.'

'Perhaps Mr Higgin—?'

'My Albert were taken with the typhoid two years ago,' she said sharply.

Woods hesitated. Despite the woman's truculent attitude he felt a pang of sympathy for her. It couldn't be easy for a widow to run a business single-handed on this street and bring up a son at the same time. Young boys were a handful and a constant worry to their mothers. Or so Betsy kept telling him.

'So young Nathanial here is now the man of the house?' He smiled at the lad and reached out to ruffle his spiky hair. 'You've done well, Mistress Higgin. He's turned out a fine young man. I realised this yesterday when he first came to collect us from Bow Street. Many lads try to play pranks on the Bow Street officers but no one doubted for a moment that your son was serious and honest.'

The boy blushed red to the roots of his carrot-coloured hair at the compliment. But Woods' praise for her son didn't seem to have any effect on Jacquetta Higgin. Wielding a large flat knife, she deftly cut the dough into several portions and shaped them into loaves. She covered them with a cloth and pushed them aside.

'I've done my best with the boy,' she said, stiffly, as she wiped her hands on her apron. 'It ain't been easy – especially with so much evil temptation on the doorstep, the gin and the women.'

'I understand,' Woods said. 'I have two lads of my own. Nathanial's about the same age as my Eddie. They might be peas in a pod, although our Eddie doesn't have such a magnificent head of ginger hair. May I compliment you, Mistress Higgin, on the lovely colour that you have bequeathed him?'

The smile dropped from her face and her fingers went instinctively to her own head. She pushed back some trailing, faded, ginger tendrils. 'My 'air is strawberry blonde,' she said, sullenly.

Fifteen years of marriage was enough to warn Woods that he was now on dangerous ground. 'Quite, quite,' he said quickly. 'Now let me ask you some questions.'

'Look, 'ave you any idea what it's like tryin' to live around 'ere and run a business in these 'ere parts?'

'No,' he replied, 'why don't you tell me?'

'It's difficult, Constable. Difficult. Apart from the disruption from the lewd women and the drunkards from the taverns, the local crooks demand payment from traders like us. If we want to stay safe, we 'ave to keep our mouths shut and our eyes closed. There's more criminal activity goin' on 'Art Street every night than in the whole of London.' She waved her hand dramatically in the direction of the city.

'Oh dear.' He had a strong suspicion that the criminals in the Seven Dials would make those on Hart Street look like amateurs but the woman was on a righteous mission and it wasn't in his best interests to contradict her. Her face had flushed the same colour as her hair.

'That place across there – Raleigh Close – it's been a flash-ken for years. Dishonest dealin's and suchlike take place every night. Prostitutes wantonly ply their trade in the Close, outside on the street and inside the rooms. And what 'ave you fancy constables from Bow Street done about it?'

'It must be difficult,' Woods sympathised, sidestepping the question. 'Especially livin' opposite such a place and havin' a young lad to bring up on your own.'

'But what I don't understand,' she continued, her voice rising with indignation, 'is why can't you do anythin' about those lewd women? It's like all the prostitutes in the kingdom 'ave pitched upon this blessed neighbourhood for a place of general rendezvous.

In fact, there are so many of 'em, they could people their own mighty colony!'

The woman clearly had a strong dislike of the Covent Garden Nuns and he wondered if this was the root cause of her reluctance to help. Did she think April Divine was just another prostitute? Was it a case of good riddance to bad rubbish as far as she was concerned?

'I will pass on your concerns to Magistrate Read at Bow Street,' Woods said. 'But in the meantime, Mistress Higgin, I'd be grateful if you helped me with our inquiries about the death of the young actress, April Divine.'

'She were an actress?'

'Yes, Mistress Higgin, she was. With the Sans Pareil Theatre, as it happens.'

'A lot of them women claim that they're actresses.'

'Well, in this case the claim was genuine. She were a respectable young woman, probably from a good family.' He saw that this news made a difference to her. 'Have you ever seen that gal before yesterday?'

'Well, I didn't get a real good look at 'er, mind but no, no, I don't believe so. I've got a good memory for faces too. I'd a remembered if she'd been in the shop. What about you, son? 'Ave you ever seen that woman afore?'

'No, Ma.'

'Poor lamb.' She patted the boy affectionately on the head and gave a huge, bosom-heaving sigh. 'No child should 'ave 'ad to see a sight like the one we saw yesterday.'

'I agree,' Woods said. 'Have you been aware of any suspicious activity over at Raleigh Close a couple of days ago? P'raps on Friday or Saturday?'

'No.'

'You see, we have reason to believe that Miss Divine was held captive over there for a while.'

'What? A prisoner?'

'Yes, she may have been kidnapped for ransom.'

'Ooh, that's not right, poor gal.' Mistress Higgin's plump face frowned with concern. Woods knew that she was thinking hard.

'Is there anythin' else you can think of, which might help us, Mistress Higgin? I'm sure that you want to help us find the villains that sent that poor gal to kingdom come, as much as we want to track them down.'

'Well, there is one thing . . .'

'Yes?'

'Nathanial? Go into the back for a minute, will you, son?' The young lad opened his mouth to protest but then saw the determination on his mother's face. Reluctantly, he dragged himself off through the curtain and disappeared into the rear of the bakery. Jacquetta Higgin lowered her voice. 'If anyone were usin' that place to keep a prisoner, they would 'ave needed permission from that rat, Darius Jones. "Dirty Dar" we call 'im.'

'Who's he?' The name was vaguely familiar.

"E's a pimp, Constable Woods, a whoremaster. There's no nice way to speak it so I'm tellin' you straight.'

'I appreciate that, Mistress Higgin.'

"E runs several gals on this street and makes frequent use of Raleigh Close for their trysts. If the poor gal was 'eld prisoner in there, Dirty Dar would 'ave known about it and 'as been paid to keep away from the place for a while.'

'You have been most helpful, Mistress Higgin.' Relief flooded through Woods; at last they had something to go on.

'You never 'eard it from me, you understand?'

'Of course.' He pointed to a tray of fresh pastries at the end of the counter. 'Before I go, may I pay you for one of those delicious-smellin' raisin tartlets?'

She beamed as she took his coin and handed him the pastry. 'I saw you were a man who likes his food, the second you walked in,' she said. 'Don't forget to tell those other constables at Bow Street about Jacquetta 'Iggin's bakery, now will you? 'Ere, have a free one for that detective pal of yours. 'E were real clever to work out the mystery of that wailing bird. Funny fellah, though. I didn't understand 'alf of what he said.'

'He's very clever,' said Woods, 'and educated. He speaks like a toff sometimes and he knows too much of that Latin.'

'Oh, that reminds me, Constable. I don't know if it will 'elp you, but there 'ave been an awful lot of Frogs on this street recently.'

'Frogs?'

'Yes, Frenchies. Ruddy furriners. I've 'eard them jabberin' away in their nasty language outside in the street while I've been tryin' to get to sleep.'

'French? Are you sure?' He remembered the Spanish *escudo* Barnaby had discovered beneath the floorboards of Raleigh Close.

'Well, I've had no education like your detective, Constable. But I know the King's English when I 'ear it, and that were definitely not the King's English they were talkin'.'

Rather than go straight to Bow Street, Woods decided to try and locate Darius Jones. Woods remembered him now. A tall, bald man with features ravaged by opium addiction, the Bow Street officers had been aware of his illicit activities for some time but the man was as slippery as a jellied eel and they had never managed to find enough evidence to convict him of any crimes. Although it was still early in the morning, several of the sleazy taverns and gin shops were open for business. Many of the wagon drivers who had brought in the produce for Covent Garden had driven through the night. Still swathed in their thick coats and scarves, they were now slumped at the rickety tables, red-eyed and exhausted in front of a flagon of ale and a meat pie. Each time Woods entered a tavern, a hush fell on those assembled when they saw his distinctive uniform.

'I'm looking for a Darius Jones,' he informed the barmen and patrons alike. 'He's not in any trouble with the law but I need to speak to him.' Each time his enquiry was greeted with sullen silence or growls.

Frustrated, he decided that he might have better luck with one of the Covent Garden Nuns, who were already milling around in groups outside the taverns beside the piles of stinking refuse and dank puddles that littered the cold, uneven cobbles. They were a miserable bunch: thin, and clad in gaudy, ill-fitting and frayed clothes, their rouged faces lined with poverty and hunger. Several of them hugged their arms to their sides and stamped their feet to ward off the chill. One of them took long swigs from a bottle of brandy.

'And what can we do fer you, Constable?' cackled the oldest of the group as Woods approached. The sharp smell of body odour and stale alcohol made him stop in his tracks, but the women surrounded him.

'I'm looking for your pimp, ladies: Darius Jones. Do you know where I can find him?'

'Why d'ya want Dirty Dar?' asked one.

'I have some business to conduct with him.'

The women shrieked with laughter. 'Business, eh? D'ya want our services, Officer?' asked one. 'We do a special rate fer you Runners.'

'I'm sure you do,' he replied jovially, 'and no doubt it is worth two groats.'

The women laughed again.

'Martha and I can do you the beast with the two backs for an extra shillin',' the swaying girl with the brandy bottle offered. She was toothless when she grinned, her gums black. 'Yer look like the kind of fellah that can handle two of us at once, a big fellah like you.'

'Maybe another time, ladies,' he said. 'But I need to speak to Mr Jones right now. Do you know where he is?'

'Oooh! Listen at him wi' his "ladies" and his "Mr Jones"!' The eldest woman, their leader, spat onto the ground. She had badly dyed blonde hair and her powder and rouge were caked into the lines of her face. Beneath it, Woods thought he saw a hint of disease. 'We do our own pimpin' now, Officer,' she said.

'Aye,' muttered the other women.

'We ain't seen hide nor hair of Dirty Dar for days. In fact, we've been usin' his lodgings to conduct a little business of our own and it's been good to keep all of the profits for once.'

The women giggled, obviously pleased with themselves.

'What's your name?' Woods asked her.

'I'm Peg,' she said. 'And this 'ere is Martha. Izzie is the drunken tosspot who's about to fall over – and the little one's Kate.'

'I'm pleased to make your acquaintance, ladies,' he said. 'Have any of you been inside Raleigh Close since Thursday?'

'Now why would we go into that creepy old cesspit when we can use Dar's nice warm bed?' asked one. The others laughed. 'Those days of stumblin' around Raleigh Close in the dark are over fer us.'

'Is this about that dead gal you Runners found there yesterday?' asked Kate, the youngest and quietest of the cackling group. She was little more than a child, he realised sadly.

'Yes, treacle, it is,' he said. 'Do any of you know anythin' about her?'

The mention of the dead actress had the same effect as a bucket of cold water on the whores. Their faces dropped into a collective scowl.

'Was she one of us?' asked Kate. The girl looked terrified.

'No, she was an actress from the Sans Pareil.' The sigh of relief in the group was audible: the prospect of a killer on the loose, who was partial to murdering prostitutes, was terrifying to them.

''Twas nothin' to do wi' us, Officer,' said the older whore. 'We were as surprised as you Runners when her body popped out from beneath them floorboards.' Some of them must have been in the crowd, he realised. 'And I doubt it were anythin' to do with Dirty Dar, either. We ain't seen him fer days.'

'Eeh! You don't suppose he's been murdered too, do you?' said one of the group.

'What, that slimy old bastard? Naw, he'll be foxed somewhere in a gutter. Let's make hay while the sun shines, gals – our miserly buttock-broker will be back afore we know it.'

Woods' mind was spinning. A missing pimp? Was there a connection? And then he remembered something else.

'I've changed my mind, ladies,' he said. 'I think I would like a bit of company.'

Peg grinned. 'Why you naughty boy, Officer!' she said. 'And yer supposed to be workin' too! Now what do you fancy? We can provide all manner of services for an hour or so.'

'Yes,' slurred the swaying Izzie. 'Yer can lie in state wiff all of uz if yer wants.'

'Oh, it will only take a few minutes,' he said blithely.

Peg blinked in surprise. 'Well, I'm sure we can draw it out for a bit longer than that, Constable. It'll be a shillin', anyways.'

'Good,' said Woods. 'But I warn you, it takes a lot to get my juices flowin' these days.'

'Bit of a dry bob are you, Officer?' asked Peg. 'Don't worry I'll get those nutmegs and that sugar stick of yours workin' again.' She leered provocatively at him, grabbed her ample bosoms and bounced them up and down. The other women fell about laughing at her antics.

They were a cheerful bunch of whores, Woods decided, and probably relieved that their pimp was gone. He pulled out the coin and handed it over to Peg. 'I think it might be best if you accompany me back to Bow Street, madam. You sound just the kind of gal I need.'

'Bow Street?' She recoiled and he wondered if she had spent time in their cells. 'What kind of a knave's trick is this?'

'I've a fancy for a bit of dockin' at work. I think the risk of being caught swivin' at Bow Street might just get my old juices in a frenzy again. There's an unused room around the back. I'll give you another shillin' if you'll come with me to Bow Street.'

'Very well,' said Peg and hooked her arm into his. 'But no funny business, mind – I don't want you arrestin' me for trespass once you've done.'

Chapter Nine

Lavender knew that Lady Caroline was a late riser and he was reluctant to take her bad news about her stepdaughter when possibly in a state of déshabillé. He went briefly into Bow Street to deal with the charges for the silk-snatcher he had apprehended the night before at the theatre and then decided to visit April Clare's lodgings. His route took him straight across the bustling Covent Garden market.

Inigo Jones' grand Italian piazza was now a heaving, stinking mass of humanity and commerce. A row of forty-eight small shops, brick-built with slate roofs, and many of them with cellars, had been erected on the south side of the piazza. Contrary to intended original usage for the market, many of them were now occupied by bakers, haberdashers, cook shops, retailers of Geneva and other spirituous liquors. This section served the lower orders of London society and even at this early hour some of the crowds were disorderly and drunk. Housewives and servants strolled along the aisles examining the stalls, which were piled high with mountains of potatoes, turnips, swedes, dried herbs, stringy beans and sprouts. The stallholders who shouted out their wares were desperate to drown out their competitors and thus yelled until hoarse. Their customers argued about the high prices and complained about the poor choice. Occasionally a fight broke out.

At the western edge of the square were the better-class fruiterers and the florists. Here the choice was wider, colourful, exotic and more expensive. Aristocratic ladies and their liveried servants examined the hothouse blooms, and the plums and grapes. Imported breadfruits, oranges and lemons from the South Pacific islands sat side by side with new and strange fruits and spices from the East Indies. Lavender skirted this side of the piazza and veered round a fat woman with a tray of buttonholes and posies. He paused briefly in front of an Italian puppet play and smiled as he remembered how, as a young man, he had once expended a shilling, which he couldn't afford to spare, to purchase a bunch of dahlias for his child-hood sweetheart. He made a mental note to purchase some flowers for Magdalena the next time he called on her.

April Clare's lodgings were on a dank street behind the market, on the top floor of a dismal house. The upper window frames in the overhanging eaves were rotten, and dark streaks of grime ran down the walls from the broken guttering above. The elderly landlady who answered his knock at the door said, 'No gentleman callers!' and tried to slam it in his face. Lavender pulled out his badge of office for her to examine in the dim light. She glared at his tipstaff for a long time with her rheumy eyes before she finally shuffled aside and let him in.

'You said she's dead?' The old crone leant heavily on the banister at the bottom of the staircase as climbed up the steps.

'Yes, I'm sorry to be the bearer of bad news,' he called down over his shoulder before he turned a bend in the stairwell and disappeared from sight.

'Who'll pay me the rent she owes?' she wailed after him.

As he approached the door of April Clare's attic chamber, Lavender realised that it was ajar and had been forced open. Cautiously, he pushed the door and entered the freezing garret. The room had been ransacked. The mattress had been lifted off the bed and rested on its narrow edge against the window. Clothing from the open closet was strewn across the floor and the drawers of the dresser had been pulled out and upturned. Hundreds of sheets of paper were scattered across the debris like confetti. When he examined them closer he realised that they were the loose sheets from the actress's play scripts. Someone had been here before him and they had been looking for something.

Lavender sifted through the wreckage of April Clare's life, searching for clues to her intruders. What had been so special about the young actress that led others to imprison her and ransack her room? What was she involved in?

He decided to send Woods, or another constable, back later. They could ask the other tenants in the house if they had heard the door lock shatter and when. They may have also seen someone climbing up to the top floor. But he doubted these inquiries would yield much information. Despite the fact that the old crone downstairs with her red eyes and bristly chin looked a bit like Cerberus, the canine guard to the gates of Hades, Lavender suspected that she was useless as a gatekeeper and probably a bit deaf as well. The building seemed to be deserted and the door to the chamber was rotten and warped. It would have yielded quickly.

He straightened up and resolved to return to Bow Street, find his constable and then go on to Lincoln's Inn Fields. He had put off his visit to Lady Caroline Clare for long enough.

However, Lavender was in for a shock when he walked back into Bow Street Magistrates' Court, looking for Ned Woods.

''E's out the back in the courtyard,' said one of the clerks at the desk. ''E's in trouble with one of those 'ell-cats from 'Art Street.'

The man grinned from ear to ear but refused to enlighten him any further.

There was a large crowd of cheering grooms, patrol officers and other constables gathered in a circle at the rear of the police office. In the centre of the cobbled courtyard was a furious middle-aged, red-faced whore, screaming abuse at Woods.

'You dirty smut!' she yelled as she tried to pummel him. 'You're sick, you! Sick in the 'ead! You should be in bleedin' Bedlam!'

Woods grinned from ear to ear across his broad face and did his best to dodge and parry her blows.

'Desist, madam!' Lavender shouted as he pushed his way through the crowd. 'What is the problem here?'

'Are you 'is guvnor?' demanded the woman.

'Yes.'

She pointed furiously at Woods. 'Well 'e needs lockin' up – the depraved bugger! Sick! Sick 'e is!'

'What's happened?'

''E brought me back 'ere for a quick strum of his fiddle.'

'What?' The question came out as more of a splutter. Fighting back laughter and incredulity he struggled to formulate his next question. 'Constable Woods did what?'

'Come wi' me, 'e says,' the woman continued. 'Come with me. I know a quiet room at the back of Bow Street. Nice and quiet it is. No geezer will disturb us . . .' The grooms were in hysterics. Her voice rose to a furious crescendo.

'What happened?

''E took me into the bleedin' morgue!' she screamed. 'Full of stiffs it is – and stinkin'! Great dead eyes staring up at me!' The other men in the yard were now bent double with laughter. Tears streamed down their cheeks.

Somehow Lavender kept his face straight. 'When you said he "took you" in the morgue, madam, exactly what do you mean?' One of the grooms started choking.

'You dirty bugger!' screeched the harridan. 'I 'ave my standards! I'm not layin' in a room with dustmen nor plasterin' my warm guts to a corpse!'

Lavender's lips twitched. 'Is that what my constable asked you to do, madam? Lie with the corpse?'

'No, I didn't.' Woods grinned and nimbly dodged another blow to the head. 'I have me standards as well. I simply asked Peg, here, if she recognised that corpse we dragged out of the river the other day – and she does. Come on, gal. You've had your fun and you've been well paid for a few minutes' work.' His voice rose with authority. 'Off back to Hart Street with you now.'

For a moment it looked like the furious woman would refuse to leave but then she spat onto the ground and strode away. 'You're debauched – the bleedin' lot of you!' she yelled over her shoulder. 'Rot in 'ell!'

Disappointed that the fun was over, the other officers and grooms drifted reluctantly back to their duties. Most of them were still laughing.

Lavender relaxed and allowed himself the luxury of a grin. 'You tricked her here to identify a corpse?' he said. Woods nodded. 'Did she know the dead man we pulled out of the Thames?' Woods nodded again. 'And you brought her back here to identify him with the promise of some business?' 'Well, she wouldn't have come to identify him if I'd asked her straight, would she?' Woods grinned. 'Those gals don't go out of their way to help the law.'

'What made you think she might know the dead man?'

'There's a missin' pimp on Hart Street,' Woods said. 'And we've got an unidentified body in the morgue. I just had a hunch it were him.' Woods was still grinning. He rubbed his red forehead.

'Gawd's teeth! Peg doesn't half pack a good punch, when she's riled.'
He nodded towards Lavender's swollen eye. 'By the look of that
shiner, you've been on the wrong end of someone's fist as well.'

Instinctively, Lavender's hand went up to his bruised eye socket.
'I had a spot of trouble with a silk-snatcher at the theatre last night,'
he said. 'So, who is the dead man?'

'He's called Darius Jones; he's that pimp from Hart Street.'

'And how did he end up in the river?'

'I don't know, but I think there's a connection with our dead
actress.'

'Oh? That sounds intriguing. We have to go and visit the stepmother of the dead girl now. You can tell me the details on the way.'

Lady Caroline leased rooms in the basement of an imposing house
in one of Lincoln's Inn Fields' leafiest streets. The area was out of
fashion since the burgeoning developments in the West End and
the house had a jaded grandeur to it. The cracked limewash and
peeling paintwork on the exterior of the building added to the aura
of faded glamour and dwindling fortune. A cold wind swirled up
the winter debris that littered the weed-strewn cobbled street.

However, the inside of the apartment was warm and beautifully
furnished. Exquisite oil paintings of landscapes and framed gilt litho-
graphs jostled with each other for space on the walls of the hallway,
interspersed with tiny cameo portraits suspended on brass chains
from the picture rail. The maid led them through to the back of the
house where a large glass orangery had been attached to the house.

Sunlight streamed down through the vaulted glass ceiling. Half-
finished canvases were stacked, row on row, against the lower walls
of the hothouse. A great easel stood in the centre, ringed by assorted
furniture. There were tables littered with discarded paintbrushes,
tubes of oil paints, rags and glasses of water. Flowers and platters of
fruit were scattered about the tiled floor.

Lady Caroline was cleaning brushes in front of the easel when they entered the orangery. A plain, green turban held back her unruly red hair and a simple, paint-splattered, dun-coloured pinafore protected her white muslin dress.

'Detective Lavender!' she exclaimed, graciously. 'What a pleasure to see you again so soon – and your charming constable.'

Two young men sat on the mismatched daybeds and chaises longues amongst discarded fans and ostrich feathers. They glanced up when the maid announced Lavender and Woods' arrival. Lavender recognised the foppish Henry Duddles but the other young man, who wore a black velvet yarmulke on his dark head, was unknown to him.

'You know Duddles, of course?' she continued. 'This is Solomon Rothschild, my nephew. Will you take tea with us? You can tell me how you came across that black eye. I'm sure that you weren't so colourful when we met last night at the theatre.'

Lavender nodded to the other men and swallowed hard before he began. 'Unfortunately, Lady Caroline, I'm the bearer of terrible news.'

The smile faded from her face. 'Oh?'

'I think you need to sit down.'

'What has happened?' She remained standing by the easel, her eyes narrowed with concern and her back rigid. He had no alternative but to continue.

'We have recovered the dead body of a young woman and I'm sad to tell you that we believe it to be your stepdaughter, April Clare.'

For a split second there was absolute silence in the studio. Lady Caroline took a sharp breath and Lavender saw her eyes widen with horror. A second later, she staggered and fell against the easel in front of her, which crashed to the ground. He leapt forward and managed to catch her before she fell on top of the shattered easel and canvas. Both young men jumped to their feet but it was Rothschild who helped him lead the half-conscious woman towards a pale yellow chaise longue. Duddles hopped from one foot to the other wailing. 'Caro? Caro!' he shrieked. 'Help! Someone! She's dying!'

'Find some smelling salts,' Lavender instructed him sharply.

'Stay calm, fellah,' said Woods.

Lady Caroline raised her head. 'No. No smelling salts. I'm fine,' she whispered. 'Oh, what a terrible thing to happen! Poor April!'

Solomon sat down beside her on the silk daybed and put his arm around her shoulders. Lavender handed Lady Caroline his own handkerchief and sent Woods to find the maid and organise some sweet tea.

After a few minutes, Lady Caroline made a determined effort to stop crying. She turned her pale face towards Lavender and demanded to know what had happened to her stepdaughter.

'Perhaps you should lie down for a while,' suggested Duddles.

'Do stop fussing, Henry,' she snapped. 'I need to know about poor April.'

Briefly, Lavender told her the facts. Unfortunately, there was no way to soften the horror of how they had discovered April Clare's body. Caroline recoiled, sank back into her seat and sobbed again. But when the tea arrived, sipping the beverage seemed to calm her.

Lavender took her hand in his. 'You have to believe me, Lady Caroline,' he said. 'I had no idea April Divine, the actress, was connected to you when I met you last night at the theatre.'

'I do believe you,' she said, and sighed. 'I was the one who insisted she used a stage name.'

'Can you tell me more about her?' he asked.

Lady Caroline dabbed her eyes. Lavender saw the pain in them. 'April always was a wild girl, charming – but wild,' she said eventually. 'She dreamed of a theatrical career from a young age. Of course, while her father was alive this was impossible; the daughters of barons do not become actresses. But there was nothing I could do to stop her going onstage after he died. I had a premonition that this would end badly.' She raised both her hands in a gesture of resignation. 'But who am I, Detective, to stop a young girl from following her heart?'

Lavender knew she was thinking about her elopement with Victor Rothschild. 'I'm sure you were an excellent stepmother,' he said, softly. 'She was lucky to have such a tolerant guardian.'

Lady Caroline gave a short strangled laugh. 'I was far too tolerant,' she said. 'Both girls were out of control when I married their father. April was the worst. Harriet has had poor health since she was a child and was the more malleable of the pair.'

'Do they have any other family?'

'No. I am all they have – apart from each other, of course. Anyway, when Baron Clare died, April cultivated a friendship with Mrs Jordan—'

'Dorothy Jordan, the actress?'

'Yes. Mrs Jordan must have seen some talent in April because she became her patron and introduced her to the manager of Drury Lane Theatre. At that point I withdrew any opposition I had to her ambition, but I did insist that she use a stage name to protect her sister from malicious tongues. Harriet has made a respectable marriage to Captain Nesbit Willoughby and lives quietly in Wandsworth. I was quite surprised that April agreed to my request. She wasn't always that agreeable.'

'Did you hope to see her at the theatre last night?'

Lady Caroline shook her head. Several red curls were now plastered to the side of her face with wet tears. 'I knew she wasn't in *Mary: Maid of the Inn.*'

'We had heard good reviews of the show,' Duddles explained. 'Caro wanted to see it.'

'Lady Caroline, when did you last see Miss Clare?' Lavender asked.

She blew her nose on her lawn handkerchief and stared thought-fully ahead. 'It must have been a few weeks ago,' she said. 'Both she and Harriet were invited to my soirée last Friday night – but neither of them turned up.'

Lavender felt the hairs stand up on the back of his neck. The surgeon had said that April Clare had possibly died on Friday night.

'Where is Mrs Willoughby now?' he asked. 'Did either of your stepdaughters send an apology or an explanation for their absence? Have you seen Mrs Willoughby since Friday?'

Caroline Clare's forehead creased and her lower lip trembled. 'Such a lot of questions, Detective!' she exclaimed in distress.

'I'm sorry, Lady Caroline.' He softened his voice. 'I appreciate that this must be very difficult for you. I can always come back later, when you feel more composed.'

'No, no,' she said. 'I want to help you in any way I can. We must find out who is responsible for this – this – this atrocity.'

He waited a moment for her to clear her throat and her thoughts. 'Are you aware if Miss Clare had any enemies, Lady Caroline? Or a beau?'

'No, neither,' she said. 'Although I would have been the last to know: the girls were always close and secretive. Neither of them let me know that they weren't coming to my gathering.'

'Have they been in contact with you since then?'

She sighed and leant back against the daybed. 'No, they haven't. An apology or an explanation would never have crossed their minds. You have to understand, Lavender, that when I was married off to Baron Clare, the girls had been motherless for quite a few years. At first, they hated me. But I gave them a lot of freedom and put up with their mean little pranks and eventually we settled into a mutual understanding. I didn't interfere with their lives; and they kept out of mine.'

'I see,' Lavender said.

'This arrangement has worked quite well for some years now,' Lady Caroline told him. 'I don't see much of them but I always add the girls to my guest list when I throw a soirée. There were a lot of people here. To be quite frank, I didn't notice they were missing until the next morning when Solomon commented on their absence.'

'Thomas Lawrence, the outstanding British portrait painter was amongst the guests,' Duddles volunteered, his voice rising with excitement. 'Along with various peers and their wives and that new chap who does interesting things with glazes – John Constable, I think he's called.'

'Same name as me then,' Constable Woods said suddenly.

The other men glanced up at Woods curiously but Lady Caroline didn't notice the awkward pause.

'It was odd though,' she said. 'The girls sent a note that said they would arrive together in Harriet's carriage; their invitations had definitely been accepted.'

'And you have not heard from Mrs Willoughby since Friday night?'

'No. Oh, my goodness!' Suddenly she reached out and grabbed his arm. Her watery eyes widened with shock. 'You don't think that anything has happened to Harriet, do you? She's not also lying murdered in an abandoned building, is she?' He heard the panic in her voice.

'No,' he soothed. This thought had crossed his mind. 'I'm quite sure that Mrs Willoughby is safe. But Constable Woods and I will go straight to see her and we will send you word that she's well.'

'Yes, yes – please do. And please be gentle when you tell Harriet about April. They were close. Harriet has never had a robust constitution and is very delicate. Tell her that I will be along as soon as I can.' Large tears rolled down her pale cheeks.

Lavender picked up his gloves and rose to leave. 'Again, please accept my condolences, Lady Caroline, and if there is anything we can do to help, don't hesitate to ask.'

'Just find the evil fiend who did this, Detective Lavender,' she said. Her voice cracked with anger. 'And make sure he swings for it at the next assizes.'

Chapter Ten

'Are you thinkin' that we may have two murdered women on our hands?' Woods asked as they walked back onto the chilly, crowded streets of Covent Garden.

Lavender frowned and his jaw tightened. 'I'm alarmed to discover that April Clare was in the company of her sister on Friday,' he confessed. 'And that Mrs Willoughby hasn't been seen since. I propose that we saddle up and go straight to Wandsworth. If she's there, then at least she will be able to shed some light on the events of Friday night.'

Lavender grabbed Woods and managed to push him into the doorway of a shop just in time to avoid a spray of muddy water as a fast-moving carriage raced by. There were yells of anger from less fortunate pedestrians who had not been as alert and quick-thinking.

'This case is becomin' a real mystery,' Woods said, as they resumed their steady pace. 'We've got the dead daughter of a baron buried beneath the floorboards of a rotten buildin' in one of the seediest parts of London – and the body of the pimp who used the same buildin' for a snoozin'-ken for the Covent Garden Nuns. Both of them are on a slab in our morgue. I still think that the dead gal and the buttock-broker were connected in some way. What do you think?'

'I don't know,' Lavender admitted. 'But I doubt they knew each other. My suspicion is that both Miss Clare and Darius Jones were somehow in the wrong place at the wrong time.'

'And in the wrong shoes,' Woods interrupted. 'Don't forget those ruddy shoes.'

'Ah, yes – shoes,' said Lavender. 'And boots.'

'Boots?'

'Yes. I promised to go to Bushy House and collect Magdalena's reward from the Duke of Clarence. This may be a fortuitous arrangement. I would welcome the opportunity to question Dorothy Jordan about April Clare. Lady Caroline said that the Duke's mistress had become the young woman's patron.'

Woods grinned. 'That were a clever little trick your Spanish widow pulled on the Sailor Prince and his floozy.'

The sides of Lavender's mouth twitched in amusement. 'Once again, Ned, she's not my Spanish widow. And it may be her last little money-earning ruse,' he added. 'She has threatened to take up honest employment now.'

Woods' greying eyebrows rose. 'Lord help us!' he said. 'She weren't thinkin' of becoming a school ma'am, were she? I'd pity any nippers in her schoolroom. I still have bad dreams about how she cuffed that tobyman she helped us capture on the road to Barnby Moor.'

'I don't know what she's planning,' Lavender said. 'But I find the thought rather disconcerting. Oh, by the way, please tell Betsy that we will take up her kind invitation to supper for tomorrow night.'

'She'll be delighted,' said Woods.

'And ask her if she knows of a shoemaker called Kinghorn and Naylor.'

'I will do.'

Lavender frowned as he was jabbed in the side by a wicker pannier carried by a plump shopper. Ever wary of thieves, he kept his hands over his pockets. His mind returned to their case. 'It would help us if we knew exactly how April Clare had died. Damn—' He stopped abruptly in his tracks and pulled out his pocket watch.

'What's the matter?' Woods asked.

'Sir Richard Allison said he would have completed the autopsy by noon. It is already half past midday. I suspect we may have missed him. We had better return immediately to Bow Street before we go to Wandsworth, in case he's still there.'

'Fair enough.' Woods good-natured face darkened. 'Although I doubt that cocky little sawbones would wait around for us.'

Woods was right. The Bow Street clerks informed them that Sir Richard had finished his autopsy several hours earlier and had expressed great displeasure that Detective Lavender had failed to turn up for the results. He had left instructions for Lavender to visit him at Guy's Hospital the next day.

'He could have just left a report on your desk,' Woods said. 'Does the fellah not respect the fact that we also have a job to do?'

Lavender sighed. It was an inconvenient and an unnecessary delay but his priority was to continue straight to Wandsworth. He was very concerned about the safety of Mrs Harriet Willoughby. 'Saddle us a couple of horses, Ned. I'll just report to Magistrate Read before we set off.'

'By the way, sir,' the clerk added as Lavender passed. 'There were a foreign woman looking for you earlier.'

'A foreign woman?' *Magdalena?*

'Yes, quite a looker she is,' the clerk said. 'And charming. She's upstairs now with Magistrate Read.'

Magdalena is with Read?

Lavender took the stairs up to the magistrate's office two at a time. He heard the silvery peal of Magdalena's laughter as he pushed open the door. She was seated elegantly in the old chair opposite

Read's desk, smiling and gesticulating elegantly as she elaborated on a story. Teresa sat at the back of the room. He smiled at her as he strode across the floorboards. On the wall above Read were two soot-blackened oil paintings of the Fielding brothers. Sir Henry and Sir John glowered down from their heavy frames. Was it Lavender's imagination or were the founders of the Bow Street Runners scowling even more than normal at the intrusion of the two foreign women into that hallowed office?

James Read was clearly enraptured with Magdalena. Pink spots glowed on his usually pallid cheeks and he didn't take his eyes from his visitor in order to acknowledge his principal officer. Lavender bit back a smile.

'Ah, Lavender!' said Read, eventually. 'Glad you can join us.' He sounded anything but glad, Lavender realised. In fact, Read looked annoyed at the disturbance. 'Doña Magdalena has presented me with an interesting proposition that I'm to place before our colleagues at the Home Department.'

'Really?' Lavender said as he took the seat next to Magdalena.

'Yes.' He heard the excitement in Magdalena's voice. 'I have offered my services to teach Spanish to your operatives who go to work in my native country. You have told me yourself that you have sometimes been sent to Spain on police business and I know that someone has taught you excellent Spanish. I hope that the Home Department may have a use for my skills. I thought that Magistrate Read would know about this.'

Lavender smiled. She had chosen wisely. Although nominally only the magistrate at Bow Street, James Read had a finger on the pulse of most Whitehall departments and the language school was one of them. Lavender remembered the hours he had spent in a cramped, dusty, airless room in the old palace battling with Iberian verbs and grammar. His teacher, Professor Quincy, had been an old, wizened fellow with a moth-eaten wig.

'I have explained to Doña Magdalena that we may not have a vacancy,' Read said cautiously.

'I'm sure you will do your best to help me, Magistrate,' Magdalena said, as she rose gracefully to her feet. The two men also stood. 'I will leave you now as I'm sure that Detective Lavender has business to conduct with you.' She gave both men a beautiful smile and held out her hand. Read pressed it to his lips.

'It has been a pleasure to meet you, Doña Magdalena,' he said.

'Likewise, Magistrate Read,' she replied.

'I will escort you out,' Lavender said. 'There are some drunkards downstairs in the hallway who maybe a nuisance.'

'I trust you're not referring to our clerks?' Read said jocularly, and then bowed his head once more over his paperwork.

Lavender escorted the women down the stairs. This new development had caught him unawares. Magdalena obviously didn't let the grass grow beneath her feet when a notion lodged in her mind.

Magdalena stopped halfway down the stairs. Sir Lawrence Forsyth, the duke's aide, blocked the way. He bowed his head. 'We meet again, Doña Magdalena,' he said. 'How delightful, although I'm surprised to find a lady of your breeding in this den of iniquity.'

Magdalena flashed him a confused glance; she didn't remember Forsyth from the night before. It wasn't surprising. Forsyth was the kind of man who would always disappear into the wall hangings of a room.

'Good morning, Detective.'

Lavender nodded curtly at him. 'Doña Magdalena, may I present Sir Lawrence Forsyth, aide to the Duke of Clarence.'

'Ahh.' Realisation dawned on Magdalena's face. 'You were at the Sans Pareil last night,' she said. 'Did you enjoy the show?'

Forsyth smirked. 'Which one, madam? The one on the stage or the more dramatic performance you gave in the foyer?'

Lavender felt his hackles rise but Magdalena took it as a compliment. She smiled. 'I was glad to be of assistance to the duke.'

'Quite so,' said Forsyth. 'I take it that your injured knee has fully recovered from the incident? The silk-snatcher fell over your leg with some force.'

'Yes, thank you. My knee has quite recovered.'

'Well, if you will excuse me,' Forsyth said, 'I have business with Magistrate Read.' He stood to one side of the stairwell and let the women and Lavender pass. 'Lavender, if you care to call at Bushy House later today, Mrs Jordan has passed on to me a reward for Doña Magdalena.'

Lavender nodded and continued down the stairs after the women. He was annoyed by Forsyth's manner and irritated by the fact that he would now have to wait until Forsyth had finished his business with Read before he could have a few minutes of his own with the magistrate. He was desperate to travel on to Wandsworth. But Magdalena's excitement as he flagged down a cab soon brought a smile to his face. 'See Stephen,' she said, her eyes gleaming. 'I too have the skills to become an independent woman.'

Whatever Forsyth's business with James Read, it didn't take long to conclude, and Lavender was able to gain an audience with the magistrate within five minutes. However, a few moments inside Read's office were enough to reveal that Read wasn't in a good mood. Nor was Lavender's ongoing case about the dead actress now his main concern. Read wanted to talk about Magdalena. He fixed Lavender with a quizzical stare and bombarded him with questions.

'Is this the woman you met when you went up to Northumberland to look for that missing heiress last year? Wasn't she involved when your coach was attacked by highwaymen? Didn't her husband die at Talavera?'

'Yes, to everything,' Lavender replied. 'Doña Magdalena was instrumental in helping Constable Woods and I overcome that band of tobymen.' He didn't mention that she had also saved his life in the ensuing gun battle.

'She's also the one who fled Spain after she shot dead several of Joseph Napoleon's officers, isn't she?' Read's voice rose as he delivered the accusation. Lavender sensed his antipathy towards Magdalena and wondered what had brought about the change in his attitude. She seemed to have him eating out of her hand only a few minutes ago.

'Allegedly. I've never been told the details of that incident.'

'Did you put her up to this?' Read asked suddenly. 'Is this "Spanish teaching" your idea?'

'No. She has come up with this little scheme by herself.'

'Well, I don't know what the Home Department will think about a woman teaching Spanish to our foreign operatives. It is a most irregular suggestion and bound to raise a few eyebrows. Do you intend to marry her?'

Lavender glanced up sharply and saw that Read was watching him for a reaction. 'Doña Magdalena is a good friend of mine,' he said. 'She's not in a position to remarry at the moment and is still grieving for her late husband. But she does need an income; everything she owns is currently in the hands of the French and she has a child to support. The world is changing, sir. Last night I met three different but intelligent women at the theatre. All of whom work to support themselves – and Dorothy Jordan keeps a prince and ten children at Bushy House.'

Magistrate Read shrugged. 'Dorothy Jordan is a strumpet; respectable women don't work for a living. What Doña Magdalena suggests would still be an irregular arrangement. And you haven't answered my question.'

Lavender remained silent. He had no intention of answering it.

Read threw up his hands in frustration and sighed. 'Look Stephen, I'm just a simple man of the law and I know little to nothing about women, or the shifting mores of society – as Mrs Read will confirm. In fact, I tend to leave matters of that nature to Mrs Read's discretion; I find her guidance in such matters invaluable.'

'I have no doubt that Magdalena's language skills will be a great asset to the British government,' Lavender replied. 'She's very intelligent, has an excellent ear for languages – and sharp eyes as well.'

'On top of this she's a Catholic.' Read frowned.

'Oddly enough, the best speakers of the Spanish language tend be Catholics.' Lavender could barely keep the frustration out of his voice.

'Touché,' said Read. 'You have me there, Stephen. But perhaps championing this woman is something you should think about more carefully. Prejudice against Catholics is rife in England at every level, from the street hawkers down in Covent Garden to the politicians on the benches of Parliament.'

'Yes,' snapped Lavender. 'Yet the Prince Regent of our country married a Catholic.'

'Not officially.' Read narrowed his eyes and frowned. 'You would be well advised not to mention that in public. Prince George could never present Mrs FitzHerbert to the country as his wife.'

'So he bigamously married Princess Caroline instead?'

Read's frown deepened. 'Are you deliberately trying to provoke me, Lavender? You know damned well that his marriage to Mrs FitzHerbert was banned under the Royal Marriages' Act.' His voice hardened. 'You also know that there is a world of difference between how a Hanoverian prince can behave and how you yourself need to conduct your life. Your association with this woman, charming though she is, may do irreparable damage to your career.'

Lavender froze. *Was Read threatening him?* 'As a principal officer at Bow Street I'd assumed that I had reached the pinnacle of my career.' The icy tone in his own voice matched Read's.

'Yes, but such an association, no matter how platonic, gives rise to gossip and speculation. You may find yourself sidelined by various clients and barred from carrying out some investigations.'

Realisation dawned on Lavender with a flash. 'This has come from that weasel, Forsyth, hasn't it?' Lavender snapped. 'He's made a trip up to town especially to tell you about the theatre last night and let you know that one of your officers is escorting a Catholic widow about town.'

'He felt it was his duty.'

For a moment Read couldn't look him in the eye. Lavender was seething. He wanted to chase after the devious Forsyth and wipe the self-righteous smile off his face. How dare that ridiculous man try to stir up trouble for him and Magdalena? Lavender fought back his anger and tried to bring the conversation back to something less personal. He needed to diffuse the tension in the room created by that dandyprat, Forsyth.

'Does Professor Quincy still teach Spanish for the Home Department?'

Read eyed him suspiciously. 'Yes, although they tend to use a room in the language school on Hart Street these days.'

'How old is Quincy now?'

Read narrowed his eyes and frowned. 'I can see where your thoughts are going. Quincy's health has been a cause for concern for some time.'

'Look, sir,' Lavender said with as much sincerity as he could muster. 'I know that you're concerned for my happiness.' This was a lie. He knew damned well that Read's overriding concern was for the reputation of Bow Street Magistrate's Court. 'But whom I choose to associate with in my private life is my business and I will deal with any consequences of my friendship with Doña Magdalena, as and when they arise. But this doesn't affect the fact that Doña Magdalena's skills – and her discretion – could be invaluable to the Home Department. If you, and they, can't appreciate this fact and overlook her religion, then you're not making decisions in the best interests of the country. Besides which, she takes her maid with her everywhere as a chaperone so there will be no impropriety.'

Suddenly Read grinned. 'She takes that little maid everywhere? How unfortunate for you, Stephen!' He laughed. 'That must make the courting a little awkward, eh? There's nothing like a little *dueña* glaring at you from the corner to dampen your ardour while you're trying to enjoy a bit of relish.'

Lavender shrugged as the other man cackled. He was just grateful that the tension between them had lifted.

Another thought seemed to suddenly strike James Read. 'She's very observant, you said? And discreet?'

'Yes.'

'And her loyalty to the British Crown is without dispute?'

'Nobody hates the French more than Doña Magdalena and she is makes every effort to fit into English society as best she can. She's well aware that England will be her home for some time and is grateful for the sanctuary she has found here. Her son is at an English school.'

'Mmm. Well, we'll see what the Home Department thinks. We may just have a use for Señora Morales after all.'

'What do you have in mind?'

But Read wouldn't be drawn into divulging any further details. 'Tell me, how are you progressing with this case of the dead actress? Oh, by the way, the news-sheets have heard about the story. I had a reporter here earlier, trying to get information about the case. I didn't tell him anything except the basic facts but I suspect that he will probably elaborate on them. If you still have any family to notify about the girl's death, I recommend that you do it before they sit down and read the grisly version over tomorrow's boiled eggs and breakfast kippers.'

Chapter Eleven

Lavender was relieved to hear from the housemaid who answered the door at Mrs Willoughby's home in Wandsworth that April Clare's sister wasn't only alive but also in good health. The girl told them that Mrs Willoughby was taking tea in the parlour.

Both he and Woods froze with shock when the maid showed them into the room.

'Gawd's teeth!' Woods exclaimed. The blood drained from his face. 'It's a ghost! A damned spirit!'

April Clare's sister sat in front of the fireplace, glanced up and frowned at their whispering. Harriet Willoughby was an animated version of the corpse they had left on a slab back at Bow Street. The two women were identical in every way, from their thick, glossy raven hair and creamy complexions down to their curvaceous figures. Lavender understood Woods' initial superstitious reaction and shared his shock. It was as if the dead girl had been reincarnated and was now sat calmly in this neat little parlour in suburban London.

'I think that Lady Caroline forgot to mention something important,' he whispered.

'Have you come from my stepmother, Detective?' Mrs Willoughby asked. 'I heard you whispering. Is everything well with

Lady Caroline?' Her large, dark eyes stared dolefully across the room at him. He detected a slight puffiness and redness in the rims. *Had she been crying?*

Lavender cleared his throat. 'My apologies, Mrs Willoughby. Yes, we have just come from Lady Clare's home. Unfortunately, we have some bad news for you about your sister, Miss April Clare.'

Suddenly, her shoulders shook and the woman dissolved into ugly sobs. Lavender and Woods exchanged a startled glance and moved swiftly across the carpet towards her. Her distress was genuine but Lavender wondered what had upset her; he hadn't told her about April's death yet. He reached for his handkerchief then realised that it was still sodden from Lady Caroline's tears. He gestured to Woods who pulled out his own grubby handkerchief and offered it to the distraught woman. She took it gratefully with a trembling hand.

Afternoon tea was set out on a silver tray on a nearby table. Lavender poured a cup of the steaming beverage and held it out to her. 'Here, try to drink this. It may help,' he suggested. 'Do you want sugar?'

'Yes – no – yes,' she stammered. A little confused, Lavender took the silver tongs and dropped two cubes of the fine white crystals into the china cup before placing it in front of her. Grasping the drink with both hands, she raised it to her lips and gulped it down. Eventually she sat back and stared up at him with swollen eyes.

'April is dead, isn't she?'

He was taken aback. He abandoned his carefully prepared speech and said quietly, 'I'm afraid so, Mrs Willoughby. We found her body in an empty house in Covent Garden yesterday.'

'I knew it! I knew it!' The young woman now collapsed into a new spasm of tears. Alarmed at her grief and remembering Lady Caroline's warning about Mrs Willoughby's delicate constitution, he sat down beside her on the sofa and took her hand in his.

'Is Captain Willoughby at home?' asked Woods. He had wandered across to the window to examine the large brass compass, mounted on gimbals that glinted in the light streaming through the lace curtain. 'Should we send for him?'

The mention of her husband had a strengthening effect on the distraught woman. 'No. Captain Willoughby has been away at sea for nearly a year,' she said between sniffles. 'He's in the Indian Ocean aboard HMS *Boadicea*.' She pointed above the fireplace to a magnificent oil painting of a thirty-eight-gun warship in full sail and at a jaunty angle on choppy seas. 'He commissioned that painting on his last voyage.'

'Is there anyone else we can fetch?' Lavender asked. 'Lady Caroline said she will be calling soon but perhaps there is someone we can call immediately?'

She shook her head and did her best to compose herself. 'I will be fine until my stepmother arrives.' Her face crumpled again. 'Oh, Detective! I'm so glad you're here! I have been frantic with worry over the last few days and had no idea what to do!'

'What's happened, Mrs Willoughby? And how did you know that your sister was already dead?'

She fell silent. Lavender squeezed her hand again and was conscious of the ticking of the clock on the mantelpiece in the short silence that followed. He decided to try gentle questioning. She seemed to be struggling to find the right words. 'Did you see Miss Clare on Friday night?' he asked. 'Lady Caroline said you were due to travel to her soirée together.'

'Yes. April arrived just after lunch. She had a few days when she wasn't needed at the theatre. She often spent time with me during these lulls. Her lodgings are rather drab and uncomfortable and I'm so desperately lonely since Nesbit went back to sea.' She sighed. Her beautiful eyes stared vacantly ahead. Lavender had the impression that she was looking for inspiration or trying to retrieve a memory.

'We ate a light supper here and then dressed for the party. I had hired a hansom cab for the journey, as Captain Willoughby and I don't keep a carriage.'

'What happened on the journey?' Lavender prompted gently.

'We crossed the river and were just approaching the Five Fields area when our cab was set upon by highwaymen.'

Lavender grimaced. The dangerous marshland known as Five Fields, south of Hyde Park, was a notorious stamping ground for tobymen and footpads. He felt her hand tremble again. The experience must have been traumatic for the two sisters.

'But they didn't want money or jewels. They wrenched open the door of the cab and reached in for April.' Her voice faltered. 'I heard one of them yell: "Get the actress!"'

'Could you see their faces?' Lavender asked.

'No. No – they wore masks.'

'Did any of them sound like foreigners?' Woods asked. He moved across to perch on the arm of the chair.

She glanced up at him, confused. 'They dragged April outside and disappeared with her into the gloom.' Large tears rolled down her smooth cheeks again, then she started to babble again. 'It happened so fast, Detective. I heard April scream . . . I have never felt so wretched in my life when they rode away with her. So useless . . . so utterly helpless . . .'

'There was nothing you could have done, Mrs Willoughby.' Lavender waited until she was more composed. 'Did they say anything else?' he asked. 'How many of them were there?'

'Three. Four, maybe. One of them said: "Go back home. Stay away from the law. We'll be in touch." That's how I knew they wanted a ransom.'

'Did they get in touch?'

'No. I haven't heard a thing from them – nothing. But I knew . . .'

'What did you know?'

'I knew she was dead.' The starkness and simplicity of her statement and the utter certainty in her tearstained and tragic face made the hairs stand up on the back of Lavender's neck.

'We're twins you see, detective. We're connected. I felt her life force go out several days ago. She's left me. Left me for good.'

Lavender saw Woods turn pale and shuffle uncomfortably on the arm of his chair. He shared his constable's discomfort. Although Lavender didn't believe in most aspects of the supernatural he had never been able to discount the existence of a strange, unnatural bond between siblings who had shared a womb.

'What I don't understand,' Woods said, 'is how they knew which one of you were which?'

'I was wearing a partial veil,' Mrs Willoughby said. 'It was dark and I was – I was at the back of the coach on the far side. April was nearer the door they opened.'

'So the kidnappers were not intimate with you or your sister. They didn't know either of you personally,' Lavender said thoughtfully.

'How do you work that out, sir?' Woods asked.

'They didn't know that her sister was an identical twin but they had followed Miss Clare and knew what she looked like.'

'With respect, sir,' said Woods. 'Half of London will know what Miss Clare looked like. She's a famous actress.' Mrs Willoughby gave him a grateful, weak smile.

Lavender fell silent for a moment, mulling over these latest revelations. He had always suspected that April Clare had been kidnapped and held prisoner in Raleigh Close. This evil scheme had been carefully thought out. Someone had known that the actress planned to spend time with her sister and then travel to Lady Caroline's. She had obviously been followed here and the villains had seized their chance to kidnap the actress in the remote and dangerous Five Fields. It was well planned and premeditated. The fact that

Darius Jones, the pimp who used Raleigh Close for his nuns, had been drowned in the Thames could still be a coincidence. But if it wasn't a coincidence, then these villains were more brutal and calculating than Lavender had previously imagined.

But something had gone badly wrong at Raleigh Close. The actress had died before they could claim a ransom, or even contact her relatives. These criminals had not gone to all this trouble to simply murder April Clare; they could have done that when they stopped the coach at the Five Fields. No. They wanted something. But what?

Damn that surgeon, Allison. If Sir Richard had waited for them at Bow Street, they would already know how April Clare had died. Then Lavender remembered the ransacked lodgings of the dead girl and he frowned. That didn't fit with the normal behaviour of criminals intent on abduction.

'What happened next?' Woods asked. 'And what was that rascal of a cab driver doin' while you were attacked?'

'The cab driver was as scared as me,' Mrs Willoughby said. 'They held a pistol up to him. The man was shaking.' She grimaced at the memory.

'Why didn't you report the abduction of your sister to the constables?' Lavender asked.

'I was too scared,' she said. Her head drooped with shame. 'They had told me not to go near the law. I knew they must want money. I have a little money. I thought that if I did what they said and paid the ransom, then April would be returned to me safely.'

Lavender sighed at her naivety. Kidnapping was a crime more common than most Londoners were aware and it could be vicious. Only last summer, two innocent young boys had been taken from a wealthy family in Mayfair. The ransom had been paid but both boys had still ended up with their throats cut. The gang responsible had disappeared back into whatever sewer they had crawled out of, and so far they had eluded capture. Was it the same gang, perhaps?

'I came home and waited,' Mrs Willoughby wailed. 'Hoping beyond hope, for some news – or a message. It has been interminable!' She began to sob again. 'I'm so glad you're here, Detective – the last few days have been so awful, so lonely. I know you've brought me terrible news but at least my torment is over, and poor April is at peace. I've never been so frightened in my life.'

'Did you notice anything else out of the ordinary on that night?' Lavender asked.

Mrs Willoughby shook her head, too overcome with grief to speak.

'If you'll excuse me, sir,' Woods said as he stood up, 'I think I'll go and talk to the servants. They may have seen or heard somethin'.' Lavender nodded. 'Another suggestion, sir – we should track down the driver of this cab.'

Lavender raised his head sharply. 'Do you think he may have been in collusion with the kidnappers?'

'It's a possibility, sir. Most cabbies know how dangerous the Five Fields are, and most of them avoid the area like the plague. His choice of route is suspicious. He would have been better advised to take a different route and stay south of the river until the Westminster Bridge.'

'He was very young and frightened,' Mrs Willoughby said.

'Bloody coward,' muttered Woods, as he disappeared out of the room.

'Mrs Willoughby, did Miss Clare have anyone in her life who may have wished her harm?' Lavender asked. 'A jealous rival, perhaps?' Mrs Willoughby shook her head. 'Did she ever confide in you about a sweetheart or a beau?'

Again this was met with a negative response. Lavender asked a series of questions about the dead woman but he gleaned no further information. He wondered how much Mrs Willoughby had slept since her sister had been wrenched from her life. He was relieved when Woods reappeared with a pale-faced maid.

The maid wrung her hands in her apron. 'Oh ma'am!' she exclaimed. 'I'm so sorry to hear about Miss April! She were such a lovely woman.'

Mrs Willoughby rallied slightly. 'Show the detective and the constable out, Ruby,' she said. 'And then return to me.'

'Very good, ma'am.'

'We'll be in touch soon,' Lavender promised as they left.

'This is dreadful news about Miss April, dreadful,' babbled the servant as she led them to the door.

'Had you no idea?' Lavender asked sharply. 'Didn't your mistress confide in anyone about her terrible ordeal?'

The girl blinked up at him in surprise. She had a large pair of cornflower blue eyes to match her soft, country accent. 'Why, no, sir. I knew nuffin' about Miss April's kidnappin' until yer constable 'ere just told me in the kitchen.'

'Thank you for your help,' Lavender said. 'By the way, does your mistress usually take sugar in her tea?'

'Why, no, sir.'

'Well, I would recommend that she does today,' he said. 'Sweet tea is the best thing for shock. Insist that she takes a couple of lumps.'

'Yes, sir.'

The two men pulled on their hats and left.

Chapter Twelve

It was mid-afternoon and both men were hungry. They decided to have a meal before they retrieved their horses from the ostlers. Lavender led Woods into the busy town centre of Wandsworth. People made their way slowly down the street, staggering home beneath the weight of their purchases: heavy baskets, bolts of fabric and bulging sacks. There was a strong and attractive smell of hops and barley from the Thames-side brewery that masked the stench of the fetid river. A steady stream of brewer's drays, hauled by the rippling muscles of huge, broad-shouldered shire horses, passed them in the street. They waited for a momentary break in the traffic and then crossed the road, drawn to a brightly lit tavern on the quayside.

The taproom heaved with brewery workers and grimy stevedores, amongst other labourers. Lavender and Woods pushed their way through the throng until they found a table and a couple of stools at the back of the smoky tavern. Beneath the hum of conversation could be heard the incessant clink-clink of dice being shaken in a glass as patrons played the age-old games of 'Bones'.

Lavender sat down, took off his hat and loosened his greatcoat. The crackling log fire sent a welcome blast of hot air to warm his frozen face. When the barmaid arrived, they ordered food and a tankard of ale. Woods poured most of a full jug of thick gravy onto his meat and potato pie. He then proceeded to demolish the meal with relish.

Lavender smiled and asked: 'Is Betsy keeping you short of food again?'

'You what, sir?' Woods asked. His ruddy cheeks protruded like a rodents as he chewed.

'Never mind. Tell me what you discovered from the Willoughby servants.'

Woods belched with satisfaction and wiped the greasy gravy from his mouth with the sodden handkerchief he had retrieved from Mrs Willoughby. 'There's three of them: a cook and a couple of maids. They saw and suspected nothing. They were aware that Mrs Willoughby came home alone and early from her Lady Caroline's party but she claimed to have a headache, so the servants thought nothing of it. According to the servants, Mrs Willoughby has sat quietly in the parlour for the last three days. No one has called at the house and no one has seen or heard anything suspicious in the neighbourhood. The servants weren't aware of anyone watching the house on the night of the kidnapping or of anyone loitering outside.'

'Well, April Clare's movements were followed closely,' Lavender snapped. 'Someone must have seen something.'

'I think the household has been distracted,' said Woods. 'The nursemaid told me that their nipper has been colicky and they've all been upset and disturbed by his cryin'.'

Lavender was startled. 'There's a child?'

'Yes, Mrs Willoughby has a baby boy, called Charlie. He's about the same age as my Tabitha. Eight months, I think.' Woods paused with a fork of pie halfway to his mouth. His eyes widened. 'You don't think it were somethin' to do with that mynah bird, do you?'

Lavender smiled. 'No, Ned, I don't. But it had crossed my mind that the sisters may have played one of their pranks on Lady Caroline last Friday.'

Large furrows appeared in Woods' broad forehead. The meat pie continued to hover in midair. 'What? You think that they may have swapped clothes and pretended to be each other?'

'It had crossed my mind,' Lavender said, 'though God knows why. It might have been the way she gulped down that sugared tea – and I failed to see any sign that Mrs Willoughby was as "delicate" as Lady Caroline had described. Yes, she was upset but she seemed quite robust and healthy to me. I've no doubt that to swap identity would have been an easy trick for the sisters to play. Anyway, Mrs Willoughby is obviously whom she claims to be. Sir Richard told us that the dead twin had never borne a child and the Willoughbys have one in their nursery. The woman we have just interviewed was Mrs Harriet Willoughby, the mother of the child.'

Woods nodded and swallowed his food. 'You could have knocked me down with a feather when we walked into that room. Those women are identical.' He jabbed the fork in Lavender's direction for emphasis.

'*Were* identical, Ned,' Lavender said softly. 'One of them is dead now and we still don't know why.'

'Is it just a kidnappin' gone wrong, do you think?'

'I don't know.' He sat back thoughtfully and applied his mind to the unsolved mysteries that still surrounded April Clare's death. The gloom of the warm, cosy tavern was probably as good a place as any to think. Had it been a kidnapping for a cash ransom? If so, why had the villains ransacked April's lodgings? Or had they? Was that just a coincidental burglary?

'The Willoughbys are financially comfortable,' Lavender said aloud. He always found it helpful to share his thoughts with Woods. 'A naval captain makes a good salary. But I don't think they're particularly wealthy. Baron Clare left his family very little money. Miss Clare chose to support herself on the stage, and the baron's widow, Lady Caroline, never has any cash to spare despite the income she makes from her art. She struggled to pay Bow Street for the services I rendered a few years ago when her former lover blackmailed her. She juggles her creditors. Kidnapping April Clare would never have made anyone rich; the ransom would not have been huge. And the kidnappers seem to have gone to a lot of trouble to organise this abduction.' He shrugged. 'Perhaps things will become clearer when we track down Sir Richard and find out how the girl died.'

'Are you goin' to see him now?' Woods asked.

'No, while we're so far west of London, I thought I'd ride on to Bushy House and have a word with Mrs Jordan about her young protégé, April Divine. There is also something I need to retrieve from them.'

Woods stood up and brushed the pastry crumbs off his coat. 'What do you want me to do?'

'See if you can find this cab driver and question him.' Lavender rose to his feet and pulled on his gloves. 'Oh, and Ned . . .'

'Yes, sir?'

'When you do find him, make sure you let his governor know what a coward he has been and that one of their customers is dead.'

Armed with the address of the coaching stables used by Mrs Willoughby for carriage hire, Woods soon tracked down the establishment. Situated at the rear of the Brewers' Arms tavern, the low buildings with their arched entrances were arranged around three sides of a cobbled courtyard.

Woods took a cursory glance over the split stable doors. The piles of fresh bedding straw, refilled water troughs and the healthy-looking bays and chestnuts that stamped and snorted in their stalls, all reassured the experienced patrol officer that the place was well run and the owner knew his horseflesh. The emptiness of the stables also suggested that the business was a thriving concern: most of the cabs, coaches and horses were out on the streets. He picked his way carefully across the cobbles through piles of steaming horse dung, in search of Fred Tummins, the thin and elderly owner of the stable yard.

Completely bald beneath his hat, Tummins had a bulbous nose and several disfiguring warts across his face. Despite his physical frailties, there was nothing wrong with the old man's mental capacities and he was quick enough to realise the gravity of the situation Woods described to him. Tummins was horrified when he heard about the attack at the Five Fields and the kidnapping of April Clare. He was also annoyed that his young and inexperienced coachman had behaved in such a cowardly fashion and not reported the incident to him on his return. Woods didn't feel that it was necessary to mention Lavender's threat, as the old man was distressed enough.

The young coach driver was currently out on another job and Woods realised that he was lucky to be absent. Despite his small stature, Tummins looked like he could be formidable when riled. Woods bit back his disappointment when he realised that he would have to return the next day at first light to interview the coach driver.

'He's not scarpered, has he?' Woods asked. He had not ruled out the possibility that the lad was involved in the kidnapping or had taken a dawb from the villains to keep quiet.

'No, no,' Tummins reassured him. ''E's just takin' a customer to Westminster at the moment; there's a late sittin' in Parliament tonight. I'll make sure 'e's 'ere for you to speak to first thing in the mornin'.'

Woods raised his eyebrows with slight surprise. Obviously, Tummins had some exalted customers on his books. 'Let's just hope he doesn't take the poor bugger through the Five Fields,' he commented. 'We don't need a dead Member of Parliament on our hands, as well. I'll need your coachman to take me out to the location of the kidnappin'. The kidnappers may have left some clue to their identity at the scene.'

'Of course, of course – and I'll come with you. I can't tell you 'ow sorry I am that this 'as 'appened, Constable.'

Chapter Thirteen

The tall, elaborate wrought-iron gates at the entrance to Bushy House, the residence of the Duke of Clarence, were wide open. Lavender rode through them without challenge from a gatekeeper and was instantly aware of the spacious grandeur of the deer parkland attached to the house. The tree-lined drive was nearly two miles long and probably the widest road he had ever seen. Now skeletal and leafless against the backdrop of the darkening sky, the great avenue of chestnuts had been laid out to a design by Sir Christopher Wren. Lavender caught a glimpse of the glimmering silver of the well-stocked fishponds that littered the park. A herd of red deer who had grown confident with the failing light had come out to feed on the vast lawns. In the gloom he could just about make out the famous fountain at the end of the drive, which encircled a statue of the Goddess Diana. He turned off the drive in order to approach Bushy House, whose tall chimneys rose through the treetops.

A group of children raced around the grounds playing with hoops and poking at toy boats on the ponds. They were well wrapped up in coats and scarves. He knew that the older FitzClarence boys had already been sent away to the army and the navy, but there still seemed to be a lot of youngsters in the grounds of Bushy

House. Lavender assumed that the younger FitzClarence children had invited their friends over to play. They happily ignored him.

He tied his horse to low branch of a tree and mounted the sweeping stone steps of the imposing four-storey house. Thanks to the coming and going of the children, the front door was also ajar. He pushed it open and entered. No footman stepped forward to challenge him. Grateful that he wasn't personally responsible for the security and safety of the king's third son and his large family, Lavender walked to the fire blazing in the immense stone fireplace and warmed himself. He was curious to see how far he could get into the premises before he was noticed. He had almost five minutes to stand and admire the soot-blackened collection of old family portraits, which wound up the plastered walls of the carved oak staircase, before a passing footman finally noticed his presence.

Lavender asked for an audience with Mrs Jordan and was led into an antechamber to wait. Yellow silk curtains tied back with tasselled cords framed the deep-set windows. He walked across and admired the narrow glass-fronted bookshelves that climbed up the inside of the alcoves. He decided that if he was kept waiting much longer, he would take out one of the leather-bound volumes and read.

When the door opened, he was surprised and displeased to see Sir Lawrence Forsyth stride into the room. The duke's aide puffed out his chest and glared up coldly. 'I suppose you have come for the *señora's* reward, yes?' The man clutched a cloth purse in his hand.

Lavender gritted his teeth and pushed his fists into the pockets of his greatcoat. 'If it pleases Mrs Jordan to bestow it when I see her—' he began.

'Mrs Jordan is busy,' Forsyth interrupted. 'As is the duke. I have been charged with giving you this.' He handed over the cloth purse. Lavender could tell by its weight that there wouldn't be enough to cover the cost of one boot for Magdalena, never mind a pair.

Obviously, the duke and his mistress were not quite so magnanimous in the cold light of day. *Never mind*, Lavender thought, *I'll top up the coins in the purse myself.*

'You may go now.'

'I need to see Mrs Jordan on a matter of police business.'

'What police business?' Forsyth blinked. Was that a hint of fear Lavender saw in the aide's close-set eyes?

Lavender's felt his lip curl. 'It is a matter I need to discuss with Mrs Jordan – alone. Please escort me to her.'

'What? Am I a footman now?' snapped Forsyth.

'I don't know,' Lavender said forcefully. 'Are you? What exactly is your role here at Bushy Park, Sir Lawrence?'

Forsyth drew himself up to his full height, which was still less than five foot. 'I am aide to Prince William,' he announced. 'His Grace is an admiral in the King's Navy. It is an onerous position, fraught with responsibility for the security of the nation. I assist him with secretarial duties and do my best to ease him of some of the more mundane aspects of his role. I take exception to your attitude, Lavender.'

Lavender was well aware that the duke's position in the navy was honorary and his rank was purely titular. Although he had seen active service in the navy as a young man and served in New York during the American War of Independence, where President George Washington had once approved a plot to kidnap him, the king's son had been a landlubber for the last twenty years. Lavender vaguely remembered some scandal about the prince who'd ignored orders and sailed for home while in charge of HMS *Valiant*. The navy had taken great pains to cover up his act of mutiny. Whereas most naval officers would have been court-martialled, Prince William had been permanently brought ashore and given a dukedom instead. Although he wasn't familiar with Forsyth's naval career, Lavender had a sneaking suspicion that it was probably unremarkable: the man didn't look or sound like he was capable of effective command. Telling tales like a schoolboy was more his style.

'It is *Detective* Lavender,' he replied, sharply. 'I am a principal officer with the Bow Street Magistrates' Court and I have a matter of extreme importance to discuss with Mrs Jordan. Now are you going to impede police business or arrange an interview with Mrs Jordan? There might be consequences if you insist on the former.'

The small man flushed angrily and opened his mouth to protest but Lavender had had enough. 'If security is part of your remit, Forsyth,' he said. 'I suggest that you review the arrangements here at Bushy House. I entered the grounds of this estate, walked through the front door and stood in the hallway for a full five minutes before anyone noticed my presence. If I had been an assassin or a foreign operative working for Napoleon, I could have murdered the duke and his entire family and robbed the place blind before anyone even knew I was here. I suggest that you look to your business and let me look to mine.'

Forsyth gulped, turned pale and hurried to the bell pull by the fireplace to summon a footman.

Dorothy Jordan and the Duke of Clarence were relaxing in front of a fire in their drawing room when Lavender was ushered into their presence. The duke was reading a daily news-sheet and Mrs Jordan had a novella in one hand and a pair of pince-nez in the other. She hastily pushed her reading glasses down the side of her chair cushions when he entered. He smiled at her vanity.

Two young curly-haired children played with a toy horse at their parents' feet on the thick Turkish carpet. The room was tastefully furnished with a collection of oval side tables and cream chintz chairs and sofas. The furniture blended well against the pale green silk wallpaper, which rose up to the decorative moulding of the white cornice. A huge gilt chandelier with dozens of flickering, creamy wax candles hung from the ornate plastered ceiling. Lavender's eyes flicked to the marble bust of Sir Horatio Nelson, which took pride of place on a plinth in the centre of the window bay. He knew that Nelson had been a friend of the duke.

Mrs Jordan wore a flattering lavender muslin gown, which enhanced her complexion, and a pair of jade earrings that reflected the green of her eyes. She was draped gracefully across her cushioned chair. Lavender had to admit that the scene in the room presented a charming picture of domesticity, with the famous actress at the centre. The role of royal mistress clearly suited her; she had made it her own over the last twenty years.

'Detective Lavender,' she purred, in her soft Irish accent. 'How delightful to see you again – and so soon. I trust that Sir Lawrence has dealt with the matter of the *señora*'s reward for felling that thief?'

'Indeed he has, ma'am, thank you,' Lavender said as he bowed to the duke. 'Unfortunately, I now need to speak to you on another, more serious, police matter.'

'Good grief!' The actress raised both her voice and her eyebrows dramatically. 'What on earth could that be? You haven't been naughty again have you, William?' she asked.

The duke burst out laughing and his double chin wobbled. 'I say, Dora, you're a wag! She's a great comedienne, ain't she, Lavender?'

Lavender smiled. 'Mrs Jordan always lives up to her reputation for comedy.'

'Have you seen her perform on the stage?' the duke demanded.

'Yes. I once saw Mrs Jordan as Viola in *Twelfth Night* and a great performance it was too.' The actress smiled and bowed her head modestly.

'Shakespeare? Pah!' spat the duke. 'It is her role as Little Pickle in *The Spoiled Child* where she excelled. Did you never see that? Captured my heart with that role, Dora did. No woman can wear a pair of breeches and strut across a stage like my Dora.' The duke's eyes misted over at the memory. For a moment there was a respectful hush.

'But to business, Detective,' said Mrs Jordan. 'How can I help you?'

'It may be best if the children weren't here,' Lavender said cautiously.

'Of course.' She indicated to the hovering footman, who immediately moved forward and ushered the children out of the room. They wailed and complained as they were taken away from their parents and the warm fire.

'I trust this is serious enough to warrant upsetting my children,' said the actress, coldly.

'I'm sorry for the inconvenience, Mrs Jordan,' Lavender said. 'But there has been a disturbing development at the Sans Pareil Theatre and I don't think the children need to hear about it.'

'What has happened?'

'One of the young actresses, whom I believed you personally sponsored, has been found dead in mysterious circumstances.'

'Good grief,' said Mrs Jordan, this time without the exaggeration. The woman was shocked. 'Which one? Which actress?'

'Miss April Divine, otherwise known as April Clare; the daughter of the late Baron Clare.'

'How awful! Poor April! What on earth happened?'

Lavender hesitated for a moment but was relieved to see that Mrs Jordan remained dry-eyed. For that he was grateful. He quickly related the circumstances of April Clare's death. The duke and his mistress winced but listened intently. Mrs Jordan did her best to answer Lavender's questions.

'I haven't seen Miss Clare since last summer,' she told him. 'Yes, I helped her to find her position with the Drury Lane company but I understand that she took some time off from the theatre after the fire last year. She approached me again at the end of August for an introduction to Jane Scott at the Sans Pareil, and I was happy to oblige. April was a promising young actress with a great future.'

Lavender was struck by Mrs Jordan's high opinion of April Clare's ability, and compared it to the differing version he had received from Jane Scott the night before. He had no idea if it had any significance but every piece of information was valuable at this stage in the investigation. 'Are you aware if April Clare had a lover, Mrs Jordan? Or a sweetheart?'

The actress smiled and waved her hand dismissively in the air. 'Every actress has their admirers, Detective.'

'I'll say!' interjected the duke. 'There's many a time I've nearly challenged some love-struck popinjay to a duel for being overly fond of my Dora.'

She smiled across at him fondly. 'I can't remember if April ever associated with one young man in particular,' she continued. 'But— No, wait! There was a young man to whom she was close at Drury Lane. I have no idea who he was or what became of that relationship.'

'Thank you, Mrs Jordan,' Lavender said. 'And a final question: you said that Miss Clare took some time off from her acting career after the Drury Lane fire. Have you any idea why?'

'Oh, yes. I can help you out there, Detective.' Mrs Jordan beamed with confidence. 'When she came to ask for an introduction to Jane Scott she told me about it. She had spent some time with a sick and elderly aunt in Gloucester. She was such a kind young woman, very worthy of my support. It is so sad to hear that she's now dead.'

Chapter Fourteen

Wednesday 21st February, 1810

Dawn was only just breaking over the smoking chimneys and spires of London when Lavender left his lodgings in Southwark. Not that he or anyone else would see the dawn today – or the top of the crenelated tower of the Church of St Saviour and St Mary Overie. A damp, sulphurous fog had descended over the capital. It cast the whole city into gloom and muffled the usual sounds of the river and road traffic. Even the squawking seagulls that constantly wheeled overhead were subdued this morning. Lavender sighed and pulled his coat tighter around his shoulders against the bitter cold and damp air. A rat skittered out from under his boots, but apart from the odd beggar lying half out of a doorway, he saw very little other life at this ungodly hour. Occasionally, a shadow loomed out of the gloom in front of him but few other people were abroad apart from nightwatchmen and villains.

A few night lanterns still glimmered on the dripping walls of the houses and an occasional warm pool of light from a drapeless window spilled down onto the cobbled road to illuminate his path. He moved from one pool of light to another, picking his way carefully round the stagnant puddles and indiscernible piles of refuse that littered the street.

Lavender was tired and the weather reflected his mood. It had been a long journey to Bushy House and he hadn't returned to his rooms until midnight. His mind had been troubled by this case and he had barely slept. The mounting controversy about his relationship with Magdalena also bothered him. Finally, he had thrown back his crumpled blankets with irritation and clambered out of bed to dress and break his fast. That was one good thing about operating out of Bow Street, he decided. The place never closed. Such was the level of crime in the capital that the police office was a hive of activity every hour of the day and night. He might as well be at work, he decided. Perhaps he would be able to think more clearly there.

So much about April Clare's kidnapping didn't make sense, and Dorothy Jordan's comments about the actress' aunt in Gloucester had only added to the mystery. Lady Caroline had been quite clear that the sisters didn't have any other family except her. Besides which, he had heard nothing about the young actress to suggest that she was selfless enough to give up her career to nurse an elderly relative.

His pace slowed when he reached the low wall with the high iron railings that skirted the churchyard of the Church of St Saviour and St Mary Overie. The peaceful, leafy graveyard had been one of Lavender's favourite places since he was a child. His maternal grandfather had once been dean of the church and so his family connection with the place was strong. As children, Lavender and his sisters had raced each other through the grounds, hidden amongst the gravestones and clambered up the trees.

More recently, he had appreciated the tranquillity of the churchyard, especially in the summer when it was alive with birdsong and the gentle hum of bees. It was an oasis of calm amongst the noise, filth and crowds of the bustling city. It was a good place to think.

And, of course, this was where Vivienne was buried.

Lavender's hand lifted the latch of the creaking iron gate and his feet trod his well-worn path between the crumbling stones to her grave. Condensation dripped from the tree boughs onto his hat and shoulders. With each step, his boots sank into the soft, muddy ground. He stopped beside her gravestone. Instinctively, he bent down, reached out with his gloved hands and pulled away a few weeds at the base. Then he straightened his back and gazed down sadly at the final resting place of his dead fiancée.

He hadn't visited Vivienne's grave for several months but the familiar ache of longing and misery still settled in his chest when he thought of her laughter, her love of life and those futile plans they had made together. Everything had been destroyed in a matter of days. Her life, their love for each other and their future, together with the child she was secretly carrying. Everything was snuffed out by a cruel disease.

A lump formed in his throat and he allowed himself a few moments to wallow in the thought of what might have been if Vivienne had survived the ravages of cholera. He imagined her warm and alive in his arms. He could smell her hair and the smooth softness of her lips as she kissed him. He remembered the silkiness of her fair hair. If she had still been alive, this morning her hair would have been tousled from a night of passion in their marital bed. Her smile would have been sleepy as she kissed him goodbye.

They would already have an infant in the cradle, maybe two. Who were those faceless children that death had denied him? He tried to imagine what they would have looked like. The smiling cherubs he created in his mind were both fair like Vivienne with compassionate, blue eyes. Had it only been two years?

He shook himself, glanced up and followed the line of the lofty tower of the Gothic church as it disappeared into the mist above. He heard his mother's voice in his head: *It's time to move forward, Stephen. Time to learn to live and love again.*

He chased thoughts of Vivienne and his ghostly infants out of his mind and made himself think of Magdalena. He remembered the warmth of her hand in his, the warmth of her breath on his cheek at the theatre. He thought of her gorgeous smile, her quick wit and the way that she arched her right eyebrow whenever she was sceptical. How she lifted her chin and tossed back her head when she laughed.

Lavender's argument with Read yesterday and Forsyth's blatant interference seemed to have brought the matter of his relationship with Magdalena to a head. Could he and this exotic foreign aristocrat ever share a life together as man and wife? What kind of a wife would Magdalena make? He smiled again as he thought about the differences between her and his first love, Vivienne, a gentle schoolmistress.

He couldn't imagine that Magdalena would ever rise with him at this ungodly hour to make his breakfast. There would have to be willing servants in Magdalena's household, lots of them. But that wasn't a problem; he could afford servants now. It was about time he did something with his money. That he needed to provide a comfortable home for himself and a future wife was the obvious course of action to take. He wondered what it would be like to wake up next to Magdalena in their bed. He thought of her warm, curvaceous body beneath her nightgown and for a moment he imagined what it would feel like. Then he shook his head to chase away the tantalising image.

Above him, the sky lightened. A weak ray of sunlight forced its way through the fog and illuminated the gravestone in front of him:

Vivienne Thompson, aged 24, died June 14th, 1808

'Forgive me, Vivienne,' he said quietly. But his voice, thick with emotion, still seemed to resonate across the silent and dismal churchyard. 'I have to go now, my love.' Yet, his hand still lingered on her headstone. He wanted to say more but it sounded so hollow, so pointless. 'I'll never forget you,' he whispered.

He turned up the collar of his coat, pulled his hat down further onto his head and resumed his journey.

Alfie, the young coachman, was as young and immature as Mrs Willoughby had indicated. *He's barely shaving*, Woods thought, when presented with the lad the next morning. Thoroughly dejected, the boy hung his head in shame while they questioned him about the kidnapping. A shock of greasy hair fell forward to cover his pimply face. Meanwhile, Fred Tummins glowered beside him and shuffled from one rickety leg to the other.

The lad's account of the kidnapping matched that given to them by Mrs Willoughby. 'She told me to say nowt,' the lad insisted in his own defence. 'She said I must keep me gob shut or else 'er sister might get 'urt.'

'Bloody saphead,' Tummins muttered angrily.

'How many of them were there?' Woods asked.

'I dunno, three, four maybe?'

'And all they said was: "Get the actress"?'

'Yes, no – oh, I dunno. It were dark, mister, and I felt grievously queer. I thought they would fell me there and then and give me an earth bath.'

'That ain't no "mister"!' shouted Tummins. He cuffed the lad on the back of the head. 'This gentleman's a Runner from Bow Street and you call 'im Constable, d'you 'ear?' Alfie yelped and rubbed the back of his head.

Woods decided that nothing more could be gained from interviewing the lad in the stable yard so they mounted their horses and set off for the Five Fields, with the dejected young man leading the way.

This is a godless place, Woods thought. Soaking wet and muddy underfoot, their trip was hard going for the horses. Pockets of silvery mist limited their vision. Occasionally Woods caught sight of a copse of stunted trees in the distance but there were few other distinguishing features to help the young coachman isolate the spot. No farmhouses. Not even a roadside gibbet. As far as the eye could see it was a dull, uneven canvas of marsh grass, spiked reeds and treacherous bogs, loved only by waterfowl and highwaymen. Today, even the moorhens and cranes were silent.

Finally, Alfie reined in his horse and stopped. He had been slumped miserably in his saddle since they left Wandsworth.

'I think it were about 'ere, guvnor,' he said. 'I can't tell fer sure, but I reckon it were about 'ere.'

Woods and Fred Tummins reined in beside him. Tummins glanced around at the desolate landscape then he scowled, leant across and angrily cuffed the pimply youth on the back of his head again. Alfie yelped and a shock of greasy hair fell forward over his eyes.

'What do yer mean, yer "think"? Is this where they 'eld up the coach, or not?' the older man demanded. 'In God's name, Alfie, why did you bring 'em wimmen this way? Why didn't yer tek 'em south of the river and cross at Southwark?'

The young man rubbed the back of his sore head. He looked like he was close to tears. 'It were quicker!' he whined. 'I wanted to get back fer another fare. Yer always tellin' us to 'urry up and get back to the stables.' He bowed his head again and sank into sullen silence.

Woods glanced down at the rutted mud track that served as a road. His sharp eyes scanned the immediate area for trampled reeds, hoofprints in the churned up mud, anything that would indicate that this was where a terrified woman had been dragged from a coach. Nothing.

Woods sighed. This was a fool's errand and he knew it. The lad didn't have a chance in hell of remembering exactly where the kidnappers had held up the carriage and kidnapped April Clare. For a start, it had been pitch-black on the night they were attacked. How this young and inexperienced coach driver had managed to stay on the road at night was a mystery. He had hoped that the trip out to the scene of the crime might jog the lad's memory, but it seemed not.

'I'm sorry, Constable,' said Fred Tummins. 'I think we've wasted yer time.'

'Never mind,' Woods replied cheerfully. 'The lad's done his best. I'll stay here a while and have a look round. Before you go back though, is there anythin' else, *anythin'* you can remember about those villains? Anythin' they said or did, which might help us in our investigation?'

Alfie glanced up. 'Well, they threatened me with my life if I followed 'em. I were in a cursed funk.'

'Yes, we know that,' snapped Tummins. 'You've already told us about your pathetic cowardice, you saphead. There's no need to mention it again.'

Alfie looked downcast then suddenly his face brightened.

'Oh, wait a minute.' The lad stared straight ahead at the watery scene and frowned. He was trying to pull some memory from the recesses of his mind. 'As they rode away I heard one of 'em ask: "Does she 'ave it on her?"'

'Does she have it on her?' Woods echoed. This was a new development.

'Yes, and one of the others shouted back something like: "'Ow should I bloody well know!"'

'Did they have foreign accents?'

The boy looked startled. 'No, no accents. One of them sounded a bit plummy if anythin'.'

'Plummy?'

'Yes, posh, like a nob.'

Woods frowned. 'Just one of them?'

'Yes, the others spoke normal, like me and you.'

'In which direction did they ride off?'

'East, towards London.'

'Thank you,' said Woods. 'You've been very helpful.'

Alfie's face brightened. 'Can I go back to Wandsworth now?'

'Yes.'

The lad needed no second bidding. He wheeled his horse around in a flurry of flying mud clarts and he cantered off back down the road. Fred Tummins hesitated a moment and glanced awkwardly in Wood's direction. The old man's face was lined with worry. 'I'm so sorry about this, Constable,' he said. ''E's young and foolish but 'e's not a bad lad.'

'Really?' Woods said, coldly. 'You can vouch for him, can you? You'll swear on the Bible in a magistrates' court that your coachman is not in league with these kidnappers and part of the gang?'

Tummins' rheumy eyes widened with horror. 'Is that what you reckon 'appened, Constable?'

'It has crossed my mind.'

The old man paused for a moment to digest this latest unwelcome piece of news.

'Well, yes, I would stand up for 'im in court,' he said, quietly. 'A saphead the boy may be, but 'e's no criminal. The lad's my son. I'll bid you good day, Constable.' With that he dug the heels of his boots into the flank of his horse and set off back to Wandsworth.

Chapter Fifteen

Guy's Hospital for Incurables was a more cheerful building on the outside than its name suggested, Lavender thought as he strode towards it with Woods at his side. Built in the classical style it consisted of three imposing wings around a cobbled courtyard. Elaborately carved ionic pillars supported the huge triangular stonework frieze above the entrance. Lights blazed behind the great arched windows on the ground floor. It was another city establishment that never seemed to sleep. Lavender hoped that Sir Richard would be available to see them, otherwise he would leave an apologetic message for missing the surgeon yesterday and call back mid-morning.

The inside of the hospital didn't live up to its grand exterior and the sickly sweet miasma of disease and camphor hit them in the nostrils the moment they entered the gloomy hallway. Woods' broad face creased in disgust and his nose wrinkled. Several new patients crowded around the desk. They groaned and wailed while they waited to be assessed by the medical staff. Some were bent double with pain. Others were half carried, half dragged to the hard wooden benches by family and friends. A young woman in the later stages of labour screamed. Meanwhile, a thin child vomited repeatedly into a bucket held by its mother. The hospital was the place of last resort for the desperately ill and dying of London. Few of the patients admitted with cholera, fever, consumption or advanced venereal disease came out alive from Guy's Hospital; the spread of infection and disease within the hospital itself was often to blame for its high mortality rate. Yet Guy's was a highly respected teaching hospital and had gained a worldwide reputation for innovative medical research and techniques. The surgery they undertook, although risky, often saved lives. Surgeons like Sir Richard donated their time freely to the hospital and were revered by their patients (which, Lavender suspected, probably accounted for the man's demigod behaviour and arrogance towards other mere mortals).

A clerk informed them that Sir Richard had been there all night, touring the cramped and poorly ventilated fever wards. He was now resting in his office in the Surgeon's House.

'A sleepless night in this here hospital won't have improved that sawbone's temper,' Woods commented dryly, as they made their way through the hospital. Lavender wondered if he had been wise to bring his constable. Woods' dislike of Sir Richard was obvious and he suspected that the surgeon would make a fuss over the fact that they weren't there to jump to attention when he had finished the autopsy the previous day. There was much to do. They still needed to follow up on inquiries the other constables had made at April Clare's lodgings and someone needed to interview the actors at the Sans Pareil.

However, Lavender was soon glad of Woods' company. Sir Richard made them wait for half an hour outside his office before he would give him an audience.

'He's makin' us pay for yesterday,' Woods said. 'We weren't there to dance attendance on him durin' and after the autopsy.'

'Then let us endure our penance patiently,' Lavender replied. 'Tell me again what that young coachman overheard the kidnappers say.' They sat on an uncomfortable bench in a cold corridor. An orderly in a bloodstained uniform ambled passed them, mopping the stark wooden floorboards with a pail of dirty water.

'They said: "Does she have it on her?"'

'What did he take this to mean?'

'I don't think he took it to mean anythin'. The lad was petrified and didn't even remember the incident until we got out into the Five Fields.'

'Can Alfie Tummins be trusted, do you think?'

Woods shrugged his broad shoulders. 'It's a queer thing to say if it ain't true.'

Lavender was thoughtful. 'It suggests that Miss Clare had something the kidnappers wanted.'

'Yes, it does. Perhaps this crime weren't about money, after all.'

'That would be fortunate because I suspect that Mrs Willoughby and Lady Caroline have little money between them.'

Woods nodded. 'Then there's the attempted burglary in her lodgings. Perhaps that weren't about theft either?'

'Yes,' Lavender agreed. 'Well remembered, Ned. The room had been ransacked: drawers pulled out, papers thrown everywhere and the wardrobe emptied. It is possible that whoever broke in was looking for something.'

'It must be something important if they're prepared to go to such lengths to recover it.'

'Absolutely,' Lavender said. But before they could speculate any further a clerk arrived to let them know that Sir Richard would see them now.

The ancient floorboards creaked ominously as they entered the office and approached the surgeon. Bookcases dominated every wall of the room. On some shelves were heavy medical tomes with Latin titles or rolled scrolls with diagrams of human anatomy. Evil-looking knives, scalpels, drills and hooks glinted on others. In one corner, a complete human skeleton hung on wires from the ceiling. The wires were too long to stretch out the bones in a normal posture and it slumped forward, arms dangling down like those of a chimpanzee Lavender had once seen in a travelling fair. A sickening row of human hearts and fresh entrails rested in pools of blood on trays on a side table. There was the slight hint of rotting flesh in the air.

Sir Richard glanced up from the document he was writing and put down his quill. His eyes were red with lack of sleep. 'Ah, Lavender – and Constable Woods – I thought you would be along today. Glad you could make it so early. We need to talk. We have a bigger mystery to solve than I anticipated. Take a seat.'

Lavender had expected a far colder reception and was surprised by the surgeon's uncharacteristic geniality. Intrigued, he sat down and waited for Sir Richard to elaborate. Woods took a seat at the far corner of the room. The surgeon's use of the word 'we' was encouraging. Was this the first time Sir Richard had had to perform an autopsy on a woman he had known in life? Lavender wondered. Did the fact that he had seen April Clare act and heard her sing make him feel more connected with this victim?

'Been in a fight, Lavender?' Sir Richard pointed towards his eye.

Instinctively, his hand went to his face. The swelling had gone down but he had seen in his shaving mirror that the skin around the eye was still bruised. 'It's nothing. A silk-snatcher resisted arrest, that's all.'

'My, you fellahs are busy. Anyway, the actress, Miss April Divine, wasn't murdered,' Sir Richard began. 'She died from natural causes – albeit in unnatural surroundings.'

Lavender nodded. 'We have discovered that her real name was April Clare. She was the daughter of the late Baron Clare of Rochdale. What caused her death?'

'This,' said Sir Richard. He reached over for a silver tray that held a bloodied heart and plonked it on the desk in front of

Lavender. The cloudy blood and plasma swirled from side to side within the tray, some of it slopping over the side and forming a pool on the desk. For a moment Lavender was startled. He had often seen diagrams of the human heart, but he had never seen one so close up. The three exposed tubes of the aorta jutted out of the heart then flopped down like the scarlet coxcomb of a cockerel. In fact, this lump of bloodied meat could have been a recently skinned and mutilated fowl bird.

'Is that Miss Clare's heart?' Lavender asked in surprise.

'Of course,' said the surgeon. 'I extracted it during the autopsy yesterday and I plan to use it in a lecture on anatomy I will give this afternoon.' Lavender was momentarily speechless. 'But don't worry, Detective,' Sir Richard continued cheerfully. 'She won't miss it now – and neither will any of her grieving relatives. I sewed her back up afterwards.'

'Quite.' Lavender cleared his throat. The man's casual – almost flippant – attitude to the dead never ceased to amaze him. He also found it disturbing that Sir Richard systematically removed organs from the deceased for his lectures. He was unsure about the legality of this situation.

'So what is, or was, the problem with her heart?'

'This.' Sir Richard reached for another grisly specimen and placed it next to April Clare's organ for comparison.

Lavender stared. 'I'm sorry, Sir Richard, I don't see—'

'Look at the size of her heart, man. Can you see it now?' The surgeon podded at the flaps of tissue on either side of the specimen with a silver scalpel. Each jab made more blood seep from the tissue. 'The walls of both the left and right side of the heart had become thin and stretched,' he explained, 'resulting in a considerable increase in the size of the organ. It is dilated cardiomyopathy, better known as an enlarged heart. This young lady was gravely ill and her heart could have given way at any time.'

'I can see the difference now,' Lavender said. 'We now know that Miss Clare was brutally kidnapped. Could the trauma of her abduction and captivity in the squalor of Raleigh Close have contributed to her death?'

'Almost certainly. That level of strain on her heart would have been unsustainable during such a terrifying event.'

'What about if she had borne a child?' Woods asked suddenly.

Sir Lawrence frowned at him. 'I've already told you, Constable – this dead woman has never borne a child. But in a hypothetical situation, yes, a pregnancy and the ensuing birth would have probably killed her; her heart would never have stood the strain.' He turned back to Lavender. 'Did the kidnappers ever ask for a ransom?'

'No.'

'If she died soon after they took her to Raleigh Close then that would have thrown the kidnappers' plans into a right mess,' Woods said, 'and it explains why they never made a ransom demand. They simply stuffed her corpse beneath the floorboards and hurriedly left the scene.'

'Yes,' said Sir Richard. 'Kidnappers they may be, but murderers they're most certainly not.'

Lavender frowned, sat back and exhaled heavily. His mind was whirling with the implications of this latest revelation and the faint ferrous-tinged smell from the dead girl's organ made him feel nauseous.

'This explains why there were no obvious marks on the corpse or signs of violence,' Woods continued.

Sir Richard pushed the morning news-sheet across the desk. 'Are you responsible for this, Detective?'

Lavender glanced down. There, in thick, black typeface, was the headline: *Actress Brutally Slain*.

'No,' he said sharply.

'Well, some ignoramus has been blabbing to a reporter,' Sir Richard said, coldly. 'This inaccuracy needs correcting as soon as possible.'

Lavender scanned the article and frowned at its lurid and dramatic tone. He had no doubt who was the source of the information: the melodramatic writing style of Jane Scott was all over the piece and the Sans Pareil Theatre was mentioned three times. Miss Scott clearly knew the value of publicity and was happy to exploit the death of one of her cast for financial gain.

'I'll see that the paper prints a correction and gives the proper facts in tomorrow's edition,' Lavender promised. 'Thank you for your professional expertise, Sir Richard. At least now we have solved the riddle of the poor woman's death.'

'Ah, but as one mystery is solved,' said the surgeon, 'another rears its head.'

'What do you mean?' Woods asked.

Lavender heard the irritation in his constable's voice. He wondered what new revelation the surgeon was about to leave them with today. Sir Richard had obviously spent too much time at the Covent Garden theatres; each autopsy had now become a major drama.

'Are you gentlemen familiar with the symptoms of dilated cardiomyopathy?'

'No,' said Woods. 'But I hope that you're goin' to tell us that the patient's feet shrink and their shoes don't fit any more.'

Sir Richard raised his eyebrows and frowned. 'I'm not in the mood for humour, Constable,' he snapped. 'Dilated cardiomyopathy is a progressive disease and sufferers experience shortness of breath, fatigue and palpitations, amongst other things.'

'Oh?'

'Yes, it is a very debilitating and leaves the patient unable to carry out mundane tasks such as walking or climbing stairs. Most can't live an ordinary life and for a case as advanced as this, the misery and exhaustion must have been severe.'

Lavender stared hard at him. He knew what this new revelation meant but he let Sir Richard put it into words.

'Quite simply, Lavender, it would have been impossible for April Divine, or April Clare as you now call her, to have held down such an active, lively career as an actress at the Sans Pareil. There is your mystery – our mystery. The woman who performed at the theatre last month for Lady Allison and I didn't suffer from advanced dilated cardiomyopathy.'

'That fellah is only one step away from the bodysnatchers who haunt the Cross Bones Graveyard,' Woods announced angrily as they strode across Westminster Bridge towards Covent Garden. 'Lord save us from his kind! I tell you, that fiend would rip out your innards before you can draw your last breath.'

Lavender smiled and let Woods continue his rant. He stopped, leant over the stone balustrade and peered down at the black water below. He could just make out the bulbous oak hulls of tall ships that loomed out of the mist. It was quieter out here on the bridge away from the frantic activity on the riverbank. The heaving water slapped against the stone arches of the bridge below him. He heard the faint, monotonous creak of metal oarlocks from the river taxis. These and the occasional rumble of wagon wheels and the cry of an invisible seabird wheeling high above them in the fog were the only sounds that ruptured the eerie silence.

'I just hope that when I peg it Betsy gets the lid nailed down on my wooden surcoat before any of Sir Richard's kind come snoopin' around my corpse.'

'If she's any sense, she will sell you off piece by piece to Sir Richard.' Lavender grinned. 'There's enough of you to make a tidy sum.'

'Don't you go puttin' that notion in her head!' Woods exclaimed, in genuine alarm. 'Especially when you come to our house for supper, tonight. We've had another incident with the lads and apparently it's my fault. I'm in enough trouble as it is.'

Lavender turned his head. 'Oh?' The untamed liveliness of the Woodses' boys was a constant source of vexation for their diminutive mother, and their antics amused Lavender. But Woods would not be drawn about his sons' latest indiscretion.

'You hadn't forgot that you and Doña Magdalena are due at our house for supper tonight, had you?' Woods asked. 'Betsy will be cross if you forget.'

Lavender smiled. He had forgotten but the prospect of an evening with Magdalena was a cheering thought. 'I wouldn't dream of letting Betsy down,' he said. 'Her home-cooked fare is the highlight of my existence.'

Woods grinned. 'She said to tell you that the cobbler, Kinghorn and Naylor, is on the Strand.'

'Please thank her for me, Ned. I will pay them a visit about those shoes and see if we can establish who they were made for.'

'Do you think that those twins changed places again?'

'I don't know what to think,' Lavender confessed. 'The dead woman was clearly very ill – and Miss Clare took an unexpected break in her career last summer. When she finished work at Drury Lane Theatre last February she appears to have disappeared until the end of August when she asked Dorothy Jordan for an introduction to Jane Scott at the Sans Pareil. Was it ill health that forced her off the stage? Was the story of a sick aunt merely a lie to account for her absence and avoid speculation rising about her health? Yet Sir Richard seemed adamant that the woman whose body we recovered couldn't have performed at the theatre last month.'

'The gal lied to Mrs Jordan about where she had been,' Woods said. 'Lady Caroline was quite clear yesterday that them gals didn't have any other family except her.'

'And Sir Richard was also adamant that the dead girl had never borne a child – so the child in the Willoughby nursery must belong to the living sister.'

'It seems to me that Sir Richard is adamant about quite a few things,' Woods said coldly. 'What if he's wrong?'

Lavender paused for a moment and considered this option. A lively breeze began to clear the mist. It also stirred up the miasma from the murky waters beneath them. The stench of rotting vegetation reached his nostrils. He was well aware that Woods' bias against the surgeon had prompted his last remark, but could it still have value? Did Woods' prejudice make him more objective about the abilities of Sir Richard? Had Lavender placed too much store on the word of the surgeon?

Lavender shook his head. 'If he's wrong,' he said, 'then it will be the first time I have known it to happen. Sir Richard can be difficult and repulsive, I know, but I have never known him to be wrong.'

As the fog continued to clear and the weak sunlight pushed its way down to earth, the city took shape before them. The great dome of St Paul's Cathedral dominated the skyline. Buildings were sprawled out endlessly along the curving riverbank. For once not obscured by clouds of smoke, the buildings glittered in the weak light. As far as the eye could see, there was a multitude of little boats criss-crossing the Thames like water-skaters and tall ships lying at anchor.

'I will go back to see Mrs Willoughby again today,' Lavender said. 'And Lady Caroline. We need more information about April Clare. I will call back at the Sans Pareil this evening to speak to the other actors. Hopefully, someone today will be able to cast light on some part of this mystery.'

'Do you want me to come with you?' asked Woods.

'No. But can you follow up on the inquiries the other constables made at April's lodgings? Magistrate Read promised me yesterday that he would send some men round to question the other
tenants about the intrusion into April's room. The more I think
about it the more I'm come to the conclusion that the break-in is
linked to the kidnapping. Those men were after something, and it
doesn't seem to be money.'

Woods nodded. 'It sounds to me like she were mixed up in
somethin' dangerous.'

Lavender agreed. 'God knows where this investigation will lead
us.' He turned up his collar against the cold and shivered. Below him
a boatman hauled in oars dripping with slimy weed, and reached
out for the swaying wooden ladder which led up to the jetty.

'"Earth hath not anything to show more fair,"' Lavender said.
'"Dull would he be of soul who could pass by a sight so touching
in its majesty . . ."'

'You what?' Woods' eyes widened.

'It's part of a poem by William Wordsworth,' Lavender
explained. 'It was written a few years ago about this view from
Westminster Bridge. The same view that we can see now.'

Woods glanced about uneasily as if he half expected the poet to
pop up behind them. 'Wordsworth, eh?' he said. 'Wasn't he one of
those romantic poets who see pretty things in a pile of muck and a
clump of daffydils?'

Lavender smiled. 'Yes, he loves London and feels that this man-
made terrain before us can be compared to nature's grandest natural
spectacles. He describes the river as the mighty heart of the city.'

Woods greying eyebrows rose cynically and the corner of his
mouth twitched. 'North Country lad, ain't he?'

'Yes.'

'Well, speakin' as one of those born within the stench and racket of the East India Docks, I could tell him a thing or two about our Mother Thames.'

Lavender grinned. 'What would you tell him?'

'That there is nothin' "fair" about Mother Thames. She's a foul open sewer and a deep and treacherous bitch. If he took a leap into her arms, she would drag him under within seconds and then poison him for the hell of it.'

Lavender smiled again. 'Well, it's not Shakespeare, but I do believe we'll make a poet of you yet, Ned. Your grasp of personification is excellent.'

Alarm flashed across Woods' features. 'My what?'

'Never mind. Come on, back to work.'

Chapter Sixteen

Magdalena was surprised but delighted when Stephen called round that morning. He apologised for his unexpected arrival and handed her the purse, which he said the Duke of Clarence had given to him at Bushy House the previous day. She poured the coins out into her palm and was pleased to see that there were two guineas in the purse as well as a few copper coins. The presence of the copper coins was curious but she dismissed them from her mind as soon as she saw them.

'This is wonderful!' she exclaimed. 'How generous the duke has been! I will be able to buy two pairs of new boots with this money – and a pair for Teresa. Would you like a new pair of boots, Teresa?'

The little maid said nothing but flushed pink with excitement.

Stephen smiled at their delight, but Magdalena saw in his eyes that he was troubled by something. He looked as smart as ever in his pristine cravat, brushed black coat and gleaming leather boots, but he was obviously upset about something. She wondered if there were problems with the case of the dead actress. Stephen had told her about the connection between the two women and it had saddened her nearly as much as it had saddened him. She had already written a letter of condolence to Lady Caroline.

'Fetch our cloaks, Teresa,' she said in Spanish. 'We shall visit the cobblers immediately.' Teresa raced off towards their closet, behind the ragged curtain that discreetly hid the bed at the other end of the room.

'Would you mind if I accompanied you?' Stephen asked. 'I'm on my way to Wandsworth but need to visit a shoemakers called Kinghorn and Naylor on the Strand, with reference to my case. That may a good place for you and Teresa to purchase some boots.'

She tilted her head on one side, lowered her lashes and smiled at him through half-closed eyes. 'Why Teresa!' she said. 'I do believe that the detective wants to see our ankles.'

Stephen's lips curled into a smile. 'Alas, you have discovered my devious motive, Doña Magdalena,' he said.

'Well, maybe just this once you may view our ankles, Detective Lavender,' she replied with mock grandeur. 'It is your reward for bringing me the duke's money. But you must not make a habit of it. No doubt, you will ask to see our elbows next.'

'You're so kind to a poor flesh-starved man,' he said and winked roguishly at Teresa who had just reappeared from behind the curtain with their cloaks over her arm. The maid let out a strangled squeak and suddenly seemed unstable on her legs.

Magdalena laughed. 'You must behave with Teresa, Stephen,' she said. 'Or she will have an attack of the vapours and I will have to revive her with the sal volatile. She's most fond of you.'

'Well, I'm glad there are some women who still are pleased at the sight of me.' He sighed. 'I've feel like I've been the harbinger of bad news for half the female population of London over the last few days.'

Magdalena patted his arm reassuringly. 'But you will be the bringer of good news when you solve the mystery of the poor girl's death – which you will do, eventually.' She turned away as Teresa held up her cloak.

He smiled and pulled a dusty woman's shoe out of his coat pocket. 'This is the reason I want to visit Messers Kinghorn and Naylor.'

'*Dios mío!*' Magdalena froze. 'Is that the dead girl's shoe?'

Confusion flashed across Stephen's face. He hastily replaced the shoe in his pocket. 'My apologies, I shouldn't have brought it to your attention.'

Magdalena relaxed, laughed and placed a reassuring hand on his arm. 'Do not worry, Stephen. Teresa and I are not as – how do you English say it? – squeamish about death in the way of most our sex. Unfortunately, we have seen too much of it in our short lives. We're grateful for your kindness and will happily allow you to take us to the shoemakers. However, we also have to visit the shop of Mistress Evans on Long Acre. Mrs Jordan was most particular in that recommendation.'

Their cab driver frowned when they asked him to take them to Mistress Evans' shoe establishment on Long Acre.

'Do you not know of it?' Lavender asked.

'Yes, I know the old scold well enough,' the man replied. 'But yer may change yer mind and want to stay in the cab with the ladies.'

'What did he mean?' Magdalena asked as the three of them squashed themselves in the rocking vehicle.

'I don't know,' Lavender replied.

The cab driver pointed out Mistress Evans to them from a distance. Her 'establishment' wasn't a shop but a wooden stall on the pavement on one of the seedier stretches of Long Acre. It displayed a dismal selection of worn-down, second-hand shoes and boots and factory clogs. The clientele who gathered around her were some of the poorest women of London, including several of the Covent Garden Nuns. Mistress Evans herself was unclean, slatternly and obese. She sat on an upturned barrel next to her stall with a tankard of ale in her hand. From her disjointed movements and glazed eyes, it was obviously not the first drink she had imbibed that morning.

'Ah, as the duke reminded me yesterday,' Stephen said, sharply. 'Mrs Jordan has a great reputation as a comedienne.'

If this was Dorothy Jordan's idea of a joke, Magdalena decided it wasn't very funny.

'Drive on,' Stephen instructed the cabbie. 'Take us to Kinghorn and Naylor on the Strand.' Magdalena could see that Stephen felt the insult as keenly as she did.

'Why did she do that?' she asked quietly. 'Why did Mrs Jordan recommend that dreadful woman to me?'

He took her hand in his and squeezed it. She liked his touch. 'An attempt at humour, perhaps?' he suggested.

'Don't lie to me, Stephen.'

He sighed. 'She was probably jealous of the attention the duke paid you and thought she'd have a little revenge. I saw the look of anger and envy she gave you at the theatre.'

'I did nothing! I don't want her silly old duke.'

'No, you didn't do anything,' Lavender said wisely. 'But Dorothy Jordan becomes less and less secure about her position as the duke's mistress. Every beautiful and attractive young woman is a threat to her.'

'What do you mean?'

'There are rumours that the duke will be forced into marriage to try and secure the succession to the throne.'

'But I don't understand,' she said. 'The Duke of Clarence has two older brothers and a niece who are before him in line to the British throne.'

'Yes, but both of those two elder brothers are estranged from their wives and every hope for the House of Hanover rests on the shoulders of a fourteen-year-old girl. The old king and queen had fifteen children but they only have one grandchild: Princess

Charlotte. There is talk that the Duke of Clarence and his brother, the Duke of Kent, may be soon obliged to marry to provide more heirs.'

Despite her disappointment, Magdalena felt herself smile. She knew he was trying his best to distract her from Dorothy Jordan's little trick.

He turned around and stared straight into her eyes. 'Besides which, Magdalena, you're young, beautiful and vibrant – everything that the faded actress no longer is.'

'I'm beautiful, am I, Stephen?' she asked, quietly.

'Very beautiful,' he confirmed. 'Very beautiful.' Then he winked, leant forward and kissed her lightly on her lips.

Beside them, Teresa squeaked with surprise.

Their visit to Kinghorn and Naylor was far more successful. The shoemakers' names were carved in elaborate script across the lintel of the low door of their tall, timber-framed establishment. Either side of the door were large bow windows: one displayed men's footwear, the other women's. Magdalena paused before the wonderful arrangement of brightly coloured women's court shoes and slippers and let herself be distracted for a moment by their loveliness. The satin slippers, delicately dyed in pale lavenders and pinks, had no heels and sat next to others made from leather of robin's-egg blue. Some had ribbon laces and ties, some didn't. She was especially attracted to a pair in yellow leather that had been cut away to reveal an insert of white satin, embroidered in blue, pink and green. Stephen smiled and waited patiently.

Magdalena tore her eyes away from the delicate shoes to the lines of boots which were displayed in a row behind the colourful slippers. She was pleased to see that they were also attractive and of good quality.

'Is this shop more to my lady's liking?' Lavender asked.

She gave him a dazzling smile. 'Most definitely, kind sir. Although I suspect that once we enter the premises we will have trouble persuading Teresa to leave.'

'Only Teresa?' he asked. His eyes twinkled with humour.

She smiled and pointed to a corner of the window. 'Look at those, Stephen!' At the edge of the display was a pair of high-heeled, embroidered brocade evening shoes with silver buckles. Apart from the filth, they were identical to the one he had shown her earlier. 'I think that we will all find what we need for at Messers Kinghorn and Naylor.'

He frowned. 'Mmm, I had hoped that the shoes were individually made for patrons of this shop. It would appear that they're not this unique.'

'Well, let's find out,' she said as she pushed open the door. A tiny bell tinkled above their heads as they entered.

A matronly assistant with a severe hairstyle, a sombre brown gown and a shoehorn dangling from a chain at her waist, moved to assist them. 'Good morning, madam – and sir,' she said. 'Is it shoes for the lady you require?'

'Boots,' Magdalena informed her.

'This way, please madam.' The woman led her away behind a pretty but discreet curtain, which divided up half the shop. The curtain was there to ensure that no prying eyes could watch the female patrons as they hitched up their dresses and revealed their stockings while trying on footwear. She smiled to herself at the thought of Stephen's disappointment on the other side of the barrier; his 'reward' had been denied him. However, she soon heard him in conversation with one of the male proprietors of the shop. The two men disappeared into the cobbling workshop at the rear of the premises.

Seated comfortably on a padded gilt chair, with Teresa beside her, Magdalena decided on a pair of brown kid leather ankle boots for herself. They were decorated with a rose-coloured rosette just below the laces. She chose a plain, black pair for her delighted maid. The total cost for both pairs of boots came to ten shillings and sixpence. She handed over one of the guinea pieces given to her by the duke and pondered about whether or not to treat herself to a pretty pair of striped silk dancing slippers with a black leather-covered heel and black silk trim. She eventually decided against the purchase, as her financial situation was so precarious she dared not risk frittering her money away on a pair of slippers she might never wear.

Stephen reappeared at her side. She knew by the frown on his face that he had not gained the information he sought.

'This shoe is one of the most successful items of footwear made by Mr Kinghorn,' Lavender explained, as they walked out into the cold street. 'And its popularity goes back over several seasons. He does make them for individual clients but he also made several pairs for display in the shop and in the window. I checked through his records but didn't recognise any of the names of the women for whom he had a commission to make these shoes. And he has no idea of the names of any of the ladies who may have bought one of the pairs on display.'

'That's a shame,' Magdalena said.

'Nor has he ever heard of the actress, April Divine. He's not aware if she's one of his regular customers. Nor does he have any idea why her shoes no longer fitted her.' His face was dark with disappointment when he led them back out into the busy street. Three hansoms went past them, nose to tail, while a cart and four horses clattered by in the opposite direction. He flagged down the last cab, which was for hire, and helped Magdalena and Teresa up into the vehicle.

'Perhaps she purchased the shoes from one of the second-hand stalls in the market,' Magdalena suggested. 'That may account for why they didn't fit her properly. I had also wondered if they might have been defective and simply stretched out of shape.'

'Those are good suggestions,' Lavender replied as he sank down into the seat beside Magdalena. 'Though according to Mr Kinghorn, he has never had a complaint or a pair returned to him.' He sighed. 'I have a niggling feeling that these ill-fitting shoes are important to this case. But I might be wrong. I'll take you home and then continue on to Wandsworth to see Mrs Willoughby again.'

'Never mind,' Magdalena said. 'At least Teresa and I have had a successful outing.'

Lavender smiled. 'You are happy with your purchases?'

'Oh yes, my new boots are beautiful. However, I was a little disappointed that I had to take a pair in a bigger size. My feet grew when I carried Sebastián and they never returned to their normal size after his birth . . .' She paused as a strange look flashed across his handsome face. His head snapped up and his eyes widened. 'Stephen? What is the matter?'

'Of course!' he yelled. He leapt to his feet and rapped loudly on the roof of the cab with his gloved fist. He looked like he would explode. 'Magdalena, you're a genius!'

'Stephen? What is it?'

The cab jerked to a halt and he reached for the door handle. Before he stood up, he fished in his pocket for some change and dropped it in her lap. 'I'm sorry,' he said. 'But I must ride out to Wandsworth immediately. Take this cab home – I'll get another back to Bow Street and collect my horse.' His eyes gleamed with excitement. Then he was gone.

Instinctively, Magdalena leapt to her feet and followed him. 'Stephen! Wait!' Holding onto the door for support, she stepped down into the cold street after him. The crowds on the pavement hurried past, veering to avoid them. 'Stephen, what is it?'

He smiled and stepped back towards her. 'You have just solved a mystery that has been bothering me for days.' Then without warning he leant down, pulled her forward and kissed her full on the mouth. The speed and passion of the kiss took her breath away and her body exploded in a flush of pent-up desire. Groaning slightly, she tilted her head back, willing him to ravish her face and her throat. Disappointment swamped her when he pulled away as quickly as he had accosted her.

'Thank you, Magdalena,' he said, his voice husky and his breathing erratic. One moment she was drowning in the pools of his dark, excited eyes, the next a draught of cold air swirled around her as his warm body moved away and he was gone.

Magdalena climbed back into the carriage in a trance. She neither knew nor cared if Teresa had just witnessed their kiss. Slumping back against the hard wooden seat of the cab, she raised her gloved hands to her still-tingling lips and smiled.

Chapter Seventeen

Lady Caroline was taking tea with Mrs Willoughby in her parlour when Lavender arrived. Both women were now dressed in black mourning gowns trimmed with velvet ribbons. Mrs Willoughby wore a see-through chiffon overgown atop her white silk dress. Lady Caroline had a fetching black lace cap, decorated with seed pearls, on top of her thick auburn hair. They made an elegant and sombre picture but Lavender wasn't in the mood to appreciate it. Part of him was fuming at the deceptions they had practiced upon him. The women were leant forward, deep in discussion, when he entered the room. They sat back, unsmiling, and eyed him warily.

He waited until the maid had left and then bowed. 'Good morning, Lady Caroline,' he said, pleasantly. 'And to you too, Mrs Willoughby.'

Then his voice hardened and sliced through the warm room like a knife: 'Or should I say, good morning, Miss Clare?'

There was a stunned silence. The younger woman froze in her chair and said nothing. She stared silently up at Lavender, her dark eyes large and luminous. Was that fear that shone in their depths? He hoped so.

Lady Caroline slowly put down her teacup on the side table. Her hand shook and the cup rattled in the saucer. She cleared her throat. 'Detective Lavender, how delightful to see you again. But what on earth do you mean?'

'Please don't try to continue the pretence, Lady Caroline,' he snapped. 'As you well know, the woman sitting opposite you is not Mrs Harriet Willoughby. Mrs Willoughby is dead. This is Miss April Clare, actress extraordinaire from the Sans Pareil Theatre.' He took a few steps across the thick carpet and glared down into the pale face of the younger woman. 'And what an excellent part you have played over the last few days, Miss Clare. Do you deny it?'

The young woman took a deep breath. 'No,' she said, quietly. 'I'm April Clare.'

'Why in God's name did you pretend to be your twin sister?' he shouted. 'What are you hiding?'

'Detective Lavender, take a seat, please,' Lady Caroline pleaded. 'Let us get you a cup of tea.'

He wasn't in the mood to be distracted or placated. 'Don't you want us to track down those responsible for your sister's death?' he demanded. April Clare nodded. 'Well, how on earth do you think we can help you if don't tell us the truth? We have spent the last few days investigating the death of the wrong woman! How long did you intend to carry on with this charade? And for God's sake, why do it in the first place?'

'Detective, *please!*' Lady Caroline sounded genuinely distressed. 'Sit down, take some tea with us and we will try to explain.'

He turned to reply and was struck with a fresh flush of anger. 'Did you know about this, Lady Caroline?' he demanded. 'Are you party to this deception, as well?'

'No,' she said firmly. 'I arrived yesterday afternoon to offer my condolences to Harriet and quickly realised that this was April, not Harriet. I have spent the last two days trying to persuade her to tell you the truth and ask for your help.' She reached out a bejewelled hand for the china teapot and poured out a fresh cup. 'The girls have swapped clothes, mimicked each other's hairstyles and pretended to be each other since they were little,' she continued, 'But I have always been able to tell them apart. Not that I let them know this, of course. They enjoyed their little game and I always went along with it.'

'Well, I'm not enjoying this,' Lavender snapped. He turned back to the actress. 'I have a good mind to arrest you, Miss Clare, for wasting my time.' The younger woman still said nothing but he thought he saw a glimmer of distress flash across her face. 'You lied to us,' he continued. 'My constable and I have been seriously misled about the identity of a dead woman and have probably wasted valuable time trying to solve the case as a result. On top of that, a reporter from the newspaper has now told most of London that the actress, April Clare, is dead.'

'Ah, yes,' said Lady Caroline. Fine frown lines appeared across her forehead and she paused, her hand resting lightly on the handle of the milk jug. 'I read the article this morning at breakfast. This is most, most unfortunate . . .'

'So, just how long did you intend to carry on with this charade?' Lavender asked the actress. 'You have obviously fooled the servants. They believe you are Mrs Willoughby. Was it your intention to steal the rest of her life? What about when Captain Willoughby finally returns from his latest sea voyage? Were you hoping that after such a lengthy absence he wouldn't notice you had taken your sister's place in his house and his bed?'

'Detective Lavender!' Lady Caroline let the silver teaspoon fall with a clatter onto the tray. 'Please take a seat and let April explain.'

He paused. Perhaps he had gone too far remonstrating with the blasted woman but he wasn't accustomed to people behaving in such a devious fashion while he tried to help them. He ignored

Lady Caroline's gesture to sit next to her and chose a low-slung armchair opposite the fireplace, which kept him apart from the women but gave him an excellent view of their faces. He flicked a piece of dust from his breeches and waited.

Finally, the actress spoke. 'I had no plan,' she said, simply. 'I didn't think ahead. I just knew it was safer if I pretended to be Harriet – for both her and me. I have never been so scared in my life, Detective; you have to believe me about that. I was terrified.' She turned her large eyes up towards his face and he saw tears glistening on her long lashes. Despite his anger, he felt a stab of sympathy; there was no doubt in his mind that the two sisters had been through a harrowing ordeal. In that, at least, she was sincere.

'It was— It was exactly as I told you and the constable yesterday morning,' April Clare began. 'Except, as you have already determined, my sister and I swapped clothes and were pretending to be each other in order to play a trick on Lady Caroline.' Her hand went to the high ruffled neck of her sister's gown and she pulled it away from her skin as if it irritated her. 'I was wearing Harriet's clothes, a sombre dress and a short veil, and Harriet had on my more – how shall I say it? – my more distinctive clothing beneath her cloak.' She paused.

'And you also swapped your shoes?' he prompted.

'Yes. The silver embroidery on my shoes complemented that on the dress I gave her. She didn't want to wear them because she said they didn't fit her properly, but I insisted.' Her eyes clouded over with pain at the memory of the disagreement.

'You always were more forceful than your sister.' Lady Caroline sighed. 'You could persuade her to do anything.'

'What happened next?' Lavender asked.

'It was as I told you yesterday, Detective. On the way to Lady Caroline's soirée the coach was attacked and a group of men threw open the door. "Get the actress!" they shouted. They pulled out my sister, threatened me and the coach driver and . . . and . . .' She looked like she might dissolve into tears again at the memory.

'And what did you do?' he prompted.

'I came back here. When I entered the house, I was distraught but I claimed to have a migraine. Ruby, the maid, immediately assumed I was Harriet and chivvied me up to her bedroom. I was too upset to protest and the next morning when she continued to address me as "Mrs Willoughby", I just let her. I didn't know what to do for the best. Those kidnappers wanted April Clare, the actress, and I didn't want it known that they'd kidnapped the wrong woman. I thought that might endanger Harriet's life. I just sat here and waited for them to get in touch with their demands so that I could get her back.'

'There you are, Lavender,' said Lady Caroline, as she passed him a cup of tea. 'A perfectly reasonable explanation. Sugar, Detective?'

He glanced at her, looking for that twitch of the lips or a glint in her eye that would suggest that she was being ironic. There was none. Either these women were blithely unaware about what was normal and 'reasonable' behaviour in most families, or Lady Caroline was a better actress than her stepdaughter. And he hadn't even touched on that other deception they had carried out yet – the one that was sleeping innocently upstairs in the nursery.

He picked up his cup, held up his hand to refuse Lady Caroline's offer of sugar, sat back in his chair and regarded them both dispassionately. 'So tell me, Miss Clare, what exactly do you propose to do now?' he said.

The women exchanged startled glances.

'I don't know,' April confessed.

'What do you suggest, Detective?' Lady Caroline asked. Neither of them had expected him to throw the problem back at them.

'You never thought through the consequences of your actions, did you?' he said, slowly.

'No, I didn't. I'm so sorry for all the problems I have caused.' April Clare whispered and he was pleased to see that at least she had the grace to look embarrassed by her foolishness. 'But you must believe me, Detective, when I said that I was motivated by fear for my life – and fear for poor Harriet.' If this was another perform-ance, then it was a good one. He almost believed her.

'Did the kidnappers find out the truth that they had taken the wrong woman, do you think?' she asked. Her body trembled and her voice rose to a crescendo. 'Did she die because they realised she wasn't me? Did they kill her because of that?' She stared up at him, imploring him to answer in the negative.

'Mrs Willoughby didn't suffer for long,' he said. 'I have had the results of the autopsy from Sir Richard Allison this morning. Your sister's weak heart gave way sometime on Friday night. She wasn't murdered. The shock of the abduction killed her within a few hours. Continuing your deception only served to protect your own life; it didn't help your sister.'

April Clare's pretty face crumpled and she sobbed quietly. Lady Caroline leant forward, gave her a handkerchief and patted her knee affectionately. 'We must take some comfort from that, April,' she said. 'At least Harriet's terrible ordeal was short-lived.' The strength in her voice seemed to help her stepdaughter, who sniffled and dried her eyes.

Lady Caroline now turned to face Lavender. 'I have to confess that I'm at a loss about what to do now, Detective,' she said. 'Poor Harriet needs a funeral but the world thinks that she's April. And if we announce that there has been a terrible mistake, and that it was Harriet who has died, then I'm concerned that this might place April's life in great danger once again. Those scoundrels were clearly after her from what she has told me. It was April Clare the actress they intended to kidnap. Would they seek her out again, do you think?'

'Yes, I think they would,' he said, 'because Miss Clare has something they desire.' He sipped at his tea while they absorbed this latest revelation, grimacing slightly at the taste. Coffee was his preferred beverage.

Both women stared at him in surprise.

'I don't understand, Detective,' Lady Caroline said.

He drained his cup and put it down. 'This morning my constable tracked down your coach driver from the other night. His account of the events of that evening match your own. However, there is one thing he has told us which you have not.'

'Which is?' April Clare's voice was emotionless.

'That as they rode away, one of the kidnappers asked if "she had it on her".'

'What does that mean, Lavender?' Lady Caroline asked.

'I don't know,' he replied. 'I hope that Miss Clare can tell us. What do you have in your possession, madam, which would prompt a group of scoundrels like that to kidnap you?'

The clock on the mantelpiece ticked loudly as he and Lady Caroline waited for the actress to answer.

'I have absolutely no idea,' the young woman said. 'I never heard this conversation. I was cowering inside the carriage.'

'No?' Lavender was disappointed. 'You definitely have something those kidnappers want, Miss Clare. I'm sorry to tell you this but someone has also broken into your lodgings and ransacked the place.' She took a short sharp breath. 'I'm not sure when this happened, or if it is a coincidence but someone appears to have been searching for something in your rooms.'

'Good grief.' Lady Caroline again leant towards her stepdaughter. Her voice became resolute and businesslike. 'April, come on now. You must think and think hard.'

But the pale young woman just stared back at them.

'Tell me about your friends and acquaintances – and your lovers,' Lavender said. 'And tell me the truth. Are any of them entangled in the criminal underworld of the city? What are they involved with? What are *you* involved with?'

'Nothing!' she protested. 'I live quietly. I'm focusing on my career. Yes, I have friends at the theatre but they're just normal people, silly at times, yes – but criminal? No.'

'What do have in your possession that would lead to such a heinous crime?'

'I don't know.'

'And your lover?'

'I have no lover,' she snapped. She dropped her gaze beneath his glare. 'I, I was once close to another actor at Drury Lane.'

'His name?'

'Mr Seamus MacAuley. But the relationship came to nothing and he returned to work at the Theatre Royal in Cork after the Drury Lane fire. As you know, I moved to the Sans Pareil.'

Not immediately, you didn't madam, he thought. But he decided to leave the issue of Mr Seamus MacAuley alone at this point. It would be easy enough to find out if the man was still in Ireland. He softened his tone. 'Think, Miss Clare, think carefully. Is there anything out of the ordinary that has happened over the last week or so? What have you acquired in that time which these scoundrels might desire?'

Suddenly, realisation flashed across her face. 'Well, there is something . . .'

'What?'

'I didn't think it was anything important.'

'Everything is significant at the moment.'

'Wait a minute.' She rose gracefully to her feet and went across to a cabinet on the far wall of the room. She opened a drawer and removed a huge sheaf of papers. She carried it back to her seat and placed it on her lap. Lavender recognised the typescript from the papers he had seen scattered in her lodgings. It was a play script from the Sans Pareil.

She licked her finger and leafed her way through the rustling pages. Her hand shook. 'This is my script for *The Necromancer*. I brought it with me last Friday to read it over the weekend. I needed to refresh my memory of the lyrics for some of the songs. When I picked it up on Friday afternoon I was surprised to find—'

'To find what?' Lady Caroline shuffled to the edge of her seat.

'This.' April pulled out a sheaf of paper from amongst the pile and offered it to him. He saw at once that the paper was a different quality to the others in the pile. 'I didn't think it was anything unusual at first . . .'

Lavender scrutinised the page of writing. It contained a handwritten column of random numbers. There was only one word at the bottom of the page: *Victor*. It had a line drawn through it. He frowned. 'What is this?'

'I don't know exactly,' Miss Clare said. 'I just found it amongst my script, which I'd placed in Captain Willoughby's bureau. I assumed it belonged to him and had become mixed up with my own papers.'

'Why did you think it was Captain Willoughby's?'

She gave him a brilliant smile, leant forward and pointed to the word *Victor*. 'Because, Detective Lavender, that was the name of one of the ships in the fleet. They captured it from the French and renamed it. Captain Willoughby wrote and told my sister about it. The ship was only a few years old and it was a great prize. He enjoyed the irony that the British navy were now using a French ship against the French.'

'Why is there a line through the ship's name?' Lavender asked.

The actress shrugged. 'I have no idea.'

Lavender stared back down at the paper in his hand. *Are those columns of numbers degrees of latitude and longitude?* he wondered.

'If this is not one of Captain Willoughby's papers, then how on earth did it end up with your play script?' he asked.

'I have no idea,' she replied.

Lady Caroline's face flashed with irritation. 'Think harder, April,' she said. 'We need to get to the bottom of this.'

'I keep my scripts safe in my lodgings when they're not with me in the theatre,' Miss Clare said.

'So this pile of papers travels with you to the theatre sometimes?' Lavender asked.

'But of course! I took it with me on Thursday when I last performed,' said the actress. 'I left it in the green room for a while.'

Lavender had to think for a moment. The green room. Often used, as he observed the other night, as a reception room for visiting dignitaries. 'Whereabouts in the green room at the Sans Pareil did you leave the script?'

'On a table beneath the window.'

'Was there anything else on the table?'

She smiled again. 'There's always something on that table, Detective. Actors are messy creatures. It's cluttered with old props, discarded grease paint sticks – and random papers and news-sheets.' Her eyes widened. 'Why I do believe that may be where I picked up this piece of paper. Do you think it is significant, Detective? Is that what the kidnappers wanted from me?'

He frowned and glanced back down at the paper in his hand. *Victor*. HMS *Victor*. Why did the name of this ship seem familiar to him? Where had he heard it before?

Suddenly he remembered. A dreadful realisation flooded over him. He glanced back down at the innocuous piece of paper. Captain Willoughby was not responsible for the neat line drawn through the words HMS *Victor*. This list did not belong to him.

'Good God,' he exclaimed.

'What's the matter, Detective?' asked Lady Caroline.

Lavender stared at the crackling fire in the hearth as his mind raced to try and make sense of this latest discovery and connect it to the brutal kidnapping of Harriet Willoughby. The two women waited patiently for his reply, their faces etched with concern.

If his suspicions about that slip of paper were correct, then April Clare was in far greater danger than either he, or she, had ever imagined. Other lives may also be in grave danger. And the significance of this discovery could have national repercussions. Any lingering annoyance at the woman's earlier deception now disappeared from his mind and was replaced with nothing but concern for her immediate safety. He must return to Bow Street as soon as possible and seek out James Read.

'I have no idea what it is at present,' he lied. 'But I do know where I can find some answers to this mystery. I need to take this paper with me. In the meantime, Miss Clare and Lady Caroline, you must stay indoors and take the utmost care of yourselves. I shall send down some constables from Bow Street to watch the house. I think it is best that you have some extra protection until we know what we're dealing with.'

Both women sat back, startled. April Clare turned pale. 'Are we in danger, Detective?' she asked.

'You may be,' he said. 'The gang of men who kidnapped your sister may have now given up their search for this document, now that they think that April Clare is dead. Alternatively, they may try to gain entrance here to continue their search.'

'Is this why poor Harriet died?' Lady Caroline demanded. 'For a piece of paper?'

'It may well be.'

Miss Clare leapt to her feet and threw her hands over her mouth in horror. 'What have I done?' she asked dramatically.

Lavender and Lady Caroline also rose to their feet. Lady Caroline walked swiftly across the carpet and put a comforting arm around her stepdaughter. 'Don't worry, April, I shall move in here with you to protect you – and I'll send for Solomon and Duddles to come and stay, too. We must trust in Detective Lavender.'

Despite his anxiety for the women's safety, the corners of Lavender's mouth twitched at the thought of Duddles trying to fend off a gang of determined criminals intent on ransacking the Willoughby household. 'The Bow Street constables will be on the street within an hour,' he said as he reached for his gloves.

'Thank you, Detective.' Miss Clare was visibly relieved.

'I will also arrange to have the body of Mrs Willoughby returned to you, so that you may organise a quiet and discreet funeral.'

'What should April do?' asked Lady Caroline.

'Keep on with the deception,' he advised. 'Tell nobody who you really are; keep up the pretence that you are your sister. I will return as soon as I have some news and I will instruct you about how we're to proceed at that point. I will see myself out.'

'Thank you, Detective Lavender,' said Lady Caroline as he gave them a short bow. 'But before you go, please tell me how you worked out that April was pretending to be Harriet.'

He paused and stared back at the beautiful young actress. Black suited her, he realised – it gave her creamy complexion a luminous quality. Was there a hint of unease behind those dark eyes? Perhaps his brusque questioning about her former lover had unnerved her? But this wasn't the time to expose all of her deceptions. He had a gang of murdering villains to catch.

'When Sir Richard Allison discovered the full extent of Mrs Willoughby's frail health, I realised that it was impossible for the dead woman to have conducted such a lively and successful career on the stage.' With that, he bowed again and left the house before they questioned him further.

Chapter Eighteen

It was raining softly when Magdalena and Teresa returned to their lodgings but Magdalena barely noticed the drizzle. She couldn't stop thinking about the passionate kiss she had shared with Stephen. She was shocked at her own reaction. She lowered herself down into one of the chairs by the window and stared out at her favourite view of the street, trying to calm her reeling mind. *I have been without a man for too long*, she told herself. But deep down she knew that this was more than just carnal desire: she had feelings for Stephen Lavender.

Stephen's spontaneous burst of passion had startled her out of her naïve complacency and she knew it. His physical magnetism was indisputable. Her mind relived every nuance of his closeness, his masculine scent, the warmth of his lips on hers and the faint brush of the stubble re-emerging on his close-shaven chin. Since their first meeting last November, she had enjoyed his company, basked in his kindness and relished his humour and intellect. Their 'friendship', as she called it, had been a welcome distraction from the loneliness and isolation of her exile. His influence, knowledge and advice had helped her adapt to her new life in London and made her plight bearable. But she was a young widow, not a virgin, and she could no longer deny the excitement and heightened passion that was coursing through her veins at the thought of him.

Behind her, Teresa clattered around making coffee, but Magdalena didn't hear her. She removed her gloves and ran a hand over her still tingling lips. She closed her eyes and tried to imagine what kind of lover Stephen would be. She was sure that he would lavish far more attention on her than her late husband, Antonio, had. Her imagination whirled in wicked delight and she struggled to shut out the fantasies of steamy love-making with Stephen that leapt unbidden into her head.

But with the excitement also came caution. Marriage was out of the question, of course. She would ruin his life if she married him. Perhaps she should take Stephen as a lover while she was in London? Why not? Other women took lovers, she told herself. She went through the list of her acquaintances who would either notice or care about such a lapse into depravity. It was deplorably small.

'Doña Magdalena, there is a message from Señor Read at Bow Street.' Teresa's voice cut through her fantasies like a pail of cold water.

'Thank you.' Magdalena took the note from her maid and tore it open. She hadn't even heard the knock at the door when their landlady had brought up the note and passed it to Teresa. Magistrate Read was brief and to the point:

Doña Magdalena,

You have been engaged to deliver lessons in the Spanish language at the language school on Hart Street, each afternoon at 2 o'clock, commencing tomorrow. Your remuneration shall be four shillings per week. Please call on me at Bow Street an hour before your first lesson as I have another confidential matter I wish to discuss with you.

James Read

Magdalena couldn't restrain her satisfaction. Four shillings a week wasn't much but it would feed her and Teresa and pay their rent. The teaching and preparation would relieve some of the interminable boredom of her life, while she waited for her son to come home from school each term. Yes, there was still the money to find for Sebastián's school fees next year but Magdalena had become adept at dismissing that problem and was happy to believe that somehow it would resolve itself. Magistrate Read's final sentence intrigued her, but before she had time to ponder on its meaning, Teresa interrupted her thoughts again.

'We have visitors.' Teresa pointed out of the window.

Magdalena glanced up. Through the streaming rainwater on the window she could just see the glint of black bombazine and tortoiseshell hair combs, as Juana and Olaya Menendez alighted from a carriage on the street below.

'*Dios mío!*' she exclaimed. 'We're popular today, Teresa.'

Five minutes later, the two Menendez sisters sat stiffly on hardback chairs around the spluttering fire in the grate. It was still chilly in the room and the sisters retained their high-necked cloaks, which were damp from the rain outside. Magdalena compared their severe hairstyles and dark, foreign clothing with the lighter colours and softer, more feminine styles preferred by English women like Lady Caroline and Dorothy Jordan.

To distract them from the poverty of her surroundings and to fill in the time while Teresa prepared more coffee, Magdalena showed off her new boots and praised the generosity of the Duke of Clarence. The sisters made appreciative noises about her choice of footwear but her ploy to distract her guests only partially succeeded. The sisters' sharp eyes still took in every detail of her lodgings: the draughty floorboards, the shabby furnishings and the limp and faded curtain that divided the room and hid from sight the bed Magdalena shared with Teresa.

'It was a pleasure to see you again at the theatre, Doña Magdalena,' said Juana. 'We weren't aware that you had settled in this part of London.'

'Or that you had emerged from your mourning so soon,' said Olaya. There was a short pause while Magdalena tried to decide whether the woman's comment was designed to be critical or had just been tactless. Juana frowned and gave her sibling a withering glance. Olaya seemed to shrink inside herself for a moment.

'As you saw, it was a melancholy play.' Magdalena fought back the sudden flash of anger that consumed her and she kept her tone measured. 'I felt that it suited my mood and my situation.'

'Quite so, quite so,' said Juana. 'Although some may believe that widows should shun public gatherings for two years, there is perhaps a case for partaking of such solemn entertainment.'

Teresa finally brought the coffee in their mismatched china cups. She had also arranged small pieces of seed cake on a tiny plate.

'Ahh,' Juana said. 'This is good. I far prefer coffee. The English preference for tea is a mystery to me.'

Magdalena smiled. At least in this, she and Juana had something in common.

'I understand that tea is a good remedy for stomach upsets,' Magdalena said. 'However, I am also baffled about why they drink so much of it here.' Thankfully, Stephen preferred coffee.

'They must suffer a lot of gut-ache,' said Olaya. She helped herself to a second piece of cake. *Thank goodness their brother didn't accompany them*, Magdalena thought. *We don't have enough crockery or cake for more guests.*

They made her recount the incident with the silk-snatcher and the duke.

'Of course, it's scandalous the way the English lords parade their concubines in public,' Juana pronounced, 'such a poor example to set the lower orders. They say Mrs Jordan is a woman of the basest origins who made her living strutting across the stage in men's clothing and has moved from the bed of one man to another all her life.'

Magdalena shrugged. 'Our Spanish nobles are no better. During the early years of my marriage, before Sebastián was born, Antonio and I spent some time with my relatives in Madrid. They introduced us to life at court and I was a frequent visitor to the vast palace of El Escorial. I quickly became aware of the scandalous and the illicit liaisons that carried on behind the gilt bedroom doors of the palace.'

Olaya's eyes widened and both women leant forward to hear more. It gave Magdalena great pleasure to let them wait. She was no huge admirer of Mrs Jordan after her unpleasant little trick, but if there was one thing she hated more than anything it was the sense of superiority that many of her fellow émigrés displayed over the English, whom they felt were godless and sinful.

'You're referring, of course, to the affair between Queen Marie Luisa and Prime Minister Godoy?' Juana suggested in a breathless whisper. 'Was it true? Were they lovers?'

'Would you like more coffee, Olaya, or perhaps some bread and honey?' Magdalena asked. The younger sister nodded and smiled. Olaya was easily distracted, Magdalena realised, especially with food. The girl was plain but not quite as sour-faced as her older sibling. However, her corsets were struggling to restrain her expanding waistline.

Juana finally sat back in her chair when she realised that Magdalena wasn't going to enlighten them further. Irritation flashed across her face. 'It must be quite a disappointment for a woman who has spent time in the palace of El Escorial to find herself living here,' she snapped.

Touché, thought Magdalena.

'I must confess, Doña Magdalena, that I don't like this area and the people within it – especially the trading men on the street. When we alighted from the carriage I smelt their rank underclothes and walked in fear of their hands reaching out for me. I feared their touch.'

Magdalena almost choked on her coffee and struggled to hide her laughter. This dried-up old spinster must have a nose like a ferret if she could smell the men's underclothes. And Juana was spending more time thinking about their smalls than they ever would spend thinking about hers. Juana was quite safe from groping hands.

'Felipe has found us a lovely house in which we can wait out the war,' Juana continued. 'It's in a pleasant area. The house is tall and elegant, with more bedchambers than we require. We also have a cook and several servants. Despite the dismal weather in this country, we're quite comfortable in our exile.'

'That's nice,' said Magdalena.

'Sometimes Felipe assists other émigrés who have also found themselves in difficult circumstances by letting them stay with us. He's so considerate and kind to help those less fortunate than us. He's a true Christian, a true Catholic. Perhaps I will ask him to let you stay with us.'

'You can't imagine how distressed we were to hear of Don Antonio's death,' Olaya suddenly blurted out. She drained her cup and passed it to Teresa for a refill. 'Our brother, Felipe, was particularly upset.'

'May God guard the souls of the departed.' Juana crossed herself as she spoke.

'Amen,' said Magdalena. She was grateful for the interruption provided by the younger woman. It gave her a moment to recover from the shock of Juana's suggestion. Is that why they were here?

To offer her charity? Yet only two nights ago, Juana and her siblings had snubbed her at the theatre.

'Felipe had always felt close to Antonio, he regarded him as the brother he never had,' Juana continued.

Again, Magdalena bit back her urge to laugh. Despite his faults – and he had many – the energetic Antonio had been a good judge of character. He despised Don Felipe, whom he considered as lazy and hedonistic. Antonio always referred to the sisters as a pair of twisted old geckos. In a society where men stuck together, her husband had spurned the company of Felipe Menendez and ignored his overtures of friendship.

The Menendez family were never part of the ancient *hidalguía* to which Magdalena and Antonio belonged. The Menendez were the new rich, who had grown wealthy and idle on the gold stolen from the natives of the Americas. '*His rings won't fall off,*' Antonio had said many times about Felipe Menendez and his idleness. The family treated their servants badly and took only a self-serving part in politics. They had no social conscience, made no effort to improve their land for the benefit of the community or to adopt modern agricultural practices that might improve the lives of their illiterate peasants. Thanks to the languid attitude of families like that of Felipe Menendez, Spain had become a fractious, underdeveloped, economic backwater. No wonder Bonaparte and his French pigs had walked all over them.

'Antonio and I were always very fond of Don Felipe,' she said.

'I'm sure that he will be pleased to hear that,' Juana said. 'But I think that your late husband would have been distressed to have seen you fallen so low in fortune. You and Teresa must come and stay with us for a while. You would enjoy the comfort – and the warmth. It would save you some money.'

'Thank you for your kindness,' Magdalena said graciously. A few months ago she would have leapt at the opportunity to live off the charity of this wealthy family, no matter how much she disliked or distrusted them. 'However, I'm sorry,' she said. 'But I must decline your kind invitation. I'm about to commence some employment which I hope will improve my circumstances.'

'Employment?' Juana looked like she had been struck.

'Yes, I will be giving Spanish lessons to the staff of the British government.'

'Teaching?' Olaya spluttered crumbs across the table.

'Yes, Detective Lavender helped me gain this employment.'

'Ah, this Detective Lavender,' Juana said slowly. Her eyes narrowed. 'He's the policeman, yes?'

'He's a highly respected principal officer at Bow Street Magistrates' Court,' Magdalena corrected her. 'You saw the familiar ease with which the Duke of Clarence addressed him? Well, Detective Lavender is a man of influence.'

Teresa placed a plate stacked with bread and honey in front of Olaya. 'He also likes to kiss,' her maid said suddenly.

Magdalena gave the startled sisters a beaming smile. 'Yes, he's forever kissing my hand – and Teresa's,' she said. 'His manners are impeccable.' She really must have a word with Teresa as soon as possible. For someone who didn't speak much in either Spanish or English, her maid chose the most inappropriate moments to suddenly become articulate. The sisters lowered their eyelids. Magdalena knew that they didn't believe her.

'Does he come to your window at night?' Olaya asked, her mouth once more crammed full of food.

Magdalena smiled at the thought of Stephen up a ladder at her first-floor window, wooing her in the traditional Spanish custom. That would raise a few eyebrows in the neighbourhood. 'Detective Lavender is a good friend. He found out what had happened to Antonio. Without his help I would never have known of my husband's death at Talavera.'

'A friend like that must be valued,' Juana said. 'Come, Olaya, we have taken up far too much of Doña Magdalena's time and encroached for long enough on her hospitality. We must return in time for evening prayers.'

Olaya cast a last, lingering glance of regret at the unfinished plate of food then rose to leave with her sister.

'Do you still find a place and an opportunity to pray and take Mass in this heathen country, Doña Magdalena?' Juana asked as she fastened her cloak.

'Oh yes, I pray all the time,' Magdalena lied blithely and pointed across the room to the curtains which hid their sleeping quarters. 'I have a devotional corner where I keep my Bible and the family reliquary. But I don't have a priest to take my confession.'

'That is another reason why you should come and stay with us for a while,' Juana said. 'Felipe has found us a priest, a Father Hernandez. I'm sure you have much to confess,' she added, with a sly glance. 'But it's good to hear that you had time to remember to pack your religious items before your dramatic flight from Spain.'

And with that final curt statement, she turned on her heel and marched out of the door, Olaya trailing in her wake.

Magdalena breathed a sigh of relief when the rigid figures of the Menendez sisters finally disappeared down the stairwell. However, her relief was short-lived. She was shrewd enough to realise that there must be a reason why those dreadful women had called on her today. Two nights ago they had turned their back on her at the theatre. There was something behind this sudden flush of friendship and she doubted it was her brief popularity with the Duke of Clarence. She wasn't sure what had prompted their renewed interest or offer of hospitality, but their quick departure after the discussion about Stephen left her uneasy.

Chapter Nineteen

Lavender, Woods and Magistrate Read stared silently at the innocuous piece of paper on the desk. The longcase clock ticked gently in the background. Dusk was falling and the gas-lamp lighters would soon be out but Lavender could still hear the cries of the market vendors outside in the cold streets of Covent Garden, shouting out their wares. London never stopped. This was the time of the day when frugal housewives would arrive at the fruit and vegetable market in the hope of buying produce at reduced prices and the fruiters and florists vied with each other for customers, desperate for a last few coppers.

Read and Woods were silent for a considerable time. They had a lot to think about, Lavender realised. They had been shocked when he told them about April Clare's deception and how she had been masquerading as her dead sister for the last few days. However, when he explained how genuinely scared the woman had been and that he believed the kidnapping had been an attempt to retrieve the document that lay on the table before them, their irritation had quickly turned to concerned curiosity.

'What *has* this woman got herself mixed up with?' Read took off his wig, tossed it onto the desk and scratched his close-cropped head. He pointed an ink-stained finger from his other hand at the sheet of paper. 'What do you think it is?'

'I think it's in code,' Lavender said. 'A code that gives the location of ships. The location of our naval fleet in the Indian Ocean, probably. I have no idea about how accurate it is – or how relevant.'

Read frowned. 'If you're right, then we have a grave situation before us.'

Beside the magistrate, Woods scratched his stubbly chin. The glow from the flickering oil lamp on Read's desk illuminated the tired confusion on the faces of both men.

'Miss Clare had put her play script into Captain Willoughby's bureau?' Read asked.

'Yes.'

'Well, it may simply be one of his old papers that had become mixed up with her script. It is not inconceivable that a naval captain might be thinking about navigation and jot down a list of the degrees of latitude and longitude.'

'That's what she thought, at first,' Lavender said. 'But I don't think that Captain Willoughby wrote that list. He sailed away from England over a year ago and that list has been written since November.'

'How do you know that?'

'Because of the line drawn through the word "Victor". HMS *Victor* was a French ship called the *Iéna*. We captured her from the French in 1808 and renamed her HMS *Victor*. But she's no longer one of ours. The French recaptured her in November last year. I read about it in the news-sheets. One reporter likened her to an inconstant mistress because she was forever swapping from one master to another.'

'We're grateful for your prodigious reading and excellent memory, Stephen,' Read said.

Lavender glanced up, suspecting sarcasm but the magistrate's praise was genuine. It seemed their earlier disagreement had been forgotten in the light of this new and disturbing development.

'The *Victor* has been crossed off this list because she's no longer part of our fleet. She's back in the hands of the French,' Lavender continued. 'Captain Willoughby couldn't have made this mark on a paper back in England because he was on the other side of the world when the ship was retaken.'

Read observed him shrewdly. 'That is one explanation, I suppose, but you put a lot of significance into a single line through one word, Stephen.'

'Don't forget that somebody has gone to extreme lengths to retrieve this document,' Lavender insisted. 'Every mark on it has significance. These villains have kidnapped the woman they thought had taken it, ransacked her lodgings and possibly murdered Darius Jones so they could gain undisturbed access to Raleigh Close in order to hold their victim prisoner. This list is significant to someone.'

'What is so damned important about a piece of paper with a few degrees of latitude and longitude marked on it?' Woods jabbed a finger in the direction of the paper on Read's desk. 'Why would those coves kidnap and terrify two innocent gals in order to get it back?'

Read sighed. 'We won't know the answer to that question, Ned, until we have determined exactly what the paper is. But if Lavender is right, and this document does give the whereabouts now – or at some point in the future – of our naval fleet in the Indian Ocean, then the situation is more serious than I ever imagined.'

'Why?' Woods asked.

'Because such information is classified,' Lavender explained patiently. 'If it landed in the hands of the French, then the lives of thousands of our seamen and officers may be in danger.'

'Gawd's teeth!' exclaimed Woods. He sat back in his chair in horror. His gaze flicked between Lavender and Read. 'Have we stumbled across a Froggie spy ring?'

'I don't know,' Lavender said. 'But a document like this shouldn't be lying around the green room of the Sans Pareil Theatre. Someone has been careless.'

'That woman in the Hart Street bakery, that Jacquetta Higgin, claims she heard foreigners talkin' outside her shop one evenin',' Woods reminded them. 'She thought they were French.'

'Do you think that somebody who works at the theatre is involved?' Read asked.

Lavender shrugged. 'There has to be some connection to the theatre. That is the only other place where Miss Clare took her play script; the paper before us must have become caught up in her script when she put it down in the green room.'

'I thought Admiral Lord Nelson had destroyed the French fleet at Trafalgar.' Deep furrows embedded themselves into Woods' broad forehead. 'Why would it matter if anyone knew where our ships were in the South Seas? The French have no ships left. Britannia rules the waves!'

'Not quite,' Lavender said smiling. 'The French still have substantial frigate squadrons at the Île-de-France and Île Bonaparte in the Indian Ocean. They use these islands as raiding bases to disrupt our trade links with British India. The East India Company sends millions of pounds worth of goods back to London every year. The Royal Navy is dominant in these waters and protects the heavily laden East Indiamen as they sail home. But French warships have become a real nuisance; they capture or sink trading vessels and isolated British frigates.'

'So this case is about ruddy piracy as well as spyin'?' asked Woods. He had raised his eyebrows so high they disappeared beneath his hair.

Read smiled. 'No doubt Napoleon Bonaparte would call it an act of war, rather than piracy, Ned,' he said. 'Remember that not all wars are fought on an Iberian battlefield under the command of Viscount Wellington. Some wars are more subtle, more remote – but still as devastating to our island nation.'

'We need to verify this document,' Lavender said. It had been a long day and he was tired.

'I have a contact in the Home Department in Whitehall,' said Read. 'Captain Sackville will know what it is. I will pass it across to him first thing tomorrow.'

'What do you want us to do?'

'Go home,' Read replied. 'Miss Clare is safe under the watchful eyes of our constables and there is nothing else you can do tonight. Things will be clearer in the morning when my contact has had a look at this document. Call on me at midday after I have finished my early session in court. Then we will know how to proceed.'

'Let's get a brandy,' Lavender said as he and Woods pulled up their coat collars and descended down the steps of the building onto Bow Street. Despite his exhaustion, Lavender's mind was still in turmoil with the day's events and he welcomed the opportunity to wind down for a while in front of a blazing tavern fire with Woods' company and a large glass of brandy. 'It's early yet and Betsy doesn't expect us all for supper for a while.'

'I can't be long,' Woods warned. 'And neither can you. Don't forget you have to collect Doña Magdalena. I'd better get back and give Betsy a hand. She'll be mad if you're late.'

'Just one brandy in the Nags' Head, Ned,' said Lavender. 'I have something else to tell you. Besides which, I know Betsy well enough to realise that she won't appreciate any help from you; you'll just get under her feet.'

Woods thought for a moment and glanced down Hart Street at the welcoming glow that emanated from the small-paned bow windows of the Nag's Head tavern. 'All right,' he said. 'But just one drink, mind you. I'll get the rollin' pin across my lugholes tonight if I stagger home fuddled with brandy.'

It was quiet in the Nag's Head. Centuries old, the ceilings of the public house were low and smoke-blackened, the windows small. Behind the bar, tiers of mirrored shelving displayed a wide range of brandies and other spirits in a wonderful array of glass bottles that glittered in shades of emerald and sapphire. The light from the chandeliers full of dripping tallow candles reflected in the glass and went someway to lifting the gloom in the ancient tavern. The place was popular with the Bow Street officers and the landlord nodded to them in recognition as they strode across the uneven floorboards towards the back of the inn where they found a couple of vacant settles next to the stone fireplace.

Woods sat and stretched out his legs. His boots were still splattered with mud from his ride to the Five Fields. 'I can't believe that the gal pretended to be her dead sister,' he said. 'She had me fooled.'

'It was an accomplished act,' Lavender said. 'But she had good reason to lie. She was scared for her life.'

'I know what it is you want to talk to me about.' Woods gave Lavender a conspiratorial wink across the hearth. 'It's about that arrogant sawbones, Allison, isn't it? You want to tell me that I was right and the jumped-up little dandyprat got it wrong, didn't he? Mrs Willoughby has had a child.'

Lavender smiled. He took up the poker, leant forward and stoked up the small fire in the grate. 'Actually, Ned, he was right. I believe the child in the Willoughby nursery belongs to April Clare – not Harriet Willoughby.'

'What?'

A barmaid with a stained gown and a mob cap on top of her thick mop of unruly hair appeared by their side. She poured them both a large glass of glinting amber liquid. She gave Lavender a beaming, toothless smile when he tossed her a coin and told her to leave the jug.

'I don't understand,' Woods said. 'How is that possible?'

'You remember that April Clare previously worked at Drury Lane Theatre before the fire?'

'Yes.'

'Well, she had an admirer there, another actor; an Irish fellow by the name of Mr Seamus MacAuley.'

'Where does he fit into the kidnappin'?'

'He doesn't. He returned to Ireland after the Drury Lane fire and works in the Theatre Royal in Cork. As far as Miss Clare knows, MacAuley is still there but I have already written to them to confirm this. We need to eliminate him from the inquiry. Lovers can behave erratically – especially if there has been a tiff. There have been several examples of spurned men kidnapping women. But I don't suspect that MacAuley had anything to do with this case; I think he is safely in Ireland. However, I do suspect that when MacAuley returned to his native country he left April Clare with more than a broken heart.'

Woods stared hard at him; trying to understand his meaning. As realisation slowly dawned, his constable's jaw slackened and his mouth gaped open with surprise. 'You think he left her with child?'

'I'm quite sure that he did. That would explain Miss Clare's mysterious absence from the theatre during last summer. There is no sick aunt in Gloucester. I believe that April Clare took the time off from her career and disappeared out into the provinces in order to give birth to a child.'

'And her sister, Mrs Willoughby, agreed to bring up the actresses' by-blow as her own?'

'Yes.'

'But why the secrecy and the lies? London actresses, married and unmarried, have children all the time. That tragedy queen, Sarah Siddons, has several – and Dorothy Jordan had a few before she even got with the Duke of Clarence.'

'Yes, actresses have illegitimate offspring,' Lavender said. 'But the daughters of barons do not, especially if their sisters have married respectable naval captains. The scandal would have been huge. It was essential for the reputation of both sisters – and Lady Caroline – that Miss Clare's indiscretion didn't become common knowledge.'

Woods nodded. 'Ahh – how did you work it out?'

Lavender took a long drink from his glass, sat back and undid the buttons of his greatcoat. Their corner of the tavern was warming up nicely. He found the scent of the woodsmoke and the gentle crackle of the fire soothing. As the brandy warmed his innards, he felt the tension ease from his tired body and mind.

'It was those ill-fitting shoes that finally solved this riddle for me,' he said. 'Magdalena told me that when she carried her son, her feet grew larger. Suddenly it made sense. The two women may be identical twins but April Clare had slightly larger feet after the birth of her child. When the two women swapped clothes to play their little trick on Lady Caroline, poor Harriet Willoughby got a pair of shoes that didn't fit.'

'Gawd's teeth!' Woods exclaimed. He burst out laughing and held up his glass in a toast to Lavender. The amber liquid swirled, caught the light and glinted. 'Well done, sir! Mystery solved.' Woods drained his glass, poured more brandy and sat back. 'I'll tell you what though, I'm surprised that Captain Willoughby agreed to this. I can't imagine that many respectable naval captains would have voluntarily taken in their sister-in-law's nipper as their own.'

Lavender glanced at his constable through partially veiled eyes. 'Perhaps Captain Willoughby doesn't know the truth,' he said slowly. 'Maybe he thinks that the child in the crib in his Wandsworth house belongs to him and his wife.'

'What?' Woods' drink slopped onto the flagstones. He reached for the earthenware jug and poured himself another. 'You think those women have gulled him?' He looked incredulous.

'Think about it, Ned,' Lavender said. 'Captain Willoughby sailed away at Christmas last year. It would be easy to fool him. In the summer a child is born. If Mrs Willoughby pretended to be with child and padded out her clothing, who was to know any different? All she had to do was disappear with her sister into the provinces when the birth drew close and return with an infant. How would anyone know whose baby it was?"

Woods seemed to have lost the ability to formulate his words and Lavender suspected that it wasn't simply due to the influence of the brandy. Eventually, Woods said thoughtfully: 'The, the servants assumed that the little nipper was Mrs Willoughby's baby, hers and the captain's.'

'Just as I suspected,' Lavender replied, with a certain amount of satisfaction. 'Lady Caroline said that April Clare could persuade her sister to do almost anything.'

'But wouldn't Lady Caroline have recognised this as a ruse? I'd be surprised if they pulled the wool over her eyes.'

'Oh, I imagine that Caroline Clare knew all about it. In fact, she probably thought up the idea in the first place.'

'But why would Mrs Willoughby agree to deceive her husband like this?' Woods' broad face was crumpled with concern, his eyes glazed with confusion and liquor.

Lavender shrugged. 'Well, I'm not going to pretend to be an expert on the fairer sex.'

'You're not,' agreed Woods.

'But I have a theory. You heard Sir Richard Allison when he said it would be dangerous for Mrs Willoughby to bear a child? Well, perhaps the good captain wanted a child and an heir. If Mrs Willoughby pretended that Miss Clare's child was her own, then she removed the need to endanger her own health with a pregnancy. I'm quite sure that Lady Caroline would have seen sense in this arrangement. She was keenly aware of Mrs Willoughby's delicate health and despite her alleged disinterest in her stepdaughters, I know that she is genuinely fond of the young women. Yes, I definitely think Lady Caroline had a hand in this.'

'Well, I'll be damned!' Woods said. 'This is a rum do. Did you confront them with your suspicions?'

'No, I decided to leave the matter as it was. This particular deception has no bearing on the case, apart from the fact that the issue of the child made it more difficult for me to determine that April Clare was masquerading as her sister.'

Woods shook his head and sighed. 'There's many a cuckolded man in England has a child in his home which is not his – but this is the first time I've heard of a case where some poor geezer has been landed with a nipper that's neither his – nor his wife's.'

'As we've agreed, I'm no expert on women—'

'No, you're not.'

'But I have begun to notice that women have their own ways of ensuring their survival.' He lowered his voice. 'Sometimes they can take a shocking course of action.' He stared into the glowing embers of the fire and thought of Magdalena.

'Well, I think it's wicked to deceive a fellow so,' Woods slurred.

Lavender smiled and drained his glass. Despite his earlier protestations that he would remain sober, his constable had already downed half the jug of brandy. It was time to head for home. Lavender would shave and change before collecting Magdalena. He was looking forward to an evening in her company.

But Woods wasn't ready to go yet. 'How many other poor blokes has this happened to, do you think?'

'I don't know. What do you mean, Ned?'

'I mean that my Betsy has two sisters. She's very close to them both; thick as thieves them gals.' Lavender realised that Woods was working himself up. His shaggy brows crinkled together in consternation. 'You and I were away in Maidstone when my little Rachel were born. What about if Betsy and one of her sisters—? You don't suppose—?' He left the questions dangling in midair and looked up beseechingly at Lavender.

Lavender rose to his feet and laughed. 'No, I don't suppose,' he said firmly. He buttoned up his coat and hauled Woods up onto his feet. 'And you must be foxed to think so. Chase that thought right out of your mind, Ned. Betsy's never played that trick on you. And if she suspects for one minute that you think such things – you'll have a lot more than the rolling pin to worry about!'

'Do you know what the worst of it is?' Woods said as they staggered back out into dark cobbled street. The cold night air hit their faces hard but Woods didn't seem to notice it. He spun round dramatically and stared hard at Lavender.

'No. What's the worst of it?'

'That Allison, that bloody little sod of a surgeon, was right all along.'

Chapter Twenty

Lavender was surprised but relieved that Magdalena left Teresa behind when they set off for supper at Ned and Betsy Woods' house.

'I gave her the night off,' Magdalena informed him as he helped her up into the cab. 'Normally, Teresa would sit in the kitchen with the other servants while we dined but I don't think that Betsy Woods has any servants.'

Lavender bit back a smile. The family didn't have a dining room either as far as he recalled; most meals were taken in their back kitchen at the battered wooden table in front of the warm fireplace and range.

Magdalena looked ravishing tonight. She wore a dark, burgundy dress, embroidered with black silk and further adorned with black lace and an intricate swirling pattern of glistened jet beads. The rich wine colour of her gown was just visible below the neckline of her black cloak. It enhanced her complexion at her throat and in her face. She smiled and leant her warm body next to his.

'I have some good news,' she said. 'Magistrate Read has been in touch with me; I'm to begin teaching Spanish at the Hart Street language school tomorrow afternoon.'

'Well done,' Lavender replied. 'I know this is what you want to do and I'm pleased for you.'

She gave him a brilliant smile and she squeezed his hand. In fact, she was very physical throughout the journey. Her hand seemed to be forever fluttering to his arm. At one point, she lightly flicked a speck of imaginary dust from his breeches. He smiled to himself and wondered if his spontaneous kiss earlier that day had ignited her passion. He was tempted to kiss her again to find out. Unfortunately, the journey to Oak Road was short and they were already late and he didn't want to start what he couldn't finish. There would be plenty of time to explore her warm lips again on the journey home – and any other bits of her glowing flesh that she was prepared to allow him to caress. He intended to take full advantage of Teresa's absence.

Woods greeted them at the door in his Sunday best waistcoat, breeches and cravat. He had also run a comb through his thick hair. Apart from his shining eyes, he showed no sign that he had been chirping merrily only a few hours ago due to the influence of the brandy. 'Welcome, Doña Magdalena,' he said. 'Please follow me into the parlour and partake of a warmin' glass of Madeira.'

Lavender bit back a smile at this unusual formality; he suspected that Betsy had told Woods what to say.

Woods took Magdalena's cloak, threw it over the end of the stair bannister and, to Lavender's surprise, led them into the dreary room at the front of the house. Half-panelled in dark wood with claustrophobic brown-paper hangings reaching up to the smoke-stained ceiling, the parlour was a dull and drab room at the best of times. The family only used it at Christmas, Easter and funerals. They preferred the large, cheerful kitchen at the rear of the house. Even with the fire crackling in the grate the room looked glum. In addition to this, the mismatched and uncomfortable collection of furniture had been pushed back against the walls to allow for a round, bow-legged Queen Anne dining table and four spindly chairs to be centred in front of the hearth.

Someone is going to get hot, Lavender thought as he glanced at the seat immediately in front of the fire.

The pungent smell of beeswax polish now overpowered the musty odour he normally associated with the parlour. The table was already laid with Betsy's best crockery and cutlery.

Woods squashed himself past the chairs and reached for the decanter stood on top of Betsy's precious piano. He poured out four glasses of the ruby-coloured spirit. There was just room for one of them to move around the table at a time. Lavender stood back and allowed Magdalena to follow Woods. First, she smoothed flat her silk gown, careful not to snag it on the furniture.

'Thank you, Constable Woods,' she said graciously, as she took her drink. 'But I must go to the kitchen and see if Betsy needs any help with the food.'

A look of alarm flashed across Woods' face. 'She asked me to keep you in here. She said you're a guest and weren't to think about helpin'.'

Magdalena smiled. 'Nonsense. Is she in the kitchen? I must assist her.' She squeezed back passed Lavender and exited the parlour.

'Where's the table come from?' Lavender asked when Magdalena had left.

Woods groaned. 'Betsy borrowed it from a neighbour. She made me carry it in here when I came in from work – and the blinkin' chairs. Apparently, we can't feed Doña Magdalena in the kitchen.' The physical exertion had taken its toll. Woods' broad face was ruddy and still glowed with perspiration.

Another thought suddenly struck Lavender: the house was unusually quiet. 'What have you done with the children?' he asked. 'Have you bound and gagged them?'

'They're upstairs,' Woods said. 'Betsy asked Elizabeth to come round and sit and play with them for the evenin'.'

'Ah,' Lavender said. 'So Elizabeth is here, is she?' This was an unforeseen development but there was no time for further questions because the two women appeared in the doorway bearing platters of food.

'Good evening, Stephen,' said the tiny mistress of the house. He leant down and planted a kiss on Betsy's soft red cheek. He felt the tension in her jaw muscles below her skin. Betsy was clearly out to impress Magdalena tonight and the strain showed. Like Woods, she wore her Sunday best: a white poplin gown with a faint grey stripe. He noticed that she had a few spots of cooking fat on her ample bosom.

'I'm so glad you could come tonight and bring Doña Magdalena,' she said as she placed an oval serving dish in the centre of the table. 'Although I don't appreciate that you took Ned into the tavern after work – tonight of all nights to send him home foxed!' She gave him a withering glance, which Lavender knew would have felled most men on the spot. Woods grinned sheepishly at him across the room. 'I had to make him two jugs of coffee to sober him up,' she added.

'Ah, I'm sorry about that, Betsy,' he said, trying to hide his smile. 'You know how it is at the sharp end of crime – we always have some important issues to discuss.'

'I know there are too many taverns in Covent Garden which offer temptation for weak-minded tosspots,' she said and glowered at her husband.

'The table looks beautiful, Betsy,' Lavender said, cheerfully. He pointed towards the crystal vase of hothouse flowers which stood in the centre. 'You have done us proud tonight.'

Distracted, she flushed and pointed to the chair next to the fire. 'Well, get yourself sat down then. We can't let the food go cold.'

Normally, Lavender would never remove his coat and loosen his waistcoat buttons in the presence of a woman, but the close confines of the room were unusual circumstances. Drastic action was required in order to save himself from overheating and to save Betsy's pride. His hostess had not noticed the unsuitable proximity of the table to the hearth. After divesting himself of his coat, he slid sideways into the chair in front of the fire. The heat immediately burned through the material of his shirt into his back. Wood's followed his example, took off his own coat and eased his bulk into the chair beside him.

Magdalena sank gracefully into the seat opposite. She leant across the table and stroked the smooth lawn of his sleeve. 'What a beautiful shirt, Stephen,' she said, 'and so well laundered.' She was touching him again. He struggled to hide his smile.

Betsy removed the cover from her china serving dish. 'It's just lamb cutlets,' she said. 'Nothing too fancy.'

'It smells delicious,' Lavender said.

'Ned? Please serve Doña Magdalena first.' Woods picked up a large silver serving spoon, leant across the table and heaped the meat onto their plates, while Betsy dished out the vegetables.

'Oh, please call me Magdalena,' Magdalena said. 'We're all friends here. There is no need for formality.'

'If you like,' said their hostess.

'I've been trying to get Ned to call me Stephen for years when we're off-duty,' Lavender said. 'But he can't seem to manage it.'

'Doesn't seem right, sir,' Woods said. 'And it's too much for my brain to remember, all this switching from one name to another.'

'You had no difficulty calling me Stephen when I first started work at Bow Street as a constable and it was your task to teach me the job.'

'Yes, but you should have heard what he called you when he got home on a night,' Betsy said.

Magdalena spluttered with laughter and hastily covered her mouth with her napkin. Their hostess glanced at her shaking shoulders and smiled. 'We've known each other for a long time, my dear. And although I don't say it often, we're very proud of Stephen's rapid rise through the ranks to principal officer.'

'Taught him all I knew, I did,' said Woods.

'Well, that wouldn't have taken long,' Betsy said. 'Ned. More Madeira, please for Doñ— for Magdalena.'

'I'll get it,' Lavender said, grateful to be able to move away from both the fire and the attention. There was no way that his burly constable would have been able to get round that room now that they were seated.

By the time he had refilled the glasses and passed their hostess her drink, the others had already begun their meal. Lavender knew by Woods' stiffness and the confused expression on his face that something was wrong. He took a forkful of the lamb, chewed then stopped in concern. The meat had a very strong nutty flavour that made it bitter. It was palatable, but only just. He glanced at Magdalena. She calmly ate her meal, her features composed.

'This is an unusual flavour, Betsy,' he said. 'I know it's not mint or rosemary. I can't work it out.'

'Ha.' She grinned. 'So I have foiled the great Detective Lavender, have I?'

He smiled. 'Absolutely. This is a mystery I can't solve.'

'I have cooked the lamb in the Spanish fashion tonight,' she announced grandly. 'In honour of Doña Magdalena's company.' Magdalena gave Betsy a gracious smile. 'Yes, Doñ— Magdalena told me that Spanish food is highly spiced, so I have spiced this lamb.'

'What did you use?' Woods asked.

'Well, when I looked in my pantry the only spice I found was the nutmeg I use for the egg custard.'

'You put nutmeg in lamb cutlets?' Woods' jaw dropped, his face incredulous.

Betsy bristled, pushed a greying curl back beneath her cap. She opened her mouth to argue.

'It is delicious, Betsy,' Magdalena interrupted. 'It reminds me of the lamb dishes we cook back home in Oviedo.' Lavender doubted that this was true but he respected Magdalena's diplomacy. He forced himself to swallow another mouthful of the nutty lamb then changed the subject.

'How are the children, Betsy – especially my sweet little god-daughter?'

She raised her eyebrows to the ceiling. 'Humph! Baby Tabitha is the best behaved of the lot of them,' she announced. 'But those boys will be the death of me!'

'What have they done now?' he asked, smiling.

'What have they done? What have they *not* done?' Her voice rose into a crescendo of frustration. 'They only tried to shoot poor Rachel, that's all!'

Lavender choked softly on his lamb and took a hasty swig of Madeira to clear his throat. It did a good job of neutralising the strong flavour of the spice.

'It wasn't as bad as all that, Betsy, love,' Woods suggested. He was immediately silenced by another withering glance from his wife.

'I blame you for this, Stephen Lavender,' Betsy said hotly.

'Me? What have I done?' He looked up, wide-eyed and inno-cent. Magdalena was laughing quietly to herself.

'Do you remember when you were attacked by tobymen on the way to Barnby Moor?'

'Yes?'

'Well, when you disarmed the one who was travellin' inside the coach with you, my lump of a husband here pocketed his pistol.'

'Ah yes, I remember he used it to great effect on the tobymen to save our hides,' Lavender said. 'And a few days later he used it to quell the excitement of a gang of rioting farmers.'

'Well, that is as maybe,' she replied. 'But that pistol should have been handed into the Nottin'hamshire constabulary as evidence after the attempted highway robbery – and don't you try to deny it, Stephen.' She jabbed her fork across the table in his direction. 'I've been a constable's wife long enough to know how these things work. You were remiss in your responsibilities.'

'Guilty as charged, m'lady.' He grinned.

'So a few days ago our Rachel starts screamin' blue murder upstairs – and when my old legs finally got me up there, I found Dan holdin' her down and Eddie tryin' to shoot the poor gal in the heart with the pistol.'

'There was no shot or powder in it,' Woods mumbled. His cheeks bulged with food. 'She were never in no danger.'

'Not that that makes any difference,' Betsy snapped. 'Anyway, I've removed the pistol from the house. None of them can use it now.' She turned back to Lavender and sighed. 'I've bred a couple of sister-murderin' heathens, Stephen.'

'Your boys are fine, Betsy,' he said. 'There's many a time I plotted to murder my own sisters – and look how I turned out.' He suddenly realised that this might not have been the best thing to say in front of the outspoken Betsy. She knew him too well. Before she replied he hastily added: 'They'll make you proud one day, Betsy. Mark my words, they're fine boys.'

She didn't look convinced but her ruddy cheeks flushed anew with the compliment.

The rest of the meal turned out to be far more successful. Betsy was a superb cook when she wasn't trying to experiment with continental cuisine. For dessert they had a delicious bread and butter pudding, liberally sprinkled with sugar and served with a steaming rum sauce. There was a plate of marzipan sweetmeats, glazed with rosewater and sugar. While Betsy prepared the desserts in the kitchen, Lavender leant back and dampened down the damned fire. The back of his shirt was soaked with sweat.

Magdalena ate more of the sweetmeats than Woods. Betsy noticed this and he could tell that she was delighted that Magdalena appreciated her cooking. The tension dropped from the little matron's jawline and she beamed from ear to ear.

The Madeira had flowed freely and they all showed signs of slight intoxication. While Betsy was out of the room, Woods entertained Magdalena with the tale of how he and several other constables had struggled to restrain a frisky young bullock that had escaped from Smithfield market and terrorised shoppers and stallholders alike.

'You should have seen the local parson run when that bullock got behind him,' Woods said. 'He lifted his cassock above his knobbly knees and bolted down Cock Lane and round Pye Corner quicker than Nelson could scuttle a flamin' French warship.'

Magdalena laughed.

'Language, Ned – don't you start cussin',' warned Betsy as she re-entered the room.

'I'll tell you what, Betsy, love,' Woods said. 'If sir will help me push back this damned table so you can get to the piano, we'll have a song or two.'

'Yes, Betsy – give us a song!' Lavender said. Betsy was a wonderful singer with a wicked sense of humour. He rose to his feet and helped Woods push back the table to make some space in front on the piano.

Betsy blushed and refused but Magdalena was also delighted with the idea and urged her to entertain them. 'Perhaps we should let our guest sing for us,' Betsy said. 'I'm sure that Magdalena is very accomplished.'

'That's right, Magdalena,' Lavender said, with a wink. 'It's a British tradition that guests sing for their supper. You must pay your dues after that sumptuous meal.'

She gave him a sideways smile. 'You tease me, Stephen,' she said. 'No, no. I'm a dreadful singer and a poor musician. Please play for us, Betsy.'

Finally persuaded, Betsy sat down on the stool in front of the instrument, placed a few pieces of sheet music in the rest and stretched her accomplished fingers out over the ivory keys. She trilled out a scale to warm up. Woods pulled up a chair next to her.

'I'll turn the page for you Betsy, my love,' he slurred.

Betsy began gently with a Robbie Burns Scottish love ballad and her sweet, mellifluous voice held them enraptured. She paused dramatically after the first verse then, to the delight of her audience, she launched into the second verse – in a Scottish accent.

Magdalena rose from her own chair and sat down on the sofa next to Lavender. 'She's really talented!' she whispered in his ear.

His arm slid surreptitiously behind her and rested on the back of the sofa. 'Just wait until Ned joins in,' he replied.

Sure enough, by the third verse Woods had added his own deep baritone to Betsy's faultless soprano and made a passable job of keeping time with his wife and the melody. They had their backs to Lavender and Magdalena but he knew by their closeness and the occasional glance they exchanged that they were thoroughly enjoying their duet. Woods inevitably fumbled turning the page of sheet music but the slight delay only seemed to amuse Betsy. Their voices rose in harmony to a strong finish with the chorus.

'Bravo! Bravo!' Magdalena shouted.

Lavender pulled back his arm and applauded loudly. 'Encore!'

'Let's sing "None Can Love Like an Irish Man",' Woods suggested.

Betsy cast a glance at Magdalena. 'It's a tad bawdy,' she said.

'Please! Please sing it to me,' Magdalena said. 'I love your music. This is better than a night at the theatre.'

'Well, if you're sure.' Betsy smiled at the compliment. 'I don't need the music for this one,' she said and launched straight into the lively ditty.

'The turbaned Turk, who scorns the world,
May strut about with his whiskers curled,
Keep a hundred wives under lock and key,
For nobody else for himself to see;
Yet long may he pray with his Alcoran;
Before he can love like an Irishman.'

Betsy switched to a strong Irish accent for the second verse and Woods' booming voice joined her in the last line: 'Before he can love like an Irishman!'

Magdalena laughed and clapped her hands in time with the lively rhythm.

Emboldened by the Madeira, Lavender slid his arms around her slender waist and pulled her closer to him. She started with surprise but didn't resist. Meanwhile, the oblivious couple at the piano continued to belt out a rousing rendition of the popular song.

'The London folks themselves beguile,
And think they please in a capital style,
Yet let them ask as they cross the street,
Of any young virgin they happen to meet,
And I know she'll say, from behind her fan,
That there's none can love like an Irishman.'

It felt so good to have Magdalena's warm body next to his. She leant into Lavender and rested her head lightly on his shoulder. He felt her soft hair brush against his cheek, its sweet perfume intoxicating. He raised a hand and stroked the smooth skin of her face, brushing back a glossy tendril of silky hair that had escaped from her hairpins. Unable to resist, he kissed her lightly on the top of her head. She glanced up at him and smiled, a mischievous light dancing in her dark eyes. A wicked smile played against the edges of her lips. She knew the effect she had on him.

'Ehm, em.'

The music had stopped and Betsy was watching them quizzically from the piano stool. Beside her, his tipsy constable grinned from ear to ear and, unseen by his wife, he gave Lavender an exaggerated wink.

Magdalena saw it. She laughed, pulled away and smoothed down her gown. Lavender lifted his arm and rested it on the back of the sofa, above her shoulders.

'My apologies Betsy,' he said. 'Your music filled me with such passion that I couldn't help myself. I grabbed Doña Magdalena and I fear I may have compromised her.'

'Well, you can put her down now, you devilish rake,' Betsy said tartly. 'And try to behave yourself. The poor gal doesn't need to be pawed like that after a big meal.'

'Oh, I don't know,' said Woods. 'I think sir might have the right idea.' Before his diminutive wife could protest, he scooped her up off her stool and into his own lap. He screwed up his eyes, pursed his lips and tried to force a kiss on her. She wriggled, shrieked and pummelled his chest with her fists to keep him at bay.

'You great drunken fool!' she shouted. 'Now look what you've done, Stephen Lavender – you've set him off!'

Lavender and Magdalena burst out laughing. His arm encircled her waist once more and she made no effort to pull away. Betsy finally escaped Woods' clutches by beating him across the head with a rolled-up sheet of music.

'I think it may be time for us to go home, Stephen.' Magdalena's voice was husky, her skin still flushed and her pupils enlarged. Home. Home meant a cab ride with Magdalena – alone in the dark. He would pay the driver extra to take them the long, leisurely route back to her lodgings. The prospect excited him. Yes, it was time to leave.

Suddenly, the door opened and a slim, dark, pretty girl stood in the entrance. It was Elizabeth. Her quick eyes took in the scene and widened with surprise when she saw Magdalena sitting so close to Stephen, with his arm around her waist. A delighted smile spread across her young face. Magdalena shuffled nervously and tried to move away. Lavender relaxed his hold and reclaimed his arm.

Elizabeth grinned. 'I'm off home now, Betsy,' she said. 'The children are asleep.'

'Thank you, Elizabeth,' Betsy said. 'We're most grateful for your help tonight.'

'It sounded like you've had a wonderful time,' the young woman said. 'I heard the laughter and the music upstairs. And look at you, Stephen,' she added mischievously. 'It's not often we get to see you in your shirtsleeves with a woman by your side. Nice to meet you, ma'am.'

Magdalena nodded stiffly but didn't reply.

'Goodnight, Elizabeth,' Lavender said.

'Goodnight, everyone!' the girl called as she turned and left.

Magdalena rose to her feet and smoothed down her dress. They heard the front door slam. 'Well! Your nursemaid is rather forward,' Magdalena declared, indignantly. 'Is it normal for English servants to make such comments?'

Betsy laughed. 'Oh, that's not my nursemaid,' she said. 'That's Elizabeth – Stephen's youngest sister. I asked her to help keep the children out of our way tonight.'

'Now you can see why I was often tempted to murder my sisters.' Lavender smiled as he rose and fastened the buttons on his waistcoat.

'That was your sister?' Magdalena looked horrified.

'Yes, don't worry about it,' he said as he reached for his coat. 'Elizabeth is the best of the whole bunch.'

Magdalena clapped a hand to her mouth, her face contorted with distress. 'I'm so sorry, Betsy,' she wailed. 'I have embarrassed you; that was so rude of me. I have made a fool of myself and ruined the whole evening.'

'Nonsense! We have had a wonderful time, haven't we, Ned?' Betsy smiled, stepped across the room and gave Magdalena an affectionate hug. 'Please don't worry about it, my dear. I often get mistaken for a woman who has servants.'

The men laughed but Magdalena still looked inconsolable.

The journey home wasn't as Lavender had hoped. Magdalena resisted his attempts to pull her back into his arms when they took their seats in the cab.

'I'm tired, Stephen, and must return home to sleep. I have a busy day tomorrow – and a lesson to prepare for my Spanish class.'

Sighing, he sat back and examined her strained profile in the semi-darkness of the cab. She had no need to still be embarrassed about her comment, as Betsy was amused rather than insulted. Something else must be bothering her.

'Are you still upset by Elizabeth's sudden appearance?' he asked.

'Of course!' she snapped. 'What must she think of me! I was nearly sat in your lap. Such intimacy seemed fine with Betsy and Constable Woods – they know of our, of our friendship. But in front of a perfect stranger? Your unmarried younger sister? Thank goodness she didn't arrive a few moments earlier! No doubt she will go home and tell the rest of your family how she found us – so compromised.'

'Please don't worry about that,' he said. 'My mother is always telling me that I work too hard and need to have more fun.'

'Fun?'

He could have bitten his tongue off.

'Is that what I am to you, Stephen?' she yelled. 'A lewd squeeze in a darkened room? A bit of fun?' She half rose in the swaying vehicle and he thought for a minute that she might try to leap out of the moving carriage. He grabbed hold of her arm, pulled her back down but she shook him off.

'You're far more to me than that, Magdalena' he said firmly. 'And if you will give me some time, I will prove it to you. I'm incredibly fond of you – and my affection grows stronger by the day. What Elizabeth saw was just that, a demonstration of my affection. She will understand.'

Magdalena paused to consider his words but they didn't have the softening effect he had hoped. 'I doubt that your mother, a church dean's daughter, will see it that way,' she said icily.

'Trust me, Magdalena. I will make this right. I will send a note to Elizabeth tomorrow. I will tell her to say nothing to anyone else.'

'It is probably too late! My reputation is all I have left, Stephen.'

He nodded. Magdalena was right: it was her reputation that would suffer if they weren't more careful. He knew it was time for him to take action to resolve this situation and formalise their relationship. The awareness of this responsibility was sobering.

'In a while,' he said, 'we will laugh about what happened tonight. My mother is a kindly, loving woman – as you will discover when you eventually meet her. And she married my father for love.'

She seemed to stiffen at the suggestion. 'You seem so close,' she said. 'I never realised that Ned and Betsy Woods were familiar with your family.'

He sighed again. 'We law-keepers are not popular in London,' he said. 'As a result, the families of the Bow Street police tend to be close to each other and support each other as best we can.'

'It is a different world,' Magdalena said sadly. 'A world to which I do not belong.'

Despite his best efforts, she refused to speak for the rest of the journey home.

Chapter Twenty-one

Thursday 22nd February, 1810

Captain Brandon Sackville's long frame was sprawling in a chair opposite Magistrate Read's desk when Lavender finally appeared at their meeting. It was just after midday and Lavender knew he was late. Woods was already there, perched on another chair. When Read introduced him, the captain retracted his booted legs from where they had been stretched out in front of him, stood up and shook Lavender's hand.

'Your reputation precedes you, Detective Lavender.' He spoke slowly with the soft burr of a Devonshire accent. Even without his uniform he had the unmistakable bearing of a military officer.

'As does yours, Captain Sackville.' This was true. Still only in his late thirties, the blond, curly-haired naval officer had risen quickly through the naval ranks. He had an impressive reputation for leadership, navigational skill and bravery in battle. Briefly, Lavender wondered what had enticed him back on land to work in the fusty corridors of the Admiralty and Whitehall. The captain's slow, measured way of talking obviously masked considerable intelligence.

'You're late, Lavender,' Read said sharply.

'Yes, my apologies for that,' Lavender replied. 'I had some private business to attend to this morning which took longer than I expected.'

'Private business?' Read frowned with displeasure.

'Let's get down to the issue in hand, gentlemen,' said Sackville. He pulled out the innocuous sheet of paper that April Clare had found within her play script and spread it out on the desk. Lavender took the vacant chair beside him.

'I will come straight to the point,' Sackville said. 'The document that you have recovered is very worrying.'

'What is it, exactly?' Lavender asked.

'It didn't take our decoders long to work it out,' Sackville said. 'The code is amateurish but it's an alphabetical list of our fleet in the Indian Ocean. It gives their last known location with a few details about each ship's artillery capability. Some of the entries have the number and poundage of the canons on each deck.'

'That'll be why the *Victor* was at the bottom of the list,' said Woods. 'Because it's alphabetical.'

The other men glanced up and Sackville smiled. 'Exactly, Constable, and the fact that the *Victor* is mentioned suggests that the author of this document needed to update his reader that the *Victor* is no longer a British ship and is back in the hands of the French. They had a pattern to this code. I suspect that the author regularly provided this information.'

A shiver ran down the back of Lavender's neck at the implication of Sackville's last sentence. 'How much damage could this do to our fleet? Suppose we hadn't been able to intercept it, what would have happened if it had found its way into the hands of the French?'

Sackville shrugged his broad shoulders and flicked a speck of dust from the black velvet cuff of his burgundy coat. 'It's difficult to say. Our ships move around constantly, of course – unless they're laid up for repair – and it would have taken several weeks for this information to have landed in the hands of the French. But the Indian Ocean is vast and anything that gives a general idea of the whereabouts of our vessels to our enemies is something that causes the Admiralty concern.'

'Heaven and hell!' exclaimed Woods. He slapped his hand down hard on Read's desk and made them all jump. 'We've uncovered a bloody spy ring!'

Sackville smiled again. 'So it would seem, Constable.'

'What do you want us to do? Lavender asked.

'Well, it is quite obvious that someone at the Sans Pareil feeds information to our enemies,' Sackville said. 'As Constable Woods has said, we have a spy in our midst. The list accidentally became mixed up in Miss Clare's play script last Thursday and was missed by its owner virtually immediately. Less than a day later, her poor sister was kidnapped in an effort to retrieve this document. Somebody in that green room last Thursday night had a connection with this piece of paper. They had either put it on that table – or they had arranged to collect it from there. We need to find this spy.'

Lavender frowned. 'I shall obtain the names of everyone who was in the theatre last Thursday. Jane Scott, or her father, will be able to provide those easily enough but I suspect it will be a long list. There are not only the actors and actresses but also the stagehands to investigate – and possibly visitors . . .'

'Remember, Stephen,' Read warned, 'even Miss Scott and her father are suspects at this point of the investigation.'

Lavender's frown deepened. 'Yes, it will be a slow process to rule out everyone from our inquiries . . .' His voice trailed away as his mind explored other possibilities.

'Well, that would be a good place to begin,' Sackville said.

'Unless we took another approach to the investigation.'

'You've got that funny look in your eye,' Woods said to Lavender. 'Like you're about to hatch a plot.'

They all stared at Lavender in silence while he thought.

'Spit it out, man,' Read said, eventually. 'What are you thinking?'

'I'm concerned that if Bow Street officers investigate the cast and crew of the Sans Pareil, then we might scare off our quarry,' Lavender explained. 'If he gets wind of our investigation, he will be on the next boat to France before we can identify him.'

'That would be unfortunate,' Sackville said. 'We need to smash this operation and round up the perpetrators. Do you have a suggestion?'

'Yes, I think I do,' Lavender said slowly. The plan was still only half formed in his mind but it grew by the second. 'I think we need to flush out this infiltrator. Let him reveal himself to us.'

'That's assumin' the spy is a man, sir,' Woods said. 'From what I've learnt about women this week, I wouldn't be surprised if this sneaky budge wasn't a gal.' His face was rigid with indignation.

The other men stared at Woods. For a moment it looked like Read was about to ask Woods to explain his last comment but then the magistrate obviously thought better of the idea. He turned back to Lavender. 'How do you propose to do this, Lavender?' he asked. 'How will you flush out him – or her?'

'I'm not quite sure just yet; I need to think some more. But I do believe that it might be time for the dead actress, Miss April Divine, to rise up from the ashes like a phoenix.'

Lavender sensed the stony atmosphere between the two women as soon as he was shown into the late Mrs Willoughby's drawing room in Wandsworth. Swathed in their organza mourning gowns, Lady Caroline and April Clare sat stiff-backed and silent on opposite sofas by the fire like a pair of black-ash bookends. Their forced intimacy had taken its toll on their fragile relationship. Both looked angry, as if they had been arguing.

Relief flashed across Lady Caroline's face when the maid announced Lavender.

'Oh, Detective Lavender – thank goodness you're here! We had begun to think that you had forgotten about us.' The jewels in her rings flashed as she offered him her hand.

He raised it to his lips. 'How can any man forget about you, Lady Caroline?' he said, smiling.

'You must be serious, Lavender,' she admonished. 'We have a lot to discuss.' But a faint pink spot had appeared on her high cheekbones.

He turned to April Clare and bowed politely. She didn't offer her hand and appeared to be further angered by his banter with her stepmother. April's pretty face darkened.

'We have done as you asked,' Lady Caroline said. She waved him over to the empty chair he had occupied the day before. He sat down. 'We have arranged a quiet and discreet funeral for poor Harriet tomorrow morning. And I have written to Captain Willoughby – and his lawyer here in England – to apprise him of the sad news of the death of his wife.'

'Quiet and discreet!' snapped Miss Clare. 'You have notified half of London!' She turned angrily to Lavender. 'I had to stop her placing an announcement in *The Times*, Detective!'

'It is only fitting,' Lady Caroline wailed. 'Poor Harriet was the daughter of a baron! It is terrible to have to make her funeral such a cloak-and-dagger affair!'

'It would be even more terrible if the kidnappers discovered their mistake and came after me again! You might as well place an announcement that Miss April Clare is still alive – come to Wandsworth and kill her now!'

'Really, April!' Lady Caroline said, exasperated. 'I begin to think that you don't care one jot about what has happened to poor Harriet – all I hear from you is concern for yourself.'

'Now, now, ladies,' Lavender said quickly. 'I have some good news – and a plan – which I think might help.' Both women turned to stare at him. April Clare still looked like she would explode with anger but she remained silent.

'There has been a development,' he said. He took the list out of his coat pocket and laid it on the occasional table beside the actress. 'I now know what this document contains, and yes, I have to report that it is as serious as I suspected.'

'Good grief!' Lady Caroline said. 'You mean it is classified naval information?'

'Yes, and I have no doubt that Mrs Willoughby was kidnapped in an attempt to retrieve this piece of paper – and your lodgings, Miss Clare, were ransacked for the same reason.' The actress paled and she sank back in her chair as if to put as much distance between the document and herself as possible.

'However, I have a plan, which, if it works, will mean that the kidnappers leave you alone for good – and will allow you to resume your life.' April Clare sat up straighter, tilted her head and listened.

'It is time, Miss Clare, for April Divine to rise from the ashes of death and strut the boards of the stage of the Sans Pareil once more.'

Lady Caroline gave a short laugh. 'The detective plans to resurrect you like Lazarus,' she said. 'How intriguing! Do tell us more.'

Carefully, Lavender explained the plan he had worked out earlier with Sackville, Read and Woods.

Chapter Twenty-two

Thursday 22nd February, 1810

Despite his wife's instruction that he was to remain objective when dealing with the fascinating Spanish *señora*, Magistrate Read allowed himself a moment or two to appreciate Doña Magdalena's elegance and beauty when she glided into his office. He could understand why Stephen Lavender was so besotted with the damned woman. She was stunningly attractive, with a curvaceous figure, a flawless golden complexion and wide, luminous eyes fringed with long dark lashes. Glossy black ringlets and curls framed her pretty face and intelligence shone in her eyes. She appeared to be in her mid-twenties but he knew that she had an eight-year-old son away at boarding school so he suspected she was probably a little older, possibly in her late twenties – a year or two younger than Lavender. He cleared his throat, bade her take a seat and tried to force his mind back onto the business that lay ahead.

'Thank you for the teaching position, Magistrate Read.' Magdalena smiled at him like an old friend, and revealed two perfect rows of small, pearly teeth. 'And I have to confess that I'm intrigued by the mention in your note of the confidential matter we needed to discuss.'

Her English was excellent, Read noted. Her voice was deep and her accent slight. He was due in court in twenty minutes and was wearing his wig and sombre black gown. Most people found his official garb intimidating but not Doña Magdalena, it seemed. The woman was obviously made of strong stuff. *Let's see if you're still smiling in ten minutes, madam*, Read thought.

'Does Detective Lavender know you're here in my office at this moment?'

Her smile dropped from her lips and was replaced by a slight look of confusion. 'No. You said in your note that this was a confidential matter; I felt it wise to tell no one of our appointment. As you can see, I have even travelled without my maid.'

Good, she has passed the first test, at least.

'I will come straight to the point, Doña Magdalena,' he said. 'I may have another proposition to put to you, which may be more lucrative than Spanish lessons.' Her dark eyebrows arched upwards. 'However, first, we need to discuss your politics.'

She gave a short, surprised laugh. 'My politics?'

'Yes, madam, I'm curious about where your sympathies lie. Are you an Absolutionist, a Liberal, a Godoyista or a Fernadista? Speak plainly.'

'I tended to leave matters of state to my late husband,' she said warily.

'Yes, I'm well aware that Señor Garcia de Aviles had political ambition. But surely you had an opinion of your own, an intelligent woman like yourself? I understand that you had an uncle in one of the Cortes Generales. Politics is in the lifeblood of your family. You can't be immune to it.'

Magdalena's face registered surprise and her eyes flitted to the innocuous dun-coloured folder that lay on Read's desk beneath his folded hands. 'I see that you're well informed about my background, Magistrate Read,' she said slowly. The thought didn't seem to alarm her. 'Yes, Antonio was ambitious. My family's political connections were part of the attraction when his father approached my father about our marriage.'

'Your marriage was arranged?'

'Of course.'

Her calmness with the convention of an arranged marriage was unnerving. It sounded so cold, unemotional and alien to him. However, when he allowed his memory to return to the hazy days of his own courtship and marriage to Charity he was vaguely aware that he had little to do with it. He remembered mentioning to his mother that Miss Charity Gilroy had a pretty smile and nice eyes and the next moment he was betrothed. Charity and his mother had 'arranged' everything between them – even their introduction in that ballroom. He suspected that he wasn't the first man to be waltzed into a marriage he didn't see coming. But he took comfort that such a strong affection had grown up between him and Charity over the years; he knew they had an amicable and supportive relationship.

'Were you happily married?' This had nothing to do with her politics, of course but he was curious.

She waved an elegant gloved hand in the air, dismissively. 'We were as content as any other married couple in the world, Magistrate. Antonio was a kind husband, if a little distant. We spent the first few years of our marriage in Madrid. After our son, Sebastián, was born, I lived quietly with Antonio's parents on their estate near Oviedo. My own father was dying and I needed to be close to him at that time. Antonio was often away in Madrid. After Sebastián was sent away to school, I found it too quiet and dull in the country. I wasn't happy; I missed the excitement of the city and I missed my son.

'I went briefly to Madrid but the capital was now a dangerous place. Bonaparte imprisoned our foolish king and put his own brother on the Spanish throne; riots and mutinies broke out all over the country – especially in Madrid. I had only just left the city when Murat's cavalry trampled thousands of innocent men, women and children in the streets and shot to death thousands of others. It was carnage.'

'How did you feel about these events?'

'How did I feel?' she snapped. Her face flushed with anger. 'How does any right-minded person feel about such acts of atrocity?' she demanded. 'But I had a foreboding that things would go wrong from the moment our inept government and foolish king allowed Bonaparte and his French dogs to march across our land to invade Portugal. Even I, a mere woman, could see that this would be a disaster. It was only a matter of time before the despotic tyrant and his dogs turned around to bite us.'

'I see you have no love for the French, Doña Magdalena. But do you hold any particular affection for your deposed kings and Godoy?'

'No, none. You asked me earlier which faction of Spanish politics I favoured,' she said. 'I think I can answer your question now: none of them. You would probably call me a realistic, Magistrate Read, rather than a devoted follower of one group or other. My main concern has always been the safety of my son. His future wellbeing and happiness were placed in danger by the foolish actions of our leaders. Of course, Antonio immediately allied himself with the rebels. He fought against the French at the battle of Bailén and glorified in our Spanish victory. He also allied himself with the Cádiz Cortes, the government in exile.'

'My sources tell me that Don Antonio was quite vocal in his opposition to the French invasion of your country and earned a well-deserved reputation for gallantry and bravery in battle. That must be of some comfort to you.'

She looked anything but comforted. A tendril of hair had escaped from her pins. She angrily pushed it back up into her bonnet. 'In an occupied country, reputations for gallantry in battle impress men and silly young girls,' she said. 'They do not protect the terrified wives and children left back at home at the mercy of the invaders.'

This was a perspective that he had never considered before and he suspected that it wasn't one that entered the thoughts of most Englishmen or women. After all, they had not been invaded by the French. Well, not yet anyway. Every coastal town and port in Britain was on high alert.

'What happened to your family?' Read asked.

Magdalena sighed and lowered her head. For a moment Read thought she would refuse to tell him. It didn't really matter. He already knew most of the details of her flight from Spain. British foreign operatives regularly updated the Home Department with information about influential Spaniards like Antonio Garcia de Aviles. He had already heard rumours that Magdalena had shot her way out of the country.

Then Magdalena raised her face and stared straight into Read's eyes. 'As the numbers of French soldiers in Spain increased, the rumours of French reprisals against the families of the revolutionaries became worse. Whole families disappeared overnight or were hanged, their homes and land razed to the ground. I became scared for Sebastián, Antonio's parents and myself. I pleaded with Antonio to arrange us passage to the safety of England but he refused. We weren't to desert our home, he said. We were quite safe on our remote estate. But I wasn't convinced.' Her voice rose as she relayed her frustration.

'Eventually, I decided to act. I arranged the passage to England for Sebastián and myself. I pleaded with Antonio's parents to come with us, but they refused. They never questioned the judgement of their brilliant son; they never thought for one moment that his conspicuous, outspoken opposition to Joseph Bonaparte might endanger his family.

'On the morning Sebastián and I were due to leave, Antonio's parents were away visiting his sister. We had packed the carriage and were about to depart when four French soldiers rode up the drive.'

'What happened?'

'We opened fire on them; they were killed. I had already armed my servants and we had the element of surprise. The French had not expected resistance from a woman, a child and two old people.'

'Did you take part in the shooting?'

'Of course I did. I was fighting for my life,' she said. Her large eyes were expressionless but he thought he saw a slight tremor in her lower lip. 'I have a pistol and my father had trained me to be an excellent markswoman. We left immediately, raced like the wind to the coast and I arranged the passage to England for Sebastián, Teresa and myself.'

They regarded each other across the desk. She twisted her hands nervously in her lap, pulling at the material of her gown. He realised that she was trying to assess the impact of her confession and, despite his reservations, Read felt a pang of sympathy for the woman. He had convicted many heartless female murderers in his courtroom over the years and Magdalena Morales was not of their ilk. She had been forced to kill in order to save her own life and that of her child. He recognised the difference and sensed her remorse and fear. Her composure was a thin veneer beneath which she was scared and probably wracked with guilt.

'Does Stephen Lavender know about this?' he asked.

'I think he suspects the truth – and he knows that I can shoot to kill.'

He frowned. This was a new development. 'Is this something to do with the highwaymen who attacked your coach at Barnby Moor?' He heard the alarm in his own voice.

'Yes, Stephen's pistol had jammed and one of the highwaymen was about to discharge his shot into Stephen's face. I shot the villain through the temple.'

'Good grief, I had no idea.' Agitated, Read's hands picked up and smoothed back the feathers on his quill while his mind churned over with this latest information. No wonder Lavender was infatuated with the woman if he owed her his life.

'You think that I'm unnatural? That I'm unwomanly?' Her beautiful eyes bored into his across the table. 'You must understand, Magistrate Read, that I will do anything to protect my son. Even commit a cardinal sin like murder.'

He shuffled uneasily in his chair. The longcase clock in the corner of the room gently chimed the quarter hour and reminded him of the case he was due to judge downstairs in the court. He brought the conversation back to its intended purpose. One thing was for sure: this woman was more than suitable for the job he had in mind.

'Well, I must thank you, Doña Magdalena, for the service you have already given to the British Crown when you saved the life of Detective Lavender. His loss to Bow Street Magistrates' Court would have been a great blow – at both a personal and a professional level.'

Magdalena nodded, her eyes narrow. Flattery and charm would be wasted on her. He needed to keep the conversation businesslike.

'As I mentioned earlier I have a proposition to put to you that might prove lucrative in addition to your teaching. Your son is at an expensive boarding school, I understand?'

She nodded again. 'It was the only one that would overlook his religion and accept him.'

His mention of her son had been well timed; he had her undivided attention and she looked less hostile now.

'Do you regularly mix with the other Spanish émigrés who have fled to England? I understand that you Catholics are a closed group.'

'Sometimes. Sometimes I meet other Spaniards or are invited into their homes. Unfortunately, some of them are wary of me because of the rumours of how I escaped to England.'

'Yes, I can understand that,' Read said with feeling. 'However, you may still be able to help us. The British government is concerned about the proliferation of French spies in London – we worry that some of the Spanish émigrés may be feeding information back to the French.'

Magdalena gasped in surprise. 'But we fight side by side against Joseph Bonaparte on the battlefields!'

'Not all of your fellow countrymen and women appreciate the support given by Sir Arthur Wellesley and his army,' Read said. 'And not all of them hate the French with the same passion as you do, Doña Magdalena. There are many who are sick and tired of a war that causes economic devastation to Spain and they would like peace at any cost, even if it means submitting to the yolk of the Bonapartes. The British and Spanish alliance against the French can be uneasy at times and it is important that we know whom we can trust.' He pulled out a piece of paper from the file on his desk and laid it face down. Read saw curiosity flit across Magdalena's face.

'This is a list of Spaniards who live in London and who have come to the attention of our Home Department for one reason or another.'

She gave him a slow smile. 'If you want me to assassinate them, Magistrate Read, then I'm sorry to disappoint you. I only shoot in self-defence.'

He glanced up sharply and saw the self-mocking smile on her lips. 'Such a thought never entered my mind, Doña Magdalena,' he said. 'No, we would simply like you to report back to us about them. We would like to hear about any opinions they express, the company they keep and any journeys they plan to make.'

'You want me to spy on them?'

'In short, yes. We would like to hear about everything they do and say, even what they eat for breakfast.'

She was thoughtful for a moment. 'If you think that this would help the war in Spain come to a speedier conclusion, then I will assist you. Please show me the list.'

'There are two final things I need to insist upon before I show you the list. Firstly, this conversation needs to remain confidential. Nobody must know that you're helping us in this way,' he continued, 'Especially Stephen Lavender.'

For a moment, he thought he saw doubt flash across her face. But then she nodded. Read wasn't entirely sure how Lavender would react to Magdalena's involvement in espionage, but he suspected that he wouldn't be pleased. Read had been surprised by the stubbornness his usually genial detective had shown concerning this woman and by the icy-cold glint that had set in Lavender's eyes when Read had dared to criticise their liaison.

'And the other thing is that I think you should tell Detective Lavender the truth about your escape from Spain. He deserves your honesty.' Magdalena's beautiful eyes narrowed and clouded with alarm. 'If you don't tell him, then I'm afraid I must.' She swallowed, and nodded again.

That might bring the man back to his senses and dampen his ardour, Read thought with a small glow of satisfaction.

Satisfied that Magdalena would comply with his terms, Read turned over the paper. A large smile illuminated her face as she read the names spread out before her.

'Oh, I think I will be able to help you, Magistrate Read,' she said slowly. 'Now, how much did you say that you intended to pay me for this service?'

Chapter Twenty-three

The Sans Pareil Theatre was different in the daylight, Lavender realised – it was less magical. The porter had told him that the cast were in rehearsal but had allowed him to enter anyway. He walked unobserved into the back of the stalls. The company used fewer candles to light the auditorium for a rehearsal and as a result the upper circle, the boxes and the far corners of the vast chamber were shrouded in shadow, the gilded, ornamental carvings dulled. As the actors and actresses strutted across the stage, they seemed smaller and more insignificant without their elaborate costumes and garish make-up. With no soft-bodied audience to absorb the noise, Lavender was now conscious of the thud of each booted footstep across the hallowed boards and the actors' booming voices echoing around the empty stalls and boxes of the auditorium.

Jane Scott had seated herself in the third row of the stalls. A dark blue turban held back her wiry hair; a flowered overdress covered her dark gown. She had kicked off her shoes and sat cross-legged, peeling an orange while directing her actors at the same time. 'Good heavens, Bill! Do you have a memory in that head of yours?' she demanded as one of the actors forgot his lines again.

'Sorry, Miss Scott!' Bill called down off the stage cheerfully.

'Oh, do us all a favour and shake out some of the sawdust that's between your ears then,' she replied acidly. The rest of the cast laughed.

Jane Scott clapped her hands to get their attention again. 'Now, now,' she said sternly. 'Let's try to finish this act and work together, shall we?'

The actors redid the scene, word-perfect. Lavender smiled. Jane Scott ran a tight ship. He stood and watched for a while as the act jerked awkwardly towards its finale.

'I suppose that this will have to do for now.' Jane Scott sighed. 'Let's break for some refreshment and I hope that you return more alert than you have been this morning.'

Lavender saw his opportunity and assuming a cold professional attitude, he walked towards her.

'Detective!' She rose to her feet and wiped her orange-juice-soaked hands on her gown. 'What a surprise. Have you more news about poor April?'

'Yes,' he said, not returning her smile. 'May we talk in private?'

She led him back to the same office where they had talked on his last visit. The smell was as cloying as it had been last time he visited the dark, narrow, backstage corridors. Lavender's ears caught the hum of conversation and laughter from the actors in the green room. It was directly in front of him at the end of the corridor. The door was open and he could see the table against the far wall where April Clare had put down her play script. Good. This would make Woods' role easier.

Once in the privacy of the office, Jane Scott removed a dusty pile of folded velvet curtains, and a jester's hat complete with jingling bells, from the only chair in the room. She sat down gracefully, smoothed her gown and folded her hands primly in her lap. 'How can I help you, Detective Lavender?'

'I have some good news – and two pieces of bad news for you, Miss Scott.'

Her hand fluttered to her bosom and her face whitened and emphasised the outline of the smallpox scars beneath her powder. She blinked up at him. 'Oh dear. Perhaps I should hear the good news first to cushion the blow?'

'Very well. The good news is that your actress, Miss April Divine, is not dead.' He paused to let the full impact of his words sink into the startled brain of the shocked woman. She gasped, gave a short laugh, shook her head in disbelief and asked him to repeat himself.

'Miss Divine is not dead. But alas, her identical twin sister, Mrs Willoughby, is. That is the first piece of bad news. Where you aware that Miss Divine had a twin sister?' he asked.

Speechless, sheshook her head.

'It was a natural mistake to make when the surgeon examined Mrs Willoughby,' he continued. 'He didn't know that Miss Divine had a twin either, and he assumed that he was examining the body of the famous actress.'

'Quite,' Jane Scott spluttered. She took a deep breath and blurted out her next few sentences. 'This is wonderful news. I'm so pleased that dear April is still alive – but it's distressing to hear about her sister. Where is poor April now?'

'Miss Divine is very upset. She has been staying with her stepmother, Lady Caroline. The funeral takes place tomorrow morning but she hopes to return to work for Saturday night's performance of *The Necromancer*.'

'Of course, of course,' she said. Frown lines suddenly appeared above her thin eyebrows. 'Poor April,' she said, thoughtfully.

'My second piece of bad news concerns this,' he said. He pulled the crumpled news-sheet out of his pocket and placed it face down on the table between them. He smoothed it out until the headline, *Actress*

Brutally Slain, was visible. 'As it turns out, poor Mrs Willoughby died from natural causes and – of course – she's not an actress. Somebody was ill-informed when they spoke to the newspaper.'

'Ah.' Guilt flashed across her features.

'Yes,' he said sternly. 'The paper will need to print a retraction. The story you gave them was incorrect.'

She flushed with embarrassment and gathered up the offending news-sheet. 'Of course, Detective, of course. I will contact the reporter today. I will make sure that the newspaper prints an amendment in tomorrow's edition.'

A tiny paragraph at the bottom of the page, no doubt, Lavender thought.

'That would be one approach to take,' he said, slowly. 'However, there is another way to undo the damage of that premature article and further the interests of the theatre at the same time.'

'There is?'

'You have been most fortunate.'

'I have?'

He paused for a moment to let her dangle on his hook for a bit longer. 'Yes, Miss Divine has come up with an idea which may help the Sans Pareil and alleviate any problems caused by your mistake.' Her eyes were alert, attentive and fixed on his. 'Miss Divine has suggested that you allow the news-sheet to make a big story about her miraculous resurrection. She feels that it would only enhance her career – and increase attendance at her performances in the theatre – if they reported the full story about how she was assumed to be dead.'

Jane Scott's eyes lit up and she clapped her hands together in glee. 'Of course! What a clever girl April is! The news-sheet will sell out in a matter of hours with a story like that on the front page – and so shall we! The actress who rose from the grave will become the talk of London. They will flock to see her performances!'

Lavender hid his smile and let her enjoy her moment. The queen of the lurid melodrama stood up and paced the floor of the office, her mind bursting with ideas. 'We will have to give April a part in *Mary, the Maid of the Inn*,' she said. 'I shall organise a reception to be held in the green room for her return on Saturday night.'

'There is one last thing, Miss Scott,' he said. 'Although Mrs Willoughby died from natural causes, we're still not happy about the other circumstances of her death.'

'No? Oh yes – that dreadful place where she was found. Yes, I can understand that, Detective.'

'As a result, we have decided to provide Miss Divine with some discreet protection for a short while. I would appreciate it if you would allow one of my constables into the theatre under the pretence that he's a labourer, in order that he can watch out for Miss Divine's safety.'

'Certainly, Detective. I'm more than happy to help in any way I can.'

'No one must know that he's a policeman.'

'Of course not, you have my word. I shall be discreet.'

Lavender stared at her smiling face and was tempted to say something cutting, but he held back. If their plan was to succeed he needed the cooperation of Jane Scott. He needed her to weave her influence with the news-sheet reporter, whom he hoped would maximise the sensation about April Clare's return to the theatre and inflame the public's imagination. It was important to his scheme that by Saturday most of London was talking about the actress, April Divine. He needed the whole city to know and marvel about the fact that she had risen from the dead and was returning to the Sans Pareil for Saturday evening's performance. Despite any nagging doubts he still harboured about this female theatre owner, he recognised that he needed Jane Scott's skills and her flair for publicity.

Lavender decided to call at the language school and see Magdalena before he returned to Bow Street.

No one received him as he entered the deserted hallway of the dilapidated non-descript building on Hart Street. He heard the low murmur of voices from one of the rooms; the unmistakable chant of students declining French plural and singular nouns. But apart from this and the muffled noise of the traffic outside, the place was eerily quiet.

He knew from his own lessons that the Spanish classrooms were on the second floor and he ascended the narrow, wooden staircase. When he turned the corner on the first-floor landing, his face broke out in a grin. Above him, he heard the unmistakable sound of Magdalena berating her students.

'No, no, no!' she shouted. She accompanied each syllable by rapping a wooden stick across the top of a table with a sharp thwack. 'Pay attention! The *ser* and *estar* verbs are different. Both are the same as the English verb: "to be." Both *soy* or *estoy* mean "I am" – but you use them in different circumstances. Try again. *Estoy viajando a Madrid* – I am journeying to Madrid.'

He heard a deep chorus of male voices repeat: '*Estoy viajando Madrid.*'

'*Tu estas viajando a Madrid,*' she said. 'You are going to Madrid.'

'*Tu estas viajando a Madrid,*' echoed her students.

The door to the classroom was ajar. Lavender paused outside and watched Magdalena. She stood in front of a blackboard mounted on a portable wooden frame. Teresa sat on a stool, needlework in hand, beside a cheerful fire burning in the grate on the opposite wall. There were no drapes at the tall, rectangular windows, no carpet on the bare floorboards and the walls were plain and dirty. But at least the room was warm. Magdalena had taken off her coat and rolled up the sleeves of her dress for the lesson, revealing the smooth golden skin of her arms. In front of her, four men sat bolt upright around an ink-stained table, their parchment, quills and slate tablets scattered across the surface. Several of the men had also removed their coats and slung them over the back of their chairs. Magdalena had a pointed stick in one elegant hand, which she waved in time to the rhythm of her carefully articulated Castellano.

No one noticed Lavender's arrival. Everyone was focused on Magdalena; the men hung on every word that fell from her soft lips. He smiled when he realised that after the ponderous teaching of Professor Quincy, Magdalena's arrival must have been like a breath of fragrant air to these men – or possibly, quite a shock. He recognised two of the older operatives: Williams and MacDonald. Williams seemed less keen to join in with the verb chanting than MacDonald, who was concentrating hard. Lavender had only had a brief acquaintance with both of them. These men had spent their lives in the shadows of Europe, flitting quietly in and out of one country or another at the bidding of the government. They were shadows themselves: glimpsed today, invisible tomorrow.

But at the moment, they were ordinary men struggling to keep up with the quick brain, quick tongue and even quicker stick-brandishing right wrist of the feisty Magdalena Morales.

One of the men stumbled over his pronunciation and received a sharp rap across his knuckles for his mistake. Startled, he yelped and drew back his hand. But he didn't make the same mistake twice; the next time his pronunciation was flawless. Lavender had to stop himself from laughing out loud as MacDonald earned himself a swipe across the back of his hand. At this rate, Magdalena would to earn herself the reputation as the best whip-hand in Covent Garden, which would be a considerable achievement in an area dominated by at least four notorious and exotic 'ladies' who charged a fortune for flogging their customers.

'*Estoy viajando a Madrid!*' she said. 'I am journeying to Madrid. *Tu estas viajando* – you are journeying to Madrid. Remember: it's a journey, not a permanent situation.'

'I never realised that *soy* and *estoy* are so different,' moaned one of her younger students.

Magdalena nodded. '"*Yo soy Doña Magdalena*" means "I am Doña Magdalena" – forever. It is my permanent state. This is why we use *estar* and not *ser* to ask after someone's health or where-abouts. "*Como está*" means "how is he?" or "*donde está*" means "where is he?" – at this *precise* moment. Now, Mr Williams, shall we try again?'

The man named Williams shuffled in his seat and cleared his throat. '*Yo soy Señor Williams y soy viajando a Madrid.*'

'No!' The stick crashed down on the table again. '*Estoy viajando a Madrid!*'

'But I *am* Señor Williams – and I am the person travelling to Madrid,' the man protested, frowning. 'I won't change on the way like Saul on the road to Damascus.' The other men guffawed. 'At least, I don't expect to.'

Magdalena sighed. 'I think you have missed the point, Señor Williams. You are not going to be travelling to Madrid forever and ever – it is not a permanent situation.' She sighed. 'Perhaps we should leave it there for today, and try again tomorrow.'

There was an audible sigh of relief and the tension lifted. The men pushed back their chairs and reached for their coats. Magda-lena stood back and waited for them to leave. Meanwhile, Teresa also rose to her feet and packed up Magdalena's papers.

'My! How parched is my throat?' said one of the younger men loudly. 'Is your throat parched, Doña Magdalena? I think I shall retire to the coffee house on Garrick Street for a beverage. Would you care to accompany me?'

'Oh, aye?' MacDonald said. The other men laughed and encouraged the youngster. Someone whistled. Lavender felt his right hand clench into a fist.

'May I purchase you a cup of chocolate, Doña Magdalena?' the young man asked.

Everyone turned to the blushing Magdalena for a reaction; she appeared to be lost for words. Lavender decided that it was time to make his presence known.

'Stephen!' she exclaimed in surprise when he stepped into the room. Magdalena looked pleased to see him.

'Good afternoon, Lavender,' MacDonald drawled in his familiar Scots accent. He shook Lavender's hand. 'What on earth brings a Bow Street detective to our fusty little school? They're not sending you back to Cadiz, are they?'

'Good afternoon, MacDonald,' he replied. 'No, I'm here to see Doña Magdalena. I wish to talk to her for a moment.'

'Oh, aye?' MacDonald said, and grinned across to his teacher. 'You can wait your turn,' he drawled. 'There's a few of us that would care to know this wee lass a bit more.' Then his face became serious. He made a short bow in Magdalena's direction. 'It has been a pleasure, lassie,' he said. 'I have learnt more from you this afternoon than I have in the last month with old Quincy.'

MacDonald gestured to the younger man who had propositioned Magdalena and who was now scowling at the back of the room, desperate to get Magdalena alone. 'Come on, Barrington. I'll gan with you to the coffee house on Garrick Street – it would seem that Doña Magdalena has a prior appointment.' He waved for Barrington to leave the room. 'Away, laddie.' For a moment it looked like the young man would stubbornly remain to press his suit on Magdalena but Lavender gave him a glowering stare and the Romeo finally retreated.

'The lesson seems to have gone well,' Lavender said once the door was closed behind them.

Magdalena's eyes gleamed. 'Oh, Stephen, I have really enjoyed myself. It isn't easy – but I felt so, so challenged. It was such fun and I feel that I have been useful.'

'I can understand that.' He smiled, pleased to see her in such a good mood after the upset of the night before. 'MacDonald seemed impressed by your teaching.'

'He's the most accomplished,' she said. 'His accent is excellent. I must go straight home, though. There is much preparation I need to do for tomorrow's lesson.'

'Of course,' he said. 'I merely stopped by to ask how you were.'

'That was most considerate of you, Stephen.' She gave him a brilliant smile.

'I also wondered if you wanted to accompany me to the funeral of Mrs Willoughby tomorrow morning. I know that Lady Caroline would appreciate the gesture and see it as a kindness.'

'Of course!' Concern flashed across her face mixed with a little guilt. 'I had quite forgotten about poor Lady Caroline and her sad loss. Yes, of course I will go with you, Stephen. What time?'

'I will call for you at nine o'clock in the morning. Afterwards, I would like you to accompany me somewhere else. I want to show you something.'

'Show me what?' Her dark eyes widened with curiosity. 'Where are you taking me?'

'It's a surprise,' he said, smiling. 'You will see tomorrow.'

Chapter Twenty-four

Magistrate Read, Captain Sackville and Constable Woods were waiting for Lavender back at Bow Street.

'How did it go?' Sackville asked.

'Perfectly,' Lavender replied. 'Miss Clare is excited at the prospect of returning to her old life and keen to cooperate with our plan. I have left the shipping list with her. She will put it back into the folds of her play script and leave the whole manuscript on the table in the green room when she returns to work on Saturday night.' He turned to Woods and smiled. 'You start your new job as a caretaker at the theatre at ten o'clock in the morning.'

Woods nodded and grinned.

'You have done well, Lavender,' Read said.

'Yes.' Sackville laughed. 'Yes, this bacon-brained scheme might actually work.'

Lavender pulled another sheet of paper out from his inside coat pocket. 'It's worth trying,' he said. 'In the meantime, Miss Scott has made me a list of all the actors, actresses, workers and visitors whom she remembers were present backstage at the theatre last Thursday night.' He handed it over to Read.

'Did she ask why you needed such a list?' Sackville stood up and walked behind the magistrate's chair in order to read the document over his shoulder.

'Yes, but I said I couldn't explain at the moment. She accepted this and promised to be discreet. I thought such information might be useful but Jane Scott has no idea whether the list is comprehensive or not.'

'Well, it is something to start with,' Sackville said. 'I'll take it now, thank you, Magistrate Read, and hand it over to the Home Department.'

Read didn't look up. He continued to scan the list Lavender had provided. 'I wonder what the Earl of Thornaby was doing backstage that night?' he said. 'Freddy has never struck me as a follower of culture and the arts.'

'Miss Scott told me that Lord Thornaby is enamoured with the beautiful singing voice of Miss Helene Bologna, their Italian actress,' Lavender said. 'I understand that he hovers by the stage door at the theatre most nights hoping for an audience with the lady.'

'And Baron Marsdon?'

Lavender hesitated. Lord Nicolas Marsdon was a judge at the Old Bailey and also an old friend of Read's. 'The same,' he said.

Read looked up in alarm. 'The same woman?'

'Yes.'

'Good grief! I wonder if his wife, Fanny, knows about this infatuation.'

'Not if he has any sense,' Woods said, wisely.

Read leant across the desk towards the constable. 'Make sure that you take care of your morality while you're working in this den of iniquity, Woods,' Read said suddenly. He had two pink spots on his cheeks and Lavender realised that he was rattled by the news that a respected friend and colleague was behaving like a moonstruck calf over a foreign actress. 'The place seems to be riddled with vice and sin festers within those walls like a putrefy-ing sore. Those women are sirens, Ned. They have silken tongues and are skilled dissemblers. Don't let them draw you into their sinful, ways.'

Woods' eyes were round as saucers. 'I'll do my best, sir,' he said.

'Remember, you, too, have a wife.'

''Tis hard to forget that at times, sir.'

Smiling, Sackville gently eased the list out from beneath Read's hand. 'I will take this now and the Home Department will begin discreet inquiries into the people mentioned here. Did you remem-ber to add Miss Scott and her father onto the list, Lavender?'

'Yes,' Lavender said. 'There is one more thing, however.'

The other men glanced up.

'Spit it out then, Stephen,' Read snapped. He was still upset about Baron Marsdon.

'You may have noticed that the Duke of Clarence and his party were also at the show on that night, and, as is their custom, they went backstage to congratulate the cast.'

'So?' Read's voice cut through the shocked silence like ice. 'What is the point you're making?'

The other men were rooted to the spot. Lavender saw concern etched across Woods' features. Time seemed to stand still. Lavender chose his next words carefully.

'We're looking for members of a spy ring that passes on naval information to the French. We can't overlook the fact that because of his position as admiral in the navy, His Royal Highness, Prince William – and his staff – are privy to some extremely sensitive infor-mation.'

Woods whistled low under his breath.

Magistrate Read almost choked on his words. 'Good God, Lav-ender!' he spluttered. 'This is the second time in two days that you have dared to make slanderous and treasonous comments about a member of the royal family! Do you dare to suggest that the king's own son is a traitor and is passing on secrets to the French?'

'Of course not,' Lavender said.

But Read hadn't heard him and continued to rage. 'Are you aware of the enormity of what you're implying? You're an officer of the law, for God's sake! Sworn to protect this realm! Even thinking such a thing about a member of the royal household could – and should – land you in the Tower!'

Lavender's voice was calm and measured. 'I'm merely pointing out that we seek someone in this nest of vipers who has a naval connection – and because of the gravity of the situation, I don't think we can afford to dismiss anyone whose name appears on this list of potential suspects; nobility or commoners.'

'If such an accusation against the Duke of Clarence were even whispered abroad,' Read warned, 'it could bring down the House of Hanover! Last summer the press was full of rumours that the jezebel, Mrs Mary Anne Clark, had used her sexual influence over the Duke of York when she was his mistress to secure army commissions for money. How much more do you think the British public will take? Do you want to see our country ripped apart by revolution like the French? Shall there be guillotines in Hyde Park to decapitate the royal household? Do you wish to see the rise of British despots like Bonaparte?' Read paused dramatically while the other men absorbed his words.

'I just want to get to the bottom of why an innocent woman was kidnapped and scared to death in a freezing, derelict building, miles from her home and loved ones,' Lavender said. 'I want justice for Harriet Willoughby – and yes, I will take that at any cost. I have sworn to uphold the law, not the House of Hanover.'

'We all want justice for the damned woman!' Read yelled. 'But you go too far sometimes, Lavender.'

'Do I?' Lavender said. 'Well, to be honest, my instincts tell me that Prince William is not involved.'

'Well, thank God for that!' Read snapped.

There was a short silence. The relief in the room was palpable. Sackville and Woods had watched the angry exchange between the two men like the spectators at a tennis match, their heads turning from one player to the other, their mouths gaping open.

Now Lavender pointed at the list in Sackville's hand. 'However, I wouldn't trust Sir Lawrence Forsyth, as far as I can toss the poisonous little dwarf.'

'Bit of a whiddler, is he, sir?' Woods asked.

Now it was Sackville's turn to look startled. 'Sir Lawrence Forsyth is a highly respected lieutenant in His Majesty's navy,' he said, 'and a trusted employee. The poor man's ship went down and he was held by the French as a prisoner of war for years in despicable conditions. I can't see him trading secrets with Boney. The fellow must hate the French more than we do – and he has been commended for his bravery!'

Lavender frowned. The news that Forsyth had had such an illustrious and well-respected career in the navy explained why he was now in a position of such great trust. But Sackville's suggestion that Forsyth was brave didn't seem right. As far as he was concerned, the man was sly. Thinking back to their conversation at Bushy House, Lavender also realised that Forsyth was easily intimidated. These weren't characteristics of a 'brave' man; they were the weaknesses of a man who could be pressured or bullied into betraying his country.

'I know what this is about.' Read smirked and slammed his fist down on his desk with jubilation. 'It's personal, isn't it, Stephen? Forsyth came to me telling tales about your relationship with that Spanish widow. He's got your back up and you want revenge.'

Lavender shrugged. He wasn't going to give Read the pleasure of rising to his bait. He just hoped that his comments had planted the seed of suspicion in Sackville's mind. 'I don't like the fellow but that doesn't cloud my judgement. Captain Sackville is right. Everyone on this list needs to be investigated. I was merely airing my concerns that we shouldn't overlook anyone who was backstage at the Sans Pareil last Thursday – no matter what their rank or military exploits.'

The Menendez carriage was again waiting on the street outside her lodgings when Magdalena arrived home. She grimaced. The last thing she wanted right now was to spend another boring hour with Juana and Olaya Menendez. She needed some time to herself to think about her first experience teaching; to consider Magistrate Read's offer; and to muse about the secret trip Stephen had in store for her tomorrow.

To her surprise it was Felipe Menendez who stepped out of the carriage to greet her, not his sisters. Tall, and swathed in a voluminous greatcoat with three tiers of capes, he cut a striking figure of wealth and elegance against the backdrop of her dilapidated street with its piles of refuse, ragged inhabitants and peeling paintwork.

He bowed low over her hand. 'Please forgive the intrusion, Doña Magdalena,' he said in Spanish. 'However, when Juana told me about the conditions and circumstances you had to endure through living in this area' – he paused and cast a disdainful glance across to the shabby market stalls with their drooping awnings – 'I was so alarmed, that I had to come and see for myself.'

'How kind of you,' she replied and felt obliged to add, 'Would you care to come up to my rooms and take a coffee with us?'

Menendez nodded and Magdalena led the way. Her room was freezing but Teresa hurriedly lit a fire and busied herself making coffee. Menendez politely enquired after her health and that of Sebastián and they made some small talk about their neighbours back in

Spain, the poor harvest on their estates and the effect of the interminable war. Then Menendez took a leisurely look around the inside of her home. She realised by the way the nostrils twitched below his long nose that he didn't like what he saw. While he examined every cobwebbed corner of her lodgings she amused herself by examining him. Despite her reservations about the Menendez's character she couldn't help but admire his prominent cheekbones and the sleek sheen of his ebony hair. He was a very attractive man with intelligent and slightly hooded eyes. It was such a shame for Juana and Olaya, she thought. Felipe had inherited all of the family's good looks and left none for them. It was also a shame that he didn't smile more often; he and Juana shared a certain sourness of expression in their unguarded moments.

'I'm sorry to see that your circumstances are so reduced now, Doña Magdalena,' he said. 'Don Antonio would be distressed that he had left you in such squalor.'

She bristled at his impertinence; she preferred to believe that she lived in simplicity rather than squalor. Besides which, she knew that Antonio had been so angry with her in the final months of his life that he wouldn't have cared a damn about her blessed circumstances.

'How much did Don Antonio leave you?' he asked, suddenly.

She wasn't sure that she had heard him correctly and asked him to repeat the question.

'How much money have you got?' he said with a hint of irritation. 'How many *reals* do you own?'

She lowered her eyelashes to hide the anger in her eyes while she considered how best to respond to such base rudeness. 'Not many in England,' she finally said. 'Most of what I own is back in Spain in the hands of the French.'

'Does that include your late father's estate in Langreo? Do the French have that too?'

Deciding that vagueness was probably the best policy to deflect him, she sighed and threw her hands in the air in a gesture of confusion. 'I have no idea. You will have to excuse me, Don Felipe. Antonio dealt with issues of money and finance. I really have no idea – and I'm struggling to find out about what is left of my property and wealth in Spain.'

He lowered the veiled lids further over his eyes. She sensed that his mind was calculating something. 'You will need help when the war is over, to reclaim what is yours.'

'Most probably.'

'You women are foolish when it comes to money and inheritance,' he continued dismissively. 'None of you ever know what it is you own. People will try to cheat you all the time.'

She forced a look of bewildered sadness onto her face. 'Yes, you're right, Don Felipe. I will probably need help to put my affairs into order once we return to a liberated Spain. I just find the whole thing upsetting. Thank you for your concern.'

'I would see it as my duty to help you in these matters, Doña Magdalena. Don Antonio would have expected no less from me.'

'Again, that is kind of you, Don Felipe. Very neighbourly.'

A broad grin of satisfaction spread across his handsome face. Suddenly he leant forward and took her hand in his. She tried to pull it away but his grip was like iron. 'Perhaps we should consider the possibility that we can be more than neighbours?'

'What— What do you mean?'

Fortunately, Teresa appeared at that moment, with a tray of steaming coffee and mismatched china crockery.

Don Felipe released Magdalena's hand and took his cup without a glance at or a word of thanks to Teresa. He sat back in the chair. Across from him, Magdalena shuffled uncomfortably in her seat, conscious that his eyes were lazily undressing her.

'You're a mature and very beautiful woman, Doña Magdalena,' he said. A lascivious smile now played on his lips as his veiled eyes once again shamelessly travelled over her breasts, her curvaceous hips and long legs. Magdalena felt like a prize heifer in a cattle market.

'Thank you, Don Felipe,' she said through gritted teeth.

'But you're also a realist. You know how the world works. Your estates, which border mine, are extensive. Then there is your father's estate to consider. A woman could never manage such responsibility alone.' His voice assumed a businesslike tone. 'You will need a man, a protector, when you return to Spain. Firstly, you will need to re-establish your right to your land – and then you will need help to manage the estates, someone to handle the finances and make the decisions.'

'You may be right,' she said, warily. She had a strong suspicion what he would say next and braced herself.

'Yes, you will need to remarry. You need a husband.'

She opened her mouth to mention that she was still grieving for Antonio but his next statement took her breath away.

'And I'm in need of wife.'

Not even three years of practising deceit at the Spanish court had prepared Magdalena for that. She hardly knew the man. Her composure slipped and she choked on her coffee.

'Is this a proposal, Don Felipe?' she asked lightly, once she had dabbed her coffee-spattered cloak with her handkerchief. She desperately tried to think of something she may have done or said in the past, which had led him think that she might welcome such an outrageous offer.

He shrugged. 'It is something to consider, to think about,' he said, casually.

'But I'm older than you Don Felipe!' she exclaimed.

He shrugged again. 'There are only a few years between us. You may no longer be a young girl, Doña Magdalena, but you're still an attractive woman. I assume you're still fertile? You and Antonio only had the one child. Why was that?'

She sat in stony silence; every fibre of her body was screaming in outrage at his rudeness and arrogance. When she didn't reply another lascivious smile spread across his face. 'Well, no matter. We're both well endowed – with land.' His meaning was clear.

'I thank you again for your interest in my welfare, Don Felipe,' Magdalena replied. 'You're too kind to this poor, *old* widow. However, I'm still too wracked with grief for Antonio to even think about remarriage. I need more time to mourn for him.'

Felipe shrugged. 'There is time,' he said, 'plenty of time. I doubt that the war will be over this year. I suspect that you may be living in penury for some time longer, Doña Magdalena. The constraints of your situation may become intolerable.' He narrowed his eyes and watched her reaction to his next words carefully. 'And I assume that Don Antonio made no provision for Sebastián's school fees for next year?'

'I'm sorry that you feel that the war may drag on longer,' she said, desperate to change the subject.

'Yes, Viscount Wellington is a fool,' he said. 'The English have lost their advantage and retreated into Portugal for the winter. Our own resistance is in disarray.'

'That is disappointing.'

The padded shoulders of his cape rose again in another dismissive shrug. 'The Cádiz Cortes were foolish to put their trust in the British.' Suddenly he stood up and fastened his greatcoat. 'Take up my sister Juana's invitation, Doña Magdalena,' he said. 'Stay with us for a while at our home in Bedford Square and we shall get to know each other better.' He flashed a looked of distaste at the shabbiness of the room. 'Leave this miserable place and enjoy our hospitality, our comfort.'

'I will . . . consider it,' she replied, relieved that he was departing. She held out her hand. He ignored it, leant down and cupped her chin in a firm grip. Before she could protest he had forced his mouth down onto hers. Her body recoiled at his touch. The hard insistence of his emotionless kiss sent a shiver of distaste down her spine. She gasped as his slimy tongue probed into the secret recesses of her mouth like the antennae of a fat snail.

She pushed him off. 'I must protest, Don Antonio,' she said angrily as she forced herself to her feet. 'You presume too much!'

The sardonic smile returned to his lips. 'Methinks the lady doth protest too much,' he said. 'This Detective Lavender, he's your lover, yes?'

She bristled with indignation. 'Really, Don Felipe! Of course not!'

'If he isn't, then he wants to be. But it is no matter.' Felipe gave that annoying shrug again and Magdalena had to clench her fists to stop herself slapping his face. 'You're a widow, not a virgin. You should foster your acquaintance with Lavender,' he said vaguely. 'He may be useful. He has access to many people and places with information which could be useful to us.'

His sudden change of tack threw her for a moment. 'Who is *us*?' she asked.

He smiled, his eyes veiled once more behind his lowered lids. 'Us – or we – are those in Spain who want to see this blessed war ended once and for all,' he said quietly.

Don Felipe took her hand, raised it halfway to his mouth then paused and stepped closer, intimidating her with his masculine presence and strength. Once again she felt the hairs on the back of her neck stiffen. 'And that includes you, Doña Magdalena,' he whispered. 'Doesn't it? Don't try to pretend that you're resigned to this miserable existence in London. You want to go back home – and the sooner the better. Listen carefully to what this Lavender fellow has to say and report it back to me.' Before she could reply he kissed her hand, gave a short bow and strode out of the room.

Her mind in turmoil, Magdalena sank back into her seat, her heart pounding. She stared bleakly ahead. For the second time today a man had sought to enlist her into his services as a spy. Had this really happened? And what on earth had led Menendez to think that she would consider a marriage proposal from him? Had someone taken a quill and etched 'desperate *señora*' across her forehead as she slept?

Teresa returned to her side after closing the door behind Menendez. 'Humph! More kisses!' she said in English. 'Him? Him I don't like. You marry Señor the Detective.'

Chapter Twenty-five

Friday 23rd February, 1810

Lavender and Magdalena attended the short service in the Willoughbys' local church. It was a sad and dismal affair. The lesson was read by a vicar with the quietest and most monotonous voice Lavender had ever had the misfortune to endure. Then they stood around for half an hour in the mud, drizzle and blustery wind of the graveyard while the vicar intoned some more.

The congregation shuffled from one foot to another as their boots sank into the sodden ground. The hems of the women's cloaks and gowns quickly became darkened with damp. Everything around them was muted into differing shades and hues of grey: the crumbling walls and ancient slate tiles of the church and the darkening clouds in the sky above. A line of carriages waited for the mourners on the lane beside the church. Occasionally the jangle of harnesses would reach their ears as a horse stamped on the cobbles.

Magdalena stood in dignified silence beside Lavender, her gloved hand resting lightly on his arm. Her dark, modest clothing did nothing to hide her regal poise or the alluring sway of her hips when she walked. Even the veil over her gleaming black hair only added to her mystery. A gust of wind swirled around her skirts.

He pulled her closer to him to shelter her from its blast. She smiled at him from beneath the veil.

While the vicar droned on, Lavender's eyes scanned the crowd of mourners and the road beyond the low, church wall. The occasional wagon and carriage rumbled past the line of waiting vehicles at the churchyard gate. There were only a couple of family friends at the funeral and an officer from the Admiralty to represent Captain Willoughby. It had crossed Lavender's mind that one, or more, of the kidnappers may turn up at the service to see the truth for themselves. The morning newspapers had told a dramatic story to the world and this was the first time in a week that April Clare had left the house in Wandsworth.

Would the kidnappers be able to resist this opportunity to confirm the truth of those sensational headlines? Jane Scott had played her part well; the vivid and melodramatic story of April Clare's resurrection had appeared in nearly every morning newspaper. He imagined that quite a few Londoners must have choked on their kippers or dropped their porridge spoon on their waistcoats if they had attempted to eat their breakfast and read at the same time.

The kidnappers must now be aware that they had taken the wrong woman. Their trap was set.

Magdalena squeezed his arm to attract his attention. She regarded him quizzically. 'Who are you looking for?' she whispered.

Lavender smiled and shook his head; she missed nothing.

'Ashes to ashes,' the vicar intoned, and the relieved congregation stepped forward to throw dirt into the grave. 'Dust to dust.'

The service now over, Solomon Rothschild moved forward to engage Magdalena in conversation and Lavender took the opportunity to have a quiet word with April Clare whom he was relieved to see was quite dry-eyed.

'I saw the papers this morning,' she whispered.

'Yes, everything is ready – and Constable Woods has joined the theatre. Jane Scott was delighted with the whole idea and tomorrow night she will welcome you back to the Sans Pareil with open arms. Your part is simple but if you have any problems, Constable Woods will be on hand to assist you – and protect you.'

She breathed a huge sigh of relief and smiled. 'Thank you, Detective. You can't imagine my gratitude at the speedy way you have resolved my problems.'

'It is not over yet,' he said, more sharply than he intended. 'You still have a part to play tomorrow night.'

'Don't worry – I shall not let you down. I want justice for poor Harriet as much as you do.' Another gust of wind now whipped round the skirts of the women and threatened to blow off the men's hats. April Clare pulled her cloak tighter around her throat. 'We should get back to the house,' she said.

When Lavender returned to Magdalena's side, Lady Caroline and Duddles had joined her and Rothschild.

'I'm disappointed, Lavender,' Lady Caroline said. 'Doña Magdalena tells me that you now have another appointment and will be unable to return to Lincoln's Inn Fields for luncheon with us.'

'I'm afraid so,' he said.

'Well, in that case I insist that you both join me one evening when I hold one of my soirées. We have buried poor Harriet now and must pick up the pieces of our lives as best as we can.'

A quick glance at Magdalena's smiling face assured him that he should accept the invitation on behalf of both of them. 'It would be our pleasure to come to one of your gatherings, Lady Caroline,' he said. 'But I'm afraid that we must leave you now.' He was conscious that the funeral had overrun. There was just enough time to take Magdalena and Teresa to see his surprise before her afternoon Spanish lesson. 'Please accept our condolences once more, Lady Caroline.'

Both men bowed politely in Magdalena's direction as they left. It seemed to him that Solomon Rothschild's black velvet yarmulke remained down a little longer than necessary. His hand lingered in Magdalena's as he raised it to his lips and his gaze followed her as she turned to walk with Teresa to their carriage. He smiled. First, young Barrington at the language school; now Rothschild. Magdalena made conquests of men wherever she went.

As Lavender helped Magdalena up the steps into their vehicle, another carriage slowly trundled past on the other side of the road. A pinched, white face stared out of the window towards them: it was Sir Lawrence Forsyth. His close-set eyes widened beneath their bushy brows at the sight of Magdalena and Lavender together once more. Then a deep frown set on his face. *Not him again*, Lavender thought irritably. *The bloody man is stalking us.*

Magdalena disappeared into the swaying vehicle, oblivious to their glowering observer. Teresa waited patiently at his side for his assistance. She had also seen Forsyth. 'It is that small *hombre*,' she said. 'We saw him in Bow Street with you, Señor the Detective.'

'Yes,' he agreed. 'I remember.'

'Him? Him I don't like.'

He paused, both surprised and amused. Teresa so rarely spoke English, he felt he must appreciate the moment and encourage her. 'Why don't you like him, Teresa?'

She shrugged. 'Me know not – and him – he speak *española*.'

He frowned. 'He speaks Spanish?'

'*Si, castellano, español – mi lengua.*' She nodded her head vigorously.

Knowing that she would be more explicit in Spanish, he switched quickly into her native tongue. 'How do you know that, Teresa? What makes you think he speaks Spanish?'

She tutted and raised her dark eyes to the sky. 'It's easy if you look and listen,' she said. 'You should know this.'

'Quite,' he said, a little taken aback. 'What have I missed, Teresa?'

'Doña Magdalena hurt her knee in the theatre when she tripped up that bad man, that thief. But she only complained about it in Spanish. The next day we met him—' She jerked her thumb down the road at the receding carriage. 'We met him in Bow Street on the stairs. He asked about Doña Magdalena's knee. But how would he know her knee was injured unless he had understood her Spanish curses?'

Lavender's eyebrows raised in genuine surprise. His mind flitted back to that meeting with Forsyth in Bow Street and he realised that Teresa was right. Forsyth had given himself away; he had understood Magdalena when she was cursing in Spanish. He had no idea what this latest discovery meant to his investigation but he sensed it was significant. He gave Teresa his most brilliant smile. 'Well done!' he said. 'That is helpful, thank you, Teresa. Why – I could kiss you!'

'No!' shrieked the maid in horror. She hitched up her skirts and leapt up the steps into the carriage with the nimbleness of a Pyrenean mountain goat. She turned round dramatically in the doorway, her little face flushed with alarm. 'No more kisses!' she yelled.

Constable Woods leant against the filthy wall of the theatre corridor, gave a hacking cough and rubbed the itchy stubble on his chin. Bored, he poked his mop at a nasty stain on the floorboards and wrinkled his broad nose at the whiff of the fish wharf that emanated from his old jacket. When he had told Betsy about Magistrate Read's warning about the loose morals of the actresses at the Sans Pareil, her grey eyes had hardened. The next thing he knew, she had retrieved his old fishing jacket from the lean-to in the back yard, a filthy shirt from the unwashed laundry and had hidden his razor. She had also tried to persuade him to blacken out his teeth with paper but he had drawn the line at that. He had never looked or smelt more unattractive; which, he suspected, was exactly what Betsy intended.

Jane Scott had let it be known that she had taken pity on this poor, mute, old man and given him a job cleaning the backstage of the theatre. So far no one had questioned the philanthropic generosity of Miss Scott or seemed to care a fig for the wheezy old geezer lurking in the corridors. Not that he expected anyone in the cast or crew of the Sans Pareil to recognise him, but he knew from experience of undercover work that the more he slunk in the shadows, faded into the background and kept himself to himself the better.

Woods soon familiarised himself with the maze of dressing rooms and dark, narrow corridors backstage and eavesdropped on conversations in order to identify the different actors and actresses. As he loitered with his mop beside the door of the green room, he heard male voices approaching behind him. He lowered his head, let his jaw go slack and a bit of spittle run down his chin.

He recognised the deep tone of William Broadhurst, the company's leading man, who struck him as a pleasant, jovial fellow. Broadhurst was with another actor, John Isaacs. Isaacs had a higher-pitched, more affected voice. Head bowed, Woods shuffled to the side of the corridor to let them pass. But when they came up behind him, that princock, Isaacs, pinched him hard on the backside.

Woods spluttered, lost his balance and fell. He landed with a clatter in a pool of dirty water beside his upset bucket. He spun around to protect his rear from further assault. He also clenched his fists in anger but managed to bite back the curses that sprang to the tip of his tongue. They came out as a strangled gargle. The two actors clutched their sides with laughter. Fighting back an urge to jump up and punch Isaacs on the nose, Woods spluttered some more and grinned up at them like a lunatic from Bedlam.

Broadhurst was bent double, the shoulders of his green velvet coat shaking with laughter. 'For God's sake, John! Leave the poor fellow alone – can't you see he's a bit simple?'

'I just wanted to know if he preferred the back passage.' Isaacs grinned.

'The poor fellow can't talk, so how can he tell anyone which way he navigates?' Broadhurst asked. Still grinning, he held out a friendly hand to haul Woods back to his feet and continued to talk about him to Isaacs. 'He's clearly not interested in navigating the windward passage – or not yours anyway. All right there, fellah?'

Woods grinned again and nodded his head furiously. He wasn't really; his trousers were soaked. The two actors turned away and entered the green room. For the first time, Woods noticed the extreme tightness of Isaac's breeches and his mincing gait. 'Well, at least a mute won't run telling tales of sodomy to the Bow Street Runners,' the young actor said.

As the door to the green room closed behind them, Woods allowed himself a smile at the irony of the situation. Magistrate Read and Betsy had been so busy worrying about the immoral women in the theatre, they had forgotten to warn him about the men. Sighing, he squeezed out his mop and cleared up the pool of water around him. He had an uncomfortable few hours in sodden trousers ahead.

Woods realised, as the day progressed, that the dramatic news of April Clare's resurrection from the dead and planned return to the theatre was the main topic of conversation amongst the cast, especially amongst the women.

'Damn her!' one young actress said as he hovered near the open door of a female dressing room. 'I enjoyed playing her part in *The Necromancer* – no doubt she'll want it back now.'

'Oh, I don't think so, darling,' said another. 'It'll be too small for her now. After this little performance, April will have her sights set on the lead roles. The public will be clamouring for her. Even our darling Janey had better watch out! Only a spot in the limelight will be good enough for Miss April Divine after this.'

'Never mind our darling Janey,' purred another. 'The great Sarah Siddons will quake in her boots when she hears about this. Even she never managed to rise from the dead! What a stunt!'

Woods wrinkled his nose at the strong aroma of body odour that emanated from the dressing room and moved on. There was something else mixed with the smell: spite. Actresses, he decided, were a catty bunch of women.

And he had never known a group of men to fuss so much about their appearance as the actors. He doubted if Beau Brummell himself took so much time brushing his sideburns, plucking hairs from his nostrils and smoothing out every wrinkle and crease from his cravat. The friendly William Broadhurst seemed to be the only normal man in the troupe.

Another thing that bothered Woods was the heavy door to the green room. It hadn't taken him long to realise that this was going to be a problem. There was nowhere to hide in the cramped green room but he needed a good view of the cluttered table beneath the window. His only other option was to prop the door open and camp outside at the end of the corridor. He wedged it open for a while but it wasn't long before one of the cast members had shut it, complaining about the draught.

In the end, Woods decided that there was only one thing to do: he would have to remove the door. He waited until late afternoon when the theatre was almost deserted then he took a turnscrew from the carpenters' toolbag and loosened the hinges. The damned door was heavier than he expected and he was relieved that no one was around to watch him struggle and curse as he lowered it to the floor and dragged it to the back of the stage. He swiped his sleeve across his sweaty forehead then hid the door beneath a pile of old curtains, rope and pulleys in the void below the stage. He didn't want any interfering fool replacing it before tomorrow night.

Isaacs and Broadhurst were the first actors to return to the theatre for that evening's performance. Woods loitered over his mop and bucket in the corridor and watched their reaction to his handiwork.

Isaacs did a double take in the entrance of the green room. 'God in hell!' he said. 'The damned door's disappeared.'

William Broadhurst shrugged and sighed. 'The buggers around here will steal anything.'

Chapter Twenty-six

Their carriage drew up outside the grey-bricked terraced house in Marylebone. On the opposite side of the road, the wrought-iron railings separated them from the quiet garden in the centre of the square. As he helped the women alight from the carriage, Lavender glanced up with pride at the smart exterior of his new home. He appreciated the proportions and perfect symmetry of the building; he liked this geometric style. Three storeys of white oblong windows towered above them, all topped with a cream stone lintel. The only curve in the architecture was the semi-circular fan-window above the wood-panelled front door.

They climbed the two shallow steps and he rapped on the door with the gleaming brass doorknocker. 'I'll need some help choosing the furnishings,' he said.

Magdalena nodded and said nothing. Her eyes took in every detail of the frontage of the house, including the gate in the iron railings beside them and the flight of steep stone steps which led down to the basement kitchen.

The door swung open and Lavender's new housekeeper beamed at them from below her frilly mob cap.

'This is Mrs Hobart,' he said. 'Doña Magdalena, Mrs Hobart.'

'Welcome to Westcastle Square, sir – and ma'am.' She bobbed Magdalena a curtsey. The heat inside the house was welcome after their cold journey and the even colder funeral service. 'I've lit the fires, as you instructed, sir,' Mrs Hobart said. 'You'll see the house at its best today.' She took their damp cloaks and led them downstairs to the cheerfully tiled kitchen in the basement. It was an impressive well-lit and ventilated room that smelled of freshly baked bread and strong coffee. Before they went any further, Mrs Hobart insisted they take a seat at the well-scrubbed kitchen table, drink some coffee and try out her warm scones with a little homemade jam.

They didn't need a second invitation. The coffee was particularly welcome to Lavender. Mrs Hobart chatted amiably as they ate and drank and pressed a second plate of scones onto Teresa. He and Magdalena left the young girl chatting in broken English to Mrs Hobart while they explored the rest of the house.

'I'll have a fresh pot of coffee waiting for you when you've finished looking around,' Mrs Hobart said.

Magdalena was quiet as he led her from floor to floor, and room to room around the house. There were four large bedrooms upstairs and several reception rooms led off from the spacious hallway. An ornate, curved staircase wound its way up the centre of the house to the servant's attics on the top floor. Despite the dullness of the day, light still poured through the tall windows and the skylight at the top of the staircase with its coloured glass inserts. The previous owners had left several tasteful window drapes, carpets and random items of furniture. 'They have emigrated to the Americas,' Lavender told Magdalena. 'I assume that they were unable to take everything with them on the ship. Obviously, we need to purchase some more furniture and paintings and ornaments to make the house more comfortable.'

Magdalena nodded. 'It will be my pleasure to help you choose them, Stephen. What about Mrs Hobart?' she asked. 'Did the previous owners leave her as well?'

He frowned in confusion. 'Well, I don't remember asking for her services, but she seems to be part of the fixtures and fittings. I haven't dared to question the situation.'

Magdalena smiled. 'Have you ever dealt with servants before, Stephen?'

He shook his head. 'No – apart from Mrs Perry who launders my shirts.'

She smiled at his discomfort. 'Mrs Hobart seems a nice woman and an able housekeeper,' she said, 'and she has already worked out exactly how you like your coffee. I would recommend that you keep her for now.'

The previous owners had left a large Turkish rug, which covered the floorboards in one of the front bedrooms. An abandoned cream chaise longue was pushed up against a wall near the fireplace where a warm fire crackled gently in the grate. Magdalena crossed to the window, pulled back the white lace curtain and looked down into the square outside.

'This is a beautiful room,' she said. 'The whole area is so peaceful and pleasant.'

Lavender moved to stand by her side. 'I understand that those gardens are very pretty in spring,' he said. 'They're also popular with the neighbourhood children. I'm sure that Sebastián will make many friends, very quickly if he came to live here.'

'Why would Sebastián come to live here?' She stared at him in surprise.

'Because I hope that you and Teresa will be living here when he comes down from school at the end of term.'

'I don't understand.'

'Let me explain,' he said, slowly. 'I have a lot of money lying idle in the bank, Magdalena. I decided to invest in some property, which is why I have bought this house. But at the moment, I'm quite comfortable in my rooms in Southwark and they're convenient for my place of work at Bow Street. I had a fancy to let the house for a while and I would be honoured if you and Teresa would move in here – with Sebastián, of course.'

Her mouth formed a perfect circle with surprise then she laughed and patted his arm. 'That is so kind and generous of you, Stephen – but I could never afford to rent this beautiful house! I can barely afford the lodgings I already have.'

'You wouldn't have to pay for it. I don't need the money.' Her eyes widened but she said nothing. 'There is no rent to pay, Magdalena. Removing you from that dreadful street in Spitalfields would be reward enough for me.'

Her hand fluttered to her breast and her mouth seemed to struggle to formulate her words. 'But I would be beholden to you!' she exclaimed. 'I'm not sure . . . I couldn't possibly . . . To live here rent free?'

'Yes, that is what I hope.'

A frown line appeared between her eyebrows. 'If anyone found out about our arrangement, then everyone would assume that I was your mistress,' she said bluntly.

'Ah.' *Damn*, this wasn't an objection that he had foreseen. 'My apologies, I never meant to imply—'

She held up her hand to silence him. 'I know that you meant no offence, Stephen. You're the kindest, most thoughtful man I have ever met.'

'Then it is agreed then? You will move in here with Teresa?'

She smiled gently at him, her eyes soft with gratitude but tinged with a little sadness. 'It is a wonderful idea, Stephen and I can't thank you enough for your kindness but I'm afraid I must decline.'

His face fell.

'Everyone in my acquaintance knows of my desperate financial situation. If I moved in here, into your home, then everyone would assume the worst – including the kind Mrs Hobart downstairs.'

'No one needs to know!' he said.

'People have a way of finding out the truth, Stephen and as I have said before, my reputation is all that I have left. I can't afford to give the gossips and the scandalmongers any cause to speculate about my morality.'

'Then marry me,' he said suddenly.

She let out a sharp breath.

Lavender stepped forward and took her hands in his. The words rushed out of his mouth. 'I know that you have said you needed more time to come to terms with Antonio's death, Magdalena, but I'm not sure that you have the time. I worry daily about the foul things that could befall you and Teresa in that neighbourhood. Marry me, move in here with me and let me protect and cherish you, as you deserve. You must have realised by now, surely, how much I have fallen in love with you?'

'Oh, Stephen!' Her eyes welled up with tears and for a moment he thought she was going to say 'yes' and throw herself into his arms. Then she pulled away from him. With her hand over her mouth, she walked across the room and collapsed sobbing onto the chaise longue by the far wall.

He was by her side in an instant, his arm around her shaking shoulders. 'Magdalena, what's the matter?' This wasn't the reaction he had expected. A slap across the face for being so presumptuous would have been more welcome – and more in character – than this level of distress.

She turned to face him and laid her head against his shoulder for a while. He smelt her hair and felt its softness. Tears still rolled unchecked from her closed eyes as she sat encircled in his arms and he waited. 'You must think I am such a fool,' she said. 'You have no idea how much I have longed to hear you say those words of love, Stephen. I have gone to sleep every night dreaming about it.'

Lavender gave a huge sigh of relief. Everything was all right; she felt the same way about him as he felt about her. He smiled and pulled her close again. 'I'd never think you were a fool, Magdalena,' he said. 'But what is it which bothers you, my love? Why the tears?'

She pulled herself back out of his arms but still held onto his hands, she looked him in the eyes. He saw the pain in hers. 'Because it can't be, Stephen,' she whispered. 'No matter how much we desire each other, our union can't be.'

His heart fell into the pit of his stomach and disappointment rose along with the bile in his throat. 'Why? Is it your religion? The difference in our class?' The words seemed to catch in his throat. 'I know that I am not worthy of your love but—'

'No!' she said. 'It is me that is not worthy of yours. I would make a poor and shameful wife for you.'

He was startled by the ferocity of her expression. He felt the blood pounding in his temple. 'That's ridiculous,' he said. 'It would be an honour—'

'Stephen – listen to me,' she interrupted.

Quietly, Magdalena told him her story. She left nothing out. She confessed that she had defied her husband, abandoned her parents-in-law to their fate with the French, and shot dead several of the French officers who had come to arrest her. She didn't look at him as she spoke. He squeezed her hand. When she had finished, she broke away from his grasp, leant forward, lifted the poker and stirred up the embers of the fire.

He felt calmer. Was this all that she fancied stood in the way of their marriage? He had had his suspicions about Magdalena's flight from Spain confirmed some time ago. Magistrate Read wasn't the only one with contacts in the Foreign Office. This was not a scandalous revelation for him.

'Magdalena, I already knew a little about what happened to you when you left Spain. It doesn't shock me. It just shows your courage and your great love for Sebastián.'

But she didn't seem to hear him. 'Antonio never forgave me for abandoning his parents.' She stared into flames. 'Once I had arrived in England, I managed to make contact with him in Spain. He sent me a letter. He refused to help me financially. He paid for Sebastián's school fees for this year but he wrote that I could rot in hell.'

A sharp pang of anger seared through Lavender, followed by a fresh wave of sympathy for Magdalena. She must have been terrified to find herself abandoned, penniless and friendless in a foreign country. He knew she had spent most of last year moving from the charity of one set of Spanish émigrés to another. 'He had no right to disown you,' he said. 'Yes, you went against his wishes but you were protecting your child – as any mother would have done. What happened to Antonio's parents?'

'They have disappeared,' she said simply. 'No one knows what happened to them after we fled. Antonio claimed that the French probably shot them in retaliation for the officers I killed.'

Lavender grimaced and realised that she was probably right. 'Your country is at war,' he said. 'Atrocities happen in war and the blame for them should be laid firmly at the door where they belong; in this case, with the French.' He felt more hopeful for himself and Magdalena. There was no new dreadful revelation within her confession, nothing that he didn't already know. 'It seems to me that your late husband also should have accepted the part he had to play in this tragedy. He was a notorious Spanish rebel. Even the British had heard about the stand he took against Bonaparte. The French would have killed both you and Sebastián if you hadn't shot them first and escaped – of that I'm sure.'

She shrugged her shoulders. 'What's done is done,' she said. 'But in saving my child I'm now branded a heartless murderess.'

'That's ridiculous,' he said.

'Is it?' She turned to face him and looked up at him with her beautiful eyes, still glistening with their recent tears. 'You saw how the Menendez family reacted to me at the theatre, Stephen. I'm not the kind of woman that decent men and women want to associate with now. What would your sweet young sister think about me if she ever learnt the truth about how I escaped from Spain? Or Ned and Betsy Woods? Or your kind, gentle mother, the dean's daughter? How would they feel if you married a woman who shoots men dead without a second thought?'

Magdalena paused, waiting for an answer. He hesitated too long.

'And your career would be ruined,' she said. 'It is bad enough that I'm a Catholic, but a heartless murderess as well? Magistrate Read already dislikes me – I can sense that.'

Read? What the hell did Read have to do with any of this? His hackles rose. It was bad enough that Lawrence Forsyth appeared to be stalking them but was Read interfering in his life as well?

'Magdalena, these are small issues which we have to overcome,' he said desperately. 'Nobody needs to know about your past and I think you underestimate the compassion of those closest to me. If the truth did ever come to light about your actions in Spain, then I'm convinced that everyone I know would understand. We shall deal with any prejudice about your race, religion and past history as a refugee. These problems are not insurmountable and shouldn't stop us from being together. If our affection is strong enough, we can overcome anything.'

She managed a weak smile. 'You're a romantic, Stephen – but I'm a realist. Your life and happiness would be over if you lost your job,' she said. 'And unsavoury wives can affect a man's career. You live to solve those mysteries, those intricate crimes that Magistrate Read passes your way. I can never come between you and your job.

And that,' she said sadly, 'is the main reason why I can't accept your kind proposal of marriage; I'm simply not worthy of your love. I would ruin your life.'

His heart sank as she rose from the seat and pulled on her gloves. He wanted to reassure her that he didn't care about her past, that he would stand up for her against Read and his own family if he had to. But at this moment in time, she believed every word she had just said; he only hoped that given some time, and some more persuasion, that she would change her mind. He knew better than to try to press her at the moment. Awkwardly, he rose to stand beside her. This wasn't the outcome he had expected when he had made this proposal. The pain cut deep and for a moment he was swamped with a wave of self-pity and injured pride. His usual confidence and articulation deserted him.

'I have been fooling myself for too long,' she said, 'and dallying with your affections. I'm not a worthy wife for a man of your standing, Stephen. You would come to regret your love for me.' Her voice was barely above a whisper. Her long eyelashes were wet with tears.

Never. His mind screamed but his throat contracted and his lips wouldn't formulate the word. He reached out for her but she brushed his arms aside.

'Can you find another cab, Stephen?' she asked. 'I think I would like to be alone with Teresa for a while.'

He swallowed hard and nodded; he also needed some time alone.

She opened the door but turned back to him before she left the room. 'I have received an invitation to spend some time with the Menendez family,' she said. 'I can't afford to turn down any offers of friendship. I think that I will take up their kind offer to stay for a few days.'

He remembered the arrogant, scowling Spaniard they had met at the theatre foyer and he frowned. Was Menendez a rival? Jealousy stabbed him in the gut and twisted the knife. Was there more to Magdalena's rejection of his proposal than she had claimed?

'Stephen . . .' she was still there, unable to tear herself away. Part of him wanted to rush forward, scoop her up in his arms and never let her go. But his wounded pride rooted him to the spot. 'It's a beautiful house . . . I can't . . . I can't thank you enough for the kindness, consideration and generosity you have shown me. But I'm not worthy of your love.' Then she was gone.

Numb, he staggered towards the window. He blinked as tears pricked the back of his eyes like needles. He hadn't felt as miserable or as wretched as this since Vivienne died. He watched Magdalena and Teresa leave the house, cross the pavement below and board the carriage. His eyes followed the vehicle as it drove out of Westcastle Square. *Is she leaving my life for good*, he wondered. Would he ever see her again? His gut wrenched again at the thought. He couldn't think properly. His mind went over and over the same few words:

Magdalena has turned down your proposal of marriage.

The words of a dead gypsy girl flooded back into his mind to haunt him: '*Who is the woman with the jet-black hair and the red-stoned ring? She's crept under your skin like the Queen of Elphame, seeking comfort beneath a rock. She's a shape-shifter and she'll ensnare you . . .*'

Chapter Twenty-seven

It was late afternoon when Lavender entered the hallowed and secret corridors of the Admiralty on Whitehall. Brandon Sackville's office was plusher than the dark, sparsely furnished police offices at Bow Street. A thick carpet covered the floor and the massive glass-fronted bookshelves which dominated two of the walls were ornately carved with Grecian pillars in the Corinthian style. Gilt-framed oil paintings of ships adorned the dark red walls.

Sackville rose from his chair behind the desk and stretched out a hand to Lavender. Lavender hastily removed his gloves and shook his hand. Papers were scattered across the desk and the captain's hands were ink-stained. His face registered surprise at Lavender's unexpected arrival but the welcome was warm and genuine. Sackville had taken off his jacket and a large tattoo of a green anchor peeped out from the bottom of his rolled up shirtsleeves.

Sackville followed Lavender's gaze. 'I have a mermaid on the other arm,' he confessed. 'The result of a foolish moment of madness in Bermuda.'

'Please excuse the interruption, Captain Sackville.' Lavender sat down. 'But a pressing matter has cropped up in regard to the case and I needed to discuss it with you.'

'You're welcome,' Sackville said. 'How can I be of assistance?'

Lavender cleared his throat. 'How is your investigation going into the suspects on the list provided by Jane Scott?'

Sackville scowled at his paperwork. 'Not very well,' he said. 'We're only partway through the list of names but there is no obvious link between the navy and anyone we have investigated so far.'

'I'll come straight to the point,' Lavender said. 'My instincts tell me that we need to further investigate Sir Lawrence Forsyth. An interesting new fact has come to light,' he said. 'I would like to see Forsyth's service record.'

A look of concern replaced the smile on Sackville's face. 'That would be irregular,' he said, 'and Magistrate Read was most insistent that you shouldn't pursue that line of inquiry.'

'Magistrate Read is frightened that I will disturb a hornet's nest and damage the prince's reputation in some way,' Lavender replied, sharply. 'He needs to have more confidence in my integrity and discretion. This informant needs to be exposed and stopped; British lives depend on it.'

Sackville regarded him curiously from beneath lowered eyelids. 'Steady there, Lavender,' he said. 'I agree with you mostly but I have to admit you seem a bit heated about poor old Forsyth and obsessed with the man. Has he slighted you in some way?'

He ignored Sackville's question. 'It turns out that Forsyth can speak Spanish. Yet his behaviour suggests that the man harbours a nasty prejudice against the Spanish themselves.'

Sackville smiled. 'Ah, so he has slighted someone you know? Perhaps your friend, the Spanish widow Read mentioned?'

Lavender's throat constricted again at the mention of Magdalena. 'Is it in his records that he can speak Spanish?' He heard the irritation in his own voice.

'Many British military officers speak several European – and Indian – languages. Their service for the crown takes them all over the world,' Sackville said. He eyed Lavender with interest now. 'And how do you know that Forsyth can speak Spanish?'

'Let's just say, he gave himself away,' Lavender said. 'I want to know if the Admiralty are aware of this linguistic ability, and if his fluency in Spanish is in his navy records. Please indulge me,' Lavender said. The two men stared at each other for a moment.

Sackville's eyes suddenly narrowed. 'Are you all right, Lavender?' he asked. 'You seem strained and to be honest, you look absolutely wretched.'

'I'm fine,' he lied. 'I've just had a miserable day which started with a funeral.'

Sackville nodded and reached across the piles of maritime charts littering his desk. 'To be honest, I had already retrieved these files to look at later,' he said. He pulled out three files from the bottom of a pile and dragged them towards him.

'Are those Forsyth's records?' Lavender asked as Sackville flicked through them.

'One of them is, yes; the other two are ships' records. Can't let you have access, I'm afraid, Lavender – but I'll check them out for you.'

Lavender hid a satisfied smile. There was only one explanation about why Forsyth's naval record already lay on the desk of Captain Sackville. His comments yesterday must have ignited the naval officer's curiosity; Sackville had quietly begun to do his own research. The captain never raised his eyes and no expression of emotion flickered across his face as he skimmed through the pages of Forsyth's naval career.

To while away the time, Lavender walked over to the window bay to admire the beautiful globe of the Earth mounted on a carved wooden frame. The detail of the terrain drawn onto those delicate paper strips beneath the varnish was intricate. He turned the globe gently, enjoying the smooth, balanced motion. His eyes rested on northern Spain. Oviedo: Magdalena's hometown. He suddenly felt hot and became conscious of the loud ticking of the clock on the fireplace. Abruptly, he turned and went back to Sackville.

'Well, there is nothing which says Forsyth speaks Spanish,' the captain said as Lavender retook his seat. 'I don't know whether to be surprised or not. You're right; it should be written in here. It's important that the Admiralty keeps an accurate record of the skills of its officer but sometimes the administration and recording is poor in this department.'

Lavender sat back down. 'Tell me about him,' he said.

'Well, there's not much to tell – and certainly nothing of note.'

'Indulge me,' he said again.

Sackville sighed and re-opened the file. 'Well, he does seem to be a bit of a Jonah,' the captain said at length.

'A what?'

'A Jonah – misfortune has definitely dogged the steps of this man.'

'How so?'

'He was orphaned in 1784 when his entire family was wiped out in a house fire in Bexleyheath. He was brought up by a distant uncle who didn't seem to warm to the boy and got rid of him quickly. He deposited Forsyth with the navy at Portsmouth in 1788 at the age of fourteen. Forsyth spent a long time as a midshipman on board HMS *Royal George* under Admiral Bridport, now retired.'

'How was his conduct?'

'There's a couple of indictments for drunkenness and brawling,' Sackville said. 'Nothing you wouldn't expect from a young man in the British Navy – and in 1793 he was briefly imprisoned in gaol in Gibraltar after a particularly nasty fight at the harbour.'

Lavender frowned. It was hard to imagine Sir Lawrence Forsyth brawling with other naval officers or sailors. The man just didn't seem to have it in him.

'Anyway, by 1796 he was Lieutenant aboard the ill-fated HMS *Berwick*.'

'What happened to the *Berwick*?'

'Wait a moment,' Sackville said. He pulled out one of the other files and turned quickly to the relevant pages. 'HMS *Berwick* had joined the Mediterranean Fleet under Captain Smith. There was a lot of movement amongst the officers for some reason and Smith was the fifth captain in charge of the *Berwick* in one year. Anyway, while they were in San Fiorenzo Bay, Corsica, there was a disaster. The ships' lower masts, stripped of rigging, were lost. Nobody could understand what happened and a court martial dismissed Smith, the first lieutenant, and the master for gross incompetence. Another captain, Adam Littlejohn, was brought in and under a jury-rig he set sail to join the British fleet at Leghorn.'

'What's a jury-rig?'

'It's a makeshift mast,' Sackville explained. 'Not very effective or desirable but the *Berwick* had orders to join the fleet. Anyway, the ship soon ran into trouble; it met the French fleet instead of the British. By noon, her rigging was cut to pieces and every sail was in ribbons. During the battle four sailors were wounded and a Captain Littlejohn was killed. This now left our friend Forsyth as the most senior officer on board the ship.'

'What happened next?'

'Forsyth decided that *Berwick* was unable to escape in her disabled state and that further resistance was useless; he then ordered that *Berwick* strike her colours.'

'So he surrendered?' *Why didn't that surprise me?*

Sackville raised a hand in resignation. 'I don't think he had much choice. Anyway, the remaining crew and officers were taken prisoner and the *Berwick* was requisitioned into the French fleet. We recaptured her at the Battle of Trafalgar but she was badly damaged and sank the following day.'

'And Forsyth and the rest of his crew?'

'Forsyth was held prisoner by the French for seven years. He was finally freed in a prisoner exchange of officers in 1802.'

'Seven years? Good God. That's a long time to be a prisoner of war.'

Sackville grimaced. 'Some of our sailors have experienced longer,' he said. 'And we've had some French prisoners in the hulks down at Portsmouth for fourteen years.'

Lavender was genuinely shocked. 'What about the rest of Forsyth's crew?'

'They're still in the hands of the French as far as I know, waiting out the war. We don't usually exchange common sailors.'

'And Forsyth's wife?' Lavender asked. 'Did she welcome him back with open arms after an absence of over seven years?'

'He wasn't married at this point of his departure. I understand that his marriage to Lady Forsyth is a recent event. He has worked on shore for the Admiralty ever since his return and has been aide to the Duke of Clarence for the past five years. The prince thinks highly of him and arranged his knighthood two years ago.'

Lavender was thoughtful for a moment. 'Seven years as a prisoner in a French gaol is a long time,' he said. 'It can harden a man, make him bitter.'

'Yes,' Sackville replied. 'And it is also an ideal opportunity to learn half a dozen foreign languages in order to while away the time.' Sackville closed Forsyth's file with a gentle but resolute thud. 'I can understand your concern, Lavender. We all want to know who is passing on information to the French. But at the moment you have to accept that we have nothing to incriminate Sir Lawrence Forsyth. I suggest that we wait and see what happens at the theatre when April Clare returns tomorrow.'

Lavender realised that Sackville had brought the meeting to an end. 'I take your point, Captain Sackville,' he said. 'But I would beg one more favour from you if possible.'

Irritation now flashed across the captain's face. 'What do you want, Lavender?'

'I have a few hours tomorrow before I need to join Constable Woods at the Sans Pareil and I would like the name and address of somebody – anybody – who sailed with Forsyth on either the *Royal George* or the ill-fated *Berwick*.'

Sackville frowned. 'As I said, most of the crew of the *Berwick* are still in the hands of the French – and most of the officers he sailed with are either dead or were dismissed.'

'There must be somebody in England who sailed with this man whom I can talk to,' Lavender's voice rose with frustration. It had been an exhausting day.

Sackville sighed, reached for his quill and scrawled out a name and address on a piece of paper. He didn't bother to sand it. He merely picked it up, gave it a quick wave to dry off the ink. 'I can see that you're not going to let this matter rest, Detective,' he said. 'There, that's the address of George Chandler in Sidcup. He was also a lieutenant aboard the *Berwick* but he had been left behind in the hospital in Corsica when the ship was captured by the French.'

'Why?'

'Because he'd had an accident and the surgeons had amputated his lower left leg. He returned home to England later on a merchant vessel and has been living in Sidcup ever since.'

Lavender opened his mouth to ask more questions but Sackville held up his hand and pointed to the magnificent oil painting of a warship in full sail that took pride of place above his mantelpiece.

'Chandler is a talented artist. The man has created a new career for himself since he was pensioned out of the navy. He paints pictures for the Admiralty and other clients. That's one of his masterpieces over there above the fireplace. By all means, pay him a visit – but I have a strong suspicion, Lavender, that your investigation of Forsyth will reveal nothing. I'll be here tomorrow afternoon on the off chance that you uncover something.'

Chapter Twenty-eight

Saturday 24th February, 1810

The marshland around Bexleyheath was bleak. Isolated buildings and disconnected settlements scattered the flat landscape. A raw wind whipped over the reed pools and dykes. Apart from a few lonely cattle on the horizon, there was no sign of life. Lavender cursed silently when he noticed that there was no church in the village either. There was only a small street of houses and the windmill, whose wooden sails creaked and groaned as they responded slavishly to the furious and bitter gusts of wind.

It had been a miserable ride out to this god-forsaken village. His outer clothes were soaked and despite the exertion of the ride, he shivered with cold. The damp threatened to seep into his bones. Yet even such physical discomfort couldn't distract from the heavy, leaden pain in his chest. He wondered what Magdalena was doing at that moment and then cursed his torturous mind. The pain of her rejection burned deeper within him than the windburn on his frozen face. Sackville might consider this trip to be a fool's errand, but at least he was doing something and burning off the restlessness that now possessed him.

Lavender dismounted, tied up his mount next to the trough and stooped to enter the low threshold of the Black Horse tavern. The inn was as deserted as the rest of the village. He took a glass of ale and warmed himself in front of the fireplace. The innkeeper was a big fellow and not much inclined to conversation but he did tell Lavender that the local church was about two miles down the road towards Welling.

'I'm trying to find out about a family who used to live hereabouts,' Lavender said. 'The Forsyths. I understand that most of them were tragically killed in a house fire over twenty years ago.'

The landlord shook his grey, shaggy head. 'Before my time,' he said. 'Sorry guvnor, I can't 'elp you there.'

Despite the refreshments and the warmth of the inn, another wave of misery swamped Lavender as he remounted his horse and turned it down the Welling Road. Perhaps Sackville had been right to suggest that he should cast his net wider for suspects. Was Magistrate Read right? Had his obsession with Forsyth become personal? He couldn't shake off a lingering suspicion that, prompted by Forsyth's interference, Magistrate Read had said something to upset Magdalena, which had caused her to reject his proposal. He clenched his jaw and felt the anger stir within him. If his instincts were right, then both men would feel the full force of his wrath.

He shook his head to chase away his vengeful thoughts and tried to focus on the dismal landscape before him. There was no church spire or tower on the horizon. Only a few stunted alder and hawthorn trees broke up the flat, dark wilderness of the marsh. The area would have been perfect for highwaymen except that the lack of traffic would have meant lean pickings for even the most opportunist tobyman. He had found his way to the back of beyond. 'Have faith, man,' he said to the wind. He dug his heels into the flank of his horse and spurred it to a canter.

After a mile, the squat church with its crumbling, buttressed walls and overgrown graveyard finally came into view. The rusty iron gate had come off its hinges and he had to lift it to enter, pushing hard against a clump of weeds. He looked around in frustration. Weathered and indecipherable headstones leant drunkenly amongst the nettles.

Lavender sighed and was about to turn back when he saw a stooped figure bent over a spade at the far corner of the graveyard. An old man with a filthy old coat and neckerchief, and a pinched, hungry face below a wiry shock of greying hair, was digging a grave. The old man touched the brim of his hat as Lavender approached. The joints of his hand were red and swollen with arthritis. 'Can I 'elp ye, sir?' he asked.

'Are you the sexton?' Lavender asked. 'How long have you worked here?'

'Yessir. I've bin here nigh on forty years – and me father were 'im that dug graves afore me.'

For the first time that day, Lavender felt his hopes rise. 'You may be the man I need to help me.'

"ow's that, sir?'

'I'm looking for the grave of a family called Forsyth. They were killed in a house fire about twenty-five years ago.'

'What? Them from over in Bexley'eath, yonder?'

'Yes, that's right,' Lavender said. His eyes narrowed as a new thought came to him. 'Do you remember the fire?' he asked.

'Why, yessir, I do. 'Twas a terrible loss of life. I dug their grave meself.' The old man laid down his spade, turned and shuffled off towards the east side of the church. Lavender followed him. He carefully picked his way through the brambles and nettle clumps and tried to avoid tripping over the raised green mounds of the graves.

The lettering of the Forsyth grave was still just about visible:

In loving memory of
Thomas Forsyth
and also of his wife,
Agnes
and their children,
Abigail, Benjamin,
Simon, Lucy and Anne.
Who departed this life on
December 9th
in the year of our Lord,
1784.

''Twere a terrible tragedy.' The sexton shook his head sadly. 'All of them nippers killed.'

'You remember the night of the fire?' Lavender asked.

'Yessir, I were there. I tried to 'elp out with the pump and the chain passin' the buckets of water. Most o' the villagers were there. The 'ouse were razed to the ground. They said it were a night candle which started it.'

'Didn't anyone survive?'

The old man nodded. 'One of the boys were still alive. We managed to pull 'im outta the rubble when part of the house collapsed. 'E were in a bad way, though – and scarred with it.'

'Scarred? How so?'

The old man bent his stiff arm and pointed to behind his own back. ''Ere,' he said, 'one of the burning timbers fell across 'is back and burnt through 'is nightshirt. 'E were screaming in agony at the pain.'

'What happened to him?' Lavender asked.

The old man shook his head. 'Some relatives took 'im away,' he said. 'I never 'eard no more about the boy.'

Lavender tossed him a shilling. 'Thank you,' he said. 'You have been very helpful.' And for the first time that day, Lavender smiled.

George Chandler's artistic studio was a spacious but cluttered room in the rear of a large stone house in Sidcup. The strong odour of turpentine and oil-based paints hung heavily in the air. It reminded Lavender of Lady Caroline's studio in the orangery at the back of her apartment but the paintings that lined the walls of Chandler's home were of magnificent seagoing vessels.

George Chandler himself looked well fed and contented beneath his paint-splattered smock. His rotund body balanced confidently on his wooden leg in front of his easel as Lavender explained his business. A beaming Mrs Chandler brought in tea and fruitcake; she was nearly as plump as her husband. Young, children with fat cheeks peeped shyly at him from behind their mother's voluminous skirts. The two men sat down to eat and drink their tea while the voluble Chandler waxed lyrical about his career in the navy. The man had loved his life at sea and missed male company since his enforced retirement. Lavender complimented him on his artwork and asked if he had heard of Lady Caroline Clare,

'Yes, I've heard of Lady Caroline,' Chandler said. 'She has a good reputation as a landscape artist but I believe that she mostly paints portraits these days?'

'She has to keep the wolf from the door,' Lavender replied, 'and I understand that this is a more profitable occupation.'

Chandler nodded. 'Shame though,' he said, 'to waste your talent like that. I've been lucky, I suppose. There's a large demand for naval-themed paintings. I paint what I love and still make a good income from it. Not everyone has that freedom or my luck.'

Luck? Lavender eyed the ex-lieutenant's stump and marvelled at the fellow's jovial good humour.

Chandler wagged a paint-splattered plump finger in the air. 'I tell you who we need to watch out for though,' he said, 'that Joseph Turner. Did you ever see *The Fishermen at Sea*, exhibited at the Royal Academy?'

'I don't think that I did,' Lavender said.

'Turner's an outstanding artist,' Chandler said. 'He's young yet – but I have no doubt that he will prove a better landscape and nautical artist than either Caroline Clare or myself. The fellow has talent in buckets.' Chandler took a large bite of his cake.

'Lieutenant Forsyth of HMS *Berwick*,' Lavender said. 'Do you remember him?'

'Of course, I do.' Chandler's cheeks bulged like a rodent's as he talked and chewed at the same time. '"Old Shorty Forty" we used to call him. Haven't seen Shorty Forty since the *Berwick* sailed out of San Fiorenzo Bay.'

'You've not seen him since then?' Lavender was disappointed. He didn't know what he had expected to discover this morning but so far there had been no new developments. Even Forsyth's navy nickname was apt for a man whose backside hung that close to the ground. 'Didn't you make contact with him when he was released by the French in that prisoner-of-war exchange in 1802?'

'Well, I tried,' Chandler said, spitting out a few crumbs. His great jovial face creased with consternation as he thought back.

'You were the last remaining officer from the *Berwick*, were you not?' Lavender asked. 'The others were either dismissed or were dead.'

'I wanted to see him and shake his hand. I thought I ought to congratulate him on surviving imprisonment by those damned French dogs. But he wasn't interested.'

'You've not seen him?'

'No. I wrote to him and suggested we met up at the Admiralty Club in town one night for dinner. He sent back a brusque note saying that he was too busy. I half expected that he had been assigned another ship but the next thing I heard, he was aide to the Duke of Clarence. Mind you, he'd always been badly bullied at sea by the other officers, so at least now he's escaped that torment.'

Lavender held his breath. 'Why was he bullied? Was it because of his scarring?'

'Scarring? You mean those burn marks he got from the house fire that killed his family?' Lavender nodded. 'No. No, the scarring was beneath his uniform – you couldn't see it. No, the other officers made his life a misery because of his baldness.'

'His what?'

'His baldness. He'd lost his hair at an early age – he said it was caused by the shock when his family were killed. It fell out in the weeks after the fire. Anyway the other officers thought this was hilarious. They ribbed him badly.'

'He is bald.' It was a stunned statement rather than a question. Lavender couldn't believe his ears.

'Bald as a pebble on the beach,' Chandler said. 'He wore a wig, of course, to try to hide it, but everyone knew. His other nickname was "Baldy Forty". He hated it and used to react with his fists to the chanting. He was forever in fights with the other fellows. Detective? Is something the matter? You look rather strange.'

'He's an imposter.'

Lavender was frozen, mud-spattered and breathing heavily. He had ridden like a fury to get back to see Sackville before the captain left his office at the end of the day.

Sackville turned pale. For a moment he seemed to be lost for words. 'Forsyth is a what?'

'The man working as aide to the Duke of Clarence is an imposter,' Lavender repeated. 'He's not the same Lieutenant Lawrence Forsyth who sailed on HMS *Berwick* and was taken prisoner by the

French in 1796. According to Lieutenant Chandler, his fellow officer was as bald as a coot. Unless Forsyth has concocted a miraculous cure for baldness – which would surely have made his fortune by now – then that man is not your naval officer.'

Sackville swore, threw down his quill and rose angrily to his feet. 'What the—? Well, who the hell is he?'

'I presume he's a French spy,' Lavender said. 'The real Forsyth probably died in captivity and they have sent you back an imposter. They have been clever. Forsyth was a nondescript man, with no close family and hardly any surviving colleagues – and he had been imprisoned for seven years. This is long enough for most people back in England to forget him. Lieutenant Chandler was probably the only man left who would have recognised him as an imposter and Forsyth was careful to avoid any contact with Chandler.'

Sackville cursed again, pulled on his coat and reached for his gloves. His handsome face was dark and contorted with anger. 'I'll get my men and have him arrested immediately,' he snarled. 'At least now we know who has leaked Admiralty information to the French.' He strode out of the door and Lavender fell into step beside him.

'I'll leave you to the arrest,' Lavender said. 'I need to join Woods at the theatre. Forsyth may have left the document on the table in the green room last Thursday night, but I doubt it was by accident. Someone else was supposed to collect it. With any luck the other party in this spy ring will show his hand tonight.'

'I can rely on your discretion, can't I, Lavender?' Sackville asked. 'And that of your constable?'

'Of course.'

'I'm sure you can imagine the scandal and the outcry if the news-sheets and the general public ever found out that Prince William had had a French spy in his entourage for the last five years.'

'Yes, sir, I understand. Please be assured that Woods and I know how to be discreet.'

They took the steps of the grand marble staircase two at a time. Suddenly, Sackville stopped dead. He spun around and Lavender saw the sudden doubt in his eyes. 'Are you absolutely sure about this, Lavender? It's one hell of an accusation.'

'If you want further proof about this imposter,' he reassured the captain, 'I have found a witness to the fire that killed Forsyth's family. He claims that the real Lawrence Forsyth suffered bad scarring on his back from the fire; Chandler verified this claim. I'm sure both witnesses would stand up in court to testify.'

'It'll never come to court,' Sackville muttered ominously. He resumed his descent of the staircase. 'When I get my hands on Forsyth, the first thing I'll do is rip the bloody shirt off his back. If there's no scarring – then I will rip off his bloody head.'

Chapter Twenty-nine

Constable Woods was fed up. He had endured about as much of preening thespians as he could stand. The men strutted around like cocks and were just as bird-brained, and the women were lewd, foul-mouthed, jealous doxies who spat like wildcats at imagined slights. It hadn't taken him long to realise that several of the cast were embroiled in jealous squabbles or simmering feuds. The only good thing about Woods' second day in the theatre was that his bruised buttocks had recovered from the twanging they had received the previous day at the nippy fingers of John Isaacs. Isaacs had lost interest in him and had found another niffynaffy fellow to torment, the new stagehand.

Woods dragged a stool out into the corridor and spent as much time as he could lolling against the wall pretending to be asleep with his mop idle by his side. He wanted to become so inconspicuous that no one would notice or question his presence. His ploy was working: no one had spoken to him all day. He had blended into the background.

During the afternoon rehearsal, two of the feuding actresses came to blows over some silly mistake one of them had made in the previous night's performance. 'You did it deliberately, you poxy old slamkin!' screamed the complainant as she leapt onto her rival, yanked at her dress and ripped off her sleeve. The screaming women whirled in a hair-pulling, face-scratching frenzy. Three of the men struggled to break it up. Woods found it hard to resist his ingrained response to arrest both of the hellcats for affray.

He decided to slink away and hide for a while in the office that Jane Scott used for meetings. As he approached the room, he heard the desk banging hard against the floorboards and the unmistakeable grunts and groans of a copulating couple.

'*Ah mon petit villain! T'es méchant, toi!*' shrieked the woman.

Isn't that French? Woods stopped in his tracks. His eyebrows met across his brow in a frown. He went through a mental list of the actors and actors in his mind and soon realised that he hadn't seen William Broadhurst for some time – or the Italian actress, Miss Helena Bologna.

'*Mon Dieu!*' the woman screamed again. Woods stepped away embarrassed. If Miss Bologna's moans of delight were anything to go by, then Broadhurst gave as good a performance offstage as he did as an onstage lover. But it was the new discovery about Miss Bologna's nationality that distracted him the most. He filed this bit of information carefully in the back of his mind; after all, they were looking for the members of a French spy ring and if there was one thing he had learnt this week, it was that the female of the species could be as devious as the male.

Woods dragged his bucket of filthy water outside the stage door and climbed up the short flight of stone steps to empty it out into the street. The chill, coal-scented air of the capital was a welcome escape from the musty odours inside the theatre. It was almost dusk and folks were hurrying to get home before it got dark. The chimney stacks and church spires of the skyline were silhouetted against a flaming-red sky and dark, billowing clouds. The lamplighters were already out and the streets were full of carriages taking home the wealthy shoppers and workers from the city. Empty wagons rumbled northwards towards the farms and market gardens of Hertfordshire and Buckinghamshire. They would be refilled with produce overnight and returned to Covent Garden before dawn. The appetite of the capital was gargantuan.

He wondered where Lavender was today and frowned when he remembered Lavender's argument with Magistrate Read over the Duke of Clarence and Read's disparaging comment about Lavender's 'Spanish widow'. That hadn't been uttered in jest. The two men usually worked well together. Read had an incredible encyclopaedic memory: he remembered nuance and mundane details about the criminals who passed through his dock and the other citizens of London who appeared in his news-sheet. And none of the other principal officers at Bow Street possessed Lavender's incredible ability to make sense of the twisted, corrupt behaviour and motives of the criminal and insane. He could unravel a case in half of the time it took the others. Read relied heavily on him and was ferociously protective of his best detective. He had brushed off several attempts by other London police offices to poach or borrow Lavender.

Woods knew that ever since poor Vivienne had died, his friend had thrown himself into his work like a demented fiend. Lavender stormed through the seedy underworld of the city, slicing through one unpleasant case after another. He solved mysteries with the same speed and precision that Sir Richard Allison carved up a cadaver. Even the criminals themselves had a grudging respect and fear for Stephen Lavender's amazing powers of detection, and everyone at Bow Street assumed that the man was married to his job.

Well, folks might be in for a surprise soon, Woods thought smugly – especially Magistrate Read. He had worried in the past about Lavender's involvement with Doña Magdalena, whom he knew was a feisty filly even on a quiet day. But he had it on good authority from

Betsy that the pair of them were well-matched and that Stephen Lavender was in love. This had calmed his fears because Betsy was rarely wrong about such things.

Magistrate Read might curl up his lip and complain about Doña Magdalena's religion, but Woods knew that once Stephen Lavender made up his mind to do something, there wasn't anything on earth that would stop him. He suspected that Magistrate Read knew this too. Still, it wasn't good for Bow Street that the magistrate and his cleverest detective were at odds.

Sighing, Woods clomped back down to the stage door and resumed his vigil on his stool. The peace and quiet in the draughty corridor suggested that Broadhurst and Miss Bologna had finished their tryst and left the office. He slumped down against the wall and pretended to be asleep. *Not long now*, he realised.

April Clare returned to the Sans Pareil just before six. She swept down the corridor in a shimmering, black chiffon gown edged with dark green lace and black beads. A fashionable black ostrich feather curled around the mound of glossy black hair piled on her head. Woods gasped. Her resemblance to her dead sister was uncanny. Then he remembered why they were here. He glanced down and noted with satisfaction that she had her play script clutched in her gloved hands. *Good.*

As soon as April Clare walked through the gaping doorway into the green room, the noise level rose dramatically. The theatre cast swarmed around her like buzzing insects.

'April! April, *darling*!' She was passed from one embrace to another. Even the three actresses who had so bitterly bemoaned Miss Clare's return now fawned all over her and squealed with delight. For a moment, she was pulled into the centre of the room and he lost sight of her. Then she reappeared with Jane Scott in front of the fireplace. Jane Scott clapped her hands to get attention. 'Quiet!' she shouted. 'I would just like to say a word or two about darling April's return to the Sans Pareil – and then we must toast her miraculous resurrection!'

'Excuse me one moment, Miss Scott,' said April Clare. 'I'll just put my play script down on the table.' The actress couldn't have timed it better. Everyone in the theatre watched in near silence as she placed her play script, containing the list of naval information, back into exactly the same place where she had left it the week before.

Good gal. Woods grunted with satisfaction and sat back to wait.

It didn't take long. After a brief speech and the toast, the party dispersed and everyone moved along to the dressing rooms to prepare for that evening's performance. Woods had counted them all into the green room; now he counted them out. Eventually, there was only one person left who remained out of sight, lurking in the shadows at the bottom end of the room. Woods sat perfectly still, leant against the wall and watched through half-closed eyes. *Here he comes.*

Gabriel Gomez, the Spanish actor, walked to the front of the green room. Woods remembered Lavender complaining about Gomez's indifferent acting earlier in the week and had identified the Spaniard yesterday. Gomez had his back to the door and the shadowy corridor where Woods sat, but Woods knew that he was rummaging through April Clare's script. Suddenly, Gomez stopped and turned towards the blazing candelabra over the fireplace. He scanned the paper in his hand and folded it before slipping it into his coat pocket. His actions only took seconds but it was enough.

Got you – you sly fox. Woods felt satisfaction sweep through him. Gomez left the green room. Woods closed his eyes, held his breath as he waited for the Spaniard's next move. The actor went into one of the dressing rooms, retrieved his coat and hat then headed for the stage door. Woods gave him a moment before he turned up the collar of his own coat, pulled his hat low over his eyes and rose to follow Gomez out onto the street. Captain Sackville's instructions had been clear: *Follow the spy to his lair so we can round up as many of this gang as possible.*

Woods leapt up the stone steps outside the theatre and joined the heaving throng on the busy street. He glanced around and caught sight of the actor weaving in and out of the crowds. Suddenly, a gloved hand reached out and grabbed him by the arm. It was Lavender.

'It's that Spaniard – Gabriel Gomez.' Woods pointed to the dark figure hurrying down the road. 'He's got the list in his pocket and I'm trailin' him.'

'Good work, Ned,' said Lavender. 'We'll follow him together.'

There was no time for any further exchange of news. It was dark; the pavement was a sea of bobbing heads, hats and bonnets. It wasn't easy to follow a black-coated, dark-haired man in a hat amongst so many others similarly attired. Sometimes they lost him in the shadows and always breathed a sigh of relief when he stepped out again into a pool of light thrown out from an open tavern door or the occasional wall lantern. They followed closer than normal, desperate not to lose sight of their quarry.

'Let's hope that he doesn't jump into a cab,' Lavender said. They closed the gap until they were less than a dozen yards behind Gomez. When they reached Shaftesbury Avenue, the Spaniard glanced back. For a moment, his eyes rested on the two police officers. He turned and quickened his pace.

'We need to split up,' Lavender said and weaved his way through heavy traffic onto the other side of the road. Gomez didn't turn round again until he reached the corner of Bedford Square. This time he looked straight at Woods and Woods saw the fear in the Spaniard's eyes before Gomez broke into a run and disappeared around the corner.

'Damn it.' Woods quickened his own pace. Lavender crossed back over the road and fell into step beside him, matching his stride. 'He knows we're on his tail,' Woods said.

They heard a house door slam as they turned the corner into Bedford Square but neither of them saw which house Gomez had entered. The elegant square, with its sides of neat brick houses, was quiet, empty and dimly lit, although candles flickered behind the closed drapes of several homes. Nothing moved except the wind-rustled dead leaves in the undergrowth of the park in the centre. There were no sounds except the distant barking of a dog and the rumble of traffic on Bloomsbury Street behind them. Their quarry had vanished.

'Where did he go?' Lavender asked.

'He must be inside one of them houses,' Woods said.

Lavender's voice rose sharply. 'But which one? Which house?'

Woods shrugged helplessly.

Fifty yards further down the pavement, the drapes at one of the ground-floor windows suddenly twitched and parted. Light flooded out onto the pavement. Gomez was framed in the window, illumin-ated by the blazing candelabra behind him. The Spaniard looked fearful and seemed to be looking for them. His eyes found them. He mouthed something, as if talking to someone else in the room. Then he disappeared as quickly as he had appeared.

'What's that about?' Woods asked.

'It's almost as if he wanted us to know where he is,' Lavender said.

'What do we do now?'

Woods never got a reply. The unmistakably sharp crack of a pistol shot suddenly shattered the evening peace. A blue flash of gunpowder flared up in the gap between the drapes of the window where they had just seen Gomez.

'Heaven and hell!' They broke into a run and leapt up the stone stairs to the front door of the house. They heard women screaming inside. Lavender pulled his pistol out of his pocket quickly followed by Woods, who muttered a thankful prayer that he had retrieved his own weapon from Betsy's hiding place. Lavender rapped loudly on the front door.

Another pistol shot reverberated around the inside of the house, fired just inside the hallway on the other side of the door. The women's screams intensified and Lavender banged harder.

'Police! Open this door!'

'Gawd's teeth, it's a massacre!' Woods exclaimed. Suddenly, Lavender stopped hammering and tried the handle. It was unlocked. The door gave way and the two policemen half fell and half ran into the dimly lit hallway.

'Detective Stephen Lavender and Constable Woods – Bow Street Police!' Lavender yelled.

The two terrified women were pressed against the balustrade at the bottom of the stairs. They screamed again and clutched each other, but neither seemed to be hurt.

Lavender and Woods turned in the direction of the pistol shots. The doorjamb and the side of the door to their left were a mass of jagged splinters. Someone had shot off the lock. Shards of wood crunched beneath their boots as they stepped cautiously into the room. Lavender led the way, the arm holding his pistol outstretched before him.

It was a man's study. Bookcases towered up the walls around them. A warm fire flickered in the grate. Before them on the thick carpet, Gabriel Gomez lay dead. His lifeless eyes stared up at the crystal chandelier in the centre of the ornate ceiling above. Blood seeped from the hole in his skull onto the white muslin of his cravat; he had been shot in the head.

Standing in front of him, with dishevelled hair and a horrified expression on her face was Doña Magdalena. She leant on the high back of a winged armchair for support with one hand. In the other, she limply held a pearl-handled pistol. Smoke still curled from the barrel.

Woods glanced sharply at Lavender who was obviously as surprised as him to see her here. Doña Magdalena stared back, her luminous eyes wide with shock. Both were oblivious to everything else in the room.

Woods cleared his throat. 'What has happened here, Doña Magdalena?' he asked.

'So glad you could join us, Detective Lavender,' said a heavily accented, sarcastic male voice beside him. Woods spun around and found himself staring into the cold eyes of a tall, good-looking foreigner.

'It appears that Doña Magdalena has just shot dead one of my tenants.'

Chapter Thirty

'What shall we do, sir?' Woods' voice was so low it was almost a whisper.

Lavender couldn't think or move. He didn't even react to Felipe Menendez's sarcasm. He stared at the woman he loved. Magdalena stared back, breathing heavily through parted lips. Her eyes were dark impenetrable pools.

Woods gave him a curious look and moved forward to take command. 'Evenin', Doña Magdalena.' He gently removed the pistol from Magdalena's grasp and opened the barrel. 'It's warm and the riflin' groove is empty.' Next, Woods squatted down next to the corpse and placed his hand at the side of Gomez's neck. 'Well, he's dead, for sure,' he pronounced.

Magdalena tore her gaze away from his own and looked down compassionately at the dead Spaniard. 'He shot himself.' Her voice cracked as if she struggled to formulate the words. The three men stared at her in silence. 'When I came through the door he was dead. He'd shot himself.'

Woods was about to stand up when he suddenly leant forward and reached out beneath the great beech-wood desk that dominated the room. When he withdrew his hand, it held a pistol: the tip of the barrel was blackened with residue powder. 'This is still warm as well,' he said. He snapped open the barrel. 'One shot fired.'

Lavender heaved a huge sigh of relief. Two pistols, both fired. Two shots. One shot had taken off the door lock; the other went into Gomez's skull.

He found his voice and turned to face Menendez. 'What has occurred here tonight?'

'As I told you,' Menendez said in that languid, annoying voice of his. 'Doña Magdalena has just shot dead my tenant, Gabriel Gomez.'

'I did not!' Magdalena's anger made her suddenly articulate. 'I heard Don Gabriel arrive home from the theatre and enter this room. Next, I heard the sound of a pistol shot and came to investigate – but the door was locked from the inside. I was concerned that someone might be bleeding to death in here – and Juana didn't seem to know where the spare key was for the room.' She glanced contemptuously in the direction of the two other women who were now hovering in the doorway. In the better light of the study, Lavender now recognised them as the two Spanish women they had met at the theatre in the company of their brother. 'So I used my pistol to shoot off the door lock. Juana and Olaya watched me.'

Lavender turned to the women framed in the doorway. 'Is this true?' He knew it was. The women both glanced nervously at their brother before nodding.

Magdalena took a deep breath as she struggled to find her next words. 'When I entered the room,' she said quietly. 'Don Gabriel was already dead – by his own hand.' She pointed to the pistol Woods had retrieved from under the desk. 'He has killed himself.'

To give himself some time to think, Lavender walked over to the damaged door and examined the splintered wood.

'Where were you when this happened?' he asked Menendez.

'I came into the room after I heard the pistols firing. I walked in to see Doña Magdalena and my sisters standing over the dead man. It was only a few seconds before you and your constable burst through the same door.'

'So you followed them into the room?'

Suddenly, there was a renewed wailing from the hallway.

'Excuse me,' Menendez said. 'I must see to my sisters. They're distressed.'

Lavender waited until Menendez was out of earshot before he moved over to Magdalena. 'Is this true?' he asked quietly. 'Did he follow you into this room?'

She nodded. 'The study was empty when I broke in. Gabriel just lay there – dead. I'd heard the first shot only moments before.' Her face crumpled and she swayed. He put his arm round her waist to steady her and pulled her close. She rested her head on his shoulder and the sweet smell of her hair neutralised the acrid stench of gunpowder that lingered in the room. 'Do you want me to take you and Teresa back to your own lodgings?' he asked, quietly. 'I know these people are your friends but you don't want to be caught up in this.'

'No, no.' He could hear the distress in her voice. 'I will stay here the night as planned. Why would Don Gabriel kill himself?' Her long, black eyelashes glimmered with unshed tears.

Lavender grimaced. Gomez had known that they were following him and he would have known why. It was only a matter of time before the Spaniard would have been arrested and hanged as a foreign spy. Gomez had chosen to take his own life, rather than face the hangman's noose. But Magdalena didn't need to know this at the moment – and neither did Menendez.

'Let me take you out of here, Magdalena,' he said, gently. 'You need to call for Teresa, pack up your belongings and leave.' He placed his arm around her and led her out into the hallway.

Menendez and his two sisters glanced up with barely concealed hostility. Lavender's hackles rose but he controlled his tone and words as he turned and addressed the older sister in Spanish. 'Señorita Menendez, please take Doña Magdalena into the drawing room and wait for us there. She has had quite a shock.'

'Haven't we all?' snapped the woman. She glared at him sourly but did as he asked. The two sisters ushered Magdalena away.

With the women gone, Lavender's mind sprang into action. He returned to the study. Woods was still kneeling by the body. 'His coat pockets are empty, sir,' he said.

Lavender frowned. 'Have you checked his waistcoat?'

Woods nodded.

Where was the list of code that Gomez had removed from April Clare's script in the theatre? The Spaniard had met no one since he left the Sans Pareil and Magdalena said that Gomez had gone straight into the study and locked the door before he shot himself.

'He must have put the list down somewhere. Help me check the desk and the rest of the room,' Lavender said.

Ignoring the corpse, which still lay on the carpet, they checked every shelf, ledge and tabletop in the room. Woods rummaged through the waste bin and Lavender rolled over the body to check the piece of paper wasn't trapped beneath.

When Menendez returned, Lavender was trying and failing to open the locked drawers of the desk. 'I have sent for an undertaker,' Menendez said. Lavender nodded brusquely. Everything about Menendez irritated him, from the man's bored and drawling voice to the sardonic glint in his arrogant eyes. 'Are you looking for something, gentlemen?' the Spaniard asked.

'What was your relationship with Don Gabriel?' Lavender asked.

'As I have already told you, Detective, he was my tenant.'

'For how long?'

Menendez shrugged. 'A few months. He needed lodgings and I was happy to assist such a talented artist. He was a fine singer; we always enjoyed his performances at the theatre.'

'But this is not his room?'

'Well, no,' Menendez said. 'The room he rents from us is upstairs. This is my study.'

'Why did he come in here to shoot himself?'

Menendez raised his eyebrows and gave Lavender a disparaging look. 'I have no idea. It was probably because this is where I keep my pistol.'

'This is your weapon?' Woods held up the pistol he had retrieved from the floor.

'Yes,' Menendez said. 'I keep it behind those books.' He pointed towards a row of red classics on a shelf of the bookcase. 'Don Gabriel knew this.'

'Why would he use your pistol to kill himself?'

Menendez shrugged again. 'You do ask the most obscure questions, Detective. I presume he used my pistol because he didn't have one of his own. And like me, he wasn't privy to the knowledge that Doña Magdalena secretes one in her petticoats. Presumably he thought it was the only weapon in the house.'

He glanced up sharply as Woods tried to force open another one of the drawers in the desk. 'There is no point trying to open those drawers, Constable.' Menendez patted the breast of his coat. 'I keep the key on me at all times – and they're locked now. Whatever it is you're looking for, it won't be in the desk.'

'Why do you think Gomez killed himself?' Lavender asked.

The Spaniard gave a low laugh. 'How do any of us know what goes on in another man's mind?' he asked.

'Was he melancholic?'

'Not particularly.'

'Was he in trouble or afraid of something or someone, perhaps?'

'I have no idea, Detective.' Irritation flickered across the Spaniard's face. 'Like many Spaniards he had fled his home country in fear of his life. But perhaps you can answer a question for me, Lavender. Perhaps you can explain why you and your constable were on my doorstep when the poor fellow decided to take his own life?'

The ensuing silence weighed heavily in the room. Menendez's face darkened to a scowl. 'I'm not stupid enough to imagine for one minute that you were here to do some late night courting with Doña Magdalena, Lavender – not with your constable in tow. So why are you here? Have you followed and intimidated Don Gabriel?' Lavender and Woods said nothing. 'Was he running from the two of you when he dashed into the house and shot himself?' Menendez asked.

Lavender said nothing.

'Your silence damns you, Detective,' he snarled. 'You two fools have driven this poor man to his death!'

'That is for an inquest to decide,' Lavender said, calmly. 'In the meantime, I would be grateful if you could let us into Don Gabriel's room. There may be more evidence in there about his state of mind.'

Chapter Thirty-one

While they waited for the undertaker to arrive, Menendez grudgingly allowed Lavender and Woods into Gomez's bedchamber. But a thorough search of the room revealed nothing except a few letters from his sister back in Spain. 'He had no other family,' Menendez told them.

It was bitterly cold when Lavender and Woods finally left Bedford Square but the wind had dropped. A full moon rode high in the night sky illuminating their path back to Bow Street. Lavender was exhausted and dejected; it had been a long day and their undercover operation in the theatre had not ended up how they had hoped. Gomez's suicide was a disappointment. The young cab driver, Alfie Tummins, had told Woods that three or four men had held up his coach and kidnapped Harriet Willoughby. So there were still more of the gang at large in the city. He had hoped that Gomez would lead him to them, but with his death the trail had gone cold.

Lavender was also uneasy at the thought that Magdalena still remained in that house. She had ignored his suggestion that she returned to her own lodgings and he had not seen her since he handed her over to the care of the Menendez sisters. He assumed she had retired for the night. He would call first thing in the morning and escort her and Teresa safely back to their lodgings. He would perform this last act of friendship for her, at least.

'I don't understand it,' Woods said as they trudged back towards Covent Garden. It was quieter on the streets now although shadowy figures still lurked in the maze of dank alleys that led off Shaftesbury Avenue. 'Where did that ruddy list of code end up? We watched Gomez every step of the way back from the theatre. He didn't stop anywhere and he spoke to no one. He walked through the door of that house, straight into the study – again without speakin' to anyone – then he locked the door, pulled out a pistol and shot himself.'

'He must have destroyed it,' Lavender said.

'But when? And why?'

'He probably threw the list onto the fire in the grate just before he shot himself.'

'Why?'

'To destroy the evidence of his involvement in the espionage,' Lavender said. He carefully sidestepped a sleeping beggar whose limbs protruded dangerously from a shop doorway. 'Gomez knew we were following him and he seems to have panicked.'

'I'll swear blind he were talkin' to someone in that study when we saw him at the window,' Woods said. 'His lips definitely moved.'

Lavender frowned. 'That doesn't make sense,' he said. 'He had locked himself into the study. He was alone.'

'Gawd's teeth!' Woods stopped abruptly, his horrified expression visible in the pearlescent glow of the moon. 'Suppose he did manage to pass along the code?' he said. 'Suppose we missed somethin' and he handed it over to another agent back on Shaftesbury Avenue while we were trailin' him? All it would have taken was a sleight of hand – we wouldn't have seen him do it.'

'I don't think he realised he was being followed until he reached the corner of Bedford Square.' Distracted from his own thoughts,

Lavender tried to work out where this new concern of Woods' was leading.

'But if he did pass it along – then all that confidential information about the naval fleet in the Indian Ocean is now in our enemies' hands!' Woods said dramatically. His tired eyes were wide and distressed. 'We may have put the lives of thousands of sailors and officers in danger!'

Lavender stopped. He placed a comforting hand on Woods' arm and smiled. 'Don't worry, Ned. It wasn't the original list.'

'It wasn't?'

'No, Sackville gave us a false list of code to return to April Clare. He knew there was a risk that this plan could go wrong; he never intended to jeopardise the safety our fleet.'

'So this document was false?'

'Yes, and if it does find its way into the wrong hands, then it will lead the French on a merry goose chase around the Indian Ocean.'

Woods sighed with relief and managed a weak grin. 'Well, thank goodness for that!'

The streets were busier now they neared Covent Garden. Cabs sped by, spraying up filth from the gutter. Staggering drunks slowly weaved their way home after a noisy night in the taverns and gin shops.

They approached a nightwatchman huddled around a glowing brazier. He clutched his lantern and stout stick in his gloved hands. The smoky charcoal fumes of the fire made him cough. Beneath his wide-brimmed hat, his eyes narrowed as Woods and Lavender approached then widened with relief and recognition: 'Evening, Detective. Evening Constable.' They returned the old man's nod.

'Does this mean that this case is now over for us?' Woods asked as they turned onto Long Acre.

'Yes – apart from the report I've got to write,' Lavender said. 'Forsyth is in the gentle care of Captain Sackville and the Admir-alty.

A dangerous French spy ring has been uncovered and their operation foiled. April Clare is out of danger and back in her beloved theatre – and most importantly, at least two of the men responsible for the kidnapping and death of Harriet Willoughby have been identified: one of them is dead and the other is detained. If there are any more French spies or villains still at large, I suspect that Captain Sackville will take care of them.'

'That's a good result,' Woods said. 'We've done well.' A sly grin spread over the constable's broad face. 'You'll have more time now to spend on that "private business" of yours.'

Lavender grimaced and turned away to hide his misery and pain. Time was the last thing he needed right now. Spare time would hang like a leaden weight in his heart as he brooded over Magdalena's rejection of his marriage proposal. He would ask Read for a case that took him out of the city for a while. He needed to keep occupied and put some distance between them both.

But Woods obviously didn't intend to let this matter drop. 'I've been wonderin' for days what it were, this "private business" of yours.'

'I have bought a house,' Lavender said wearily, 'in Marylebone.'

'Oh.' Woods glanced across at him. 'That's excellent news. Does Doña Magdalena like this house?'

'Yes,' he replied bitterly. 'She likes the house – but she doesn't like me. Well, not well enough to marry me, anyway.'

Woods stopped dead in his tracks. His face etched with concern. 'She's turned you down?'

'Yes.'

'I see.' Woods thought for a moment then his voice assumed that deep, patronising tone he always employed when he was about to impart some great wisdom about the mysterious fairer sex. 'I thought that somethin' were up when I saw the two of you together back at Bedford Square. Well, don't worry about it, sir – I'm sure she'll say yes the next time you ask her.'

'There won't be a next time.' Lavender was desperate to get back to Bow Street and retire to his bed for the night but Woods seemed rooted to the spot – and suddenly burst out laughing.

'This is not the sympathetic response I expected,' Lavender snapped.

'Oh heaven and hell, man!' Woods said between the snorts of amusement. 'You can't give up askin' the gal just because she's said no once! You really don't know nothin' about women, do you?'

'Well, you're always telling me I don't.'

'Ask her again, sir.'

'She seemed adamant, Ned; she said that this was her final decision.'

'Nonsense!' Woods exclaimed. 'It often takes several goes to persuade 'em. It took me half a dozen times of askin' to get Betsy to wed me.'

This was a genuine surprise. 'Why?' Lavender asked.

Most of Woods' face was still in the shadows but Lavender had the distinct impression that his constable blushed. 'Because she were worried about me size.'

'Your size?' Lavender choked back a laugh of his own. 'Is that what she said? What on earth did she mean?'

Woods struggled to find the words. 'She didn't rightly say but I always thought that it were something a bit awkward.' Lavender was confused. 'I thought she were worried that we might not fit.'

'Might not fit?'

'Yes, with me being so big like – and her being so small and delicate.'

For a moment Lavender was baffled then an unwanted image leapt into his mind. A strangled laugh escaped his throat as he held up a hand to stop Woods in his tracks.

'Good God, Ned. Stop. I don't want to know anything more about you and Betsy "fitting".'

'Well, I were just sayin', sir.'

'I know you were. Let's leave it there, shall we? Personally, I suspect that any qualms Betsy may have had about your size and marrying you were more to do with the rumours of your legendary appetite. Betsy was probably worried that she wouldn't be able to feed you or would wear herself out in the attempt.'

Woods seemed a little disappointed with this suggestion but soon regained his good humour. 'If you say so, sir.'

'By the way, how did you retrieve your pistol? I thought that Betsy had hidden it.'

'Oh I know all her secret places,' Woods said.

'I'm sure you do,' Lavender said wryly. 'And you have four children to prove it.'

They paused for a moment as a large drunken and noisy crowd of both men and women staggered past them.

'I would ask Doña Magdalena again,' Woods said. 'Women are Contrary Marys at the best of times.'

Lavender smiled and realised that Woods, with his gentle humour and his homespun philosophy, had lifted the lid on some of his misery. Maybe his constable was right. Perhaps a bit of persistence was all that was needed to persuade the woman of his dreams that she should be his wife.

The night clerk smiled at Lavender and Woods as they entered the grim hallway of Bow Street police office. He had been bent over a document on the desk, straining to read it by the weak light of a few lanterns and the tallow candles in the wall sconces. The place was cold and unwelcoming in daylight; at night it was downright dismal. But the clerk seemed far from disheartened by his grim surroundings. 'Good evening, Lavender,' he said cheerfully, 'Evening, Constable Woods.'

'I don't suppose that anything much will happen tomorrow, with it being the Sabbath,' Lavender said. He reached across the high wooden desk for the inkwell and quill that stood idle by the clerk's hands. 'I'll leave a note for Magistrate Read and tell him about tonight's events. I'll call on Captain Sackville first thing on Monday morning and come here later. You get yourself off home, Ned and have a good rest tomorrow – you've deserved it.'

Woods glanced around the near-empty hallway. 'It's quiet in here tonight,' he said. 'Normally this place writhes with the scum and tag-rag of the Seven Dials and the rookery of St Giles.'

The clerk nodded. 'It's not often we can see the floorboards. There's a few tosspots chirpin' merrily in the cells out the back but I think the cold 'as kept most of the felons indoors tonight – apart from that drunkard over there behind the door.' He waved in the direction of a snoring heap of rags across the hallway. 'I can't move 'im on my own. So I've just left 'im where 'e passed out. Riley will be along in a bit; we'll shift 'im together.'

'Behind the door,' Lavender said. He choked on his own words. He felt like someone had just poured a pail of icy water over his head.

The clerk pointed again. 'Yes, over there.'

'Behind the door.' Lavender cursed his own stupidity. Beneath the white muslin of his starched cravat, a vein began to throb.

'Are you all right, sir?' Woods blinked at him, concern etched across his broad features.

Lavender threw down the quill and swore loudly. 'He was behind the door all the time! Behind the bloody door!'

'Who was?'

'Menendez!' Lavender shouted. 'It's the oldest trick in the damned book – and we've just fallen for it. Quick, Ned! The stables – we need to ride back to Bedford Square and arrest Menendez.'

'Why? What's the matter?' Alarmed, Woods fell into step beside Lavender as they strode back through the corridors, hurling the internal doors aside. 'What does Menendez have to do with this spy ring?'

'He's up to his neck in it. He's probably the ringleader.'

Woods let out a curse. 'How did you work that out?'

For a brief moment Lavender stopped in his tracks and turned to face Woods who had jerked to a halt beside him. 'When Gomez dashed into the house and went into the Menendez's study, he didn't go in there to kill himself. I think that Menendez was already in the study and Gomez went to tell him that we had followed him.'

'Do you think that Gomez gave that list of code to Menendez?'

'Yes, I'm sure he did. I also think that Menendez realised that if Gomez was arrested and interrogated that he would soon reveal the names of the rest of the conspirators.'

'Gawd's teeth!' Woods' mouth dropped open.

'Menendez had to cover his own involvement with the gang – and quickly,' Lavender said. 'When Gomez turned his back to look out of the window, Menendez saw his opportunity. He locked the door and reached behind the books for his pistol.'

'I knew that Gomez was talking' to someone else in that room!'

'Seconds later, Menendez shot him.'

Woods let out a low whistle. 'But he wasn't in the room when Doña Magdalena burst in.'

'Menendez stepped back behind the door and waited until someone found the spare key and burst into the room. He didn't anticipate that Magdalena would shoot off the lock – he expected that his sisters would arrive with the spare key – but the effect was the same. Once the women entered the room their attention was riveted on the shocking sight of the dead man on the floor – none of them were aware that Menendez was behind the door. All he had to do was step forward and they would assume that he had followed them into the room.'

'Heaven and hell!' Woods exclaimed. They reached the stable block. With the help of a groom, they hastily threw saddles onto a couple of the horses and tightened up the girths.

'Remember,' Lavender said as he swung up into the stirrups, 'Sackville will want us to arrest Menendez – not shoot him.'

'We've left Doña Magdalena alone in that house with a murderer,' Woods said. 'Let's hope she'll be safe.'

Lavender's gut twisted as he gathered up the reins. 'If she's not,' he said grimly, 'if Menendez does anything to hurt her – or Teresa – then sod Sackville's instructions, I'll strangle the bastard with my own hands. '

They dug their heels into the flanks of their horses and cantered out of the yard.

Chapter Thirty-two

Magdalena lay awake listening to the unfamiliar night sounds of the house in Bedford Square. A house was never silent. Roof tiles lifted and rocked above her head; small showers of soot fell down the chimneys; floorboards creaked and groaned of their own volition. Somewhere a mouse scuttled.

A feeble swathe of moonlight floated through the chink in her window drapes but the rest of the room was pitch-black. She saw the faint glimmer of candlelight beneath the bottom of her door as a footman passed by. She waited for a moment, and then heard him in the hallway downstairs, checking the security of the huge bolts on the front door. Silence fell. The only sound now was the noisy pounding of her heart.

'The things I do for you, Sebastián,' she whispered, as she pushed back the sheets and swung out of the bed. The thought of her son gave her strength. She would need it. She had told Teresa she didn't need her help with undressing tonight – she was still fully clothed.

The house was thickly carpeted so she decided to risk wearing her boots. But she dared not risk a candle. Clutching her cloak over her arm, Magdalena slipped like a shadow onto the chilly landing and made her way towards Don Felipe's bedroom. She paused with her hand on the door handle.

For a moment her courage failed her. *This is madness*, she thought. But another voice in her head drowned out the fear and urged her forward: *Sebastián. I need the money*. The door was well oiled. It pushed open with only the faintest click. Menendez's strong masculine scent wafted out of the room. She held her breath and only exhaled when Don Felipe continued the steady rhythm of his snoring.

Thankfully, his room was at the front of the house on Bedford Square and light from the street lanterns filtered through the windows. Leaving her cloak outside and ignoring the lump beneath the bedclothes, she glanced around for Menendez's coat. It was thrown over a nearby chair. She stepped forward and slid her hand into the inside breast pocket where she knew he kept the key to his desk. She found it instantly. Silently, she backed out of the room.

So far this had been easier than she had expected. A lot easier. Don Gabriel's suicide earlier in the evening had given her an excuse to shoot off the door lock to the study and now she had possession of the key to the desk drawers. Within seconds, she was inside the study and feeling braver, she lit the desk lamp. She yanked open the doors to the desk and flicked through Menendez's private correspondence. It wasn't long before she found documents that damned him. They made for a chilling read. Magistrate Read was right: Menendez was a traitor in the pay of the French. He was a spy.

'Breeding will out,' she muttered angrily through gritted teeth as she folded the letters and slid them down the front of her bodice.

'Indeed it will, Magdalena,' said a cold voice behind her. 'Although, I'm surprised to find a daughter of the *hidalguía* has entered my bedchamber, stolen the key to my desk and riffled through my private papers like a common thief.'

She spun around. Menendez stood behind her; his hair still dishevelled from his bed and his shirt open at the neck. He twisted his cravat in his hands and his face was contorted with anger. *How did I not hear him enter the room?* She pushed herself back against the desk in alarm.

'Did your detective lover persuade you to turn into an informer against your own countrymen?' he demanded.

'You're a traitor!' she yelled into his leering face. 'You're a dancing monkey for *los cerdos franceses*!'

He laughed bitterly and stepped closer. 'I'm a realist,' he snarled. 'I know that collaboration with the French is the only way to end this accursed war and bring some normality back into our lives. But you, madam – you're a hellcat and a whore.'

Menendez gripped her shoulders roughly, spun her round and forced her face down over the desk. Paperweights, inkbottles and quills flew onto the floor. He pressed down onto her with the weight of his body and whipped his cravat over her head. She opened her mouth to scream with fear and pain but he yanked the cravat into her mouth before she could make a sound and tied it behind her head. The gag cut painfully into the sides of her mouth.

Magdalena kicked out behind her but she was no match for Don Felipe's strength. He had her firmly pinned down over the desk. Now his right hand began to roam over her body. She gasped in horror as she felt him lift her skirts and run his hands up her legs to the top of her stockings. *Does he intend to ravish me?*

She screwed her eyes up and tried to block out the sensation of his mauling hands. Suddenly, he found what he was looking for. He whipped her pistol out from the top of her boots. He pressed the muzzle of the weapon into the side of her temple.

'Did you reload it after you shot off my door lock?' he hissed in her ear. 'Shall I pull the trigger and end your life now? I've caught you red-handed trying to rob me.'

Magdalena froze.

'No.' Menendez laughed and pulled back the pistol. 'You're worth more to me alive than dead. I can think of a few other people who want to kill you – and they will pay me handsomely to return you to their clutches. Did you know that there is a reward out for your capture in Spain?' He smoothed her skirts back down over her legs. She recoiled at his touch.

'The French don't forgive,' he continued. 'They have offered a large reward for the return of the woman who shot four of their officers – and I will need that money now. Now that you have spoiled my little operation here in London.'

She swallowed hard and tried to scream but it came out as a strangled gurgle.

'Yes, I think we'll take a little trip back to Spain together.' He dragged her over to the windows and, using the cords that usually tied back the drapes, he bound her hands behind her back. Next he pushed her to the floor and tied up her ankles. She was completely helpless.

'Of course, they will play with you for a while before they execute you,' he said. 'They will torture you for information and despoil you.'

Sebastián's cheeky, smiling little face came into Magdalena's mind. As tears streamed from her eyes, she forced herself to think of his laugh and his sweet, wet kiss on her cheek. *Stephen will take care of him now. Please God, Stephen would never let her son starve.*

She was vaguely aware that Menendez left the room. The waiting seemed interminable. The ormolu clock on the fireplace taunted her with its ticking as it measured out some of the last minutes of her life. It was over. Only misery and horror lay ahead for her now.

Fresh tears seeped unbidden out of the corner of her eyes. *What a fool I have been! To risk everything – for this?* Part of her wished that

Menendez would shoot her in the head there and then. She shivered at the thought of the unspeakable horrors the French would make her suffer. *But at least Sebastián is safe.*

Menendez returned in his outdoor coat with its voluminous capes. He untied the rope around her ankles and dragged her roughly to her feet. 'Your carriage awaits you madam,' he snarled. He wrapped her own cloak around her shoulders, fastened it, pulled up her hood and dragged her into the cold hallway and out of the open front door.

For a moment, he left her standing on the doorstep while he spoke to the coach driver who was loading a small trunk onto the roof. Menendez had made a mistake. She stood in a pool of light beneath the oil lamp on the wall of the house. A few yards behind the Menendez coach a cab had drawn up at one of the neighbouring houses. The young driver looked curiously in their direction.

She shook her head vigorously and the loose-fitting hood fell back. Now her head, her face and the white gag that silenced her were clearly visible in the lamplight.

Menendez bounded up the steps and whipped the hood back over her head. 'You whore!' he hissed as he tried to drag her towards the coach. She resisted him as much as she could, refusing to use her legs to walk. Desperately, she prayed that the young cabby could see her resistance.

The coach door slammed shut behind them. Menendez threw her down into a seat then leant down and slapped her hard across her face. Tears sprang from her eyes at the pain. But a sense of triumph rose inside her along with renewed hope.

'Don't think that anyone will come to your aid, now you two-faced trollop! Your stupid, precious lover is tucked up in his bed and snoring his head off – and no one else cares for you. Do you hear me, you whore? You're just another Spanish refugee and no one gives a damn. No one cares!' The carriage jerked as it pulled away from the kerb.

Behind her gag, Magdalena mouthed the worst obscenity she knew in Menendez's direction.

Chapter Thirty-three

Lavender and Woods thundered around the corner into Bedford Square and pulled up sharply in front of the Menendez house. Throwing the reins over the park railings, they raced up the steps. Lavender hammered on the door with a ferocity that should have wakened the dead, never mind the Menendez household. Neither of them paid attention to the pale and startled coachman sat on his cab.

A dishevelled footman, with no wig and his waistcoat flapping open over yesterday's creased shirt, finally answered the door. He opened his mouth to protest at their noisy intrusion but he never managed to utter his complaint. Woods pushed him roughly to one side as the two men strode into the dim hallway.

Juana Menendez was halfway down the staircase, a lamp in her hand and a shawl thrown loosely over the shoulders of her billowing nightgown.

'Detective! How dare you force your way in here – again!' She was furious.

'Where is your brother, Señorita Menendez?'

'Felipe? Why?'

'Where is he?'

'He has gone out for a while. His room is empty.'

'Where has he gone?'

'I don't know!' she snapped. 'I'm not privy to his business.'

Lavender hesitated for a moment. He saw Juana's plump sister lurking nervously on the upstairs landing in the shadows but where was Magdalena? Surely they had made enough noise to awaken the entire household?

'I need to see his room,' Lavender said.

'You most certainly shall not! How dare you! Andreo' – she waved a furious hand at the footman, gesturing him towards the detectives – 'Andreo! Remove these persons from our house immediately.'

Woods turned to face the manservant. 'I wouldn't try anythin' on if I were you, fellah,' he growled.

Andreo took a step back.

Suddenly, there was a flash of white linen and Teresa flew across the landing in her nightgown, boots and a cheap woollen shawl. Her loose frizzy hair flew out behind her. 'Señor the detective! Señor the detective!' she screamed as she raced down the stairs.

'How dare you, you slut!' Juana Menendez screamed in Spanish. She grabbed Teresa by the hair and jerked the girl to an abrupt halt. Teresa shrieked in pain and burst into tears. 'Go back to the servants' quarters – now!'

Lavender leapt up the stairs to Teresa's rescue. The footman stepped forward at the same time – only to find his way barred by Woods' bulky figure. 'Easy fellah.'

Lavender pulled Teresa away from Juana Menendez's clutches and led the sobbing maid back down the stairs to safety. 'She has gone, Señor the detective!' Teresa wailed. 'She has gone!'

Lavender's gut wrenched again and he felt the bile rise in his throat. 'Who has gone Teresa?' he asked gently. But he knew the answer already.

'Doña Magdalena – she's not in her bed.' She buried her head in his chest and sobbed.

'There! See you have your answer!' Juana Menendez yelled. 'Your precious Señora Morales is out on a midnight assignation – unchaperoned – with my brother. The filthy whore!'

'No!' Teresa suddenly came back to life. She stamped her foot and swung back in fury to face the triumphant mistress of the house. 'No. Doña Magdalena, she loves Señor the detective! She tell me!'

'Well, where is she then?' Juana goaded. 'She's not with him now, is she? She's with my brother? Explain that!'

'I know where they are,' squeaked a nervous male voice from behind them.

Startled, everyone spun round. They stared in disbelief at the skinny young cab driver framed in the open doorway and backlit by the moonlight. Swathed in scarves against the cold, with his hat pulled low over his eyes, he clutched his whip tightly in his gloved hands.

'Alfie!' Woods exclaimed. 'Is it Alfie?'

'Evening, Constable Woods.' The lad touched the brim of his hat respectfully. 'I thought I recognised you.'

'You know him?' Lavender asked.

'Of course I do,' Woods said. 'This is Master Alfie Tummins from the cabby company in Wandsworth.'

'Oh yes?' Lavender said, icily. 'This is the young man who let kidnappers steal away poor Harriet Willoughby from his cab?'

'Well – as Constable Woods knows – I'm right sorry about that.' Tummins swallowed anxiously. 'But I can 'elp yer tonight, Constable, I can. I knows where that man took that woman.'

'How so?' Lavender demanded. Even Teresa looked up from Lavender's chest.

'I 'eard 'im tell the coach driver to take them to the wharf at Smith's timber yard next to Westminster Bridge.'

The Lambeth docks? What the hell was Menendez going to do with Magdalena at the docks?

'Are you sure, man?' Woods asked the timid coach driver.

'Very sure,' the lad replied. 'I were watchin' them closely and listenin' on account of the woman, you see.'

'The woman?'

'Yes, the pretty, dark one. She were gagged and all trussed up. She fought like a fiend but that foreign geezer dragged 'er into the coach.'

'These are lies!' Juana Menendez screamed down the stairs. 'Foul calumny!'

'Why didn't you go to help?' Lavender snapped.

'There wasn't time. They were aboard and the driver 'ad cracked the whip and set off before I could think.'

'When was this?'

'About ten minutes ago.'

Ten minutes! There was still chance to catch them.

'The next thing I knew, you and Constable Woods rode round the corner like the devil were after you. I thought the two events were connected so I leapt down from me cab and came 'ere.'

'You've done well, Alfie,' Woods said. Even in the dim light they watched the young coachman's cheeks flush red with pleasure.

'You'll tell me da?'

'Yes, lad, I will.' Woods pulled Teresa away from where she was still clung onto Lavender and pushed her towards the young coachman. 'I need you to do me another favour, son. I want you take this young gal safely to my wife on Oak Road. Tell my wife to look after her until I get home.' He gave Tummins the address and tossed him a few coins. 'You'll be all right, treacle,' he said to Teresa. 'Young Alfie here and Mrs Woods will take care of you.'

Juana Menendez's curses rang in their ears as they leapt down the steps and grabbed the reins of their tethered horses.

'Menendez has got Magdalena,' Lavender said as he swung himself up into the saddle. Fear strangled his voice in his throat.

'Not for long,' Woods reassured him. He turned his horse to face south. 'They're in a carriage – and only have ten minutes on us. We'll be at that wharf ahead of them!'

Chapter Thirty-four

Magdalena was shivering when the coach jerked to halt in front of a row of deserted warehouses and huge piles of sawn planking. Menendez opened the door and the stench of the river mingled with sawdust and rotting wood flooded into the carriage. He dragged her out onto the wharf, where bales of goods and huge piles of stacked crates towered around them. The coachman handed down the small trunk to Menendez then climbed back onto his box and drove away.

Menendez tucked the trunk beneath one arm and grabbed Magdalena roughly with the other. 'We walk from here,' he said.

Magdalena's boots slipped on the treacherous black ice. Unable to use her bound arms to steady herself she stumbled frequently. Only a low stone balustrade separated them from the deadly black waters of the silent Thames below. She thought she might break away from her captor and throw herself into the river. Drowning in the Thames seemed preferable to the fate that lay ahead of her in Spain at the hands of the French.

But Menendez tightened his grip and pulled her away from the edge. 'Careful now, Magdalena,' he hissed in her ear. 'You're a valuable commodity to me. I'd hate to lose you in the water.' Putting down the trunk, he lifted a lantern from the wall of a warehouse and signalled to his invisible allies in the Thames.

The raw wind whipped around Magdalena's skirts. Her hood blew back and her teeth chattered. She didn't know whether it was with fear or the cold. Menendez's letters to his French spymasters crackled softly against her skin. He clearly hadn't seen her hide them. They were still down the front of her bodice, stabbing her in the heart to remind her of her foolishness.

She glanced around desperately. Across the black expanse of the water the welcoming lights of Westminster twinkled and glowed but this wharf was deserted. Above her head, wooden cranes creaked and swayed in the cold wind, and their tangled rigging slapped against the beams. The bulbous oak hull of a three-masted sloop anchored halfway across the river was silhouetted against the moon. A light flashed from the prow, followed by another. It was responding to Menendez's signal. Those pinpricks of light were sealing her doom.

'Not long now,' Menendez said, the satisfaction evident in his voice. 'My friends will take good care of us on our voyage; they will be delighted to receive the list I have in my pocket – the one your stupid lover sought.'

Magdalena thought again about throwing herself into the water. Did she have the strength to knock him over the balustrade too? Could she kill them both? She shook her head and sighed: Menendez could swim.

She heard the slap of oars against the choppy water of the Thames and the monotonous creak of metal oarlocks. Someone was rowing out from the ship towards them.

'I have had a thought,' Menendez said. She saw the leering grin stretched across his face. 'As part of my reward for returning you to the French, I will ask that your confiscated estates be given to me. A neat solution, don't you think? Unfortunate for your son, but this is a far preferable course of action than marrying you to acquire them.'

Her eyes flashed. She gave a strangled groan and tried to kick him. He laughed and kicked away her legs. Magdalena sank into an undignified heap on the ground. He leant down and clutched the neck of her cloak so tightly around her throat she thought he would strangle her. His hot breath was rank against her cheek.

'You didn't really think that I would sully my family name through marrying a murdering trollop like you, did you?' Menendez hissed. 'No, I just wanted you in Bedford Square as an insurance in case your prying lover came too close to my operation.' He laughed again. 'You're too old for me Magdalena. I prefer my women to be younger – a lot younger.' She groaned and closed her eyes, desperate to shut out his mocking voice. But it didn't work. 'Even your little maid is too old and haggard for me. But it's a pity that we have to leave tonight – I would have still despoiled your precious Teresa anyway – and enjoyed it.'

She groaned with fury. If only her hands were free she would have strangled him. She had never felt more alone, helpless or furious in her life.

At the base of the wharf, the sailors from the ship hauled in their dripping oars and hailed Menendez in French. A dark figure clambered out of the wooden longboat and leapt up the slimy stone steps that glistened with riverweed in the moonlight. 'Do you have it?' he growled in French.

'Oh, yes.' Menendez pulled a folded piece of paper out of his coat pocket with a flourish and handed it over to the other man.

'Who's this?' the Frenchman asked with a curt nod of his head towards Magdalena.

Menendez hauled her to her feet. 'This is Doña Magdalena. She can't speak right now because she's gagged. She will travel back to Spain with us.'

'I don't think so, Menendez!'

Two dark-coated figures suddenly moved out from between the stacked bales on the wharf, deadly metal pistols gleaming in their hands. Magdalena gasped, unable to believe her ears and her eyes. It was Stephen and Constable Woods. They both looked strained and Stephen's face was glowering with anger. They stalked cautiously towards Menendez, their weapons steady and aimed at him. She heard the Frenchman curse and scurry back down the steps. Excitement and hope welled up inside her.

Menendez laughed cruelly. He pulled Magdalena back into him and held up a pistol to her temple. 'You're a damned nuisance, Lavender,' he said.

Is it his own pistol? she wondered as the cold barrel pressed into the side of her head. *Or is it the empty one of mine he pulled out of my boots?* Desperately, she tried to remember if Menendez had gone anywhere near the bookcase in the study where he kept his own weapon. If it was her empty weapon, then this was a bluff.

'Let her go!' Stephen and Constable Woods moved closer. They fanned out.

'One more step and I shall kill her,' Menendez snarled. But she heard the tension and panic in his voice.

'Trust a Spaniard to hide behind a woman's skirts,' Woods sneered.

But the two officers stopped in their tracks, unprepared to take a chance with Magdalena's life.

'Let her go and throw down your weapon!' Lavender yelled.

Menendez dragged her a step closer towards the treacherous steps and glanced back uneasily. The Frenchman was already clambering back into the longboat. Magdalena sensed her captor's indecision and knew that he would never be able to drag her down those slippery steps into that wooden boat. Not with her arms bound behind her. He would have to use her as a shield until he reached the top step. Then no doubt he would let her to fall into the Thames as he leapt down into the boat.

She faced a stark choice. She could either struggle like mad, try to escape his clutches and risk a pistol shot through her skull – or she faced certain death in the icy waters of the Thames.

Magdalena made her decision. With every ounce of her strength she kicked out behind her. Her heel made contact sharp contact with his shin. He yelped with shock and temporarily loosened his grip. She seized her opportunity and threw herself forward as hard as she could, twisting her body to break free. She expected the flash and sharp retort of the pistol shot that would end her life. It never came. She landed in an undignified heap on the ground, jerking her head back to stop her face smashing onto the ground.

Time stood still. Menendez raised his pistol, swung round and aimed at Lavender. A single pistol shot rang out in the cold night air. The powder flash lit up the dock.

Felipe Menendez swayed. He dropped his pistol then toppled backwards off the wharf. Magdalena held her breath. For a split second there was nothing. Then she heard the gratifying splash as Menendez's body hit the water. She exhaled. She twisted her head and caught sight of the pistol lying on the ground. Its pearl handle glimmered in the moonlight: it was hers.

Stephen was instantly by her side. Constable Woods raced to the edge of the wharf. As Stephen pulled her up off the ground and took her into his arms, he called out to Woods: 'Is Menendez dead?'

'I can't see him in the river,' Woods growled. 'And his French friends haven't bothered to look for the body – they're leavin' without him.'

Magdalena could hear the frantic slap of oars against the water.

'The buggers are gettin' away!' Woods raised his pistol and took aim.

'No, Ned!' Stephen shouted. 'Let them go. The information they've got will cause the French more trouble than it's worth. Let them take that fake document back to their masters.'

Woods grunted with reluctance but he lowered his weapon.

'And get away from the edge – they might shoot back.'

Lavender gently took the gag from around Magdalena's mouth and untied her.

'It's over, Magdalena,' he said. 'It's over, my darling.'

She couldn't speak. She just fell into his arms, buried her face in his chest and sobbed with relief.

Lavender took Magdalena back to her lodgings, wrapped her tenderly in a thick shawl and made her sit in front of the fireplace while he raked around in the cold grate and lit a fire. But she couldn't settle. She rose to her feet and stood for a while by the window looking out into the damp, dark and silent street.

He came up behind her and handed her a large glass of brandy. Her hands still trembled and she sipped it unsteadily.

'Your window to the world,' he said softly. 'Are you looking out there for more excitement?'

A slight smile played around the edges of her lips. 'No, thank you, Detective Lavender,' she said. 'I think I've had more than enough excitement for one lifetime.'

Behind them the fire blazed into life. Lavender took a large drink from his own glass and felt the fiery liquid revitalise his insides. Warmth gradually seeped back into his aching body and colour crept up into Magdalena's cheeks.

Conscious of his stare, she gently touched the bruising around her mouth, caused by the gag. When she raised her hand, he noticed that there were bruises around her wrists too. Fresh anger flashed through his exhausted mind. *He's dead*, he told himself. *He's dead.*

'I must look a fright,' Magdalena said.

He smiled. Despite everything she had been through, her first thoughts were for her appearance. 'You always look beautiful to me, Magdalena,' he said. 'The cuts and bruises will fade and the swelling will go down.' He saw her colour deepen. 'I just hope that the terror Menendez caused you will fade just as quickly,' he added.

She shrugged. 'Do you think he's dead?'

'I'm sure of it,' he replied firmly. 'I shot him right between the eyes.'

She smiled, a deep satisfied smile. 'You have repaid your debt now Stephen,' she said. 'I saved your life at Barnby Moor; now you have saved mine.'

It was his turn to shrug. 'It doesn't alter how I feel about you, Magdalena,' he said. 'My offer of marriage never came out of gratitude for your help at Barnby Moor. It came because I have fallen in love with you.' He remembered Teresa's words back at Bedford Square: *She loves Señor the detective! She tell me!* He took a deep breath and remembered Woods' advice.

Magdalena smiled again and looked down modestly. She brushed a stray lock of hair from her eyes. 'I'm tired, Stephen,' she said. 'I think I need to retire for the night.'

Lavender fought back his disappointment and nodded. But he wasn't ready to do the gentlemanly thing and bow out just yet. 'I'll just stay long enough to finish my drink,' he said. Then he winked. 'If you want, I'll come and tuck you into your bed.'

She lowered her eyelashes but her lips still smiled. She disappeared behind the faded old curtain that separated off the sleeping quarters from the main room. He swirled the amber liquid around his glass, watched it glint in the firelight and waited.

Suddenly, he heard a strangled sob from the far end of the room. 'Stephen,' she murmured.

He was on his feet instantly, striding over to her. Magdalena was standing beside the large metal-framed bed, her shoulders drooped in misery.

'What's the matter, my darling?'

'I can't get this dress unhooked without Teresa's help.'

He gave a small laugh. This was the last thing he had expected: a game. He rose to the challenge. 'I see, madam,' he said. 'So you can help the British government smash a dangerous ring of French spies – but you can't undress yourself?'

She nodded, a half-smile playing around the edge of her gorgeous lips. He knew she was lying and a wave of anticipation swept through him.

'I'll do it,' he said softly. He moved forward to the warmth of her body and her scent. 'I've always wondered what it would be like to be a lady's maid.'

Carefully, he undid the hooks on the back of the gown. It fell away to the ground, with a rustle of silk. Magdalena wore a soft, white chemise beneath her satin corset. The garment flared out from her slender waist over the voluptuous curves of her hips. Its frilled neckline was tied loosely with a pink ribbon. His fingers itched to pull the trailing end of that ribbon.

'Thank you, Detective,' she said, softly.

'My pleasure, *señora*.' He slid his arms around her waist and pulled her back against his body. She didn't resist.

'You make a good lady's maid,' she whispered. 'I may use your services again.'

He lowered his head to kiss her neck and suck gently on her ear lobe. The softness and scent of her warm skin sent a fresh wave of passion coursing through his veins.

She relaxed against his him, twisted her head and looked up. Her violet-black eyes smouldered with desire. Her tongue flicked out to wet her lips. 'Stay with me tonight, Stephen,' she whispered.

'Only if you promise to marry me,' he said.

311

Chapter Thirty-five

Monday 26th February, 1810

Lavender, Woods and Captain Sackville sat in Read's office, watching the frowning magistrate as he read Lavender's report. A folded news-sheet lay discarded at the edge of his desk. Woods was amused to see one of the headlines on the front page: *Sans Pareil Actress Back from the Dead!* Today's news-sheets had all trumpeted the triumphant return of April Clare to the stage and were blithely unaware of the greater drama that had taken place in the capital over the last two days.

The longcase clock in the corner of the room ticked slowly. The fire crackled quietly in the grate. They heard the muted shouts of the hawkers mingled with the low rumble of the incessant traffic to Covent Garden. On his left, Captain Sackville grinned from ear to ear and lounged back comfortably in his chair. But Woods was conscious that Lavender, on his right, was tense and scowling. He wasn't sure why.

'So the French agent escaped on board the ship?' Read said. It was more of a statement than a question.

'Not entirely,' Sackville said. 'Constable Woods roused the chief customs officers for the pool of London and they launched a pilot boat. They managed to get the name of the ship from its bows before it reached the East India Docks at Blackwall and gathered speed. If that ship ever returns to the Thames, my agents will be ready and the Admiralty will deal with her and her crew.'

Read glanced up at Woods. 'You did well, Constable.'

Woods bristled with pride.

'But both Gabriel Gomez and Felipe Menendez are dead?'

'Unfortunately, yes,' Sackville said. 'Menendez shot Gomez before Lavender and Woods could arrest him.'

'And Menendez tried to escape,' Woods said quickly. 'Detective Lavender had no choice but to shoot him. He fell into the river and Mother Thames claimed him for her own.' Read glanced up at his two officers. Lavender said nothing.

'It doesn't matter,' Sackville said. 'The imposter, Sir Lawrence Forsyth, is in custody and is proving to be – how shall I put this? Quite cooperative?' There was a short silence. No one asked how the Admiralty had managed to make the spy so 'cooperative'. 'You will be interested to know, Lavender, that Forsyth doesn't have scarring from burns on his back.'

Lavender nodded. There was a look of satisfaction in his eyes but still he said nothing.

Sackville cleared his throat. His next words were calculated and formal. 'The Duke of Clarence has been informed about Forsyth's deception and is, understandably, quite horrified and distressed. I trust that the Admiralty can rely completely on the discretion of everyone in this room? Should the news-sheets – or the public at large – ever hear about this story then the scandal would be devastating to both us and the House of Hanover.'

Read nodded without glancing up. 'You can trust my officers, Captain. No one in this room will ever breath a word of this shocking affair. I am more concerned at the moment about all these Spaniards in my prison cells. Who are they?'

'Oh, that's down to me.' Woods grinned from ear to ear. 'After I left the customs officer, I rounded up a few of the lads from Bow Street and we went back to the Menendez house with a prison wagon. We arrested the whole bloody household – includin' that coachman – whom we think is also part of the spy ring.'

'I can see we will be busy sorting out this lot over the coming days, Magistrate Read,' Sackville said cheerfully.

Read reached for another document on his desk. 'It says on the charging sheets that the eldest Menendez sister has also spent a night in the Bow Street cells? Do you think she's part of the gang as well?'

'It's difficult to know, sir,' said Woods. He frowned and assumed a look of concerned innocence. 'We didn't arrest the younger sister but that eldest one is a sly old tabby and a hatchet-faced old trot.'

'We don't normally lock up women just because they're ugly and have a sharp tongue, Constable,' Read said. 'Otherwise there would be no room in the police cells of London for the criminals.'

'Well, I think that Captain Sackville's men should give her a thorough goin' over,' Woods insisted. 'There may be somethin' she knows.'

'Leave it to me,' Sackville said, grimly.

Woods grinned and felt a flush of satisfaction. He had been shocked at Juana Menendez's brutality towards little Teresa; the woman deserved an unpleasant stint in the cells.

Read sighed and shook his head. 'It looks like I will have a busy afternoon in court – I'll need a Spanish interpreter, Stephen.'

'Not me, I'm afraid,' Lavender said quickly. 'You'll have to find someone else. I'm busy this afternoon. I have some private business to attend to today.'

Read's mouth dropped open but before he could close it and reply, Sackville intervened. 'Yes, you fellahs probably deserve a little time off. All in all, a satisfactory conclusion, eh Read? The Admiralty is very pleased with how this case has been resolved. Admiral

Hawkes would like me to extend his thanks to you and your officers.'

'Humph.' Read was only partially placated. He glanced shrewdly at Lavender. 'You've done well,' he said. Lavender nodded. 'And Doña Magdalena? I trust she's no worse for wear following her ordeal?'

'Fortunately, she's fine,' Lavender said. 'But that is no thanks to you.'

Woods took a sharp breath. The simmering tension between the two men was about to erupt again. He braced himself for the conflict.

Lavender pulled a wad of letters out of his coat pocket and pushed them across the desk towards Read. 'She asked me to give you these. Apparently, these are documents which prove that Menendez was in the pay of the French.'

'I'll take those,' Sackville said and reached forward to claim them. Read nodded his approval.

'I understand that some payment is in order?' Lavender stared coldly at Read. 'You persuaded Doña Magdalena to spy for you, did you not? A foolish notion on your part which nearly got her killed.'

There was an awkward silence in the room. Woods was genuinely shocked. So that was why Doña Magdalena had become involved with Menendez – and why Lavender was so furious. Read shuffled uncomfortably in his seat and avoided eye contact with Lavender.

'Ah, yes,' he said. 'So she told you, did she? Well, I will make sure that she's reimbursed for her trouble.'

'I would hope so,' Lavender said. Read didn't reply. 'This will be the one and only time that she spies for you.'

Read nodded. 'I understand.'

'In fact, I have an announcement to make.' Lavender pulled himself up straight and glanced round to make sure that the other men were paying attention. Woods held his breath.

'Doña Magdalena has agreed to be my wife. We intend to marry at St Saviour and St Mary Overie in Southwark. The first banns will be read next Sunday.'

Woods exhaled, whooped and beamed from ear to ear. Both he and Sackville reached over and clapped Lavender on his back.

'Oh, I say, old man!' Sackville exclaimed.

'Congratulations, sir,' Woods said.

'Well, this is a rum turn-up for the books! An excellent outcome to the case, I say,' Sackville added.

Magistrate Read looked anything but pleased. 'Does she intend to convert to Protestantism?' he asked, sharply.

'No.'

'And what will your family think about your marriage to a foreign Catholic?' Read's voice rose with anger. 'Don't forget that I worked with your father for years – I'll wager that he'll not be happy about welcoming a Roman Catholic into the family.'

Woods frowned. He had also worked with John Lavender and knew him to be a fair and decent man, devoted to his family.

'Actually, I took Magdalena to meet them last night,' Lavender said calmly. 'They think she's delightful.'

Woods relaxed. *Good for John and Alice Lavender*, he thought.

Read threw up his hands in a dismissive gesture. His face set in a petulant frown. 'So be it. You go ahead and ruin your career with a marriage to a Papist,' he snapped. 'The demand for your services will soon dry up once this becomes public knowledge.'

Lavender shrugged and stared calmly across the desk at the blustering magistrate. 'I've told you before – I'll take my chances with that.'

'And I shall be sorry to lose Doña Magdalena's services as a Spanish teacher,' Read continued. 'I understand that she has been an instant hit with our operatives.'

'She would like to continue with her work,' Lavender said. 'She believes it will be a worthwhile occupation for her while I'm out of town on a case and I know that you need her. Although you and I need to talk, Read, about that woefully inadequate salary you pay her for her talents.'

Woods whistled quietly. That Doña Magdalena was certainly a unique kind of woman.

'That's most irregular.' Read scowled. 'It will look like you can't afford to keep your wife if she works.'

Lavender shrugged. 'I don't care what other people think about us,' he said. 'I think I've made that quite plain.'

'Yes, but you're well matched,' said Woods. 'Betsy said so.'

The other men regarded Woods curiously for a moment, then Read began to tidy up his desk. He shuffled the papers from one side of the desk to another and picked up a quill. He scowled and his voice became laced with sarcasm. 'Well, if your union has the blessing of Betsy Woods – then who am I to object? I'm not sure that Mrs Read will be so comfortable with this marriage, though. You do realise, don't you Lavender, that she may never be able to receive your Catholic wife?'

'I'm not sure that we care,' Lavender said. 'Besides which, I don't think Magdalena will be inviting you and Mrs Read to the wedding. I don't think she has forgiven you yet for putting her life in danger – and neither have I.'

Read gasped at the insult and the quill he was twirling fell out of his hands.

'I say, you fellahs!' Sackville burst out laughing. He stood up and pushed back his chair. 'I think it is time I left. You've obviously got some talking to do to resolve things between yourselves. Woods?'

'Yes, sir?' he said.

'If this spat escalates and they pull out the duelling pistols, then you have my permission to lock them both up in the cells.'

Woods grinned. 'Yes, sir.'

Both Read and Lavender suddenly looked uncomfortable.

'It won't come to that,' Lavender said. He also rose to his feet. 'There is nothing else to be said. The matter of my marriage is decided, whether Magistrate Read likes it or not. Now, if you'll excuse me, I will take the rest of the day off – as I said, I have some private business to attend to.'

Read pushed a file across the desk towards him. 'Before you go, take this,' he snapped. 'It's the details of your next case – in Northamptonshire. There's been a series of burglaries and the authorities need some help. You should leave tomorrow. I think we may need to put a few miles between us for a while, Detective Lavender.'

Woods grimaced at the formality in Read's tone as Lavender nodded.

'With any luck, you should have the matter resolved and be back in London in time for your nuptials.'

Lavender picked up the file and glanced at him coldly. 'Oh, don't worry yourself, Magistrate Read,' he said. 'I *will* be back in town in time for my wedding. But obviously, in Northamptonshire, I'll need Woods' help.'

For a moment it looked like Read would refuse, but then he threw up his hands in resignation. 'Oh for God's sake, take him,' he snapped. 'The horse patrol has forgotten what he bloody looks like anyway.'

Woods found Lavender down by the river, sitting on a crate and staring out at the water. Seagulls circled noisily overhead but it was quieter down here away from the hustle and bustle of the market hawkers and gin shops of Covent Garden. The tide was partially out and the heaving water slapped against the muddy banks. A small group of ragged urchins prodded at the mud, hunting for shellfish. A myriad of little boats and tall ships bobbed up and down in the choppy water.

There was a cold breeze but the detective didn't seem to notice it. He stared thoughtfully across the river at the wharfs on the south bank. Woods figured that Lavender was still probably brooding about the events of Saturday night. Betsy always said that happiness spins on a sixpence, and he could see that now. If they'd arrived a few moments later – or if Alfie Tummins hadn't been on the spot to help them – then things may have gone tragically wrong for his friend. It was a chilling thought. But Woods reckoned that Lavender didn't need reminding about that right now.

'Congratulations again, sir,' he said cheerfully, as he rolled up a barrel and sat down beside him. 'Don't worry about Magistrate Read; he'll come around to the notion of your marriage in the end.'

Lavender nodded. 'I know he will.'

'I knew you'd talk Doña Magdalena around eventually. It's going to be an excitin' new life for you both.'

Lavender smiled.

'Of course this is goin' to cost me a new hat for Betsy,' Woods continued, 'and probably a new coat for myself.'

Confusion flickered across Lavender's face. 'I don't think you'll need a new coat, Ned. I suspect it will be a quiet affair; Magdalena has no family except Sebastián, and it looks like that apart from you, Sackville and my family, hardly anyone else I know approves of our match.'

'If you want me to stand up for you, I'll need to look smart.'

'Stand up for me?'

'Aye, you'll need a witness for your nuptials, won't you? And as you haven't got no brothers, I thought I'd offer my services.'

Lavender's smile broadened. 'I'd be honoured to have you as my witness, Ned.'

'Well, that's settled then. Of course the gals will have to arrange the weddin' while we sort out those thievin' joskins up in Northamptonshire.'

Lavender groaned. 'I hadn't thought about that. Magdalena won't be pleased.'

'Oh, don't worry. They'll be glad to have us out of the way. Betsy will help Doña Magdalena. She loves a good knees-up, does my Betsy.'

'My life will never be the same again, will it?' Lavender said quietly.

'No, sir. Not with a feisty new bride, a stepson, a new home and a gaggle of servants to control.' His eyes twinkled with mischief. 'It'll burn a big hole in your savin's too. I can't see as you'll have much peace from now on. Your bachelor days are over.' He shook his head in mock solemnity. 'And then of course, there's Alfie Tummins.'

'Tummins? What does he have to do it?'

'The lad seems rather taken with young Teresa,' Woods said, and winked. 'He came back to see me yesterday and asked if he could walk out with her. I think he thought that I was her da. Obviously, I must have picked up a Spanish twang to my cockney accent over the years.'

Lavender looked like he didn't know whether to laugh or groan. 'Does Magdalena know?' he asked. 'I dread to think how she would react to the news that a young coachman wants to woo Teresa. She's very protective of her maid.'

'She doesn't know yet,' Woods said, 'but I'm sure that Betsy will tell her. I sent young Tummins away with a flea in his ear, of course – but I reckon that he won't take no for an answer. So no doubt you'll find him loiterin' outside your servant's entrance when you move into your new house in Marylebone.'

Lavender smiled. 'I'm taking Magdalena up to the house this lunchtime to discuss furnishings.'

'Ooh, that'll cost you.'

'And we're attending a soirée at Lady Caroline's tonight.'

Woods whistled. 'Lady Caroline Clare? That feisty aristocratic doxy?'

'Yes. She's a bit risqué, of course, but at least she's a Catholic and sympathetic to interfaith unions. Her first husband was a Rothschild. Magdalena and I will have to seek out friends from amongst the like-minded.'

'Well, you've always got us,' Woods said. 'Me and Betsy.'

Lavender smiled. 'Then we are blessed,' he said, simply.

'I'm just glad that you decided to make an honest woman of Doña Magdalena,' Woods continued.

Lavender narrowed his eyes. 'What do you mean by that, Ned?'

Woods grinned, winked and leant towards him. 'When a man arrives home to his rooms in Southwark at three o'clock on a Sunday afternoon – still wearin' the same muddied boots and sweatstained clothin' he was last seen wearin' on Saturday night – then a good police officer can only deduce one thing. You stayed all night in her bed, didn't you?'

Lavender's expression flitted between amusement and annoyance but he didn't reply.

Unabashed, Woods sat back on his barrel and continued. 'I've always had you marked down as a bit of a dark horse, sir – with rakish tendencies. Now I know that for sure. They say that you quiet ones are the worst and you've always been the quiet, bookish type.'

Lavender struggled to keep the amusement out of his voice. 'And I've always said that your powers of detection are wasted on the horse patrol, Ned. We must get you promoted to principal officer as soon as possible.'

Woods laughed smugly and tapped the side of his broad nose. 'I have my informers in Southwark.'

'Yes.' Lavender's voice was now heavy with irony. 'I know you do. I saw your Dan loitering on the other side of the street when I climbed out of my cab yesterday afternoon. How much did you have to pay him to stand there and spy on me?'

'It's never too early for the nippers to practise for a bit of under-cover work,' Woods replied. 'Besides which, it got him out from under Betsy's feet for a while.'

'Well, make sure you tell him that next time he's undercover, he's to restrain himself from shouting: "Good afternoon, Uncle Stephen!" across the street.'

'You'll have to start thinkin' about such things yourself now, like trainin' up the nippers,' Woods said. 'It won't be long before you have one in the cradle – especially if you carry on like this.'

Lavender choked slightly and stood up. 'Lord help me!' he muttered, but he was smiling.

Sunshine forced its way through the clouds and made the tips of the choppy waves on the Thames sparkle. It was going to be a beautiful day. Cold, but sunny. Woods rose to stand beside him and for a few moments the two men remained in companionable silence, watching the river and taking in the wide sweep of the city skyline and docks on the south bank.

'What were it that Wordsworth fellah said about our Mother Thames?' Woods asked.

'"Earth hath not anything to show more fair",' Lavender said. '"Dull would he be of soul who could pass by a sight so touching in its majesty . . ."'

'Well, maybe he were right,' Woods admitted grudgingly. 'She can put on a good show, can old Mother Thames.' He paused for a minute then added: 'A bit like us, really.'

'Yes, Ned,' Lavender said, smiling. 'We've put on a show *sans pareil.*'

'English, sir, English,' said Woods.

Author's Notes

I love the theatre and acting. I enjoyed amateur dramatics as a young woman and I spent most of my teens and twenties performing in a string of productions. For me, no trip down to London is complete with an evening spent at a show in a West End theatre.

The proximity of Bow Street Magistrates' Court to the heart of London's theatre district was a fact I couldn't ignore when I began to plot this novel. I was drawn to those lively but seedy streets of Regency Covent Garden and immersed myself in research about the vibrant theatrical culture of the time.

After I decided that Lavender and Woods' latest case would begin with the suspicious death of an actress, I looked for a theatre in which to base the action. Originally, I wanted to use the world-famous Drury Lane Theatre in the novel. However, in February 1810, they shut Drury Lane for rebuilding after a devastating fire.

Swallowing my disappointment, I switched the action to the new theatre on the Strand, the lesser-known Sans Pareil Theatre – and what a fortunate decision that turned out to be. My research revealed that in 1810, the Sans Pareil (now known as the Adelphi) was run and operated by a woman: Jane Scott.

Miss Scott wasn't just the only female theatre owner in nineteenth-century London, she also wrote most of the burlettas and Gothic melodramas they performed and she starred in them too. For a historical fiction author who likes strong, independent female characters, I had landed on my feet. I'd got a real-life historical trailblazer in my book, my own Sister of Gore.

I found the information on the website of the Adelphi Theatre Calendar Project particularly helpful when researching the early years of the Sans Pareil Theatre, and I would like to thank Dr Theodore J. Seward and his colleagues for contacting me with further help. Dr Seward also pointed out that the famous image of the ornate entrance to the Sans Pareil Theatre with its Doric pillars, which we have adapted for the cover of this novel, was not built until 1814 – four years after the date of my story. In reality, Lavender, Magdalena and Teresa would have had to walk down a dark alleyway at the side of the theatre in order to enter the building in 1810. And more worryingly, so would the Duke of Clarence and his mistress, Dorothy Jordan. After much deliberation, I decided to use some artistic licence with the architecture and let my characters use the theatre entrance in the famous image.

It was inevitable during the writing of this novel that I would also be drawn to the character of Dorothy Jordan. The most famous comic actress of her day, Dorothy Jordan kept a prince and ten children out of her wages. She and Sarah Siddons, the great Tragedy Queen, dominated the stage – and the headlines – in the London news-sheets of the early nineteenth century. I've always had a lot of sympathy for Mrs Jordan, who was eventually discarded by her lover, the Duke of Clarence, and ended her days as a pauper in France. I wanted her to have a role in my novel.

With Jane Scott and Dorothy Jordan – and a bevy of other strong-minded fictional female characters – my novel was developing a clear theme. But I didn't want the book to become romanticised and unrealistic. Theirs was a tough world. I knew that there would be a high cost to pay for this liberation and independence in such a restrictive, bigoted and male-dominated society. At the risk of alienating my readers, I decided to make all of their lives challenging and show how each of them made difficult – and not necessary savoury – choices in order to survive and thrive.

As Lavender says: 'I have begun to notice that women have their own ways of ensuring their survival . . . Sometimes they can take a shocking course of action.'

I have thoroughly enjoyed returning to the world of Stephen Lavender and Ned Woods for this novel and I promise that I won't leave it quite so long before I'm back with my intrepid crime-fighting duo again.

I would like to thank Jean Gill, Babs Morton, Kristin Gleeson, Claire Stibbe and Jane Harlond for their help and support with the manuscript. I particularly need to thank Jane for all her help with the Spanish language. I would also like to thank the editing team at Thomas & Mercer for all their support, encouragement and hard work.

Finally, to you, the reader, thank you for reading my book. If you enjoyed it, please leave a review on Amazon.

Karen Charlton
14 January 2015
Marske, North Yorkshire

Bibliography

David J. Cox, *A Certain Share of Low Cunning: A History of the Bow Street Runners 1792–1839* (Willan Publishing, 2010).

Percy Fitzgerald, *Chronicles of Bow Street Police-Office*, vol. 1 (Cambridge University Press, 2011).

John C. Franceschina (ed.), *Sisters of Gore: Seven Gothic Melodramas by British Women, 1790–1843* (Routledge, 2011).

Federico García Lorca, *The House of Bernada Alba*, tr. David Hare (Faber & Faber Plays, 2014).

Stephen Hart, *Cant: A Gentleman's Guide to the Language of Rogues in Georgian London* (Improbable Fictions, 2014).

Jean Plaidy, *Goddess of the Green Room* (Cornerstone Digital, 2012).

Robert Southey, 'Mary – A Ballad', in *Complete Poetical Works of Robert Southey* (Delphi Classics, 2013).

William Wordsworth, 'Composed Upon Westminster Bridge, September 3, 1802', in *Poems, in Two Volumes* (Longman, 1807).

About the Author

Photo: © Jean Gill, 2014

Karen Charlton writes historical mystery and is also the author of a nonfiction genealogy book, *Seeking Our Eagle*. She has published short stories and numerous articles and reviews in newspapers and magazines. An English graduate and ex-teacher, Karen has led writing workshops and has spoken at a series of literary events across the North of England, where she lives. Karen now writes full-time and is currently working on the third Detective Lavender Mystery for Thomas & Mercer.

A stalwart of the village pub quiz and a member of a winning team on the BBC quiz show *Eggheads*, Karen also enjoys the theatre and she won a Yorkshire Tourist Board award for her Murder Mystery Weekends.

Find out more about Karen's work at http://www.karencharlton.com